CARNIVAL

Also by J. Robert Janes

The St-Cyr and Kohler Mysteries

Mayhem
Carousel
Kaleidoscope
Salamander
Mannequin
Dollmaker
Stonekiller
Sandman
Gypsy
Madrigal
Beekeeper
Flykiller
Bellringer
Tapestry

Non-Fiction

The Great Canadian Outback
Geology and the New Global Tectonics
Earth Science
Rocks, Minerals and Fossils
Airphoto Interpretation and the Canadian Landscape (with Dr. J.D. Mollard)

Thrillers

The Hunting Ground
The Alice Factor
The Hiding Place
The Third Story
The Watcher
The Toy Shop

And for Children

The Rolly Series
Danger on the River
Spies for Dinner
Murder in the Market

Also: *Theft of Gold*
The Odd-Lot Boys and the Tree-Fort War

CARNIVAL

A St-Cyr and Kohler Mystery

J. ROBERT JANES

MYSTERIOUSPRESS.COM

Cover design by Neil Alexander Heacox

978-1-4804-6815-3

Published in 2014 by MysteriousPress.com/Open Road Integrated Media, Inc.
345 Hudson Street
New York, NY 10014
www.mysteriouspress.com
www.openroadmedia.com

This is for Jean-Louis St-Cyr of the Sûreté Nationale
and Hermann Kohler of the Gestapo,
creatures of the imagination, lives of their own.

Acknowledgments

Each of the novels in the St-Cyr & Kohler series incorporates a few words and brief passages of French or German. Dr. Dennis Essar of Brock University very kindly assisted with the French, as did the artist Pierrette Laroche, while Professor Schutz, of Germanic and Slavic Studies at Brock, helped with the German, and in this novel, the Alsatian. Should there be any errors, however, they are my own and for these I apologize.

Author's Note

Carnival is a work of fiction in which actual places and times are used but altered as appropriate. As with the other St-Cyr & Kohler novels, the names of real persons may occasionally appear for historical authenticity, though all are deceased and the story makes of them what it demands. I do not condone what happened during these times, I abhor it. But during the Occupation of France the everyday crimes of murder, arson and the like continued to be committed, and I merely ask by whom and how were they solved?

CARNIVAL

Carnival: illusion masks reality, forgetfulness is engendered, truth hidden.

1

For some time now the train had been stopped in a cutting to the west of Belfort, in the Vosges Mountains and still in France. Crammed in on the hard wooden bench of wartime, Kohler ached for a cigarette. *Mein Gott,* had it been an hour of silence already? All lights, no matter how tiny and scarce tobacco was, had been forbidden. Louis, he knew, longed to sigh and drolly say, *C'est une attaque aérienne, mesdames et messieurs,* but soon they'd cross the frontier into Alsace, now the Greater Third Reich, soon Louis would have to be constantly reminded that speaking French in public was *verboten.*

It didn't bear thinking about, their being sent on this investigation, this *'Karneval.'* With the heat, the overcoats and the crowding, misery was compounded but *ach,* no one complained in a coach full of Waffen-SS—a *Sonderkommando,* a 'special' commando. One simply did as ordered.

'Raus, Alles.' Get out, all of you, croaked the sergeant-conductor. The snow, a metre or more deep in places, was pristine under a full moon and not a cloud up there, just stars like you'd never seen, except for the low and throaty

drone of aircraft. The RAF at 9.05 p.m. Berlin Time, 7 February 1943, one hour of daylight saving time in winter, two in summer!

In single file everyone headed up into the adjacent woods to the smell of spruce trees and their enclosing darkness. '*Merde*, this is idiocy,' swore Louis. 'We're not the target. We're in just as much, if not far more danger out here than in that damned train. Thirty degrees of frost and my shoes . . . I've no overboots!'

There had been no time to beg stores for replacements and receive the uncaring shrug of the scarcities. From Vichy to Paris, the train had taken over nine hours, instead of four. From Paris, they had had to take the southernmost route, changing to a secondary line at Dijon, due exactly to the threat of what was steadily drawing close.

Clear under the moon, the train huddled between shoulders of bare rock and walls of freshly ploughed drift. Two locomotives, one of them a booster for the grades the Vosges offered, had coal tenders and good stuff too. Little of it seen in Paris and other cities and towns in France since the late autumn of 1940, except for the chosen, the collabos and BOFs, the butter, eggs and cheese racketeers, the big shots too, the *Bonzen* and *Oberbonzen*, the 'Gold Pheasants' back home in the Reich because of all the medals and braid they wore.

A flatbed with mounted 20mm Oerliken anti-aircraft gun and MG42 machine guns, courtesy of the Luftwaffe, was operated by them, but they, too, had been ordered to vacate their posts. Treasonable behaviour to the diehards, but best not to attract unnecessary attention by raising up a stream of flak. Valuable cargo on board. Artwork, oil paintings, Old Masters, coins, antique furniture, carpets and porcelains. *Liebe Zeit*, the stuff that had been pouring out of France.

Behind the guns were the first-class coaches, behind these, two seconds, one third-, and a fourth-, all vacated, all with their passengers fighting their way up into the forest. Crazy, really. Louis was absolutely right.

A baggage truck and then two goods trucks followed, and lastly a closed, sealed truck bearing the large, crudely painted white letters N UND N, and the chalked words: KEIN ESSEN, KEIN AUSGANG. No food, no exit. No going out.

Kohler knew Louis would be watching that final railway truck. As the sound of the aircraft grew, the bombers began to pass before the moon. First came the pathfinders, then the others. Closing the gap between himself and his partner, he tugged at a sleeve. The aircraft, having begun their descent for the run-in, were probably at an altitude of 4,000 metres. There'd be a 1,000- or 2,000-kilogram bomb in each, and at least 5,000 kilograms of incendiaries, since it was a night raid and a little light would be appreciated just as it had been and still was over London and other British cities and towns, and that, too, was really crazy. Elsewhere, too, especially in Russia, Poland having been flattened in September of '39.

No clamouring for escape came from inside the *N-und-N* truck. Not a sound, but how could anyone treat another human being like that? 'Where the hell are they taking them, Louis, since we're going in the same direction?'

The *Nacht-und-Nebel Erlass* people, those taken by the Night and Fog Decree. 'Are they all dead, Hermann? Have they frozen?' came the whisper.

'*Ach*, they're listening, just as we are.'

Hermann didn't like it any more than he did, thought St-Cyr. They had both been in the Great War, on opposite sides, had had enough of the insanity and had intuitively understood this when they'd first met in September 1940 and had begun to work together. Two detectives, one from each side and fighting common crime, but known, too, for their steadfast honesty in an age of officially sanctioned crime on a horrendous scale.

'Stuttgart,' called out someone. 'Lancasters.'

Louis nodded toward the truck and softly confided, 'There's a loose board up near the roof. One of them is pushing it while peering skyward. He's letting them know what's up.'

'Us too,' breathed Kohler sadly, but the *N und N* unfortunate—mostly these were *résistants*, suspected or otherwise, and their clandestine wireless operators and female couriers—didn't add, as many now dared to hope, that someday Herr Hitler was going to get his.

After another twenty minutes, in which the frost made the needles of the spruce as stiff as barbed wire, they filed slowly back into the train, each alone with their thoughts, Louis and himself with the telex they had received from Gestapo Boemelburg in Paris: *Karneval. Kolmar. Contact Kommandant Rasche. Hangings. Apparent suicides. Stalag XIV J Arbeitslager 13 Elsass.*

Suicides, muttered St-Cyr to himself, turning to stare bleakly at the blue-washed window as the coach began to move. Hermann had been a prisoner of war in France from 17 July 1916 until well after the Armistice of 11 November 1918 and had fought in Alsace in the winter of '14–'15 under brutal conditions. He'd been transferred to a bomb disposal unit—some impulsive act of insubordination yet to be confided—and had, after his little sojourn with the trip-to-heaven boys, commanded a battery of field guns at Verdun, early in 1916.

'Big stuff,' he would always apologetically say, for this partner of his had been repeatedly subjected to it and, yes, God *did* do things like that. He'd been taken prisoner during one of the battles for the Somme and had learned to speak and write French while a POW but couldn't have known that in twenty-two years he'd have a partner to watch over and that his facility with the language had been what had brought them together. 'Destiny. Pure chance too,' he'd say with a snort, but chance so often meant everything these days and the irony was that they really did get on. Small arguments—mere differences of opinion. *Bien sûr*, the Bavarians were a stubborn lot and God must have dug deeply into the top hat to produce one of its stubbornest, but nothing serious even though Hermann was a Gestapo and had been tarred with that brush. 'Assimilated,' he'd say. 'Conscripted without a chance to refuse,' but could Boemelburg, his boss, have assigned them to this *Karneval* simply because Hermann would not only know the terrain, but that of a POW camp, or had there been that other reason?

Hated and reviled by many in the Paris SS and Gestapo, and those elsewhere in France, for always pointing the finger of truth where it belonged, were they now to be 'taught' a final lesson?

These days the blackout's constant exposure to that wash of laundry blueing over the glass made one despair of its presence ever ending. Hermann's reflection was, of course, too blurred for detail. In spite of the scar the SS had given the left side of his face from eye to chin with a rawhide whip—the matter of a small murder that had turned sour because of this partnership's penchant for pointing that finger—he still attracted the ladies as an orchard does bees, and rogue that he was, Hermann usually encouraged them. '*Ach*, how else are we to find out what's up?' he'd say. 'You should take better notice of how your partner works.'

'A carnival,' St-Cyr softly breathed and, finding a thumbprint-sized hole where some delinquent had scraped away the blueing, let the heat of a thumb melt its covering of frost and fog.

'Louis, Frau Oberkircher was just telling me about a textile factory in Colmar. Poles, Russians, and a handful of French. Lazy, all of them, and worthless. It seems our *Arbeitslager 13* manufactures rayon and Kommandant Rasche was one of my old bosses.'

Ah, mon Dieu, mon Dieu. 'In the Great War?'

'Where else?'

A 'hot box', an overheated axle bearing, emptied the train at Belfort. Having flipped up the box's lid that had been hurriedly closed by a railwayman, Kohler gingerly plucked at the packing of chopped rag waste, and using the man's glove, let some of it fall to the sooty snow. 'A two-hour delay?' he asked the *cheminot.*

The lantern was lifted. The jacket of the *bleu-de-travail,* the ubiquitous blue coveralls, was open, the gut, once that of a barrel. 'Four,' came the Occupation's vegetable-rooted grunt.

Merde alors, panicked Henri-Claude Ouelette, this 'Kripo from Paris-Central,' this *Kriminalpolizei,* had shaken off the glove and was now rubbing some of the packing slowly between a thumb and middle finger, the perfume of burnt engine oil all too evident.

Sweating, was he? thought Kohler. *Ah, bon, mon ami,* now get ready for the surprise of surprises. 'Then see what you can do, eh, but first empty that box and drop everything into the station's stove.'

'But . . . but the shortages, monsieur . . .'

'Idiot, don't argue. Just do it.'

So much of France's rolling stock had been requisitioned by the Reich, scrapyard relics like this coach and the trucks and engines had been pressed back into service and were always causing trouble. Maybe, just maybe the *Bahnschutzpolizei* stationmaster, the SS Obersturmführer or anyone else in authority wouldn't think beyond that to take a closer look.

Silicon carbide had been added to the oil-soaked rag waste. It hadn't taken him a split second to feel the sharpness. Probably done in Besançon or in L'Isle. Fortunately the bearing hadn't melted and the train been derailed or set alight. Someone had wanted to stop them and free the *N und Ns* but hadn't counted on its stopping where it had last night, thus cooling the bearing and giving it a lease on life. Of course they hadn't considered that the prisoners might well have been killed. Miraculously, too, Louis and himself had avoided being caught up in the derailment or shoot-out, but had been awarded yet another delay.

The *restaurant de la gare* and its buffet were closed until 7.00 a.m., 5.00 the old time, the station overcrowded. Coughs here, sneezes there. Kids, old people, mothers without their husbands, babes greedily at the breast or wailing their little hearts out, Wehrmacht boys, too, returning to the front from the eager arms of *les filles de joie de Paris* and dog-tired, naturally. Military police, the Felgendarmen, were on the lookout for deserters coming through from the Reich. Gestapo plainclothes were vigilant too, and God help those unfortunate enough to be caught.

'The Army's mobile soup kitchen is serving hot coffee,' hazarded Claudette Oberkircher.

'Coffee . . . ?' blurted Hermann, his mind still elsewhere.

'It's not for everyone,' she said. 'Only for our dear boys in uniform, but perhaps if . . . ' She left the thought hanging like laundry in winter.

'Use your charm, Hermann,' quipped St-Cyr. Guiding her through to a far corner, he set her two suitcases and their small grip down. Evasively this infernal chatterbox Hermann had instantly struck up a conversation with, this Hausfrau 'from home' who had *squeezed* the French half of the partnership against the ice-cold side of the carriage as if getting back at the enemy, emptily returned his gaze, her dark brown eyes misting as she said to herself, Sûreté—he knew it, always did, but would she now confess to knowing how to speak French, thinking as she must, since she had been deliberately led to believe it, that he knew no *Deutsch*? Or would she use Alsatian whose dialect was neither totally of the one or the other but that ardent distillation of the centuries of changing hands while demanding independence?

She would choose silence, Claudette told herself. These days people didn't do what she had done in that coach—talked incessantly to a perfect stranger, a Gestapo detective at that. Even those who knew each other seldom spoke, and then only in whispers.

He took out his pipe and tobacco pouch, this *Oberdetektiv* from the Sûreté Nationale with the terrible bruise and stitches above the left eye. He looked ruefully at the contents of the pouch, found his *Kippe* tin, his *mégot* tin with its collection of cigarette butts picked up here and there like everyone else and, opening it, explored the contents with a doubtful finger.

'Your . . . ' he began, struggling to find the word for *suitcases*, 'are . . . ' He couldn't even find the words for 'not heavy.'

But one must be careful these days. 'I carry little,' she said in *Deutsch*. 'The one suitcase is all but empty; the other has but a few clothes and two newspapers bearing the notices of my brother-in-law's death.'

Not understanding a word she had said, this Frenchman shrugged. Their coffee came, and for a time these two companions of hers were silent. 'The Army should use parsnips,' she said after taking a few exploratory sips. 'This is good, *ja*, but it could be much better.'

'Parsnips,' echoed Hermann who had an encyclopedic interest in all such things of the Occupation. 'Not roasted acorns and barley, and maybe with a touch of chicory if one is lucky?'

The Frenchman rolled his eyes in despair but had best be ignored. 'You do not peel them, you understand, Herr Hauptmann Detektiv Aufsichtsbeamter. Just wash in cold water and shred, then roast until black before grinding. Eighty turns of the mill, I give it until it is as fine as the flour we used to be able to buy. Then brew as you would that other stuff you mentioned. *Ach*, my little sister swore she couldn't tell the difference and said it's real!'

'Louis, what have I always been telling you, eh? Right from the start of this war you people started, you French should have listened to your friends. *Mein Gott*, Frau Oberkircher, the answers to so many of the problems they've caused themselves and us, too, are often so simple and right to hand!'

Like the lack of real coffee.

'Now don't argue,' quipped Kohler in French. 'Let's take a little walk. *Bitte, meine gute Frau*, you'll hold our seats? A breath of fresh air will do this one good.'

The Bavarian was fifty-five years old, Claudette felt, the Frenchman perhaps three years his junior. Much taller and stronger looking, a giant of a man, Herr Kohler's eyes were pale blue, the lids bagging and drooping from exhaustion, no doubt. And sometimes those eyes had been so empty when he had looked at one of the SS, his gaze had frightened her, but always when he had turned to her there had been that little rush of excitement in herself. Though those years had slipped away some time ago, Herr Kohler hadn't let their absence deter him. He was not at all like a *gestapiste,* though he did have the chin and cheekbones of a storm trooper, the scar of a terrible wound and far more recent than those that other war had left, the shrapnel. A criminal with a knife? she wondered of that scar. A dueling sword? A bullet graze had recently brushed his brow. Occasionally the thick fingers would favour it as if he was counting his blessings. No ring of course, but probably married, the hair cut close and neither brown nor black but a shade in between, like his marital status, and flecked with grey.

The Frenchman was altogether something else, even if he did wear a wedding ring he'd best change to his other hand unless he wanted to be stopped by the police and hauled in for questioning. Of a little more than medium height and blocky, he had the deep brown ox-eyes common to those people, the fists of a *pugiliste*—had he lost the fight that had given him the stitches? she wondered. The hair was dark brown and needing a trim, the moustache wide and bushy, and as for the eyebrows, must they give him a look that was so fierce?

Outside in the darkness, Louis couldn't wait. 'She's carrying cigarettes in that lighter suitcase, Hermann. How could you do this to us? She's let herself cosy up to you, knowing she's with two *Schweinebullen* and still has hopes you'll unwittingly waltz her through customs!'

'*Ach,* I wondered when you'd figure that out. She's terrified of the company we've had to keep and feels like an utter fool for having chanced what she did and has stuck to us like glue. Go easy on her, eh? Just be your generous self and thankful that she's let us know that Kolmar's *schwarzer Markt* is flourishing. That Kolmar is with a *K*, by the way, not a *C*.'

And never mind the Deutsch. Its black market, its *marché noir*. Cigarettes must now be the preferred currency in the Reich, as they were in France. 'That no-good, piano-teaching brother-in-law of hers, "that brute of a one-legged *Frenchman* and seducer of young girls," was into more than student skirts, Hermann. While helping that little sister of hers go through his things, your Frau Oberkircher, for all she wishes to disclaim and hide her French origins, came upon the mother lode of fags and felt it her duty as a citizen of the Greater Reich to confiscate the evidence before her sister found it!'

As was their custom when on short rations and in need of a quiet tête-à-tête, a cigarette was rescued from an inner pocket—Louis's this time. Kohler found them a light, and after a few drags each, they began to walk toward the centre of the old town, gripped as it was in glacial darkness.

'Silicon carbide?' asked St-Cyr.

'It was close, Louis. Just be thankful the RAF came along when they did.'

'*Ah, bon,* then it's as I've thought. During the war of 1870–71, the region's Francs-Tireurs constantly harassed the Prussians. Now it's the turn of their descendants.'

The region's irregulars, its citizen soldiers. In Vichy, not a day—was it still only a day ago?—they'd had a final run-in with the FTP, the Francs-Tireurs *et Partisans*, a Résistance group started by Communist railway workers in Lyons. Tough—real sons of bitches who had put Louis at the top of their hit list simply because he had to work with one of the Occupier.

'Even though Alsace was taken in less than five days by the Prussians in 1870, Hermann, and Paris placed under siege and France defeated within five months, not five weeks as in 1940, the people of the Vosges kept much to themselves. Let's not forget it, because we mustn't, and just to prove it to you, I'm going to take you to have a look at the Lion.'

They had had some soup and two of the regulation twenty-five gram slices of the grey National. They had each handed over a bread ticket and had left the customary two-franc donation for the Winter Relief that was run by the Secours National, the national help.

They had tried to doze off, saying little, each knowing the other's thoughts could well be in a turmoil. The future, which people seldom if ever thought about these days, was far too cloudy and troubling.

Then they had come out here, the shadows deepening as they had approached the rock face, while etched in silhouette on high, the château, the citadel, defied assault as it had during the Franco-Prussian War.

Hermann, his fedora pulled down hard, the collar of his greatcoat up and close, couldn't seem to lower his gaze. He would be thinking of the 103-day siege that had ended twenty-one days *after* the Armistice of that war, would be telling himself that Colonel Denfert-Rochereau of *place* D-R in Paris, its métro station, too, and countless streets in France, had defied the Prussians for so long, even Bismark and the Kaiser had been forced to acknowledge the bravery and agree to freeing Belfort and its immediately surrounding territory from the fate so much of Alsace-Lorraine was to suffer. Annexation.

He would also be seeing the dead of the Great War, the long, dark lines of the trenches in the snow, the gun emplacements, would be thinking of Vieil-Armand which was less than thirty-five kilometres to the northeast of them: Alsace's Verdun where, for eight long, hard months over the winter of 1914–15 and into the summer, more than 30,000 men had died, but not himself, the French 75s answering his own 77s which had raced ahead to twenty-five rounds a minute. The drumfire, the Germans had come to call those French guns: *Das Trommelfeuer;* while the French *poilus*, the common soldiers, had spoken of the other side's shelling as *la tempête de feu*, the tempest of fire. He would know, too, that his partner was all too aware of this and that its enduring memories were but one of the things that had welded the partnership, but still, reminders must always be given.

Some twenty-two metres long and eleven high, and caught against the sheer rock face below the citadel, resting on its hind quarters with right foreleg stiff and head turned a little from the rock out of which that head had been carved, the Lion, still in shadow cold, appeared as if about to roar.

'I always wondered what it would look like, Louis, but could never bring myself to see it.'

Between 1875 and 1880, Colmar's sculptor, Frédéric Auguste Bartholdi, had fashioned it largely out of blocks of that same rock as the citadel and the old town.

'The red sandstone of the Vosges,' muttered Hermann sadly, 'but there's granite to the north and northeast,' he said as if that were the answer to everything. 'Granite's far harder, Louis. It splinters when struck. Forms the busts, the heart, the guts of these rounded hills here in the south, is far worse than any shrapnel.'

He touched his face, and one knew at once where those nicks and scars had come from. Belfort the 'Heroic' lay in the Trouée de Belfort, the Gap through which the invading hordes had come. Celts, Goths, Romans and others, the Germans of course, and more than once.

'We could see the Black Forest from the summit of Vieil-Armand,' he went on. 'We could see what we called home only to then have to give up the crest of that hill to your side. Time and again we took it; time and again it was lost.'

Another cigarette was found and, once lit, passed over.

'Gerda was waiting for me,' he said, as if the girl he'd known as a teenager was still vital, the girl he had married and had two sons with.

'*Ach*, how times have changed, eh? Now I live with Oona and Giselle on those rare moments when we're in Paris, while my Gerda . . . '

Had begged an uncle with connections in the Nazi Party to help her get a divorce so that she could marry an indentured farm labourer from France who was helping out on her father's farm near Wasserburg, just to the east of Munich. And yes, both Giselle and Oona had come to love him and it wasn't difficult to see that each understood and respected the other's feelings and willingly—yes, willingly!—shared what little they saw of him and had become fast friends themselves.

'War does things like that,' muttered Kohler, having read his partner's thoughts. 'It also brings enemies like us together, so please don't forget it.'

Enemies. He hadn't said that in a long, long time, had always been planning to get Giselle and Oona out of France and into Spain.

'Bartholdi may have sculpted New York's Statue of Liberty with freedom in mind, Hermann, but that isn't why I brought you here. One hundred and three days up there in that citadel? They held fast to what they had come to believe in, themselves. That hot box was a warning to us of the Francs-Tireurs, as was the plethora of Felgendarmen and Gestapo looking for deserters in the railway station. Since this Kommandant Rasche was one of your former commanding officers at Vieil-Armand, and no doubt has remembered your usefulness, perhaps you had best tell me about it.'

Ah, damn! 'That left ball of mine . . . '

'*Sacré nom de nom,* have I not been subjected to that little legend enough? Swelled to the size of a ripe lemon? As hard as a dried one. A grapefruit perhaps?'

'You've no sympathy. I'm not at all surprised your first wife left you for a railway man from Orléans!'

'She was lonely.'

'You told me your practising the euphonium for the police band drove her away!'

'That too.'

'Then she didn't take off with a door-to-door salesman or a lorry driver? You actually lied to me?'

Hermann had caught a 'cold' in that most tender of places while in the trenches and snows of that Alsatian battlefield.

'You know what those field hospitals were like, Louis. I couldn't have some *verdammt* Wehrmacht medic amputating the necessary.'

Ah, merde!

'I went AWOL and found myself an Alsatian pharmacist's daughter who was training to fill her father's shoes even though it was heresy of her to have thought of such a thing.'

'She was pretty.'

'Sweet heaven but I couldn't have done it with her and she knew it.'

And so much for his subsequent tour of duty in a *Himmelfahrtskommando,* a suicide commando, as one of its trip-to-heaven boys.

'I could have been shot. Instead, Rasche, who headed up the court of inquiry, thought I might be useful and gave me a choice, and when I took it, six months of never knowing when the next second would be my last.'

Hence his uncanny ability to find tripwires and smell out explosives. 'Carnival, Hermann. It's from the medieval Latin for Flesh Farewell, the celebration that precedes the forty meatless days of Lent.'

'Masked girls and boys who simply want to get into mischief, eh? Costumes? Music and dancing and torch-lit parades and feasts in an *Arbeitslager,* a work camp, *mein Lieber*?'

It was a good question. 'A travelling fair too, I think. Sideshows, booths with games of skill or chance, others exhibiting the wonders of the world.'

'*Ja, ja,* the palace of mirrors, eh? Well please don't forget that this Colonel Rasche of mine could break every one of them with a simple look.'

'But does he know of the Francs-Tireurs who tried to stop our train, or simply think, as others must, that they might be out there in those hills?'

'Helping deserters to cross over?'

That, too, was a good question.

Karneval, thought Kohler. A travelling fair with games, sideshows, rides and other forms of amusement. Normally run as a commercial enterprise, occasionally held by charitable groups as a way of raising funds.

Rasche would give them no peace. Relegated to looking after *Arbeitslagern,* long past retirement and still a colonel? It didn't bear thinking about.

One hundred and twenty thousand had been expelled from Alsace in 1940; 500,000 from Lorraine—all those who had wanted to keep their French citizenship and lose their property. Only those whose families had been there before 1918 were to be considered citizens of the Greater Reich. A matter of efficiency to Berlin, one of easing assimilation and purifying the remaining stock, and then, in August of last year, introducing conscription.

Frau Oberkircher, who had grown silent at thoughts of the frontier, had probably just been caught up in things like so many others, but had bought herself a copy of today's *Völkischer Beobachter*, the Führer's paper, thinking its presence, along with that of two detectives, might just help.

Excusing himself, Louis reached across the woman and opened a fist, revealing some chestnuts. 'There are only a few left, Hermann. Don't forget to use your pocketknife. We don't want to have to visit a dentist.'

'*Ach*, we're almost in the Reich. Things will be different. There'll be anaesthetic. Cold, boiled, dried chestnuts,' he said in *Deutsch* to the woman. 'A little something for the road his girlfriend pressed upon him in Paris as we caught the train out.'

His girlfriend, Gabrielle Arcuri, a chanteuse.

'There's been no heavy breathing yet, from that love affair,' confided Kohler, widening the woman's eyes.

'Shave it, Hermann,' said St-Cyr in French, indicating the chestnut. 'Don't cut yourself.'

'We're floaters,'said Kohler to their travelling companion. 'We drift from murder to arson to missing persons, fraud and bank robberies and live in the never-never land of shadows.'

Chestnut shavings were eaten. 'I gather beechnuts in the autumn and press a lovely oil from them which I heat with onions and salt for the potatoes,' said Claudette. 'It's every bit as good as butter—better, I think.'

Certainly there were so few potatoes available in France, she shouldn't have said it, but Louis let it pass. Louis knew the woman was bringing memories back to this partner of his. At the frontier, he took the heaviest of the woman's suitcases which was opened and thoroughly searched, as he'd known it would be. At Kolmar, now spelled with a *K*, they saw her into a horse-drawn sleigh, a taxi whose mare was far beyond the needs of the Russian Front and just as aged as the few the Occupier had left in France.

Giving them a wave, her heart filled with relief and gratitude, Claudette looked back to see them standing in the Bahnhofstrasse, formerly the rue de la Gare, two very different men wondering what the future might bring.

'*Amis,*' she said, as if it were a miracle, 'but even *les très amis* must doubt one another now.'

It was curious that they each remembered where the police station was but that neither spoke of it, thought St-Cyr. Two charcoal-gas-powered lorries reminded one of Occupied Paris, their fire-boxes up front or behind and gas tanks on the roof. Long queues stood outside the shops, just as at home. There were bicycles, bicycle taxis and few, if any, privately operated cars. Here, too, people simply went on foot, but also there were fewer of them. Perhaps a third less than usual, so a population now in Kolmar of about 23,000.

Swastikas flew from many of the three- and four-storey buildings that, cheek by jowl, overlooked the former Champ de Mars, the Military Esplanade, now the *Militärpromenade*. Black wreaths trailed bunting, a noon bell sounded, but no longer was the moment of silence being observed. The workmen who had been clearing away the wreaths continued to do so as the last bell shimmered.

On 3 February, and but five days ago, Radio-Berlin had announced the defeat of the Sixth Army at Stalingrad, the first such public admission. Three days of official mourning had begun on the fourth but were now over.

' "The sacrifices of the army, Louis? *Bulwark* of a historical European mission and not in vain," or so that bastard of a propaganda minister claims, but if not in vain, then what?'

'Easy, *mon vieux*. Easy. You're in the Reich.' Hermann had lost his two teenaged sons, Jurgen and Hans, at Stalingrad, this partner of his having had to convey the terrible news to him early in January. He'd be wanting to see his Gerda, if only to tell her he was sorry for their loss. Granted, it wasn't that far and perhaps the trip could be arranged, though the delay in getting back across the frontier would be something else again.

Two direction-finding vans, with diamond-shaped wire aerials, were parked in front of the *Polizeikommandantur* which overlooked the Cathedral square. Gestapo plainclothes were earnestly talking about the sweep, just as they would have done in Paris and elsewhere in France. 'Piano study, Hermann.'

Clandestine wireless transmitters and London . . . calling London, just as in France when possible.

A dark blue Renault Juraquatre, the two-door, four-seat economy of 1937 to 39 was parked ten metres ahead and had just been washed and polished—*washed* in this weather!

'I told you, didn't I?' said Kohler. 'I warned you.'

Half-timbering gave great age, the flanking double wings of what was now an expanded cop shop rising through three and four storeys to lofty garrets, steeply pitched roofs, and paddle-shaped brown beaver's-tail tiles, the *Biberschwanzen*. No patterns were up there on the roofs to brighten the place. Just broken, crooked shutters or none at all. In the years since

1575 much had happened, but more recently the stucco had sloughed and become stained, had been shot up too, a little.

'Colmar's Hôtel de Ville had a fire, Hermann.'

Its town hall and a reminder that during the Blitzkrieg all the records had been conveniently destroyed. As a result, the town had become the home address favoured by many using false papers in France. 'Relative upon relative the remaining citizens haven't even heard of!' said Kohler with a snort.

Above them, above the swastika, a columned, railed gallery, looking like something straight out of the Renaissance, was open to all elements. Above this, there were two garret dormers, one on either side, their solid wooden shutters permanently closed and bolted.

'Hermann, before we go in there I have to tell you something. If we should run into any of my second cousins, I really don't know what I'll do.'

'Hug or hate them?'

'Or both.'

'And they?'

'Will remember the boy they teased until he fought back so hard he learned to use his fists.'

Louis had spent three summers on the farm of distant relatives near Saarbrücken.

'*Grand-maman* kept saying I would have to return until she was satisfied.'

She had lived through the siege of 1870–71 to bankroll vivid memories of the Prussians.

'Their father, my uncle Ernst, had the biggest manure pile in the village and was a real Gauleiter of the shit, Hermann. Looked up to by everyone because of it and other things. Feared, too, let me tell you.'

'Calm down. Don't be so nervous.'

'I even saw my cousin Hedda undress completely so as to give the local boys their money's worth. My look was free since I took in the cash for her. Six pfennigs, one from each of them.'

At times, even such as this, it was best to wait and say nothing.

'*Oncle* Ernst was a big man, Hermann. Not quite as tall as yourself but as strong as an ox. Gentle, though, but thorough. Rigorously so.'

'I'm waiting, aren't I?'

'*Ah, bon.* Guess who was forced to strip off for free and stand in front of all the girls and women of the village yet . . . yet afterward, no one said a thing of it. There was not one whisper or giggle. Hedda and I lived in mortal fear and remorse for days—it was as if we had been banished, but ever since then, except for that last war and this one, she and I have corresponded.'

The truth at last, but a bond, if not of distant kinship and forbidden commerce, of shared guilt, shame and trial.

'*Grand-maman* said that they had won me over and that I was a terrible disappointment to her. She had hoped I would come back hating them, and didn't even acknowledge that I had finally learned the language.'

Louis was always answering for the sins of his boyhood.

'Just remember Sainte Odilia, Hermann, then you'll realize how long such things can linger. In 700 A.D. she prophesied that evil would come via the Antichrist from the Danube.'

A tale worthy of the troubadours. Born blind, rejected by her father, Alsace's patron saint had been hidden away until baptized when a beautiful maid. Miraculously she had gained her sight and her vocation, had kept her virginity, and become a nun and then abbess of the convent she had founded. One day, in her old age when a passerby, and not a blind one, had said he was thirsty, she had touched the stone at her feet with her cane and produced a spring to which, yearly since, the blind had flocked to bathe in hope of gaining their sight!

'You shouldn't pay that legend much credence, Louis.'

'I don't. I just see the evidence of it all around me.'

The stove was cylindrical and of fluted white ceramic tile bound by gleaming straps of brass. Hands held to it, they waited in the colonel's office. Finally Hermann could no longer stand their being left alone. 'He likes to make his fish sweat before frying! He's pissed off because we're late and will never believe it wasn't my fault!'

They had been ushered past the duty desk, had been quickly led through the warren of narrow corridors, up sets of creaking staircases, down others and up again at turns, all eyes taking time out in the various offices to not only watch their progress but see what Paris had sent.

Diamond-leaded casement windows filled much of the oriel behind the Empire desk that looked oddly out of place. Frantically Hermann tried to roll a cigarette. *Mégot*-scavenged tobacco showered, messing the Aubusson under foot and littering the black sheet-iron beneath the stove.

'Let me.'

'*Verdammt!* Can't you just be patient?'

Was it all coming back to him? wondered St-Cyr. The agony of never knowing what verdict the court of inquiry would render? The distinct possibility of the firing squad—he'd never given a hint of being so troubled!

The chair behind the desk was not Empire or anything so fine. It was simply a plain, bare, mismatched wooden thing, high- and straight-backed, a railed affair without armrests. A man, then, this colonel of Hermann's, who favoured his back, but did he, in his contemplative moments, gaze off to the northwest beyond the Cathedral to the Église des Dominicains whose exquisite stained glass would have been taken down in 1939 and crated to rest in security, as had the rose window of the Notre-Dame and others? Did he know that the building of that church had begun in the thirteenth century and had continued through the fourteenth, fifteenth and well into the eighteenth? Master builders, those artisans, but did the colonel not also, as he absolutely must since it was right in the middle of the square, notice the Collégiale Saint-Martin with its glazed tiles in diamond patterns, the Cathedral's buttresses and walls inset with blocks of red sandstone among the grey so that a pattern emerged which complimented that of the roofs?

Or did he notice on the rue des Clefs, that of the keys and now the Schüsselstrasse, the formerly named Hôtel de Ville which was unique in itself and for more reasons than the false identities it had provided.

Everything on the desk had its place. Herr Rasche liked order. Pipe and tobacco pouch were to the left and as if just taken out, the bowl but half-filled. An interruption.

'Louis . . . '

Hermann still hadn't turned from the stove.

'Louis, it's my fault you're here. I . . . I just wanted you to know that.'

'Your former commanding officer is a connoisseur, Hermann.'

'Get the hell away from that desk of his before he finds you there!'

Mon Dieu, he was edgy. 'A half-bent Billiard, the brier straight-grained and waxed as it should be, the stem of ebonite just like my own, the mixture . . . '

'Don't touch it!'

'A medium-dark cavendish, Hermann. Swiss perhaps, or Dutch or Danish. Matured Virginia Old Belt with perique and a pinch of latakia to slow the little fire and add its plummy taste to the spiciness of the perique and the sugars of the Virginia. Had I the opportunity and the cash for such a treat, I'd have chosen no other.'

'*Jésus, merde alors*, just because you treasure that straight Billiard in your own pocket is no reason to think you're blood brothers with that *salaud*! Is the pouch of faded Prussian-blue pigskin?'

'It is, and unless I'm mistaken, your Kommandant is greatly concerned with these suicides. That little car of his absented itself while we were on our way up the stairs.'

Dead centre of the green, baize-coloured blotter, and to the right of the pipe, pouch and matchbox, there were two dossiers, one above the other and with the lowermost name showing in heavy black Gothic type with eagle and swastika stamp. HERMANN ANDREAS KOHLER and, yes, JEAN-LOUIS ST-CYR, and so much for their trying to discover if the colonel knew this Sûreté understood both languages. Gestapo Paris had had the dossiers flown in.

A plain, dog-eared brown notebook—one of those a schoolchild would have used before the Defeat—lay atop the dossiers, a clutch, too, of beautifully carved staghorn buttons, the set for a waistcoat perhaps. Three beechwood bobbins, still wound with thread, were there too, as was a swatch of wood-fibre cloth, the shade that of the medium blue so common among the business suits of the Occupier.

The temptation to ask, 'Does your former commanding officer enjoy hunting?' was there simply because each of the buttons depicted a different type of game.

'Louis, this map on the wall . . . There are forty-seven green flags scattered throughout Baden, Württemburg, Alsace and Lorraine.'

'The potash mines and factories near Mulhaussen, Hermann. The textile mills, and not just the one in question. Metal-working plants too, as well as coal, lumber, sauerkraut, sausage, pâté and wine. Alsace has many things the Reich needs.'

And does he like trout fishing and to tie his own flies in winter, there being three superb flies embedded in a wine cork as a little reminder of retirement perhaps?

Gently brushing the buttons, bobbins and cloth aside, Louis teased the school notebook open and looked up. Does the name Victoria Bödicker mean anything to you? He silently asked.

Finding pen and paper, Hermann quickly wrote, *Frau Oberkircher did mention her. The daughter of a dearest friend, and something about a bookshop she often helped at when this Victoria had to be elsewhere.*

Alsatian schoolteachers had been sent to the Reich in 1940–41 for indoctrination. This one had taken the personal progress record every French schoolteacher had to carry when going from school to school: the grading and comments of inspectors, no matter how damning, classes taught, days absent or late, even love affairs that should not have been allowed to interfere with one's career.

The thing had been stamped, too, by the Munich office, noted Kohler, but the girl had been chequered out of the profession, judged not indoctrinated enough.

Victoria's not French but British, he knew Louis was thinking as a faded, once brightly coloured papier-mâché ball was gently rolled across the blotter, a finger to the lips.

A carnival, Hermann. A booth, a game of *Jeu de massa-*

cre where one tries to hit the bane of one's existence: priest, schoolteacher, butcher, bully, wife or sweetheart who has chosen another.

A Game of Massacre. 'Natzweiler-Struthof, Louis. That's what it says beneath the red flag on that map. It's about forty kilometres to the southwest of Strassburg and up in the hills.'

Not just a prisoner-of-war camp, not just a stalag, but a *Konzentrationslager* under which were all forty-seven of those *Arbeitslagern*.

'Gentlemen, gentlemen, you must excuse my absence, but I've been to see if everything is as I requested. You've had a long journey and must be exhausted, poor fellows. *Mein Gott*, is it really you, Kohler? How have you been faring? Not badly, I trust? Busy, of course, as we all are, but *ach*, I do go on. Come . . . come this way, please. Inspector St-Cyr, would you be so kind as to bring my pipe, pouch and matches? A bit of lunch is in order even if we have to make do with the shortages like everyone else, but it'll give us a chance to get to know one another and in the course of it, why I can fill you in, as is my duty.'

Rasche had known the office was bugged and hadn't wanted Gestapo-Kolmar ears to hear what he had to say, thought St-Cyr, but had left the dossiers and the rest out for them to find and bring along, had known, too, that they would realize others were not to be allowed to listen in. A *Karneval* . . .

The house wasn't far from the *Polizeikommandantur*. Built in the late eighteenth century, it was on the left bank of the River Lauch and shoulder to shoulder with others of its kind. A railed porch, extending but five metres from one side to the other, was off the first storey, its plate timbers sagging. Another was off the second, yet another off the third. From there, the half-timbering ended in a steeply pitched, stepped and sway-backed roof from which a lonely dormer protruded.

'Once the house of a tanner, Hermann,' said Louis as they got out of the colonel's car. 'Look how beautifully carved the timbers and shutters are, the entrance also. Before the turn of the century, the tanners still washed hides in this river and hung them to dry in those attics up there.'

Narrow, railed walkways, placed to access each pair of houses, spanned the four-metre width of the river. Everywhere the snow had been cleared. The river ice looked thick enough for skating, and why not? wondered Kohler. Wehrmacht boys during their off-hours, probably. '*Soldatenheime?*' he asked of the nearby houses. Hostels for the troops.

'I would have thought it obvious,' grunted Rasche as the perfume of wood smoke came to them.

'Requisitioned?' persisted Hermann.

'Kohler, you ask too many questions.'

'Aren't detectives supposed to, Herr Oberst?'

'*Ach*, try to realize you're back in the Reich. Some were vacant, others donated, this one the rightful property of the family that built it.'

'And the SS, Herr Oberst?'

'Those people live elsewhere and have their offices in the former Préfecture.'

Complaining under their collective weight, the walkway's planks signalled approach, a parted curtain falling back into place while just downstream of them, a one-armed veteran of that other war looked their way from under a forage cap that telegraphed its memories, Rasche tossing the man a wave and a, 'Good of you, Werner. Any visitors?'

'*Nein*, Kommandant.'

'*Danke*. That's my former sergeant-major, Kohler. Perhaps

you remember Oberfeldwebel Lutze? Always loyal, always with his colonel's best interests at heart and his own, of course. Gentlemen, it pays to be careful these days. One never knows who is listening or watching.'

'Lutze led the search party that arrested me, Louis. A rank little—'

'Kohler, Kohler, why will you never learn? Werner was on your side and still is because I want him there.'

The *Stube*, the combination living and dining room, was warm, its aroma heady, the ample peaches-and-cream woman at the tiled *Kachelofen* about forty-five years of age: blonde and blue-eyed, the apron white, the long, layered bright red skirt colourful, it and the subdued waistcoat and pure white blouse with its lace-trimmed sleeves and bodice straight out of a storybook. Braids too!

'Yvonne, *meine gute Frau*, the two detectives I was telling you about. Gentlemen, my housekeeper, Frau Lutze, yours too. It's all been arranged. *Ach*, sit. *Bitte*, Yvonne, the *Suppe*. Beer for Herr Kohler, the Reisling for the Detektiv St-Cyr and myself. Werner had best come in. That stump . . . You know how the cold gets at it. Tell him he can watch the quay quite adequately from here.'

And that there are no secrets between them? wondered Kohler.

'Gentlemen, we'll eat and then we'll talk.'

There was no doubt they were being bribed and that the meal could well lull questions that had best be asked, but St-Cyr knew he was pleased, for what was set before each of them was as it would have been in 1937, the last time he had worked on an investigation in Alsace. The soup, a purée of split peas, ham stock, onions, garlic and carrots, had been given a scattering of freshly grilled lardons and two twists round the plate of ground black pepper—real pepper! Individual saucers of sauerkraut steamed, adding a delicate sharpness and touch of juniper to the warm, full aroma, while blue-grey ceramic pots of deep yellow mustard and side dishes of *Schniederspettel*, a lightly smoked sausage of beef and pork seasoned with caraway, contributed their notes, as did the freshly baked peasant's bread of stone-ground wheat and rye.

The Riesling was superb, its bouquet elegant, the first brush clean, crisp, not too dry or sweet, a trifle flinty perhaps but . . . *ah, mon Dieu*, to let its bouquet mingle with the other notes after all the years of the Occupation's denial was to bring tears to detective eyes.

'Kaysersberg,' he said reverently. 'The Schlossberg, Colonel. Granite is what lends the flinty taste. The slopes have a southern exposure, giving longer time on the vine and less risk of an early frost. It's magnificent. I salute you.'

Kohler downed his soup, sausage and lager as if still in the trenches, whereas the Frenchman savoured each morsel. 'Yvonne and Werner ran a very successful *Winstub** between the wars. Werner has to shop around a good deal more these days, what with the rationing and all, but still manages splendidly.'

And if that wasn't putting it mildly, what was? The big hands with their butcher-strong wrists ruthlessly broke bread, the colonel every bit as tall as Hermann but wider in the shoulders and thicker through. With the warmth, he had unbuttoned the field-grey tunic, had set formality aside. An Iron Cross First- and Second-Class were there, the Pour le Mérite, the Military Service Cross also, and a silver wound badge for three or four wounds, all from that other war. No Nazi Party button, though,

* A wine bar offering traditional fare

not even one of the phosphorescent swastika pins that were supposed to be worn during the blackout. Just an intensity that couldn't quite be hidden, the look in those dark blue eyes swift and sharp to meet each sudden assessment of himself by either of them, the robust nose flaring in challenge, the forehead wide and strong, the hair an all but vanished grey-white fuzz, the ears big like the rest of him.

'These suicides, Colonel . . . ' began Louis, not realizing what he'd done, thought Kohler, for Rasche threw back his head as if struck and gruffly said: *'Ach, mein Lieber,* not while we're eating. To honour the cook is to honour the meal.'

Louis begged forgiveness as he should, but what the hell was really going on in this cosy little nest? Werner Lutze spooned his soup as an Oberfeldwebel should while sitting directly behind his former Oberst and on the bench that ran beneath the windows. The wife sat demurely at one end of the table, this Kripo at the other, with Louis opposite the source of these 'suicides' and all three hosts assessing these two purveyors of justice from Paris with more than just a hesitant eye. Frau Lutze—formerly Yvonne what? he tried to recall—had taken far less soup so as to be ready at a curt nod from her star border, while that husband of hers watched the quay in between stealing little glances at them and at his soup. All were anxious. Yes, that was it. Wary.

'More soup, Herr Detektiv Aufsichtsbeamter?' asked Yvonne. 'A little more of the sausage and sauerkraut. It is good, yes, that you should eat.'

The Alsatian argot, if one dared to call it that, had definitely been suppressed. *'Bitte, meine gute Frau,* I'm famished.'

She took his plate, left her own and disappeared behind the stove and into the depths of the kitchen. Kohler knew she would be trying to calm herself. 'These suicides,' Louis had said and she had sucked in a breath and momentarily been unable to lift the spoon from her plate, had forced herself not to glance at the colonel.

Returning, Yvonne found the will to softly smile as she set the soup plate in front of this detective from the Gestapo, quietly accepting his, *'Danke,'* but quickly turning away. Earlier Otto had warned her that there were things they would need to know but others they must never learn.

Hans Otto Rasche was sixty-eight and well beyond the hoped-for retirement with full pension which would probably never be realized, given the way the war was turning. A man who desperately longed to simply go fishing.

Suicides, she silently said to herself as she stood watching these 'guests' of Otto's. *Ach*, the lines in his face had deepened with the worry. There were also the blotches that the sun and age had given him, the scars from the shrapnel, too, those of the granite splinters as had Herr Kohler.

Knowing what he did, why had Otto agreed to help the *Winterhilfswerk* with the *Karneval*? Had it been but a moment of weakness in a man who must still show little of it? Had he been weakened by a pretty smile or a breath of that perfume, the softness of the young, a pleading entreaty to one who could be cold even to such gestures as the nearness of the woman he had once worshipped?

The Winter Relief was an annual collection that helped to finance the Nationalsozialistische Volkswohlfahrt, the Party's Social Welfare Organization. Otto was not a member. Otto was invariably far too wary of such things. *Ach*, a generous donation, of course, to cover his back, but to agree to do what he had, there had to have been a substantial reason.

The soup plates were cleared, St-Cyr noting that the *Baeckeoffe* came in an earthenware terrine whose oval, iron strap and padlock could but have its memories for Frau Lutze. Down through the centuries here in Alsace, and in many parts of France, Mondays had been wash days, the noon meal prepared well before dawn and left to cook at the baker's while doing the laundry at the wash house. Now, of course, she would have cooked it herself, but why, then, had she insisted on locking it, unless wanting those memories to come?

Taking a beautifully worked, wrought-iron key from her apron, the woman quickly kissed it as she must have done when still a girl. Deftly the lock came away to be set on a pewter saucer, the luting paste of bread dough baked brown having sealed in the juices that would otherwise have escaped.

Garlic, he told himself as the lid was removed to reveal a top layer of sliced potatoes. Leeks, he knew were there, onions too, and carrots and cabbage, pork, mutton and beef, at least 1,500 grams of meat cut into cubes, the marinade of bay leaves, juniper berries, white wine—at least a litre and a half of that—one pig's foot, one bouquet garni, black pepper, salt, and still more garlic, the terrine filled with layer upon layer of potatoes—at least two kilos of them—the meat and other vegetables interlayered, a slab of back fat first being placed on the bottom, then the whole covered with the liquid. And the cooking time? he asked himself and answered, Three to four hours at a medium heat. Magnificent and unheard of by most at home in France and here, too, probably.

More bread was brought to sop up the juices, his glass refilled from the stoneware jug, Hermann's beer replenished, the woman making certain that everything was as it should be. Indeed, the busier she became, the less she betrayed that nervousness the colonel and her husband sensed only too well.

For dessert there was a tart whose filling was of preserved bilberries, eggs, cinnamon, slivered almonds, *crème fraîche* and honey, and whose sweet, short-crust pastry was of unsalted butter, white flour, sugar, salt and egg yolk. Pure heaven for a citizen from German-Occupied France.

Wedges of Munster cheese and real coffee, dark and absolutely exquisite, finished the repast, Rasche thrusting his tobacco pouch across the table, Oberfeldwebel Lutze having found himself a cigarette.

'These suicides, gentlemen,' said Rasche, taking a moment to draw on that pipe of his and get the fire going. 'There were two of them. The first was a week ago yesterday, but she wasn't discovered until last Tuesday.'

'Sunday, then, 31 January,' said Louis as he packed his pipe, 'but not found until 2 February. Why the delay, Colonel?'

Paris had said that St-Cyr was known to fuss over every detail, Kohler tending to jump to conclusions until cautioned by his other half.

'She went missing. We believed she had gone to Strassburg. The girl had some leave coming and understandably we thought she had taken it.'

'We?' asked Louis.

'My adjutant and myself, but also the officer who keeps the duty roster at the *Polizeikommandantur*. She was a secretary. Well, actually, gentlemen, she was my secretary.'

And now here it comes, swore Kohler silently.

'Name?' asked Louis.

'Renée Ekkehard.'

'Age?'

'Why should that matter, Inspector?'

'It's Chief Inspector, Colonel. Her age, please, just so that my partner and I hear it from yourself.'

'Was I sexually intimate with her—is that what you think? *Mein Gott*, you two. We feed you like princes and then you . . .

I'm a family man. My Hilde and I have been married for nearly forty-five years—no, it's forty-seven this coming April, the ninth!'

'Renée Ekkehard's age, Colonel?' asked Louis, unruffled.

'And then you'll get the rest of it—is this what you're thinking? Well, is it?'

'If necessary. Now, please, we're here to help.'

'Twenty-eight. She had family in Strassburg and had spoken of a need to go home for a visit. Some little matter. I . . . I didn't ask. It was personal.'

And beware all those who shout the loudest about the sanctity of their marriage vows, thought Kohler. Frau Lutze hadn't been able to stop herself from glancing sharply at the colonel as he'd ranted on about his Hilde, while Oberfeldwebel Lutze had given that wife of his a penetrating glance before turning away to concentrate on the quay as if he and his colonel were expecting company at any moment.

'Hadn't the Fräulein Ekkehard signed herself out for leave?' asked Louis.

'The girl had Sunday off but hadn't returned from lunch on Saturday. Schmidt, the duty officer, felt she and I must have been called away on business and thought nothing of it. We often were, but not that afternoon.'

'It was only when my husband noticed her skis were gone that we realized she must have left,' said Yvonne earnestly. 'We thought, a lodge in the hills, perhaps. We asked around—at least I did. One has to be so careful now. No one seemed to know until I—'

'She was one of your boarders?'

'I . . . I needed to know how many would be here for supper.'

And needed to be careful.

'Until I went to see . . . '

Rasche slid the school notebook in front of himself but kept a meaty hand pressed flat on it. 'Yvonne went to see the Fräulein Bödicker at my insistence.'

'Victoria Bödicker looks after the bookshop in her mother's absence, Inspectors. For her not to have done was to have lost the shop.'

That being the law also in Occupied France. 'And the mother?' asked St-Cyr.

'She's in the internment camp at Vittel.'

In France! 'And the school notebook?' asked Hermann, the colonel then nodding curtly at Frau Lutze who ducked her head, fought for words and then finally confessed.

'I took it. Victoria doesn't know this, so please don't tell her. Let me just put it back where I found it. She . . . she went into the shop to wait on a customer. I . . . ' Again Frau Lutze glanced at Rasche for permission. 'I found it in a drawer and thought Otto—the colonel—should see it.'

'The Fräulein Bödicker told Yvonne that my secretary must have gone out to the *Karneval* to get a better idea of what was needed,' said Rasche. 'Look, it's not usual for me to concern myself with such things, but there are always demands these days and one handles them as best one can. The ladies of the *Winterhilfswerk* Committee felt they had to have something quite different this year if they were to raise substantially more than last year. Gauleiter Wagner can be very demanding and I . . . Well, when asked, I agreed to get them a little help.'

Wagner, Gauleiter of Baden and Alsace, was an absolute bastard. 'A *Karneval*. A travelling fair?' asked Louis.

'*Ach*, the whole thing—rides, games, booths and sideshows—had been abandoned. The owner, the performers and operators simply didn't come back from the Blitzkrieg's Exodus.'

'Who went with your secretary?' asked Louis, reaching

across the table to try to do the impossible and get the notebook away from beneath that hand.

'No one. The little fool went alone. Renée was Alsatian. She belonged here. She . . . she didn't think!'

'On Saturday afternoon, 30 January.'

'Listen, damn you, she had no reason to kill herself!'

'Otto, please . . . ' began Yvonne.

'But someone had?' persisted Louis. 'It's either the one or the other, Colonel.'

'And that is why you're here at my request. Mine, you understand. Everything is as it was. I've a detail on guard. No one, unless authorized by myself, goes into that *Karneval* or comes out. The men are billeted in a nearby farmhouse.'

'Dogs?' asked Hermann.

'Of course.'

'And the corpse?' asked Louis.

'I had her cut down and covered.'

'Left exactly as lowered?'

One had best sigh heavily at this Sûreté's penchant for detail. 'She's in a pine box, Chief Inspector. It's cold enough, is it not, for her to keep and at the moment, far more secure than any morgue.'

'Autopsy?'

Verdammt! 'None. We don't normally do such things in cases like this.'

'Do so.'

Must St-Cyr make a nuisance of himself and Kohler let him? 'I'd rather you both took a look at her first. It's not that a coroner can't be produced—*mein Gott*, they're performing autopsies all the time at that university in Strassburg. It's . . . it's just that I would prefer not to submit a request until you're absolutely certain one is necessary.'

'He doesn't want to have to go through the *Konzentrationslager*'s office at Natzweiler-Struthof, Louis.'

Kohler would snort at it! 'Our *Arbeitslagern* are all under that umbrella, yes. Kommandant Zill is often away, the Schutzhaftlagerführer Kramer . . . '

'The one who keeps order, Louis. The one who does the head counts and takes care of everything else.'

'Until June of last year, Kramer was acting Kommandant of Natzweiler-Struthof but please don't think his being passed over by Zill will have upset him in the slightest. Men like Kramer are career officers in the SS and familiar with every aspect of such camps, having served in them, in his case, since 1934. Dachau, Buchenwald or Sachsenhausen, I'm not sure at which of them he cut his teeth, but believe me, gentlemen, cut them he did—'

'Renée Ekkehard and Victoria Bödicker were members of the committee that was having some of the *Karneval* things painted and refurbished,' interjected Yvonne. 'Otto had agreed to lend his support and the use of five of the prisoners. A carpenter, a glazier and three others to clean and paint, or restitch canvas that had been . . . Ah, forgive me, please, Otto, I . . . I only wanted to help.'

'I didn't formally request the loan of those men,' grumbled Rasche. 'Kramer, like so many of his compatriots, is a fanatic when it comes to paperwork, but none of those five were anywhere near that *Karneval* on that weekend. They were at the mill and at their jobs. This I know for certain.'

'And the other suicide?' asked Louis.

'Was one of them.'

2

Trees, their bare branches overhanging, lined the freshly ploughed road onto which the colonel now turned. Ahead of them, the road dipped gently into a hollow where a small bridge gave easy access to a snow-covered stream. Rasche slowed the car, but did he need to shut out the ever-increasing, sooty-grey drabness of the obvious? wondered St-Cyr.

To their left, to the west in the Vosges and perhaps no more than five kilometres, the absolute beauty of snow-covered, spruce- and pine-clad hills drew one's gaze. Below these and nearer were fields where flax would once have been grown for the textile mill, but also there were orchards, among them a cluster of houses and the white stucco and gilded spire of a church whose headstones reached well above the snow. Chapel and columbarium were there to make this Sûreté think of that last Alsatian investigation. Under French law, and they had observed it here between the two most recent wars, the scattering of the ashes was forbidden, since this constituted a violation of the burial place. Usually there was a stiff fine; occasionally the three years and the 5,000 francs it had cost an undertaker in Strasbourg who had claimed, in the autumn of 1937, that all such niches had been filled and that the bishop had turned a deaf ear to cries for more. Certainly M. Édouard Klausener had been lying to bereaved widows and eager heirs too distant to have checked up on him, but to have slept with the widow of the wealthy banker whose ashes he had just scattered, to have promised marriage when he had already tied the knot? The *imbécile*. Ashes were nothing to fool with.

'There are still trout here,' said Rasche longingly, having stopped the car on the bridge. 'The bed of this little tributary of the Fecht is surprisingly clean and of well-rounded gravel. Granite from those hills, and its sand.'

To the east, across another field, the road they should have taken ran straight alongside the compound. Behind the wire, in its southwestern corner and nearest to them, was a large, five-storey rectangular building of faded red brick with tall chimneys on either end, but no smoke coming from them. Beyond this original mill, and running in a north to south direction side by side, one after another, were the low, ground-storey factories of modern industry whose tall chimneys pillared sooty black smoke from the steam plants, but Hermann . . . Hermann wouldn't be thinking of scattered crematoria ashes or of a springtime's stolen moment. He would be ever-mindful of that double-stranded, horizontally run barbed wire at fifteen centimetre intervals which was three metres high, the top canted inwardly a half-metre so that no one in their right mind would ever attempt to climb it.

Without a word, a match was struck by St-Cyr, and when the cigarette was passed forward over the back of the front seat, Rasche noticed that Kohler instinctively reached for it. These two, he wondered. Had they grown so close? Kohler had always been trouble, but had been different than most, yes, different, but had it been wise to have asked for them? Two 'honest' detectives, 'hated' by some, the SS in particular?

Without even turning, the Bavarian handed the cigarette to the Frenchman who took but a brief drag before passing it back and gently patting his partner on the shoulder.

'Gentlemen, a quiet word before we go in there. Under the rules of the Geneva Convention governing prisoners of war, those above the rank of private are not obliged to work but can, if they wish, volunteer. From the autumn of 1940 well into '41, the men held here were French POWs—among them several textile workers from Lille and other places in the north. In '41 the camp at Natzweiler-Struthof came into being. Most of the French were moved out to other stalags and oflags well inside the Reich, but some were absolutely essential.'

'Meaning that they had no other choice but to stay, Louis, and now find themselves under Kommandant Zill and Schutzhaftlagerführer Kramer.'

'*Ach*, Kohler, please! Zill and Kramer are not above me—it's a grey area, since they are SS and I'm the Wehrmacht's representative. Among my duties as Kommandant of the Ober-Rhein,* I liaise with each of the Arbeitslager Kommandants and their staffs but can, since handling the discipline problems of each of those forty-seven camps is the prerogative of the *Konzentrationslager*, go only so far.'

And if that wasn't warning enough, what was? wondered Kohler.

'Yet you were able to obtain help for the ladies of the *Winterhilfswerk* Committee,' said Louis.

Irritably rubbing away the fog on his side windscreen, Rasche again gazed up the little valley toward the hills. 'The

* the Haut-Rhin or High Rhine area of Alsace

second of these so-called suicides ran the testing lab and was responsible for the chemical work—the dye batches, the digesters, that sort of thing. There's a staff of two that he had trained quite well for subordinate duties, but someone will definitely have to be found to replace him.'

'The date, the exact location and time, Colonel?' asked Louis.

Rasche didn't turn from looking toward the hills. 'Last Friday evening, 5 February. The men work a twelve-hour shift, but he had stayed late—the matter of a new dye batch that was coming up. When he didn't return to the barracks by lights-out—that is 2200 hours—it was felt he must have been detained. It had happened frequently. Some prisoners do enjoy losing themselves in their work. It was thought that one of the factory guards would surely fetch him. At midnight the alarm went out and they found him soon afterward. There's a toilet near the lab. He had—'

'Yes, yes, Colonel. The body?' asked St-Cyr, a hand firmly gripping Hermann by the left shoulder.

A glance at this Sûreté who asked the questions and felt so deeply for his partner would be sufficient, felt Rasche, and then the gate closing behind them as further warning.

'The dogs, where are they?' asked Hermann.

'*Ach*, they'll be in their kennels.'

'And that second victim, Colonel?'

'I had him put in the root cellar with the potatoes. It was, at that moment, the best I could do.'

'The potatoes, Louis.'

Hermann was really feeling it. 'Transport, Colonel. A busy man such as yourself can't constantly be with us.'

'It's being arranged, but for today you'll just have to be content with me as your guide.'

Constant on the air now was the muted, agitating sound of thousands and thousands of mechanical shuttles, and the rank, chemical smell of rotten eggs.

The steps were wide and of concrete, the root cellar deep and seemingly endless under the arctic light of two widely spaced fifteen-watt bulbs. Up from the earthen floor a dampness seeped, fog hanging in the fetid air. The potatoes, too many of them rotten, lay on racks of lath in tiers, the double-wrapped cord around the victim's neck, stark white, stiff, and brand-new.

He lay on his back on one of the tiers so as not to be trampled in the aisle that ran along the centre of the bunker. Not young, not old, not tall, not short—*ah, mon Dieu,* thought St-Cyr, must the images come so fast when one had to ask, had he killed himself?

With hanging it was often impossible to tell if it hadn't been the victim's intention. Perhaps forty percent of all suicides chose this method; murderers seldom, for invariably the victim fought back, leaving marks and smashing things unless drugged or drunk, but even then there were often signs of a struggle, noises too.

The face was thin, the dark brown eyes wide open but protruding slightly. Sprays of petechiae, the little blood spots usually found just under the skin of the deceased, seemed all but absent. The bridge of the nose was sharp. He had shaved early on that Friday morning, the razor dull. The tongue wasn't swollen nor bitten through. The lips, parted slightly, were plum-blue, the slipknot up tight under the right ear, the head canted to the left.

Saliva had drooled in quantity, a vital act. Most probably,

then, he had been alive as the rope had tightened. Waste had been voided but if he stank, as he must, there was no hint of this, so masked was the air. *Bien sûr,* there was nothing quite like the smell of decaying potatoes and rotten eggs.

Fully clothed, he still wore the French Army trousers he'd had during the Blitzkrieg, now much patched and crudely mended. The shirt collar was frayed but the clothes were clean, there was no dirt scaled about the throat on either side of the rope, no sign of the too-infrequent bathing one would have expected of a prison camp.

Above the rope, the neck did have its scattered petechiae; at it, the flesh was depressed, but was the ligature too tightly drawn for him to have tied it himself? one had to ask.

The backs of the hands were blotched with slate-blue to reddish-purple patches. The calves, ankles and feet would be the same. As the engine of life had ceased, gravity had simply let the heavier red corpuscles sink to the lowest spots.

'You know the colonel wants this done quietly,' he said to the corpse, 'so where, please, is it best we begin? I'm alone. I've told the guard who conducted me to this place that he was to close the doors behind me and return to his post on the gate. Where could I run to, eh, if run I wanted?'

The hands were tightly clenched, the thumbnails that dark, midnight blue all the others would show.

'You were married,' said St-Cyr, leaning well in over the victim, 'but your wedding ring isn't of gold or silver. It's been fashioned out of piece of tin and beautifully riveted. Even the edges have been curled inward so that you wouldn't cut yourself. There's an engraving—not hearts and letters but something else, something very fine. Had he Gallic and Celtic ancestors, this tinsmith-cum-jeweller? Ah, *sacré,* my light!'

Shaking the torch, he accidentally banged his head on the

rack above, cursed Gestapo stores and the Occupation, said calmly now, yes, calmly, '*Excusez-moi*, monsieur. It's the times, *n'est-ce pas*? Spare batteries are seldom available. For each new one back home, two old ones must be turned in. Certainly when in Paris, my partner is adept at substituting ours for those of other *gestapistes*, but we haven't spent much time there of late.'

Lighting a candle, taken from his pocket, St-Cyr fixed it to one of the wooden uprights. Looking down at the victim, bathed as that one was in this gentlest of lights, he said, 'May the grace of God be with you, *mon fils*. Though I am no priest, I doubt that one will ever see you.

'My partner couldn't have joined me,' he added quickly. 'Always now I feel I have to explain. You see, he can't stomach the sight of death anymore. It happens even to the best of us and he's one of them. I also don't want him heaving up that magnificent lunch. But why, please, did the colonel provide it and why was that housekeeper of his edgy, his former sergeant-major silent?'

A hanging. An 'apparent' suicide when virtually everything seen so far indicated that was exactly what had happened.

The toilet was spotless, Kohler noted, the room no more than a small closet, the porcelain throne massive, for they had sure as hell built them to last in the 1890s when the office and the original mill had begun. The dark walnut seat, lid and brass fittings were as solid as the Rock of Bloody Ages, but *Gott sei Dank*, the cistern hadn't pulled away to crush the victim.

Standing in the doorway, he let his gaze sift slowly over everything. It had been good of Louis not to have asked him to help with the corpse, good of him to have tried to keep his partner busy and away from thinking about the wire, but neither of them had realized the size of the *Textilfabrikschrijen*, the Schrijen Works. It had been almost a two-kilometre forced march just to get to this end of the administrative building. Lagerfeldwebel Jakob Dorsche was now behind him, as were the two the sergeant had delegated to escort this detective. Uneasy—all three of them were that, the guards terrified Dorsche would tear a stripe off them for some minor infraction. After all, it was his job to keep order in the camp and Dorsche should damned well have known something like this 'suicide' might happen and would definitely be held responsible no matter what.

Given the size of the factory, and at least three to four hundred POWs, Louis and he would not get anywhere without his help. Dorsche knew it too. Watchful blue eyes behind wire-rimmed specs missed little. The ruddy Burgermeister cheeks were round, the forehead a hard rampart of bone that had rammed many, the nose flat, wide and broken several times, the ears small and tight against the short-cropped, greying bristles under that cap, the fists hammers.

A barrel of a man in jackboots that gleamed, Dorsche took the time necessary to assess his visitor as cigarettes were found in this detective's innermost pocket and offered, the packet all but empty, the sacrifice evident.

'*Danke*, Herr Hauptmann Detektiv Aufsichtsbeamter. You've seen the notices, have you?'

'Pardon?'

'The fire hazard of such practices. Smoking indoors is *verboten* except in designated areas. The officers' mess, that of the men, their headquarters also, the—'

'And here I thought—'

'That this toilet would be used for such?'

Dorsche had been leagues ahead of him!

'It's not often we get someone such as yourself, Herr Kohler. The stride, the set of the shoulders—one can tell a military man at a glance, a police officer also, just as it's not hard to tell a *Kriegsgefanganer* once one has been one, but please don't trouble yourself. I also was once a prisoner of war in that other conflict, the one we lost, so in their wisdom, the OKW, after much deliberation, put me in charge of this camp.'

The Oberkommando der Wehrmacht, the High Command, and a life behind wire, but this time, *his* wire!

Now there were only two cigarettes left in the packet. Dorsche indicated the boys. 'Good fortune doesn't often come easily,' he said to them. 'Beat it. I can take care of him myself.'

A match was struck. Dorsche leaned in, and as he lit his cigarette, he said, 'A Wills Gold Flake? You impress me, Herr Kohler. Did you shoot the aircraft down or only arrest its British pilot and crew after they had bailed out and tried to escape?'

'Neither, and so much for this not being a designated area. Look, we need your help.'

'I would have thought that obvious.'

'Then I'd be grateful if you would go over everything. Who found him, the time as closely as possible, the position of the body, the rope . . . '

'And anything suspicious?'

'Even the smallest detail.'

'Like cigarette ashes in a tin cup and a man perhaps taking a contemplative moment at 2207 hours?'

One of the guards must have reported this but a sigh would be best. 'Look, I know your eyes are as good as mine, if not better.'

Ach, how humble of Herr Kohler. 'This toilet services both the laboratory and the administrative offices on this floor. The secretaries . . . there are five of them and one other woman, also the Lageroffizier, the Oberstleutnant Rudel and others of his staff, still others too. I tell you this only so that you will realize that they were in the habit of using it as well but normally not at that time of night.'

But had any of them left something they shouldn't have? wondered Herr Kohler, unable to prevent himself from glancing up at the cistern.

'There was nothing but water in it,' said Dorsche. 'I checked.'

'But what led you to do so? Apart, that is, from your normally suspicious nature?'

A shrug had best be given.

'Didn't he have a guard with him?'

Had there been a note of panic in Herr Kohler's voice? '*Kein Posten*. The one who killed himself needed no guard here and was free to come and go. Orders. . . . Who am I to question the will of my superior officers? Oberstleutnant Rudel is in charge of the *Lagerführung*.'

The camp office.

'It is he who issues the *Passierscheine und Ausweise* that allow such workers to come and go at all hours.'

The temporary passes and the more permanent ones and identity papers all such places would demand. 'And the body?'

'Was found by Gefreiter Hartmann at 0011 hours Saturday. He touched nothing and immediately notified me.'

'Who, in turn, notified the Oberstleutnant.'

'Who then notified Kommandant Rasche, as was his duty.'

'All right, we've got the chain of command. Now tell me exactly what you saw.'

'Hanging is never pleasant.'

'And I'm fresh out of cigarettes. Sorry.'

'Then try one of these. *Ach*, take two. You may need them. These days one never knows.'

They were Junos and right away they brought moisture to Herr Kohler's eyes, for they were often a Berliner's first choice and he'd once been a detective there. 'Two?' he asked, as if the truth were hard to accept and he'd been away too long.

'Sweepings. Hay, chaff, dried herbs and other things like carrot tops. With tobacco, of course, or else they couldn't legally have sold them as such, could they, a government that doesn't lie?'

Berlin, and Louis should have heard him! 'The Gauloises bleues and Gitanes we've been getting have rat shit in them. There aren't many horses left in France, so it has to be that. I use the leaves of the red beech, cured in a biscuit tin I keep buried deeply in one of the manure piles out at the racetrack, but because of the threat of terrorism from the *Banditen*, the Résistance, if you like, they've had to move the races to Le Tremblay from Longchamp. When black and crumbled, the leaves have no taste and are perfect for thinning good tobacco, if you can get it. Twenty percent. More and they're a waste; less and it just keeps getting better and better.'

A connoisseur. 'Then you'll understand that it's hard to keep paper here.'

Dorsche indicated the all but spent roll of grey, unbleached tissue most POWs would never see. 'Was he taking it for his pals?'

'When he thought he could get away with it, but when one has nothing else but the pages of one's Bible why, one does what one can, is that not so?'

It was. 'What's the ration?'

'Two packets of twenty a fortnight, or fifty grams of the loose, with papers. The POWs are supplied through their parcels from home and those of the Red Cross, so they don't always need what we bring in for their canteen, when we can get it, of course.'

And don't need it! 'Was there anything else here?'

'A little something . . . '

The copy of the magazine, *Schöne Mädchen in der Natur*, was thin, the full-page black-and-white spreads well taken. All the girls were totally naked and generously posed. They lounged, stretched, bent over backward and pressed their hands to the gymnasium's floor as they grinned.

'Every man, even a *Kriegsgefangener*, needs a little diversion from time to time,' mused Dorsche.

'Pants down when found?'

'Up. Belt and buttons tight. No signs of an erection on death as can be quite common. None of the—'

'All right, all right! Who left it and why?'

Now that was a good question, but a shrug would be best. *Ach*, the shoulders, the rheumatism . . .

Dorsche winced and Kohler let him be for the moment. Though the Nazis had a damp view of pornography, they encouraged healthy eroticism to boost the birth rate. All of the major hotels offered these above-the-counter 'health-and-art' magazines which often found their way to Paris where they were earnestly compared with photos the French produced in spite of the extreme shortages of photographic materials.

'You'd best let me keep this, Lagerfeldwebel.'

'Certainly.'

'Anything else?'

A thorough detective, was that it? 'His carpenter's nail and stone, set carefully on the floor to one side. The left. Here, you can have those too.'

'And this?'

Herr Kohler indicated the magazine and had best be told a little something to keep him happy. 'Angrily folded and jammed behind that roll of tissue in the dispenser, and wet with his tears, I think, since there was also this.'

And torn from another magazine, the upfront buff-shot of a grinning young Wehrmacht stallion, one of the 'boys' the French girls in Paris and elsewhere were having such a time with.

'He's not from here, so don't even bother trying to attach a name to him.'

The candle having burned down, the victim was again seen only in electric light. Shadows, cast by the lath and potatoes, fell on him.

'You won't mind, will you, if I take a look at these?' asked St-Cyr, gesturing companionably with pipe in hand. 'Please don't think it an invasion of your privacy and detective meddling. Think of it as a necessity if we are to get at the truth.'

On the earthen floor at his feet were the last effects, taken from the pockets. Like soldiers everywhere, Eugène André Thomas had carried snapshots of his loved ones: the wife as a girl of twenty at Paris's Lutetia Pool, then as a bride and as the radiant mother of a brand-new baby boy. One of little Paul at the age of six months, another at a year and a half, Madame Paulette Thomas holding him by the hand and delighted by his timid steps.

'Radiant still,' he said. 'But last Friday night, monsieur, you ripped her photo apart, though taking care to save your son from such a fate. Had she betrayed you?'

As always these 'discussions' were as if with the living, and everything that could be was used. 'Betrayal, *mon ami*. Certainly what has happened to her photos cries this out. Wayward wives are sadly becoming an ever-increasing problem at home, especially in the larger cities and towns where food is scarce and prices astronomical. Your rank was that of a private, though as a chemist you could have been an NCO, and I must ask, were you a bit of a rebel?'

There was no answer. 'Had Madame Paulette taken to the streets to feed herself and your son?'

Again nothing was forthcoming. Perhaps some common ground would be useful. 'Look, I know such a thought is hard, and that it takes time for one to adjust if true. Before she and our little Philippe were tragically killed early last December by a bomb that was meant for me, my second wife, my Marianne, had carried on a torrid affair with one of the Boche. Although I forgave her immediately, and was able to convey this to her, if only on one occasion, I do know what it feels like to be a cuckold. The long absences, the loneliness she had had to deal with—it was all my fault, and I readily admit it. And the bomb, you ask? The Résistance keep putting me on some of their hit lists. The Gestapo found the bomb and left it in place. Apparently neither side is content. The former think I'm a collaborator because I have to work with Hermann; the latter hate our guts for always pointing the finger of truth. Let's face it, these days no one is happy except for those who are swimming in the gravy.'

There were no photos of the parents, none of a brother or sister or in-law. The couple, it appeared, had had only themselves. 'You weren't from Lille or any of the other textile cities and towns in the northeast, as the colonel stated. You lived in Paris, in Issy-les-Moulineaux, an industrial suburb in the southwest of the city. Chemicals, leather, bronze, copper and aluminium, the National tobacco factory that employs 3,000 to make the crap they ration. The giant Renault Works is also nearby, in Boulogne-Billancourt on the Île Seguin. It's the one that makes things for the Wehrmacht, like a lot of other such concerns.'

A flat on the suburb's avenue de la Paix, at numéro 43, wouldn't be up-market, but was within a short walk of the old Fort d'Issy and the school on the rue du Fort. A good choice, one would think. Oh for sure, things hadn't been easy in the thirties for chemists like this and millions of others. They had picked up in '38, possibly a little before that, but the couple would have married in hard times, the baby coming right away, so in late '37 probably. There weren't more recent photos, even those that must have been taken just before the Blitzkrieg, but perhaps they were still pinned up beside his bunk. 'You didn't tear them, too, did you?' he asked.

Thomas would likely have received a few photos in relief parcels from home and would, most probably, have been made aware by the camp's administration that the Renault Works had been bombed by the RAF on the night of 3 March last year. Five hundred dead; 1,500 wounded, but had Paulette Thomas been terrified or had she been elsewhere on that night, having left their little son in the care of a neighbour as so many unlicenced *filles de joie* were now doing?

'Let's face it, *mon ami*, the pay of a private is next to nothing and as the wife of a common soldier, conscripted in '39, all she can hope for are the allowances Vichy doles out per child and per wife or dependent parent. Granted, after much debate and thousands of complaints, the Maréchal Pétain, our illustrious Head of State, and his ministers in Vichy where the government resides, reluctantly agreed to an additional two francs per day to ease the burden POW wives suffer when sending parcels to their husbands. After all, there are 1,500,000 of you, *n'est-ce pas*, and that's one hell of a lot of unhappy wives since almost sixty percent of you are married and forty percent have children at home. She did send you parcels, didn't she?'

They would have to find out. 'Two lousy francs,' he grated, 'at a time when five kilos of potatoes in Paris cost 2,000 on the *marché noir*, the half a kilo of sugar another 2,000. An inner tube for the bicycle of necessity everyone has to have these days, costs 250; a new tyre, 1,000 if you can get any of these items and avoid arrest, since it's illegal to deal on that market, though the Church now says one can buy but not sell on it.'

He would toss a hand at such idiocy, would add, 'There's no milk available in a country that once produced so much its milk trains were a regular feature. Granted, those wives whose incomes fail to reach 5,000 francs a year, can apply for a supplement and relief from all but the land tax, and a reduction in their rent. But to get these, one has to go down on the knees, and even then, there are over 30,000 POW wives in Paris alone who must exist on less than 1,000 francs a month.'

One couldn't do it without help and that, if not the terrible loneliness and uncertainty plus being the sole caregiver, was the problem. Two and a half years of it now.

Four hundred and seventy-one Lagermark, the 'Lagergeld' or Lager Gold, had been in a tight roll, in the right-hand pocket. Worthless outside the camp, no doubt. Certainly the money couldn't be sent home, although Vichy had said that if working prisoners could be allowed home on holiday—yes, on holiday!—they would be able to exchange the Lagermark for francs. There were eleven tens, six fifties, the rest being in fives, twos and ones and all with serial numbers well into their tens of millions.

A postcard, sent a good six weeks ago but only just received, had been forgotten in a back pocket. Saved from the bitter haste of the tearing, it said: *"Mon cher Eugène, Each day we pray for your return, each night I long for the moment we'll be together again."*

'Those aren't the words of a betrayer, Monsieur Thomas. They're those of a wife who loved you desperately.'

There wasn't much more on the postcard. Only seven lines were allowed and the censors had been at the rest. Those of the Pétain Government first, and then those of the *Lagerführung*. 'One can but imagine the humility you felt at having others read your personal mail and then delete as much as they pleased, but had she had another child? One that you were unaware of until word came through from another source, an anonymous one? Please, I must ask. You see, you wouldn't have received such a notice directly. You would have gotten the news from the Lager office, which would have received it from Vichy's Berlin office of the *Service diplomatique des prisonniers de guerre.*'

There had been little else in the pockets. A rag Monsieur Thomas had been using as a handkerchief, some notes he had been scribbling on a scrap paper—chemical equations, not written words. Two rose-coloured dress buttons had been picked up but where? A *mégot* tin had nothing in it, a last cigarette having been smoked down to its soggy end to be angrily thrust into a pocket.

'There is rust on this rag. Earlier I had to break open your fingers to remove your wedding ring, but why the rust? A little of it is smeared on this photo, the first, I believe, that was torn. Ah! Permit me my magnet. A moment. *Sacré nom de nom,* did Hermann borrow it again? He never returns anything unless reminded. I tell myself it's not that he doesn't intend to, simply that his mind is elsewhere.'

Finding the magnet, he brushed it over the skin of the fingers, yielding little, the left palm a touch more, the rag still more.

'Rust and iron filings,' he called out after having gone down the aisle to stand under one of the lights.

Along with the *carte d'identité*, there was the *Arbeitslager*'s grey *Kennkarte* or ID. The *Dienstausweise*, a mud-brown card, allowed the victim to be on Wehrmacht property. An *Ausweis* and *Vorläufige Ausweis* were passes and temporary passes, the first allowing him to be in the administrative building's laboratory and in the cellulose plant and dye works, the second, to visit the carnival site. A *Polizeitliche Bescheinigung*, a police permit, authorized him to do general maintenance and paintwork there.

All of these last three pieces of paper had been signed by Colonel Rasche.

'Eugène André Thomas, age thirty-two; born, Chartres, 2 February 1911; died, Kolmar, a mere three days after your last birthday. Hair brown, eyes brown, height 176 centimetres (5'9"), weight 72.6 kilos (160 lbs.) recorded after you were taken prisoner. Let's put it now at 56.7 (125 lbs.) give or take a kilo, but why the iron filings, why the torn photographs? Why commission a comrade to make such a ring unless you had loved your wife dearly and believed emphatically that she had reciprocated? Why the little bankroll—was it to have paid for the ring?'

Questions . . . there were always those and always far too little time.

'In short, *mon ami*, everything says you took your own life out of despair. There are no bruises to indicate otherwise, no evidence of strangulation before the rope was used. Perhaps the coroner will have a different opinion, but I didn't find any skin under your fingernails, no hairs from an assailant either, just a little dirt and grease. Oh for sure, Hermann might have something—is that what you think? Then let me tell you, with Hermann one never quite knows what he'll come up with or how far he will go.'

'Herr Kohler, *please,*' objected Jakob Dorsche.

'*Ach*, give me a minute, will you?'

Just along from the toilet, a doorway opened into the upper offices. Like the mill, the room seemed to run on and on. Rows of desks showed lots of vacancies, but also those who nailed down specific tasks: plant maintenance, supplies, sales and accounting. It wasn't hard to pigeonhole them, most looking as if they'd been with the firm for years. Beyond these desks, filing cabinets and shelves to the ceiling held the pattern books, fabric samples and order books going right back to when the firm began, since places like this never threw anything out.

Enclosed offices were to the left.

'Herr Kohler . . . '

'Didn't I tell you to leave me be?'

Lying on two of the vacated desks, beside framed portrait photos of former occupants in Wehrmacht uniforms, were bouquets of red, artificial chrysanthemums just as in Paris's Père Lachaise. Elsewhere, wreaths of vine trimmings were with baby booties, on only one a freshly folded swastika.

Immediately to the left, and just inside the door, was the secretarial pool. Three were in the uniforms of the *Blitzmädschen*, the *Bund Deutscher Mädel* or BDMs, girls from home doing their duty. Two others weren't in uniform and had obviously been with the firm for years, whereas the oldest of the BDMs was now the supervisor and kept a stern eye on the younger two who, among other duties, were the *Postzensuren* who read the POW's mail, blacked it out and sorted through the *Personalkarten*, adding notes when needed. Every POW would have one of those damned cards on file. A head-and-shoulders photo, prints of both forefingers, assorted personal data and work history, punishment too, the *Straf*.

One of the *Postzensuren* was in her late teens, the other perhaps twenty, and like all others here, they would have used that toilet and must have crossed paths every day with Eugène Thomas, but neither would meet his gaze, both just kept on working as if petrified of him.

'Herr Kohler, *please*. The laboratory is this way,' said Dorsche. 'The Oberstleutnant Rudel has said that I was to take you there, not bring you here.'

'Then I'd best pay my respects, hadn't I?'

The door to Rudel's office was just beyond the secretarial pool and tightly closed, its frosted glass bearing the name and rank in black Gothic scrip outlined with gilding.

Dorsche heaved a grateful sigh. 'He's busy.'

'He should be.'

Herr Kohler's knock should have broken the glass, but he didn't wait for an answer, simply barged in, sang out a good afternoon and then, 'Kohler, Kripo Paris-Central, Herr Oberstleutnant. I thought I'd best drop by to let you know my partner and I have arrived and are already hard at work. Fräulein . . . ?'

Dorsche buggered off and left the door open, but there was a woman in the office. Rudel, though, didn't move or appear startled in any way. Instead, he took his time to assess this visiting Detektiv. Cigarette poised in the right hand, he let its smoke curl lazily upward. A designated area, was that it?

So this was Kohler, thought Rudel. A very ordinary, not-so-ordinary man. Paris had had a lot to say about him and that 'partner' of his.

As if already bored with the interview, Rudel inhaled deeply, then let the smoke seep slowly from his nostrils. He wasn't SS, thank God, but among the awards on that neatly pressed field-grey jacket were a Spanienkreuz, the Spanish Cross, then the ribbon of the Medaille zur Erinnerung—the Commemorative for Spanish Volunteers—and a wound badge too, all from 1937 and the Revolution in Spain. Then the black wound badge of the Polish Campaign in '39, for one or two wounds; an Iron Cross First-Class too, and the ribbon of the *Winterschlacht im Osten,* the 1941–42 campaign in Russia and what was called the Frozen Meat Medal. Had he lost toes, a foot or leg? Not the ears anyway, nor the hands or any of the fingers. There was a Knight's Cross too, and Nazi Party badge, ah, yes.

'It wasn't murder, Kohler. It was suicide.'

'Karl, you know that can't be true!' shrilled the woman. 'Two suicides in less than a week? Eugène wouldn't have—'

'Sophie, Sophie . . . *Ach,* for once will you listen to me? I know you don't want to believe it possible, but he did take his own life.'

'Your name, Fräulein?' asked Kohler.

So many things were in the look she gave. Still badly shaken by the deaths, but perhaps also not liking the thought of two experienced detectives from Paris being brought in, she stood over by the windows, was in better light than Rudel. About thirty or thirty-five years of age. A blonde with rapidly misting grey-blue eyes, the hair of shoulder length and not worn in the crisscrossing diadem of the secretarial pool but as an outdoors woman would, if somewhat loose and hastily tied.

The lips were perfectly matched, no lipstick though, but when together as now, under scrutiny, they twisted down a little to the right, subconsciously emphasizing a hesitant uncertainty that, like the grief and dislike of visiting detectives, couldn't quite be hidden.

'The Fräulein Schrijen is the owner's daughter, Kohler.'

'Granddaughter of its founder,' she said sharply.

A skier too, thought Kohler. The creases under the eyes were from the winter's glare, the cheeks and chin burnished by the wind.

'Sophie has a hand in running the Works, Kohler,' said Rudel, who hadn't taken his gaze from this detective for a second.

'In my brother's absence, I'm assistant general manager,' she said, still having not moved from the windows. The shirt-blouse was white but unbuttoned enough to reveal a fine gold chain and cross that was definitely not a Nazi symbol. The powder-blue jacket and matching skirt were Swiss. She would have had to travel there on business, would have had access to all the necessary permits, but exactly what was the relationship between these two who seemed barely to tolerate each other, and why had she no liking for visiting detectives, especially if upset by these 'suicides'?

'Two deaths in less than a week, Fräulein?' he asked.

'Renée Ekkehard was a member of my *Winterhilfswerk* Committee.'

'Sophie, you weren't responsible.'

Turning quickly away to avoid looking at either of them, she said, 'I *was*, Karl! It was me who asked her if she could check on things at the *Karneval*. *Me*, Karl. I . . . I was too busy and couldn't leave. I couldn't!'

She was now all but in tears and could well have been hanged herself had she gone out there—was that it, eh? wondered Kohler. Quite obviously Rudel knew that was what she was thinking, but one had best ask, 'This *Karneval*, Fräulein?'

'This other suicide, damn you. *Ach,* why don't you call it that, since everyone else is but me? A girl of twenty-eight who had all of her life before her *hangs* herself for no apparent reason, nor gives any indication of being depressed or suicidal? She *plans* to go skiing at Natzweiler-Struthof, has been *invited* to another party there with friends from Strassburg?'

'When?'

'This coming weekend. I . . . I don't know all of the details. How could I? Only that everyone needs a bit of fun these days. Now if you will excuse me, Karl. I have work to do.'

'She's not happy, is she?' said Kohler when she had left, not closing the door but giving views of a secretarial pool and its *Postzensuren* who had obviously listened in.

'Don't be tiresome, Kohler. Both were suicides. The colonel's secretary had seen things at Natzweiler-Struthof she couldn't stomach; the other one—our chemist who ran the lab—had just discovered that his wife had been repeatedly breaking her marriage vows. Here . . . Here, you can take the letter we received from Berlin. Don't lose it. Now get out. Do whatever it is Colonel Rasche expects, but don't bother me again. I, too, have work.'

Hermann still hadn't found his way to the laboratory where three large rooms were separated by glass partitions above the workbenches. Two technicians in white lab coats were busy in the adjacent room. One was repeatedly ironing a swatch similar to the sample of fabric the colonel had left on his desk at the *Polizeikommandantur,* the other conducting a water-repellency test. Now a fine mist for a half-minute, now a close examination of the result—the beading of the water probably but girls in their late teens and temptation? wondered St-Cyr, for if ever a prisoner of war had had a cosy little nest, it had been Eugène André Thomas. Here there would at once have been immense relief from the crowding of the other POWs with whom he had to live and take his meals, then, too, the female company that had been denied the rest of the men, cleanliness too.

The technicians were Alsatian and very businesslike. Engrossed in their tasks, they were trying their best to take no notice of this Sûreté. *Bien sûr*, the colonel had said Thomas had trained them well, but had there been more than that? Such close contact on a daily basis must have produced something, but their questioning had best be left until later.

The Executive Offices were just beyond the laboratory. He had all but collided with a very well-dressed woman who had angrily rushed past him, failing entirely to hide her tears.

'Sophie Schrijen,' he muttered. The name, in typed letters on white pasteboard, had been taped to her office door beneath the Gothically lettered brass of an Alain Fernand of the same surname, her brother, the office next to it being that of her father, Yvan Léonard (Löwe) Schrijen, General Manager, Chief Executive Officer, and Owner, but had the Fräulein Schrijen been close to either of the victims? Had that been why she had been so upset, or had it simply been the presence of two unwanted detectives?

Carefully he began to arrange the contents of Thomas's pockets on the section of workbench the prisoner had used as a desk. The ID and other papers went to the left, then in an arc, the rag, the cash, the *mégot* tin and wedding ring, with the postcard text face up at the top of the arc, and the pieced-together snapshots following, especially the one of little Paul at the age of six months.

The two rose-coloured dress buttons were found and placed directly below the tin, along with the scant remains of a last cigarette. 'Rust,' he said, and drawing in a deep breath, looked slowly over the contents, trying to get a better fix on the man in his laboratory, his little kingdom, for that would have been precisely what at least some, if not all of his fellow prisoners would have felt.

'Ah, the formulae,' he muttered, and finding the crumpled scrap of paper, smoothed it out. Printed lines showed that it had been torn from the corner of a page. Victoria Bödicker's notebook? he silently asked, seeing as the colonel had left it out on his desk at the *Polizeikommandantur* and had been reluctant to part with it at lunch but had said that Eugène Thomas had been working on a new dye batch.

There were three chemical equations on the scrap of notepaper, each precisely and neatly written. The first involved a compound of carbon, hydrogen and oxygen with caustic soda. The second equation took the product of the first and combined it with carbon disulphide, the source of the stench of rotten eggs—the product of that reaction then being treated with sulphuric acid.

These equations were nothing more than the process, much simplified, of taking wood pulp, which was cellulose, and converting it to the artificial silk, the rayon the Works produced, but why write them on the corner of a notebook from which they were then torn? Why hastily scribble another formula below them, that of trinitrophenol—picric acid—used as a yellow dye, oh for sure, and as an antiseptic, but also as an extremely unstable and highly dangerous explosive? Why stuff that scrap of paper into a pocket the colonel must surely have gone through and found?

The handwriting of the trinitrophenol was decidedly different from the rest.

'Louis, he lived in despair,' said Kohler, having at last arrived.

One had best run a finger over the contents of the note, ending at the trinitrophenol, something they both knew only too well. 'For now, *mon vieux*, let's just keep it to ourselves.'

'Since Rasche must have known about it?'

'Ah, mais alors, alors, Hermann, for now the benefit of doubt, especially as these two buttons I found in Thomas's pockets are totally unlike those he left out for us to find and are from a girl's summer dress.'

'Then you'd best read this, seeing as the *salaud* failed to mention it as well.'

> "To whom it may concern,
>
> Messieurs, I feel it is my duty to report that the wife of Eugène Thomas, prisoner 220371, Stalag XIV J, Arbeitslager 13, Colmar, Alsace, has been unfaithful to him. On occasions too numerous, his little son, a boy of five, has been left with a neighbour while Mme. Paulette Thomas goes to Pigalle, les Halles and other such well-known rendezvous and does not return until the following morning. Sometimes it is noon before she gets home, sometimes later or not at all.

'Hermann, is this really necessary?'

'Read on.'

> "At other times the victorious soldiers of our German friends are seen entering her flat, the child then being shoved out the door in the cruelest of weather. An hour goes by, two hours. Sometimes she is with two men, sometimes with three."

'How can anyone give credence to such rubbish?'

'Anonymous and uncensored, Louis, but as to his having killed himself because of it . . . '

'There was also rust from iron filings.'

'*Ach*, any Kriegie worth his salt finds himself a carpenter's nail and a little stone. He grinds off a bit every day. You put the filings on your tongue and wash them down with water. Stomach acid then changes the filings to iron chloride which is absorbed by the blood, but I have to tell you, Rasche's second-in-command here is positive it's a suicide.'

'Then why, please, does a man who watches his health as closely as he can under such circumstances, kill himself even if he had only just read that letter, which he couldn't have, since it wasn't found with him?'

'The Oberstleutnant Rudel would have shown it to him earlier.'

'And yet our victim *still* takes his iron?'

'There was this, too, and this.'

One of the 'nature' magazines and a cutout from another.

'Left in the toilet for him to find, Louis. Maybe by one of the *Postzensuren*, since they were both gun-shy of me and the firm has lost several of its former staff members to the meat grinder of the present conflict.'

'A grudge, a wanting to get back at the enemy?'

'Perhaps, but for now that driver of ours is insisting that he show us a little something else.'

To the flat farmlands some seven kilometres to the east of Kolmar, the long and ever-deepening shadows of the late afternoon brought a bleakness that couldn't help but be felt. Snow drifted. The wind, down from the Vosges to the west, found each obstruction: a lonely, shaggy-maned russet mare, an orchard, a haystack, cows being driven to a barn. Two boys pulling a toboggan heaped with firewood stopped to stare at the car, while beyond them, across the barren, windswept fields where cabbages would flourish in season, the carnival lay in ruins partly enclosed by the Kastenwald, a woods whose bare branches and darkened trunks had helped to shelter what remained.

Caught, trapped, overrun, its operators and owners chased out by the Blitzkrieg of 1940, everything had been left in place, but the sight of it made one ask, is it the end of the world?

Multicoloured, much faded bunting flew in tatters. Once-gilded charioteers rode into battle. Marquee roofs of canvas, board and painted panel had collapsed, yet still there were the ruined stalls, booths, sideshows and rides. A carousel, the stark pipes of whose band organ were caked with ice and webbed with snow, awaited its riders, a zeppelin pointed skyward and dangled drunkenly by one cable, a swan chair had lost its wings and been turned upside down. There was a caterpillar . . . The Super Car Monte Carlo was still recognizable, biplanes, too, as were the Ferris wheel, the shooting galleries and the shies where one would throw a ball or coconut as hard and accurately as one could.

'The *Sitzkrieg,*' muttered Rasche. The sit-down war.

'The *drôle de guerre,*' said Louis. The phoney war.

Kohler knew both were stating the reason for the carnival's having been within less than ten kilometres of the Maginot Line and the front. From September '39, after the fall of Poland, until 9 April 1940 and the invasion of Denmark and Norway, men had languished on both sides. Then suddenly all such travel had been banned and the carnival had had to stay.

'Colonel, please go over for us exactly how and where your secretary was found and by whom,' said St-Cyr.

'Then tell us why you chose to show us the second victim first,' said Kohler.

These two, must they always suspect the worst? wondered Rasche. It was getting late. They would need the lanterns. 'I found her, and I cut her down.'

The truth at last. 'Where, Colonel?' asked St-Cyr.

'The House of Mirrors.'

Which must surely all have been broken but such evasiveness had best be stopped. 'That school notebook of Victoria Bödicker's, Colonel. At lunch you wouldn't let me take it from beneath your hand. Frau Lutze noticed this as she did everything else.'

'All right, all right. Yvonne really did feel I ought to see it, that I might well need further background on the girl. Victoria, as you know, was one of the Fräulein Schrijen's *Winterhilfswerk* Committee. Renée and I . . . '

'Your secretary, Colonel?'

'Yes! We would stop by here of a late afternoon in summer. She was fascinated by the place and loved to wander about in there. I . . . Why, I was indulgent. Staff relations, call it what you will. *Mein Gott*, the girl was like a daughter to me. A few minutes, an hour at most. When one is constantly in demand, one seeks relaxation as best one can.'

'That notebook, Colonel. It's evidence.'

'The buttons too, are they?' asked Rasche.

But not those two that were found in the victim's pockets, was that it, eh? wondered St-Cyr. 'Colonel, you deliberately left those items on your desk so that we would find them. Why did you do so, if you did not intend to let us examine them further?'

'I had merely been getting a few things together to remind me of each of the men I'd allowed to help the committee. One was the firm's fabric designer and test weaver, another a machinist and carver. Both are very capable. The carved buttons are for a waistcoat I'm having made.'

'Then please hand those items over, the papier-mâché ball also.'

Reluctantly Rasche opened his briefcase and handed them over. 'Now if you two don't mind, we had best have a look at her. Kohler, there's a screwdriver in that side pocket. Be so good as to bring it and fetch the lanterns from the boot.'

Smoke rose from the chimneys of the farmhouse where the guard was billeted. Of buff-coloured stucco and weathered half-timbering, the house had been built in the late 1880s, the lichen-encrusted, reddish-brown and spatulate tiles of its mansard roof catching the last of the sunlight. Dogs barked and Hermann, who had always loved and been at ease with such, no matter how difficult, hesitated. 'Behind the Ferris wheel,' said St-Cyr. 'Two guards, two Alsatians, each of them looking our way.'

'*Danke*. They're on the lead,' he sighed.

'Why the fright?' asked St-Cyr.

'*Ach*, after the 1918 Armistice had been signed and everyone was just waiting to be released, I used to go under the wire and would be back well before dawn *Appell*. Though one of the guards knew all about it and would always look the other way, another chose to let the dogs come after me.'

'You had only paid the one off!' snorted Rasche. '*Mein Gott*, Kohler, you continue to surprise me. Now come along. The snow's a little deeper here. We must find you some overboots, Chief Inspector. Those shoes of yours don't look good.'

'It's the glue,' muttered Kohler. 'I bought it and used it and got taken.'

'The *swarzer Markt* in France, Colonel. Hermann is an expert but an easy touch for the pretty ones.'

And hasn't changed one iota, thought Rasche. 'The *Volksopfer* might have something.'

The people's offering of winter clothes for the boys in Russia.

Quickly Louis stuffed the notebook and other things into his pockets to join the torn photographs he'd taken from the second victim, the identity papers and passes, the magazine with its pseudoerotic exposures of female anatomy, et cetera, and the anonymous letter.

The chemical formulae also, thought Kohler, not liking it one bit. Trinitro-bloody-phenol this colonel of theirs wasn't saying a damned thing about but should!

As the night came down, the sky grew clearer, its stars sharper, brighter than any he had seen in a long, long time. Was it simply Alsace and the Vosges, or was it something subconsciously within him, he wondered, this need to look up even when no enemy aircraft were there, this need to look beyond the earthly? Rasche was keeping far too much to himself. Oh for sure, he had always had a mind of his own, but why ask for two detectives if you don't want to confide everything they might need about two suicides that could just as easily have been left at that?

Torn flags were irritated by the wind. Halyards constantly struck metal and wooden standards, canvas flapped, boards creaked, swung aimlessly on chains, or banged and rubbed together. Here and there—everywhere—were sounds, especially the hollow moaning of air as it rushed through a tube or tunnel, but then, too, there was the taint of mildewed canvas and of rotting boards even in the depths of winter. Eerie . . . strange, a deserted city whose life had suddenly been snuffed out, a wilderness of silhouettes where shattered biplanes dangled, turned and swayed.

A Noah's Ark had no roof but the shadows of its animals two by two. Twin giraffes flanked the entrance. A tattered gorilla raised a fist.

In single file, the colonel leading, they threaded their way through the twenty centimetres or so of snow. 'She's not in the House of Mirrors,' said Rasche. 'I had her put in one of the wagons. Each of these'—he indicated the rides and side-show booths—'came in one or more wagons, which invariably formed part of the structure and were lived in and then used for transporting everything while en route.'

'A community. A little village of its own,' said St-Cyr, realizing as Hermann would, that the colonel must have tramped about here a good deal.

Toga-draped plaster maidens raised torches to the heavens, huge peacocks fanned their tails under starlight, an Ideal Caterpillar ride waited, its linked little train of cup-canopied carriages caught on the uphill in the broken darkness of a fallen marquee.

Wagons *did* form the walls of the House of Mirrors. Iron cross-poles had once supported its canvas roof, and from these had hung the stand-up crazy mirrors whose walkways, stairs, false turns and landings were still in place. Glass probably everywhere, thought Kohler. Those two boys they had seen wouldn't have left it for long and must have, like all the other children in the district, had free rein and a fantastic time of it.

Rasche shone his blue-blinkered torch on the shattered entrance. 'A chair was used,' he said, 'the rope thrown over one of the cross-poles.'

'Colonel, since she didn't return after lunch on Saturday, the thirtieth,' asked Louis, 'how is it that you are certain she died on the following day?'

'The girl was seen by a farm family on their way to the early Mass. They waved to her, but she appeared too cold and tired to respond. She'd been cross-country skiing.'

'All night?' asked Louis.

'Apparently.'

Hence the need for secrecy, said Kohler silently. 'Who questioned them?'

'I did. Renée was an accomplished skier. The woods, the flat-lands, the hills and mountains, each offered challenges she loved.'

It was Louis who patently ignored what was due east of them and not that far, the old frontier, the Rhine and the Black Forest, and simply asked, 'At what time, then, was she last seen?'

These two would think the worst. 'At just after dawn on Sunday. The church isn't far.'

'Had she a rucksack?' asked Kohler.

'It's still with her as is the empty vacuum flask she had filled with soup and the newspaper she had wrapped some sandwiches in.'

'Only *some*, Colonel?' asked St-Cyr.

'A good lunch, that's all. *Ach*, did you think I would try to hide the distance those skis of hers might have helped? Look, you two, I know exactly how difficult it will be for me if this should ever get out. Why else would I have called Paris, Kohler, had I not needed someone I could depend on? Renée came back here to warm up and rest and had, I am certain, every intention of returning to Kolmar. None of us would have known where she had been, not really. She could have told us anything and we would have accepted it. She was that kind of person. Totally reliable and above suspicion.'

Yet she had been out all night, thought Kohler, and wasn't this carnival a place where one might be watched by another without knowing it? 'Colonel, when I dropped in on the Oberstleutnant Rudel, he stated flatly that both deaths were suicides. This one due to despair over something the girl had seen at Natzweiler-Struthof.'

Would a sigh be best? 'Karl's forte is expedience. Three weeks before Christmas, Renée went up to Natzweiler-Struthof to ski. The *Konzentrationslager* is nearby. Skiers have gone there for years. When she came back, she was subdued and not her usually outgoing self. I thought to cheer her up, and on our return from a meeting in Neu-Breisach, we stopped in here, but she said she wasn't feeling well and would rather go home. I insisted, and it did help. She was always intrigued by the things she constantly found here.'

'And did the Fräulein Ekkehard mention what had troubled her?' asked Louis.

'*Ach*, we never spoke of it. There are some things one simply doesn't discuss. Now, please, it is this way.'

'The lanterns, Colonel,' said Hermann. 'Hadn't I best light them? One for you and Louis, and the other for myself.'

A harlequin, a hangman, a frantic young girl trapped at the end of a seedy *passage*, a lewd and laughing butcher advancing upon her, blood dripping from his hands and upraised cleaver; in the background, a high-court judge, jailer and ax-wielding executioner whose crowd of onlookers shrilled their venom.

Children also, terrified children.

Masks grinned, frowned, grimaced or were wide-eyed in horror above the wagon's mural panels but all were seen in the surrealistic blue wash of the lantern and in the full-length, distorting mirrors that stood round, their carved frames carefully repaired, the decorations lovingly restored: some with vines and succulent bunches of grapes, others with spiderwebs whose decidedly humanoid insects were not only trapped but fought back fiercely.

Palms, snakes, jungles with strange birds and bats completed the panorama, along with glasses of wine and links of sausage.

'From one house of mirrors to another,' breathed St-Cyr, the colonel having placed the lantern atop a trestle-held coffin that, in itself, hadn't been made of plain pine boards but of carnival panelboard whose ruined cartouches with their hieroglyphics in gold, silver and ruby, had faded and peeled.

Rasche, his image warped by the mirrors behind and on either side, faced him, a black-gloved hand still on the lantern. 'Though you've yet to meet him, Chief Inspector, never underestimate Löwe Schrijen. Curved inwardly, bowed outwardly—even prismatic probably—whatever glass was needed, he had it found. Frankly, I think he went too far, but you'd never convince him of that. What his daughter Sophie required for this little effort of hers she got. They simply dismantled a house of mirrors in Berlin, no doubt saving it from the bombing.'

'And then used the old frames from here.' For now one had best say nothing of the months of internment work this alone must have required, but one had to wonder at such evasiveness.

'You or me?' asked Rasche, indicating the screwdriver he had taken from Hermann.

'Myself, I think.'

'To make certain no one has tampered with her?'

'Colonel, if what my partner and I are coming to realize was at all the case, then you had best cooperate fully.'

'Renée wasn't my lover.'

'Had she one?'

'A boy she met from time to time.'

'At official functions?'

'And others.'

Sacré nom de nom, must this evasiveness continue and things go deeper still? 'His name, Colonel?'

Perhaps now St-Cyr and Kohler would begin to understand. 'Alain Fernand Schrijen.'

'The chairman's son and brother of Sophie?'

'Who else?'

3

In a cul-de-sac of shattered mirrors and lantern light at the end of a corridor, Kohler felt just as alone as Renée Ekkehard must have. Worried too—terrified perhaps, poor thing—certainly far from happy and with the sounds of flapping canvas and the like coming at her, or had there been nothing at all but an ice-cold silence on that early Sunday morning? Had it been then that she hanged herself, or had it been later on in the day, the girl waiting it out, arguing with herself until no arguments remained?

Trinitrophenol . . . *Lieber Christus im Himmel*, what had Louis and himself landed in? Rasche had, apparently, touched as little as possible here. He had even carried in a box to stand on as he'd cut her down, rather than use the chair that had been kicked away and was on its side, facing a corner.

A career soldier, nerves of steel too. Odd, though, that he should have been so calm, given that he must have been in shock and thinking only of his secretary, that 'daughter to him.'

Louis didn't know the half about the colonel; Louis couldn't. That cosy little nest with Oberfeldwebel Lutze and Yvonne and

Rasche's leavings from that other war? Trust the *salaud* to think nothing of it and come back to use her again, if only as his housekeeper!

Lutze, like others at Vieil-Armand and elsewhere during the 1914–15 campaign, had known about the affair. Maybe he had simply had his colonel's best interests at heart, maybe there had been a payoff, even love, for he'd married her. Certainly now Yvonne Lutze would have watched Renée Ekkehard and her former lover at their meals and listened in the night as well.

Yes, Louis didn't know the half of it.

Finding an empty hook on one of the corridor walls, Kohler hung the lantern up and to hell with the blackout, to hell with laundry blueing. No one was going to notice one star down here when there were so many up there.

The rope was of dark brown hemp and had all the protruding hairs of such, but it wasn't weathered, had been stored, probably in a tin trunk in one of the wagons. About sixty centimetres of it dangled from where it was doubly lapped over the cross-pole to form a loop through which the ends had been passed by a girl who had been determined not to fail, but had that really been the way it had happened?

The rope was of Manila hemp and common enough. Weatherproofed, it was flexible though still rough, and since when did a girl who wanted to hang herself not care about torn skin and rope burns too? Didn't females who did this sort of thing invariably choose a silk stocking, though these days those were often too scarce. A lisle stocking, then, or slip, scarf or chemise—hadn't he seen them all, especially the neckties of absent lovers. Whatever was at hand, but please make it soft.

The mirrors on either side of her must have showered their

remaining glass as she had kicked out violently, and she must have done, for there was little of it left, but had her wrists been tied behind her back, or had she been able to grab the rope instinctively as she would have done?

Just why would a twenty-eight-year-old who had been out all night skiing hang herself?

'There can only be one reason,' he said, and felt it deeply, everything within him suddenly collapsing. Giselle and Oona . . . Gerda too, would be taken. Gabrielle and Louis as well. All would be rounded up if this thing was what he thought it might be and wasn't handled properly.

'She was afraid she'd be arrested,' he managed. 'She knew she would talk and didn't want to.'

Or had her reasons been otherwise? Had she even killed herself?

Taking up the lantern, he stood on the box, was head and shoulders above the cross-pole and the walls, could now see over the rest of the House of Mirrors and the dark, if shattered maze of it. She hadn't just stepped into any corridor, this secretary of the colonel's. She had chosen one of the farthest from the entrance, had come in here as far as she could to hide her corpse for as long as possible, and that . . . why that could only mean she had wanted to give others in her Résistance group time to escape—was that how it had been?

Of medium height—she must have been—she had stood on that chair, but would still have had to stretch a little to flip the bend in the doubled rope over the pole. 'She was left-handed,' he said as if Louis was with him. 'The bend is to the right of the pole. Instinctively the left hand tossed it up and over, then the right grabbed it while the left fed the two ends through and yanked down hard.'

The colonel's knife had been razor sharp. Both ends of the

rope had been cleanly cut as one, but was there anything else? he wondered. 'Something,' he muttered. 'Some little thing to tell us it couldn't have been a suicide, that Renée Ekkard hadn't feared arrest, torture and decapitation.'

Because *that* was exactly what would have happened to her if she was mixed up in anything.

As the lid of the 'coffin' came away, the colonel gasped and quickly turned aside, the mirrors throwing the grimace he gave out of all proportion.

'Forgive me,' he said. 'It's just that, having not seen her in some time, I'd grown accustomed to remembering her as she'd been.'

Less than a week ago, said St-Cyr silently to the victim. The colonel won't understand my talking to you, Fräulein, but you do see that he must have been with you at least twice on that Tuesday? Once to cut the rope which is still tightly around your neck, and once to lay you out like this. 'Colonel, the coffin. Its carpenter . . . '

'*Ach*, I had to go to the Textile Works to get him.'

'Was she left alone in your absence?'

'I stopped in at the *Polizeikommandantur* and sent two of the special constables with orders not to disturb a thing. My detectives followed, but those idiots claimed it was a suicide, and don't be thinking you and Kohler are going to question those two. Just leave them out of it. The Wehrmacht guard was arranged later.'

Ah, bon, Fräulein, the colonel knows I've realized that by not accepting the conclusions of his own men, he has not only shut his mind to what they might have had to tell him, he has pissed off the whole station. Whispers . . . were there those about the two of you? Lovers . . . is this what the staff at the *Polizeikommandantur* had all been saying? That Sophie Schrijen's brother, Alain, didn't know what he was getting into by showing even the slightest interest in you?

She had lain here since, hadn't even been taken to the morgue, as she should have been. 'The knot is to the left, Colonel, and has slipped from below to above the larynx, as is consistent with her having stepped off the chair.'

Her face, once sharply featured, was livid and swollen. Sprays of dark blood spots were just beneath the slate-grey skin of her forehead. There would be more of them under the beret, over the scalp and beneath the soft brown hair that had been bobbed, and would curl outward at its ends, giving bounce to every step.

Blood spots lay under the skin beneath her eyes. They were showered over the freckled bridge of her nose and cheeks. Those once lovely lips were a dark, plum purple in the flickering light, her tongue all but bitten through. Snot, blood, saliva and fluid from the lungs had erupted to drain from the nostrils and right corner of her mouth, spattering that shoulder and the front of her ski jacket.

'Rigor has left her, Colonel,' said St-Cyr, watching him too closely. 'She wasn't tall, but a little taller than most. How far were the toes of her boots from the floor?'

St-Cyr had moved swiftly away from head to foot to look along the length of her at him. 'Thirty centimetres at least. She dropped, didn't she?'

'Yes, yes, of course, but her neck wasn't broken. Instead, the ligature slipped upward as it tightened, causing asphyxia. It took time, Colonel. Oh for sure, not much more than five or six seconds, but enough for her to have realized what was happening.'

'She kicked out. Broken glass is caught in her socks and among the bootlaces. The chair . . . '

'Was in a corner, but could it have been deliberately placed there?'

'I touched as little as possible.'

'But your detectives must have and you are upset with me for mentioning it. Why, please, were you so certain her death could not have been a suicide?'

There must be no hesitation. 'She had everything ahead of her, was happy and outgoing, believed firmly as many still do that the Reich would eventually win the war.'

'But wears a beret which is very French and now illegal? The penalty, please, for doing such a thing?'

'Look, I don't know why the little fool should have—'

'Colonel, this is a murder inquiry. Please simply answer.'

'Six months of forced labour, or in the cells if too weak to work, and a fine of 150 marks.'

'And within the former confines of the Reich?'

'Its wearing is allowed, as it always has been.'

Only in Alsace, then, and Lorraine, had it been banned. 'What was she really up to, Colonel, in spite of claiming faith in the Reich's winning this war? Was she smuggling Wehrmacht deserters through to the Vosges so that they could be hidden in France with false papers or join the partisans? We both know the Russian front is no picnic and that desertion has become an ever-increasing problem. Ask Hermann. He'll tell you the same thing.'

'I'm sure he would.'

'And the skis?'

'She loved the forest, the quiet in winter, the sight of a fox, a hawk or even a few crows or ravens. "There are always three of those birds," she used to say. It was something Celtic, she thought, something Gallic from a long time ago. They were always so silent. Suddenly they would be there watching her. Three goddesses of the supernatural who deliberately did terrible things to people, especially the innocent and the righteous. Silly of her to have believed in such rubbish. I told her some of the men used to shoot them for sport.'

'And what was her response?'

'That each facet of the Phantom Queen could and did take that form, and that to harm any was to harm all and bring down her wrath upon us.'

'You're a patient listener. You must have been, to have remembered it.'

'When Werner told me her cross-country skis were missing, I knew this was where she must have come but did nothing. I waited too long. I know it, and freely admit it.'

So now we learn a little more, Fräulein Ekkehard, and are to be reassured that your colonel really did think well of you and that, though you both may or may not have been lovers, he did consider you as a daughter. But is it the truth, that business of his having done nothing? If a lover, or father figure, surely he would have come after you, especially if there were other reasons like your helping deserters to escape?

'Colonel, why not set the lantern over there? If Hermann has finished with the location of the crime, he'll be looking elsewhere. Leave him to it and go to the farmhouse where the guards are billeted. Warm yourself. We'll find you when we need you. It may be a long night.'

Was this sympathy from a Sûreté? 'The location of the crime . . . You believe it really was murder.'

'It's too early to say, but instinct tells me she wasn't alone. Was she left-handed?'

'*Ach*, the knot. Yes, but it never affected her work and no one thought anything of it.'

But must have if murdered. 'That papier-mâché ball, Colonel. Why was it among the items on your desk?'

'We'd been practising, the two of us, the last time we were here.'

'When, please?'

And again a stickler for detail. 'The Wednesday before she died—27 January. Among the throw-booths the committee were having restored, there was one that Renée was particularly pleased with. The village bailiff, schoolteacher, old maid, that sort of thing. Though not quite completed, she insisted she take out some of the figures and we try our luck to much laughter and good fun, and in the course of this, I must have forgotten it was in my overcoat pocket.'

A game of *Jeu de massacre*. 'And the booth?'

'Is stored in one of the other wagons. Three of the men I'd assigned to help were here on the Thursday and Friday, with their guards.'

A carpenter, glazier, assistant machinist, fabric designer and the chemist, Eugène Thomas. 'Which three?'

'The firm's assistant machinist was finishing work on the chain-drive and other things, the carpenter and fabric designer busy with the booth and painting, I think. Their tasks varied so much, I . . . well, I saw no need to take note of them. It's all written down in the duty roster they kept.'

'Then for now that's sufficient. A little of your splendid tobacco, though, if you can spare it.'

St-Cyr had already gone back to work, having moved the lantern to the other end of the coffin, but would he be asking himself why the knot had been tied that way?

Of course he would. He'd see that particles of sawdust and flecks of old paint and gilding from the lid had fallen and would wonder why her eyes hadn't been closed, but would he understand the strength of will it had taken not to do so, the need that had driven him to return after the second suicide and remove the lid so as to be alone with her? To think, to decide, and finally to telex Gestapo Boemelburg in Paris for detective help.

Closing the door on Louis and the body, Rasche stepped away from the wagon. 'Renée,' he said, and finding his cigarette case, lit one and let the tobacco smoke and breath billow from him. So deep was he in thought, he didn't look up at the stars or moon, Kohler noted from the shadows. Instead, the colonel concentrated on a wagon some twenty metres from the edge of the Kastenwald. By eye alone Rasche followed a trail of footprints to that very wagon—mine, Colonel? Its door isn't closed, but what have I done with the lantern, eh? Doused it? Covered it with one of those mouldy costume dresses the *Winterhilfswerk* Committee must have gathered and rolled into bundles as if they hadn't quite known what to do with them? A wagon they had then cleaned and fixed up as a field office, but when?

Kohler was nearby, felt Rasche, but wasn't making a move and must think the worst. Would nothing remain sacrosanct? Would he and St-Cyr insist on going through her personal things? The lingerie that bastard Alain Schrijen had given her on Christmas Eve? The things she had brought back and kept from that damned party at Natzweiler-Struthof?

Would they discover that she hadn't always worn the field-grey uniform of a *Blitzmädel* but had sometimes been allowed to cheer the office up with a gaily flowered frock, high heels too, the shoes purchased in Paris in the autumn of 1938 from the Galeries Lafayette and inexpensive because she had spent nearly all of her money on that wristwatch she'd found in Bréguet's, at 28 place Vendôme. A fortune it had cost her and far more than needed for timing downhill runs or laps in the pool as she'd claimed.

And when, please, had those ladies of the *Winterhilfswerk* Committee first gotten the idea of fixing things up here, Kohler? Have you thought of that yet? Early September of last year, *mein Lieber*, but have you asked yourself why I would have agreed to allow such a thing? A wagon that becomes their campaign headquarters and a place for prisoners of war? Men who, through the camp's *Mundfunk* (mouth radio), knew very well that terrible things were happening at Natzweiler-Struthof and not just things like hanging.

Abruptly Rasche parked his unfinished cigarette on the uppermost step of the wagon and started for the farmhouse.

Kohler watched him stride away without a moment's hesitation, then went back to the wagon, closed the door, and re-lit the lantern. Louis would find him when he was good and ready.

The wagon had everything and must have been pure heaven to the POWs. There was a stove with a supply of wood—scraps from the coffin, sawn and broken-up branches from the Kastenwald, so a little foraging had also been allowed. There was even a cast-iron frying pan, a saucepan, kettle and salt-shaker, knives, forks and spoons. *Liebe Zeit*, the paradise Rasche had sanctioned but why had he done such a thing?

Three chairs, similar to the one the girl had used, were around a table. Elsewhere, a drawing board gave plans and sketches of the booths the crew had been working on, a duty roster, the schedule and a completion date of 6 March, with ticks against those items that had been completed: a bottle-throw in which wooden hoops were tossed, a paper-mâché ball-throw, not yet the *Jeu de massacre* but one with can-can dancers which, if hit, would automatically lift their skirts to much laughter; a shooting gallery also, with squirrels, hares, roe deer and wild boar, all linked by a chain drive that would flip them back up into position after being hit. Pheasants too.

Days, weeks, months the repairs and refurbishing had taken those boys that had been borrowed from that textile works, not all of them at once, but while here having the time of their lives.

The roster listed only the first names. Eugène was three down and after Martin and Gérard, and before Henri and Raymond, these last two being singled out and responsible for the Wheel of Fortune.

Among his chores, Martin had been repairing popguns that fired Ping-Pong balls, but other such guns had been found and brought in and were leaning against a corner. 'Six lever-action Winchester repeating air rifles,' Kohler heard himself saying. BB guns that fired a copper pellet that was but a shade more than two millimetres in diameter. There were tins and tins of these pellets, found God only knew where, but most probably by Löwe Schrijen.

Target shooting had always been a favourite of such travelling fairs. Gerda and he had had a time of it, competing with each other. Had she been seventeen that first time?

'Sentiment has no place in a detective's life,' he said.

Assorted tin trunks lay toward the far end of the wagon, with the bundles of mouse-eaten dresses, a pseudo-Florentine velvet being uppermost, but nothing of value, so why keep them? Scattered . . . Had they been scattered about the floor of this wagon?

Cigarette ashes filled one of those metal ashtrays that were often found in cheap restaurants but there were no cigarette butts, of course.

Shelves held rescued wooden hoops and darts—Sophie

Schrijen, Victoria Bödicker and Renée Ekkehard must have spent hours scouring the place for artifacts. Brand-new, hand-rolled papier-mâché balls awaited painting but there were buckets of those that had been found and must have been stored somewhere dry, tent pegs too, and buttons in a fruit jar, lots and lots of those and an absolute fortune if taken inside the camp and sold to the other POWs. Scraps of tin too, and bits of string—even carpenter's nails had been gathered to be wrapped, handful by handful, in bits of weathered canvas, each little bundle tied tightly, and so much for the searches by the guards at the gate of Arbeitslager 13 on return. The nails and the buttons and such would have commanded a price and been desperately put to use. Hadn't Louis found two rose-coloured buttons among the dross in Eugène Thomas's pockets? Of course he had.

There was even a beautifully honed, brand-new cutthroat razor parked discreetly behind a framed photo, sans glass, of a striptease *artiste dans costume d'Ève,* and *ach,* he'd best stop thinking in French. Nice, too, though, that photo, and well thumbed, but *sacré nom de nom,* just what had those boys been up to? To hide the razor and have it discovered by one of the guards would have meant certain death.

Beside this photo, there was an empty half-litre green bottle that had been drained of its marc or *eau-de-vie.* A toast? he had to ask. Had those committee members raised their glasses in salute to one another over what they had all but accomplished, or to something else, and had all of them been present? The three, thin-stemmed little glasses were of ice-clear Baccarat crystal and old, and obviously hadn't been found anywhere near here, but stood in a row, shoulder to shoulder as if carefully replaced.

All were dry and smelled as if unused, but had they been

washed and wiped clean, and if so, was that not why they'd been set in such a tidy row?

More and more this wasn't looking good.

Threadbare, once brightly coloured carnival tapestries covered the makeshift tin-trunk bench Renée Ekkehard and the others had used for storage. Cigarette ashes had been dribbled on a far corner, but otherwise there was nothing to indicate that anyone had recently sat here, except for the smoothness of the covering, and, yes, someone in a hurry *had* tried to wipe those ashes away.

'A suicide,' he said, gingerly peeling back the covering and opening the trunk.

Coiled Manila hemp lay atop neatly folded canvas, the uppermost end of the rope having been yanked out so that its coils overlapped, and to the right of this, as if cast aside in a hurry, lay an open-bladed, worn-handled Opinel pocketknife, the French peasant's constant companion. In just such little things were there answers. Trouble was, the colonel must have known all about it.

'To be alone with the victim is always best for me, mademoiselle,' said St-Cyr apologetically. 'You see, patience is required and my partner often has little of it. *Bien sûr,* I tell myself the Occupier invariably demands the Blitzkrieg of us both, but still there are times when the careful step-by-step is essential. And Hermann, you ask? He's improving. Working with me has been good for him, not that he always listens. A member of the Gestapo? you ask. That's not his fault, by the way, so please don't blame him for it or worry.'

She didn't respond. She just lay waiting in the soft and flickering light of the lantern. 'I need to get to know you,' he said, packing his pipe, a habit so ingrained he could do it without a glance, the colonel having parked his pouch of splendid tobacco on a corner of the coffin before leaving.

'Has he gone to the farmhouse as I said he should?' asked St-Cyr, waving out the match. 'Or has he gone to find Hermann? He hasn't quite been telling us everything, has he? There has been no mention of Eugène Thomas's anonymous letter, none either of trinitrophenol or of why its chemical formula should have been hastily written on the corner of a page in Victoria Bödicker's school notebook.'

Still there was no response. '*Ah, bon,* then, mademoiselle, let's begin with this rope. It's curious only in that after the commencement of hostilities in September '39 it would have become increasingly difficult to find. Perhaps the Fräulein Schrijen asked her father to obtain it, or the carnival owner or owners had wisely laid in a supply? I'm inclined to believe they must have, otherwise synthetic rope—rayon—from the factory would have been used. The choice, then, tells us little, except that something had to be readily available and of good enough quality. And never mind the roughness. My partner will have thought of that. It's the knot that puzzles me. The origins of it go back through the centuries, don't they? It's one of the simplest and earliest of knots and yet . . . and yet where would history be without it?'

She seemed to relax, to know that at last she was in good hands. 'Was archery not just a casual interest but a passion of yours the colonel has so far failed to mention? You see, mademoiselle, the inner part of the pads of your left middle three fingers bear such callouses. Repeated bouts of target practice aren't easy on a girl's fingers, even with the special glove that is usually worn. There are also feather cuts on the back of your right hand where the arrow has rested as you gripped the bow. A small sacrifice—it's understandable. One also uses a knot like this, though, when fitting on a new bowstring. First the noose is pulled tightly, and then a stop knot is added to prevent its coming loose, but why did you double the rope? It made the knot so large your head would have been painfully forced aside and how, please, did you manage then to tie its stop knot? You would have had to grope awkwardly for the ends of the doubled line.'

Pipe smoke billowed and as he waved it away from her, he said, 'This bowstring knot wasn't tied while you were standing on that chair. It was prepared beforehand and was easy to feed through the rope's loop once the doubled line had been thrown over the cross-pole above.'

She seemed not to want to respond, but to wait as if with breath held. 'The noose was then placed over your head, mademoiselle, and tightened. Hermann may have concluded otherwise, but for now I have to tell you that I don't think you were conscious of what was happening to you until suddenly awakening to it but even your beret, which would surely have been knocked askew, has been tidied, and why, please, would you not have worn a woollen ski cap on a night like that? The degrees of frost alone demanded it, and you were obviously an accomplished skier.'

She *had* kicked out. There *were* splinters of glass in the cable-knit grey woollen socks whose outer pair had been rolled down a little. Others were caught among the laces of her boots, just as the colonel had said.

Holding the lantern closer, St-Cyr searched among the shards. '*Ah, Dieu merci,* mademoiselle, something's caught in the back of your left inner sock, at the top. As you were taken down in haste by the colonel, the outermost sock accidentally hid this little item.'

Chance, though rare, could often make all the difference.

Holding the drop earring up to the light, he marvelled at it, was curious, pleased, so many things. 'A bit of costume jewellery one of the carnival's performers must have worn. Had you been collecting these? The bezel setting is from the *fin de siècle.* A clear, sharp amethyst, mademoiselle, its brilliant well faceted. Nothing cheap, but still far cheaper than the real thing.'

Five equally spaced beads surrounded the setting, a beautifully worked rope of silver encompassed its bottom edge. 'The stem's expanding filigree is symmetrical and instantly focuses attention on the droplet but, please, had you found it, or did someone hand it to you in a last gesture? You see, as the rope tightened, so did the fist that held this.'

'The knot, Louis. I have to see it.'

Harried, Hermann stood in the doorway with the falling snow behind him. 'What is it?'

'Trouble.'

Not taking time to explain, he pushed past to stand over the victim, grasping the edge of the coffin with one hand to steady himself and then flinging something down at her chest.

'*Verdammt,* Louis . . . '

Five neatly tied little canvas bundles now lay on her blood-spattered jacket.

'Medicinal iron,' he went on. 'They must have been carting things behind the wire for those boys. *Ach,* that's fine enough if one can get away with it, but are all of those knots the same as the one that's around her neck?'

Hermann often jumped to conclusions. 'None of those men were here on that weekend according to . . . '

'*Ja,* but who the hell was it who asked for two dumb *Schweinebullen* to dig him out of the shit? There's a cutthroat parked behind a photo. Escape, Louis. Were those boys that committee had working for them planning a little something of their own?'

A cutthroat . . .

'That scrap of paper . . . '

The trinitrophenol.

'Either this one tied those little bundles with the idea of smuggling them into the camp, or whoever did also hanged her.'

'But used a different knot, Hermann. The chair . . . '

'Didn't skid, but was carefully positioned so as to make it look like she had kicked it away. I went back to check after I found those little bundles. The son of a bitch was right-handed just as is a certain colonel who could well have tied knots like those in his sleep!'

'Hermann, listen to me, please. Renée Ekkehard was hanged using a bowstring knot, Eugène Thomas with one that was exactly the same as are around those little bundles.'

'An arbour knot?'

'Oui, oui, as is used by a fisherman, *bien sûr.* Single strand and very fast, both in the tying and the holding. Two loops, the first a little larger than the second, the working end being passed three times through the smaller, after which that loop is tightened by pulling on the side of the larger. A slip knot is then formed, which is, perhaps, as old if not older than the bowstring knot this girl must have known well how to have used but can't have, Hermann. Can't have.'

Callouses and feather marks were indicated.

'We're going to have to tell him what he already must know, Louis, that it really was murder. If he so much as gets a hint of our not doing so, we'll never see Paris again.'

'Then let's take our time. Let's flesh this killing out as much as possible.'

'Was she drugged?'

'That's what I want you to find out.'

'Then maybe I should tell you that I've already found the glasses and the empty bottle.'

'*Ah, bon,* but look further. Leave me with her for a little longer.'

Caught by the mirrors, reflected, magnified, stretched or collapsed to a pinpoint, the lantern's flame gave many lights. And all around her from on high, the garishly painted masks grinned, laughed, cried, threatened or frowned at Hermann as he hesitated, and all around her were the murals of entrapment, terror, murder and then judgement, retribution and public execution with an ax.

It wasn't good, that cutthroat Hermann had found. It was terrible. They both knew it, Hermann lifting a tired hand to indicate that he would do as asked, even to softly closing the door behind himself.

None of the rest was good either, but why, really, would it not have been possible for the men behind that wire to have simply obtained the nails surreptitiously from the Schrijen Works?

Too many men, Renée Ekkehard seemed to say. Too closely watched and harshly punished. The risk from here would have had to be taken.

'By all three of you on that committee, or only by yourself?' St-Cyr heard himself asking.

Were the bundles not clearly visible to your partner, Inspector? Is that not evidence enough if that was really what they were for?

'Then perhaps you would tell me why you concerned yourselves with their welfare, given the terrible risk of your doing such a thing? Colonel Rasche found himself in a very difficult position, didn't he, mademoiselle? He had signed and stamped the pass that allowed you to come and go freely at the Works. After hours, during them—it didn't matter, did it? A blanket pass. You had planned to visit Strassburg this weekend and he had okayed that—he must have for you'd purchased the second-class return ticket I found in your rucksack, with your papers. A skiing party at Natzweiler-Struthof, Sophie Schrijen told my partner, a visit also with your parents. A personal matter, Colonel Rasche has said of this last, but where, please, does Sophie's brother Alain fit into things, a boy who is stationed at Natzweiler-Struthof and answerable to the Schutzhaftlagerführer Kramer?'

He gave it a moment. 'Exactly *what* did you see that sickened you so much the Oberstleutnant Rudel believes it drove you to suicide? The deaths of innocent men, mademoiselle? Prisoners of war? *Résistants? N und Ns?*'

A drop-earring and a bowstring knot after a night of skiing . . .

'A little earth is frozen to the soles of your boots. You skied but walked when necessary and were, I believe, as exhausted as the colonel has stated, when you returned here early on that Sunday morning.'

But did I go to the east? Was I really conducting Wehrmacht deserters through to France?

'To the west, in the Vosges, the earth would have been buried under deep snow; to the east, over the Valley of the Rhine, which is far more populated, the snow is thinner, even in a winter such as this, the hills of the Black Forest excepted, of course.'

To the east, then, she seemed to sigh as if satisfied.

'This watch, mademoiselle. Since when does a secretary, or even an outdoor's girl like yourself, carry a man's pocket watch? Oh for sure, it's nothing but the best, though not new and made in Switzerland before that other war. A Baume et Mercier, but a watch, mademoiselle, of the kind one is perhaps loaned while one's own timepiece is in for repairs? There are several of the notations watchmakers invariably inscribe inside the back, after each little visit. The number of a replacement part, sometimes the plus or minus of an adjustment so that it can be further modified . . .'

Did the colonel know of it, having gone through my pockets before you did? she seemed to ask.

'He must have. Your rucksack also. There is something else.'

Digging a hand into the latter, St-Cyr drew out the carefully folded pages of Kolmar's *Morgenseitung* of Friday, 29 January, in which she had wrapped the lunch she had then taken with her on the following day. 'Several sandwiches. Dried, smoked sausage, mustard and Munster, mademoiselle, the absence of all of which Frau Lutze must have been well aware of yet has so far said nothing. A vacuum flask of lentil soup as well, and enough for two.'

My killer and myself—is this what you are now thinking? she asked. If so, Inspector, then why, please, would a man I had helped guide to freedom kill me? Admit it. If my death really is murder, you are looking for someone else, someone who, if I was really smuggling deserters out of the Reich, must have found out about it and then had to put a stop to it, but silently. No arrest, no accusations, nothing like those. Simply a 'suicide' because of 'something I had seen.'

'Sophie Schrijen believed it would have been herself had she come out here on that Saturday afternoon.'

But is this person, if he even exists, now planning to deal with her and with Victoria, and if so, Inspector, then why did Eugène also have to die, or was his death simply a suicide, and if so, why then did he have that scrap of paper in his pocket?

The farmhouse's *Stube* was warm, humid and stuffy. Wehrmacht laundry, grey and hanging over horizontal poles that had been strung from the ceiling timbers, all but hid the *Kachelofen*, noted St-Cyr. Two of the dogs stirred but were told to lie still by the colonel who, closeted at a bare plank table in boots, trousers, shirtsleeves and suspenders, looked grey and old and as if waiting for the inevitable.

'An autopsy,' muttered Rasche at news he had known he would have to hear.

The off-duty men had gone to bed. The two of them were alone and perhaps deliberately so, yet still the voice had best be kept low. 'Traces of a sedative will be difficult enough to find, Colonel. She's been here for just over a week now. We don't even know if one was used, but if one was, there would have to have been sufficient to have made her very drowsy, but beyond that, we have little to go on.'

Rasche laid his empty pipe aside, 'It'll have to be done quietly and that is, unfortunately, something I can't guarantee.'

The rheumy dark blue eyes were not evasive. 'At lunch, Colonel, you mentioned the university in Strassburg . . .'

The dark grey eyebrows arched. 'You don't know, do you? You can't,' he said and, reaching out to one of the dogs, began to gently stroke its muzzle and scratch behind its ears.

'The library is famous, Colonel. Some of the earliest of medieval Germanic manuscripts, the very origins of Alsace and Alsatian . . .'

The big hands had spread themselves flat on the table. 'Manuscripts? *Ach*, don't talk such *Quatsch, mein Lieber*. Those books were all taken to Clermont-Ferrand during the *Sitzkrieg* when many of the professors and their students fled to shared facilities at the university there. Now the idiots cause trouble instead of lying quietly. They even refuse to return those damned books and as a result, the Gestapo in France want desperately to put an end to them.'

'And at the University of Strassburg?'

'There is now a new and approved staff.'

'And the autopsies you told us were constantly being done there?'

'Are being done on orders from Berlin.'

'A cautious answer, Colonel. Is it that you really must go through the *Konzentrationslager* office to request one?'

Rasche pointed to his tobacco pouch and snapped his fingers for its return. He'd take a moment to pack his pipe. Maybe then this *Sûreté* would understand. 'Certainly one can be fitted into the schedule at the university, but there will definitely be talk and that would not, I think, be conducive to your investigation. Schutzhaftlagerführer Kramer is, as I have indicated, difficult at best. That goes with the job, of course, but he could, as is his prerogative, demand that the four who are left from those I delegated to help out here be taken to the quarry for questioning.'

'And the Fräulein Bödicker?'

'Could also be taken.'

'But not the Fräulein Schrijen?'

Was this infernal partner of Kohler's finally beginning to understand? 'One must proceed carefully, Chief Inspector. Leave the autopsy for now. Do all you can and then I'll see what can be arranged. Renée's parents will, of course, have to be notified and will object most strenuously. After all, the fewer questions asked, the less the attention that will be directed at those closest to the victim.'

And at those who questioned her 'suicide' in the first place!

As the colonel watched, detective shoes were yanked off, wet socks wrung of their meltwater to be flipped over one of the crowded poles, the shoes placed upside down on the stove's *Kunscht*, the little stone bench that was used for keeping things warm, even babies, so gentle was its radiant heat.

In bare feet, his overcoat, scarf and fedora hung up to dry if possible, St-Cyr rolled up his trouser legs. 'A few questions, then, Colonel.'

Paris had also warned of this.

'You've stated emphatically that we are not to question your two detectives, but could they have removed anything and not told you of it?'

Anything like a syringe or an ampoule—was that it, eh? Deliberately St-Cyr had made no mention of the Baccarat liqueur glasses and the empty bottle of marc Kohler would have found.

'Did they go over everything thoroughly, Colonel, and if so, will Hermann, who is still out there looking, find nothing?'

'They wouldn't have looked beyond the *Lach Tempel*. For them, it was fitting enough that the girl had chosen such a place.'

The Temple of Laughter, the House of Mirrors.

'The one is far too close to the SS,' said Rasche, drawing on his pipe. 'He constantly informs them of what I do, and they, of course, are a direct pipeline to Natzweiler-Struthof. The other helps him but augments his wages by taking money on the side. These days some things are best overlooked. It's enough to know of them.'

'Then who drove that girl out here? Who knew her well enough to get that close?'

Renée had a blanket pass to the Schrijen Works, and St-Cyr would have found it in her rucksack. 'Löwe Schrijen's daughter often telephoned my office. I would then hear Renée and Sophie discussing their little project. Perhaps a ride was organized, since Sophie found she was unable to come herself. Werner and Yvonne may have something when we get back to the house.'

A Schrijen lorry, would that be perfect, Colonel, wondered

St-Cyr, especially since Sophie Schrijen believed firmly she could well have been the intended victim? 'We'll want passes to the Works, will want to question everyone deemed necessary.'

'You'll have them. As to your questioning . . .'

'Colonel, you asked for us. You could just as easily have let the decision of your own detectives stand.'

'I have my reasons.'

'And I have no jurisdiction here.'

'But Kohler has.'

'Is it that you counted on his being tractable?'

'Kohler? *Ach*, what are you saying? I needed someone totally free of influences here, someone who had been a POW himself. If one is murder, is not the other? Now go and find that partner of yours. It's long past my bedtime!'

'Hermann will find us. Besides, my shoes, my feet . . . A basin of hot water. Some soap, I think, and a cigarette, if you have any.'

And refuse to part with more pipe tobacco! 'There's no soap and I'm out of cigarettes, but Herr Goebbels, who smokes as many as sixty a day, assures us that pine needles are every bit as good as soap and also help with the rheumatism. Add a handful. It costs nothing. There's a bowl of them in the kitchen by the stove.'

All of the tin trunks in the office wagon had been opened and gone through. 'Nothing. Not a damned thing,' swore Kohler.

Flea-market gleanings lay tangled in a biscuit tin, deep in the trunk that was farthest from the entrance to the wagon. Imitation pearls, diamonds, rubies and emeralds—all had been cleaned. Paste, most of them, but Marcasite too, and zircons: brooches, bracelets, rings and necklaces, the garish and not-so-garish, but had her killer found that drop-earring in this box and was that why Renée Ekkehard had had it in her hand?

Setting the lantern close, he dug deeply, yelped as blood rushed from the end of the middle finger of his right hand. 'Ah, Christ!' he panicked. 'Sepsis?' Puncture wounds were always the worst. A high fever, then delirium and no way of stopping it. Sulfa . . . would he need sulfa? Would it be of any use?

Biting hard, he sucked at the wound, found irony in the thought that after all he'd been through with Louis, and before that too, something so small could well kill him.

Spreading a piece of new canvas on the floor, he upended the tin and quickly sorted through the contents. There wasn't a match for the earring Louis had found, but the fragment of glass that had knifed him had blood on its spine and had gone in at least three millimetres. It was cylindrical and nothing like any of the shards from the mirrors. Perhaps two millimetres in diameter and maybe three-quarters of a centimetre in length, including the spine, it was of clear, medical glass.

Looking up to the shelves above, to that little row of Baccarat and the empty marc bottle, he said, '*Danke*, you son of a bitch. We're going to get you.'

On cold, clear nights Yvonne Lutze knew sounds travelled, but now with so little traffic, they came from even farther. Just when Otto turned off the main road, she wasn't sure, though soon he accelerated a little. Listening, freezing, she tried not to remember how it used to be, how as a girl she had often stood outdoors like this even in winter but upstairs, on her very own balcony, listening for her father who would be returning from the railway station, having been to Berlin,

München, Hamburg or Brussels, Paris too. *Vati* who sold the wine of others not because he had to, he had claimed, but because it was among the finest, though unrecognized as such until introduced properly.

Vati who had loved her dearly and would not have approved of her marrying Werner. Otto would have been much better, *mein kleiner Liebling*, he'd have said, but Colonel Hans Otto Rasche had already been married, that lie and fact still staying with her for he'd not just been handsome and gracious but all those other things she had admired and wanted then as a girl of nineteen when young men of her own age had been dying like flies and soon none would be left. *Vati* too.

And the child Otto had left her with? she asked and answered as always, was God's gift as her half of the bargain. Geneviève who had been a student at the university in September 1939, Geneviève who had been so serious about her studies: 'A *biologiste, maman*. I want to study biology and chemistry. Women do study such things. There are two of us girls in my class. Two, *maman*! I'm French, not Alsatian, not German.' She would never really appreciate how generations of her mother's family had come to live in this house. Werner had seen to that. Werner.

Whatever else might be said of him, Werner really did take care of things.

Otto knew where Geneviève was and fortunately perhaps the child had gone with the other students when the university had moved to Clermont-Ferrand, the letters frequent until the capitulation of June 1940, the postcards since never many and always heavily censored, and now far fewer of them.

'She's fine. She's still at her studies,' Otto had said, having made discreet enquiries, 'Don't worry.' But mothers always do.

When the little car rolled to a silent stop, Otto cleared

his throat and even though his voice was hushed, she heard him gruffly say, 'Kohler, don't forget the house will be fast asleep.'

Two suicides, two murders? she silently asked. Have they seen enough, those two detectives you asked for? The soup, the sausage, cheese and bread that girl took with her—they can't help but realize you must have known where she got them and that I had said nothing of it, not even to yourself, though you never once thought to ask me.

Renée Ekkehard, Otto. Something happened between the two of you last August. A brief moment, a mistake on your part perhaps, but whatever it was, and I'm certain of this, it left you vulnerable to that 'secretary' of yours. She never once had to force the issue, did she? She simply asked for your help with the *Karneval* and knew you would agree. A pretty girl whose shy and self-effacing modesty gave you a memory of myself perhaps, though I was nearly ten years younger than her. And now what are we to do? Wait for the inevitable? Tough it out, as Werner would? Use caution always?

Why *didn't* Sophie Schrijen go in her stead as she was supposed to? Löwe Schrijen and that son of his are bound to ask questions of their own privately and you know it too. They've people who do this for them. That's why you had to call Paris. I know it was!

And Victoria Bödicker, Otto? Why did she look at me the way she did when I asked her where Renée might have gone, asked at your insistence?

She was afraid. That business of her having to go into the bookshop to take care of a customer was simply a means of her getting away from me for a moment to give herself time. There was no one in the shop. No bell had sounded above that door, though when she came back, she did say that it worked sometimes and not at others, and that a replacement would be impossible to find.

She had realized I had taken that school notebook of hers, one you desperately needed and had asked me to get. It hadn't quite been hidden by my overcoat which was lying on a chair, but she said nothing of this. Nothing! Otto. And when I got ready to leave, she turned away to gather up the cat, making it easy for me to steal from her. Me, Otto. Me! who had never stolen a thing in her life.

Those three girls were up to something that has jeopardized us all. Why can't you admit this? Why can't you talk to me about it? I know you will want me to look through the detectives' things. I know they will ask me how Renée got to the carnival and that I will have to tell them you—yes, you—arranged for a lorry to take her. A lorry, Otto. You knew where she had gone.

In single file they crossed the catwalk, the river ice pale under moonlight, she looking down at them. Softly letting herself back into the house, she stood a moment between the heavy blackout drapes and the closed door, listening still until Werner turned over in his sleep.

Out of long habit and no matter what, he could drop off so easily when needed and sleep as soundly as a babe.

Mein Mann, Otto. Your Oberfeldwebel.

In the quiet of a house where sounds would echo, Louis laid out on one of the beds the collected bits and pieces from his pockets, and as a conjurer in a *Karneval*, passed the wave of a silent hand over them.

The two rose-coloured buttons taken from Eugène Thomas's pockets were nothing like those that had been carved by one of the POWs and left on Rasche's desk for them to find.

Carefully Kohler set the spine of medical glass next to the former.

The earring's amethystine brilliant caught the lamplight, the papier-mâché ball looking out of place and seeming to mock them, as did the tightly rolled wad of 471 Lagermark, the bobbins with thread still wound, the swatch of blue cloth, and the poor bastard's tin wedding ring, the original no doubt having been taken from him on capture.

'This investigation, Hermann,' came the whisper. 'First there is Frau Oberkircher talking her head off to you on the train, only now we find she is known to the Fräulein Bödicker and sometimes is called in to take care of that one's bookshop.'

'Frau Bödicker having been locked up in the camp for British and American women at Vittel.'

'*Victoria* being a decidedly British name.'

A hot box tells us there are partisans.'

'Feldgendarmen and plain-clothes Gestapo make a hunting ground of Belfort's railway station.'

'Looking for deserters.'

'*N und Ns* are heading for Natzweiler-Struthof.'

'A quarry, Louis, but also with well-known ski slopes nearby.'

'And a girl, a secretary and committee member, who is invited to a party there.'

'Only to witness something that could well have driven her to kill herself if we were to have believed it.'

'A cutthroat, a bowstring knot and then an arbour knot which is also used to tie neat little bundles of medicinal iron.'

Eugène Thomas's nail and stone, left on the floor of that office toilet, were silently pointed out, Hermann then tapping a forefinger against the copy of *Schöne Mädchen in der Natur* and then at the magazine photo of a lone, buck-naked, grinning German soldier.

Unnoticed until now perhaps, the boy's carefully folded uniform was on the ground at his feet, but only a corner of this showed.

'SS,' whispered Hermann. 'I didn't want to point it out to you.'

'A postcard,' breathed Louis. 'A lonely, loving wife who could well have been desperate for money.'

'A *Postzensuren* up to mischief.'

'Perhaps but for now . . . *ah, mais alors, alors, mon vieux* . . .'

'A *Karneval* to raise substantially more cash than last year since Gauleiter Wagner can be very demanding.'

'Months and months those men have been at it, Hermann, but why, please, would your former commanding officer have agreed to such a thing?'

'Since by doing so the son of a bitch left himself vulnerable.'

'And others too, others like Frau Lutz and that husband of hers.'

'Lies, lies and more of them, Louis; half-truths or none at all.'

'And only after the death of Eugène Thomas at around midnight Friday does he then decide to seek help elsewhere.'

'Knowing the chemical formula for trinitrophenol has been scribbled on a scrap of notebook paper and that he definitely can't trust his own detectives to keep quiet about it.'

'Since they've been watching him and are a direct pipeline through to Natzweiler-Struthof, knowing also, though, that it was torn from Victoria Bödicker's school notebook and that Löwe Schrijen, chairman and owner of the Textilfabrikschrijen, gives his daughter everything she needs for her *Karneval*.'

'But does so to please Gauleiter Wagner. He must, Louis. We're in the Reich and the *Oberbonzen* call all the shots. There's also a target date of Saturday, 6 March.'

And to hold anything in public, even a *Karneval,* the Gauleiter's permission would have had to have been given. Rasche had also warned them never to underestimate Löwe Schrijen, but had only reluctantly revealed that the son, Alain Fernand, had been engaged to Renée Ekkehard, his secretary who had been like a 'daughter' to him.

'A girl who skis all night, Louis.'

'Only to then be distracted by a piece of costume jewellery.'

'While being drugged.'

They hadn't bothered to unpack their grip, those two detectives. They had so little in any case, thought Yvonne. A sliver of prewar hand-soap smelled faintly of lilacs and just as faintly bore the impress of the Crillon, a luxury hotel on *place* de la Concord. The Bavarian had probably pocketed it while on an investigation in late 1940, for the Wehrmacht and the SS had taken over many of the hotels, or so Otto had said after that first visit of his. They had even built a makeshift wooden walkway above the rue Royale between that hotel and the former Ministry of the Marine, and so much for culture and architectural beauty in a city of them.

Begging herself to remain calm, she set the grip on the bed Herr Kohler had used and emptied it item by item. 'One spare hand towel,' she whispered. 'Socks with holes in them. Limited changes of underwear. Two spare shirts, an extra necktie, three handkerchiefs—St-Cyr's?' she asked, for they had been carefully pressed as if by a man, and he probably used them for collecting some of the things he did.

Two handguns were wrapped in the woollen pullover Herr

Kohler had brought and laid on the very bottom of the grip. One of them looked like the pistol Alain Schrijen had laughingly shown Werner when the boy had come to escort Renée to his father's house on Christmas Eve.

Mat-black, clean, sleek, much worn and therefore used, this one had a *P38* incised a little in front and above the trigger, a Walther too, the soft curve of the maker's name, the lie of what was now in her hand.

Well oiled, it fitted easily, the brown, crosshatched wooden grip perfect, but for a moment she couldn't move, could only stand with this thing pressed to a thigh in defeat, her shoulders slumped. Was she going to go to pieces?

'I can't! I mustn't! Geneviève,' she whispered. 'Darling, please be careful. Please don't become involved in anything no matter how strongly you feel about the way things are, just hide while you study.'

The other gun was a Lebel *Modèle d'ordonnance,* the old 1873, heavy, ugly, brutal, a six-shot revolver bearing the inscription of the Saint-Étienne Arsenal. It too had a crosshatched brown grip. Some sort of very hard wood—tropical perhaps, or was it of dyed bone?

The barrel, indeed the whole of this thing in her hand, was scratched, nicked, banged up but well oiled. Spare bullets were in a packet and heavy. Eleven-millimetre black-powder cartridges, but why should the Frenchman have such an antique when his partner had only the most modern?

Clips for the Walther pistol held eight 9mm Parabellum cartridges, and there were four spares and a full packet as well, gun oil too, and the cleaning rags, those that he had wrapped the guns in before using the pullover to hide them.

St-Cyr had slept in the box bed, he being the shorter; Herr Kohler the four poster with canopy which, like the other bed in its alcove, like the whole of this room and house, was now drawing in the light of day to glow warmly and securely from its panelled walls. Walls that showed off the lovely grain and knots of the wood and made one think always of a forest and of belonging.

Quickly, deftly, Yvonne made the beds and smoothed their quilted, chequered *Kelsch*-covered duvets and pillows, pausing at the foot of Herr Kohler's bed, the warmers now clutched. 'Cherry pits,' she had heard him mutter late last night, their light out at last. 'They radiate the heat even better than bricks, Louis, and are a hell of a lot softer.'

And then, as if he had longed for home, '*Meine Oma* taught us how to make them. The pits are gently dried in the sun. My brother and I used to turn them for her. You let the flat of your hand move lightly over them so as not to pile them up. The seed shrinks inside the stone and leaves an air space that holds the heat in longer. They're cosy too. My Gerda used to pack bags just like these.'

His grandmother and then his ex-wife . . . St-Cyr had tersely muttered something about Saarbrücken and a farm there and knowing all about it. 'Tomorrow, Hermann.'

'*Ach,* don't get fussed. I only thought it might help if you felt the warmth would last the rest of the night.'

Tomorrow, today. They had left the house, had overslept and taken only one cup of coffee each and black—had refused the milk she had offered, had said, 'We're no longer used to it,' and she had understood that to request such a thing in Paris would have been to tell others one hadn't been in France for very long and definitely draw attention to oneself.

Otto had already left by then, having taken Werner with him. Otto had known she was afraid the detectives would go through Renée's things before leaving the house, but they hadn't. Renée had used Geneviève's bedroom which was on the floor below and across the staircase landing from his. In the autumn of 1940 the girl had come from Strassburg, hadn't known anyone in Kolmar and had needed a place to stay. What else could one have done—told Otto that it wasn't a good idea, that the arrangement was contrary to army rules? Kommandant and secretary living opposite each other, their doors opening in the middle of the night. 'They had, Otto,' she murmured as if he were there beside her. 'Moonlight fills that room in summer when the blackout drapes are open as Renée had liked and had lain there all but naked, her nightdress rucked up, the white gauze of the mosquito netting you'd found for us her only defence as you stood watching her sleep, listening to her every breath. Did you see me in her, Otto, the girl I once was? Just what made you stand there so long and at other times?'

St-Cyr had left to interview Victoria Bödicker. Kohler, having taken two thick slices of bread and some Munster, had gone to the Schrijen Works in the repainted, grey-green French Army Citroën front-wheel drive that had been found for them. What remained of their presence in this room was so little, their absence filled her with despair.

'That notebook, Inspector. That page from which a corner had been . . .'

Downstairs, down, down their steepness, the front door opened, but she hadn't heard anyone cross the catwalk, hadn't heard a knock or the pull of the bell-chain. 'Inspector . . . ?' she managed from the foot of the stairs.

'My tobacco pouch,' said St-Cyr, affably gesturing an apology. 'I seem to have forgotten it.'

Though empty.

4

Wehrmacht helmets soaked up sunlight in the eastern watch-tower, while polished jackboots squeaked on hard-packed snow. Challenged at the gate, Kohler handed over the blanket pass and his papers, but Jakob Dorsche hadn't come to meet him and that could only mean there had been trouble.

'*Einen Moment, bitte,* Herr Hauptmann Detektiv Aufsichts-beamter,' grunted the Feldwebel. No youngster, he had seen enough of the Russian front to be ever mindful of it.

The cranking of the field telephone came from the guard-house. Most of the prisoners on the day shift had now been at work for hours but two lines of waiting details were under guard and probably replacement woodcutters though they carried no axes or saws and only miserable bundles tied up with rags. They were *Ostarbeiter,* eastern labourers—Poles and Russians mainly and considered *Untermenschen* (subhuman) by the Nazis.

There had been thousands of Wehrmacht POWs in the camps to which he had been consigned during the rest of that other war. Though it had never been a picnic, and they had often been cold, hungry and definitely starved for female company, there had still been a camaraderie. But here? he had to ask. Here the men just looked gaunt, lonely, forgotten, badly frightened and entirely without hope.

Uncanny as it was, he did sense trouble. It had always been like this behind the wire. A look or gesture—intuitively there would be a collective understanding that serious trouble was afoot and this thought would permeate the camp like wildfire. '*C'est une priorité, ein Grossfahdung,*' he sighed. A high-priority search. Dorsche was busy.

Had the Lagerfeldwebel been told to go through the French POWs' things thoroughly before this *Kripo* got a chance to look at them? Had orders come from Löwe Schrijen via Lageroffizier Rudel, seeing as Rasche would most likely not have wanted it done?

When he returned, the Feldwebel was less than friendly. 'Herr Kohler, you are to follow me.'

Three men sat in the panelled, memento-decorated office that faced east and was full of the winter's sunlight—Schrijen, Karl Rudel and one other. None of them were happy and all had been impatiently waiting for him, the coffee in their porcelain cups cooling, the plates of the sliced sweet and the savoury *Kugelhupf* lonely on a side table where the latest news from the centre of the world was also laid out. The *Berliner Tageblatt, Zeitung, Morgenpost* and leading daily, *Deutsche Allgemeine Zeitung. Das Schwarze Korps* too, the SS newspaper.

Löwe Schrijen did the talking.

'Well, Kohler, it's kind of you to pay us another visit, but now it's time for a few answers. Was it murder, as my daughter stubbornly believes, or suicide as Karl, here, insists?'

The accent was very much of the Ober-Rhein, the *Deutsch* so fluent he must have used it all his life. 'Both deaths, Herr

Schrijen, or just the one who died but thirty or so steps from your office?'

'Karl, you were right about him. A real smartass.'

Schrijen had kept his dark blue eyes impassively fixed on this delinquent Kripo. He may have been the son of the firm's founder but nothing had been taken for granted. Having grown up under the Kaiser, Schrijen had seen things change hands at the close of 1918 and then swing back in 1940. A survivor, a realist who had held on to the family firm throughout, he would put its welfare first. The nose was prominent and fleshy, the round, cleanly shaven cheeks ruddy, the hair thin, grey-white and cut as short as peach fuzz, the brow sun- and wind-burnt. A man of the hills and vineyards? wondered Kohler. A good fifty-eight years of age and weighing probably in excess of 130 kilos in blue serge, he filled that chair of his like concrete, the hands big, the wrists thick. A square block with Nazi Party pin and the gut of a Munich brewmaster.

It would be best to apologize but prod him a little, for men like this didn't fool around and had their own agendas. 'Herr Generaldirektor, my partner and I regret that we haven't yet been able to come to a firm conclusion about either victim. With cases of hanging it's always difficult, but if the Lageroffizier Rudel has ordered Lagerfeldwebel Dorsche to do what I think he has, that can only hinder the investigation and prolong it.'

Liebe Zeit, Kohler had a tongue after all, thought Schrijen. A peace offering and—or—the threat of a long delay!

A nod so slight it wouldn't normally have been noticed was given to the harried, greying individual in the black suit with matching tie and specs who immediately left the office, probably as quietly and unobtrusively as he'd come into it.

'Herr Bremer is my chief accountant, Kohler, and especially at times like this, my right hand. Now, please, where were we?'

'The suicides,' prompted Rudel, the jet-black hair glistening with pomade and combed well back and to the left of that high forty-year-old brow the shrapnel had spared, the eyes dark brown and swift, the fingers long and thin. A Prussian aristocrat? wondered Kohler. Of a 'good family' anyway.

Schrijen took out a small cigar and paused to light it; Rudel found himself another cigarette and crossed his knees, having to pull the right leg over the other, causing this still standing Kripo, thought Kohler, to glance at the cane—an ice ax, *mein Gott,* that the bastard had to use when walking.

The dark blue pinstripe was Swiss and immaculately tailored, no uniform today, not even a wound badge.

'Kohler,' hazarded Schrijen, looking up from his desk, 'Paris tells me you're the realist, St-Cyr the patriotic dreamer. This Works of mine . . .' He waved the cigar hand to indicate the constant source of the hydrogen sulphide and noise of shuttles, whistle blasts, log shredders and lorries that were doubtless perfume and music to him. 'It can't stop for a moment, can it? Not for anything. Had it been my Sophie, what would I have done, you're wondering? Certainly the girl's upset and understandably mistaken. *Ach,* who the hell would want to kill her? *Führerin der Frauenschaften, Direktorin der Gemeinschaftsverpflegung und der Winterhilfswerk.* A tireless volunteer in addition to everything she has to do here to fill the shoes of a brother who is in the Services.'

The SS at Natzweiler-Struthof for the last of those, but Leader of the Women's Auxiliaries of the Nazi Party for the other, the Red Cross catering service at the hospital too, and the Winter Help. A busy lady.

Rudel had, of course, heard it all before but had the decency to sympathetically nod, though he kept silent, waiting for his cue no doubt.

'When my daughter came to me with her request for help with the *Karneval*, Kohler, I had the colonel in and asked if he would agree to free up a few of the men. A day, two days a week—we would find a way to cover their tasks here. Months they've been at it. Months, let me tell you. And now what is he saying? Not one but two murders when even his own detectives, having thoroughly examined both deaths, have concluded otherwise? *Ach*, against stupidity even the gods fight for nothing!'

And a very Germanic saying. 'Herr Generaldirektor, a moment, please. Am I to understand that early last September your daughter first came to you with the request for help and that you then had to ask Colonel Rasche?'

'Who is it who stamps the passes and then signs them? Everything has to be done through the Kommandant von Ober-Rhein and, in this case, our Reichsarbeitsdienst.'

The local labour recruiting office Rasche had made no mention of since it had probably not even been asked!

'I pay the men, of course, and feed and house them as is my duty.'

Still looking puzzled, this Kripo found his little black notebook but had to borrow a pencil from the stein on the desk. 'I'd best get it straight. Colonel Rasche didn't come to you with the request, you went to him?'

'He came to see me at my request, of course, but as to the order of things, is not the chain of command necessary at all times? Sophie and her committee had already settled on what they thought best to do, but a formal request could only have come from myself to Colonel Rasche.'

'And what was his reaction?'

'Since Gauleiter Wagner had judged their holding a *Karneval* an excellent fund-raising idea, your former commanding officer could but agree to give the necessary permission.'

Having first made damned certain Rasche *would* give his sanction, those ladies on that committee had then known exactly the right buttons to push. Schrijen first, then Wagner, since the former would have insisted on telephoning the Gauleiter, then Rasche, a mere formality even though he had been the start of it all!

'The French POWs who work here are paid for their labour,' said Rudel, 'and are treated correctly as is laid out by the Wehrmacht's ordinance that covers the use of prisoner-of-war labour, so you see, Kohler, ultimately it is Colonel Rasche to whom one must go if even incidental labour is to be freed up, no matter how just the cause.'

And no one else was to blame. 'My partner and I will need to talk to those four men, Generaldirektor, and to the guards who accompanied them on each visit to the *Karneval* site. Your *Werkschutz* too.'

The work-police, and still no mention of the two laboratory assistants, thought Schrijen, or of the *Postzensuren* and other office staff Eugène André Thomas had most certainly come into contact with on a daily basis, but was Kohler keeping that to himself? 'You and your partner could be here for a very long time, *mein Lieber*. Questioning this one, that one, getting so many conflicting stories, for they'll all conflict, won't they? Men behind barbed wire like to play games to alleviate their boredom, and that is one of them. An answer here, another there and great fun in the confusion created, the testimony of their guards contradicting every one of them because the POWs will have agreed on what to say beforehand. Two suicides, two murders, or one and one, which is it to be?'

Attract the least attention possible. Leave it at suicides and go home smiling. 'We'll need to interview your son and daughter, Generaldirektor, and to have nothing but your fullest cooperation.'

The *Schweinebulle* had spoken like a man on the way to his *Heldentod*—the hero's death. Paris had said that St-Cyr and Kohler were sticklers for the truth but that if the right means could be found, the Bavarian, being close to home, might wish to pay his ex-wife a visit and be convinced to switch horses. Paris, of course, did not know everything about Herr Kohler, especially the pharmacist's daughter who had nursed him back to health before his tour of duty in Elsass with a bomb-disposal squad. 'Karl, why not leave us for a little? Come back in a half-hour. If Herr Bremer should cross your path, tell him he won't be needing any of that *Quatsch* that lady pharmacist gives him for the stomach ulcers. She's good, of course, and has her doctorate, having grown up in her father's pharmacy.

'Some coffee, Herr Kohler? Frau Macher . . . Frau Macher, refresh this, would you please?' he called out to the secretary in the outer office, his first line of defence. 'Sit,' he said. 'A cigarette? How are you getting on at that boardinghouse of the colonel's? Frau Lutze is, I gather, an excellent cook.'

'An old friend,' said the Chief Inspector of the tobacco pouch he had deliberately forgotten—Yvonne was certain of this. He stood before her in that rumpled brown fedora, threadbare overcoat, prewar trousers and shoes . . . the right one bearing a split seam and sole and leaking meltwater onto the terra-cotta tiles.

'Two pairs of socks are also needed, I'm afraid,' she heard him saying, the *Deutsch* without hardly a trace of a French accent. Removing his shoes, he went quickly past her and up the stairs but did he suspect she had just been through their things, had she put them back exactly as they'd been?

He made no sound in a house where sounds always carried: Geneviève running down those stairs to greet Otto during the interwar years when her 'fabulous uncle' would come from Magdeburg for a visit; Geneviève calling out, '*Mutti*, I can see him! He has turned onto the quay and is hurrying. He has *two* suitcases and a big bunch of flowers, has brought me a cockatoo, *Mutti*. A cockatoo!'

Otto, to give him what little due he deserved, had never forgotten the child. Money had come every now and then, money she had hated to receive though necessary.

'Madame . . . *Ach*, I would forget French is forbidden. Frau Lutze . . .'

The Inspector was right behind her. He had come down those old stairs without a sound, had avoided the third step from the first landing, the seventh too, and the one before the last and final step, but as to his having forgotten the ban on French . . .

'It's all right. We can speak it behind closed doors if you wish. My daughter . . .' *Ah, Sainte Mère*, had he tricked her into saying it?

He waited, the mildly puzzled frown neither demanding answer nor allowing one not to be given.

'Is away. A student,' she heard herself bleakly saying in *Deutsch*.

'In Clermont-Ferrand?' he asked pleasantly enough.

'Her final year.'

He did not say that it was odd the child should have gone to the university from a home like this, he simply nodded as if the information was of polite interest but of no consequence and begged her to get him a little of the colonel's tobacco, if possible.

Intuitively he had sensed that she would not want to do this, that Otto was bound to find out and discover that he had come back to question her in private unless she was very careful and did not spill any or take too much.

'A moment, then,' she managed.

He was now watching her go up the stairs. He had known Otto must have lied to her when she was nineteen and so very much in love with him—Herr Kohler would have told his partner of it. Geneviève had some of her looks at that age but was tall like Otto. 'Tall girls always have a hard time of it, *Mutti,*' the child had wept not once but often until she had realized that God must have wanted her to be the way she was. 'It is because of this that I must study,' she had concluded, as if consigning herself to scientific cloisters.

Otto had, however, taught Geneviève to love the outdoors, especially on those occasions when he had taken the child away for a day or a weekend's fishing. She had then spoken of it for months and had longed to be with him just like her mother.

When she came downstairs, the Chief Inspector was sitting at the kitchen table. To not offer coffee and butter biscuits would be impolite and might help to distract him.

'*Merci,* madame,' he said, and went on with lacing up his shoes, did not say, as Otto had warned. 'A few small questions. Nothing difficult.'

Instead, moving his coffee cup to one side, he took out a man's gold pocket watch and, opening it, placed the watch before him. 'Roman numerals and a sweep second hand,' he said, 'but it's a puzzle. Perhaps you can help.'

He had emptied Renée's pockets and her rucksack, had taken the lid off that 'coffin' Otto had had made, and had examined the girl's body.

'Renée's was in for repairs,' she heard herself saying. 'Maurice . . . Herr Springer has been fixing watches for years. Since well before I was a little girl.'

He asked the address and she told him, could not have avoided answering. 'Three the Schongstrasse. You can't miss it, though his sign was put away in 1940.'

'That's near the *Polizeikommandantur*, isn't it?' he said and saw her nod, then asked, 'The problem?' having again dropped into French, but had that been deliberate of him?

'The stopwatch. Renée has—had—a fabulous wristwatch she found in Paris, in a shop on the *place* Vendôme.'

'Bréquet's?' he asked, surprised.

'Oui, c'est très cher, mais . . .' Ah, non, she *had* spoken French like she and Geneviève had often done when Werner wasn't home, a household of two languages as most still were in secret, the French being that of her own mother. 'Renée . . . Renée had always wanted such a watch to time her downhill runs, her laps in the pool, and the archery, the speed and accuracy of the arrows.'

'Contests?' he asked, as if bemused, and now packing that pipe of his, having yet to eat a thing.

'Victoria Bödicker, the Fräulein Schrijen and Renée loved to compete with one another, for fun of course.'

Ham, bread, cheese and butter were found, and she made him a sandwich to have along with his coffee and *Bredele,* the star, round, half-moon and heart shapes of shortbread. Some of these last were flavoured with anise, and he'd known this and had not been able to resist glancing appreciatively at them.

Another sandwich was made for him to take along, and was wrapped in newspaper, prompting him to ask, 'Who picked that girl up here on Saturday, madame? *Bien sûr,* she could have . . .'

'Was she murdered, Inspector?'

'Tell me what you think.'

'How could I possibly know? I never go out to that place.'

'Never? Come, come, the girl must have spoken of it often. Weren't you curious?'

'All right, we did go there once. My husband wanted to see it. A ruin, I'm afraid. Personally I thought the whole idea crazy. To repair any of those booths would take much time and cost far too much.'

It was her turn to wait, his to decide. 'This is good,' he said of the sandwich and she knew then that he'd be thinking of the lunch Renée had taken, but he said nothing of it, nor did he push the matter of who had come to the house to give that girl a lift. He ate in silence, allowing lots of time for her to recall the *Karneval*.

'Le Tonneau de l'amour,' she said at last, the Barrel of Love. 'Werner . . . *mon mari*, insisted we go inside that thing. A tunnel, he called it because of its length, each half of which would once have turned in the opposite direction to the other, the girl entering from one end, the boy from the other, both walking toward each other and tumbling as if drunk.'

Had the Inspector seen it yet? she wondered. He gave no hint, causing her to continue. '*Docteur* Bonnet's Travelling Museum of Anatomy. It's at the very back and right against the woods.' Still there was no comment, but now he was enjoying his little meal as a Frenchman would.

'Werner insisted on forcing the entrance. It had been jammed from behind with debris. Broken glass and shattered jars . . . Formalin was all I could think of as I turned away and did not go further. Geneviève, my . . . our daughter, began preserving specimens at the age of ten, Inspector. Dead things that she would find and then dissect. Frogs, toads, minnows, mice and birds—there's an armoire in her room that is still full of such. Jars and jars I . . .'

He waited, this Sûreté, a half-eaten sandwich in hand.

'Things I still can't bring myself to move into storage.'

'You must miss her terribly.'

'Is that not a mother's duty?'

Instead of answering, he repeated the question she had earlier asked and he had deliberately left. 'Was the colonel's secretary murdered?' he said and shrugged. 'It's too early to say, but I'm almost certain someone must have picked her up here on that Saturday. You see, she would have had to change into her ski clothes, collect her skis and the lunch she had prepared ahead of time.'

No accusation of her having known of this lunch came, though she waited for it and he knew she did, and yes, Werner would have to cover for her until she was able to tell him what had been said. 'Perhaps someone did come by, Inspector, but you see I wasn't here. Saturday mornings I help my husband. Werner's very capable and has always done the marketing. At noon we stop in at the *Winstub* of a friend. Some soup, a little bread and a glass of wine, though things are always in such short supply now and the ration tickets necessary. Usually we get back here at about 3.00 in the afternoon so neither of us would have even known if she had gone anywhere, since she would have worked until 6.00 with the colonel.'

'*Ah, bon,*' he said, picking at last crumbs until she was driven to say, 'Perhaps a van came by. Herr Schrijen often sends wine from his vineyards to Karlsruhe as a gift to Herr Wagner. The Schlossberg, the Riesling . . . *Ach*, I'm sorry. I should have offered you some.'

'Wagner,' he muttered. 'He's the Gauleiter, isn't he?'

And the most feared of men—this was in the look the Chief Inspector gave, but he said no more of it, again forcing her to continue. 'Perhaps Renée did hitch a ride. Victoria . . . the Fräulein Bödicker might know.'

'Yet you didn't ask her when you went to the shop to inquire after the girl?'

On that same Saturday afternoon. 'I assumed she could not possibly have known. I . . . I could have been mistaken.'

This he did not challenge though he most certainly could have. Instead he asked for a little more coffee and decided that, after all, he would add milk to it.

'Victoria Bödicker and Renée Ekkehard, madame. They were good friends, I gather, but when did they first meet, who introduced them? All such things would be of help, even if they might seem insignificant.'

He would remember everything. He had that look about him and did not need to write a thing down. 'The ski slopes in that first winter of 1940–41. Victoria had just returned from Munich. She hadn't been allowed to continue teaching. There had been a problem with her mother's having been held in the internment camp which was at Besançon then, and after that terrible winter, was moved to Vittel and a little closer.'

The mother having kept her English passport and thus having been rounded up along with all such others. 'She visits Vittel, does she, the Fräulein Bödicker?'

And not the mademoiselle, but it would have to be said. 'Once a month, on the last Friday, Victoria leaves well before dawn and returns late the same day. Otto . . . Colonel Rasche issues her the necessary *laissez-passer* and *sauf-conduit*. Renée used to bring them home here and then either take them to the bookshop for Victoria or the girl would stop by. That way . . .' *Ah, merde,* had this been what the Chief Inspector had been after? 'That way Victoria wasn't seen at the *Polizeikommandantur* too often, a . . . a precaution Otto felt best. Renée . . . Renée went with her to Vittel last September. Perhaps he felt the girl needed a change, a little trip, or maybe it was he simply wanted to hear what she had to say about that camp. It's full of British and American women who were caught up in things.'

All of whom were trapped and left behind just like the carnival—was this what the Inspector was now thinking, since Otto had agreed to the repair of those booths and by then on that last Friday of September, the work had already begun.

Taking a few of the *Bredele,* silently asking her permission, he stuffed them into a jacket pocket, gathered his pipe and tobacco pouch and the watch he had left out all this time, and getting up from the table, sadly shook his head and said, 'It gets deeper and deeper, doesn't it, this hole the colonel has dug for himself? He agrees to find help for that committee of the Fräulein Schrijen's, since his secretary is a member of it, but avoids sending the necessary paperwork to the *Konzentrationslager,* issues passes to the bookseller, another member of that same committee who repeatedly is then allowed to cross the frontier into France, even sends his secretary along, and then lets her hitch a ride out to the *Karneval* but denies knowing anything of it at first, only to then leave her absence for several days. It's a puzzle, isn't it? A soldier through and through, yet a softness one finds difficult to understand, given the risks and the times.'

'Your colonel, Kohler,' mused Schrijen, wagging that left forefinger of his. 'Just how long does he intend to keep the body of my son's fiancée?'

And never mind that of the second victim. Left alone in the office, the secretary having closed the door and promised to hold all calls, a small cigar had been offered and accepted, coffee too, and slices of the *Kugelhupf*, both of which were fantastic and brought brief memories of that other war, of clean sheets and a pharmacist's daughter. 'My partner has only had a preliminary look at her, Generaldirektor. Louis is a stickler for detail. Patience . . . I have to constantly remind myself to have it. The French . . .'

The fists were doubled, the forearms swiftly placed flat on the desk, the look far from pleasant. 'Cut the *Quatsch, mein Lieber*. Men like myself haven't time to waste.'

'We'll need at least two days, maybe a little more.'

The eyebrows arched at such confidence, the head cocked to the right, the fleshy nose finally pinched in thought, that same forefinger lifted. 'An autopsy, is this what that partner of yours is demanding?'

God help him if it was. 'Does that worry you?'

'*Ach*, not in the slightest, though it's curious, is it not, that Colonel Rasche would prefer such a thing not to happen?'

It had to be said. 'You're well informed.'

'I have to be. Now, please, if we can't find a way through this, who can? The parents have been begging my son and me to intercede and bring their daughter home. A small funeral is requested. Understandably we see it as more, though of course they would prefer the less said the better. She was an only child. It's difficult enough.'

'And if it was murder?'

Did Kohler still need his ass kicked? 'It wasn't. You can't have read the report the *Polizeikommandantur*'s own detectives filed. My son's choice of a wife was not as I would have advised. Things troubled her greatly. Loneliness was too often preferred.

Repeated visits to a place like that *Karneval*? A young and beautiful girl wanders about among ruined sideshows on her own, picking at the rubbish of those freaks? She spends hours in the adjacent Kastenwald, speaks of ravens, has thoughts of a Gallic goddess of the Underworld who watches her constantly and waits only to torment her? Is out all night skiing—why, please, I have to wonder? A virgin? Children were what she needed and the more the better.'

Louis should have heard him. 'Generaldirektor, I understand from the Oberstleutnant Rudel that she . . .'

'Yes, yes, that she had seen something at the quarry camp. We don't ask, and my son doesn't tell us, but obviously whatever it was, in her confused state of mind it left a lasting impression. Before she killed herself, the girl wrote, *"I can't go on. Please forgive me."*'

'There wasn't a note, was there?'

Dummkopf, your ass has just been kicked. 'One of those detectives your colonel ignores found it tucked into the frame of the broken mirror nearest to her.'

'Written in lipstick or in pencil?'

'Lipstick.'

'Didn't that suggest it could well have been written by someone else?'

'A woman—is this what you're saying? The Fräulein Bödicker perhaps? *Ach*, ask her, don't ask me. Ask the colonel's detectives.'

'Fingerprints—were any taken?'

Kohler was desperate and that could only mean St-Cyr and he had good reason to believe the girl hadn't killed herself. 'Again I must defer to those detectives. I'm not a policeman.'

'But were given privileged information and have read their report, which should have stated clearly if any had been taken.'

'It's winter, Kohler. Perhaps I should have paid closer attention but the girl wore woollen gloves under her mittens, though those have since been removed.'

Schrijen must have opened the coffin and had a look himself, but more importantly, had let this Kripo know of it. 'Your son, Generaldirektor . . .'

'Was on duty when that girl chose to break his heart. As for myself and my Sophie, we were at the house in the country. I've vineyards at Kaysersberg—twelve and a half hectares of the Reisling on the Schlossberg slope, and thirty-six of the Gewürztraminer on the Kayersberg-Kientzheim. Sophie likes to keep an eye on them with me. It's a little something we do together. Friends and associates visited on the Saturday after work and stayed well into the evening. We slept in late. The fresh air perhaps. Several can vouch for our whereabouts, but of course there is no need. Personally, as the father of that girl's fiancé, I have to question the colonel's motives. Was he infatuated with the Fräulein Ekkehard? Did he try to take advantage of her? He's known for that sort of thing, isn't he? Frau Lutze for one. Formerly Yvonne Eva Ellmann, Kohler, and one of those on her father's side. Just what does he hope to gain by claiming it was murder?'

There, it had been said, and Kohler would have to think about it.

Ellmann and Jewish, ah, Christ! 'Your wife, Generaldirektor?'

'Has been dead for years though still sadly missed. My Sophie does her utmost. Here . . . Here, take a look at this.'

Swinging the chair around, he reached for a framed photo on the window shelf, took another and another. 'The twenty-sixth of June, 1940, Kohler. A lot of us wanted it to happen.'

And had managed to make it to Strassburg in time to greet

the Führer as he had stood outside the Cathedral with his generals, Keitel among them, the one who was now being referred to at home as the Lackey.

Sophie Schrijen wore a pillbox hat with a bit of net veiling the wind had teased. The light-coloured suit and high heels were perfect, the smile self-conscious as she faced the camera with her hand in that of the great one, Daddy right beside her and beaming.

'It's impressive, Generaldirektor. You must be very proud of her.'

Was this one still needing lessons? 'I am, Kohler. I am. The French . . . *Ach,* whatever else may be said of them, they're not good businessmen. Order . . . a place like this demands it. One can't be arrogant, and they are often insufferably so. Incompetence and petty jealousies have no place here. Mistresses don't flaunt their asses in our boardrooms or at official dinners and other functions. They belong on their backs or hands and knees, and that is where one should keep them. Now it is much better, *ja*. Things get done properly. In June of last year we had 169,235 members in our *Opfer,* now 227,186 and you can't do that without good business.'

The Offering, the Sacrifice. Cash given on a regular basis to keep the Party and its hierarchy going. The war effort also, of course.

'Thirty thousand of us are now full members of the Party, Kohler. Well before the military call-up of August '41, over 2,100 had volunteered. The Waffen-SS, the Wehrmacht, Kriegsmarine and Luftwaffe. You name it and we've boys there and girls too. This firm has lost five so far. Five highly valued employees to the families of whom I continue to pay wages since it may make their burden a little less.

'More coffee? Some more of the *Kugelhupf?* Frau Macher always takes such good care of me. Tireless, I tell you, Kohler. Tireless. A woman with a sense of duty that is a model to us all. Here, have another of these.'

The small cigars, the Schimmelpenninck Havana Milds, but for the road, was it? 'Generaldirektor, your son . . .'

Was Kohler like a broken record? '*Ach,* it's good of you to remind me. This is my Alain. An Untersturmführer but soon to be promoted. Schutzhaftlagerführer Kramer thinks very highly of him.'

And if that wasn't warning enough, what was? In his SS uniform, Lieutenant Alain Fernand Schrijen looked like so many: smartly turned out, a handsome young man with a nice grin, big ears and a somewhat narrower face than the sister. 'He's younger than your daughter.'

'By four years. We really miss him here at the Works. Sophie tries, though hasn't the technical background, but with the war, what can one do?'

But send him close to home where the only guns he'll see or hear are those of his fellow SS and himself. 'Did he ever visit the *Karneval* with the Fräulein Ekkehard?'

'Alain? He might have. Now wait. I think he did go out there once with his sister and the girl, but that was last autumn. Late October, early November . . . well after the colonel had agreed to let them do what they wished. The Fräulein Bödicker was also with them, I believe. Frau Macher had a picnic basket made up for the young ones. Sausage, chicken, ham and a little of the 1940 Gewürztraminer, some of our late pears . . . How could I have forgotten? The Fräulein Bödicker fortunately has someone who can come in on short notice to tend that shop of her mother's. A neighbour. A lifelong friend and widow from that other war. Frau . . . *Liebe Zeit,* what was it now? Frau Oberkircher. *Ja,* that was it.'

And yet another warning and example of his being well informed. 'This bookseller, Generaldirektor. How long has your daughter known her?'

Kohler hadn't liked the thought of his train companion tending the Bödicker bookshop. Perhaps it was a little too close for comfort. 'My Sophie, you ask? At night she often finds a need to read herself to sleep. There are bookshops and bookshops, and that was one she had settled on. Young people are best when energy is demanded, as on a *Winterhilfswerk* Committee, and my Sophie makes fast decisions—at times too fast. The Fräulein Bödicker, I asked. A rejected schoolteacher? Surely there must have been a very good reason for her not to have been accepted back into the profession, but they worked well together, and when that happens, one learns to wait and watch.'

'And you've no further concerns?'

'I always have, but if you mean, do I for a moment believe my daughter was the intended victim of an imaginary murder plot Colonel Rasche has dreamed up for whatever reason, then no. Sophie was simply too busy here and had asked the Fräulein Ekkehard to go in her stead.'

Herr Kohler didn't ask if a lift had been found for the girl in one of the firm's lorries, he didn't even ask if Sophie had arranged such a thing. He simply waited to see the other photo that had been taken from the window shelf and perhaps he had better see it.

'It's of Sophie, myself and Alain with Gauleiter Wagner on the platform at the 12 October rally in 1941 in Strassburg. The Karl Roos Platz, formerly *place* Broglie, and thousands, Kohler. Thousands. *Mein Gott*, the cheering. They must have heard it in Berlin, similar rallies being held throughout Elsass. Herr Wagner was to have been the guest of honour at my son's wedding in May. A very important man, very well liked and loved by many.'

And another warning, was that it?

'Anything even remotely connected with my Works, Kohler, and I am to be informed of it. Go where you wish, ask what you will. If you need anything, it's yours. Restaurants, theatres—those little diversions a man finds necessary especially when away from home. Anything. Just tell them Löwe sent you and it'll be taken care of. Two suicides, nothing more. Then it's back to Paris for that partner of yours and yourself, or first a little visit home if you wish it. All can be arranged.'

No problem. '*Danke*, Generaldirektor. I'll be sure to tell Louis that it's better to lie down with the lions than to hole up in some dumb old citadel and freeze.'

The street was narrow and winding and instantly it made St-Cyr think of the Middle Ages. Stepped facades of overhanging storeys, their shutters broken in places and crooked in others, climbed on either side to sway-backed, gabled roofs where tiles were loose or missing and storks could well roost in springtime. The half-timbered walls were of that faded pink, white or brown stucco, soot-stained by the centuries. Oriel windows, with leaded crown glass, looked to character, not to tidiness, reflecting shadows from their bottle-round panes while architrave carvings gave the story of each builder, those of a former wine merchant using the back-facing, S-shaped scrollwork of the Gauls, the Celts, to outline bunches of grapes.

Around one, life went on with that same suppressed interest as found in Paris and other cities in France. Always, too, it appeared, one had best look as if going about one's business especially as a dark, forest-green Mercedes tourer, a big, powerful, lonely car, was all but blocking the street a short distance away, the red *V* of its licence plate signifying *Verfügung*, by order, by decree, and a petrol allowance, whereas in France an *SP* sticker, the *Service Public*, would have been pasted inside the front windscreen.

There was a *Luftschutzkeller*, an air-raid shelter, in a cellar nearby. Two of the *Schupos*, the *Schutzpolizei*, the urban constabulary, strolled toward him, he immediately stepping to the end of a queue and wishing he had a shopping bag. The gilded, black lettering of LA CHARCUTERIE DU PABST had been scraped away to be replaced by DELIKATESSENGESCHÄFT PABST, the prewar lettering still showing faintly through.

None of the lovely wrought-iron shop signs hung anywhere. All had been either taken for scrap or hidden away.

Next door to the bookshop, which was beyond the tourer and at a bend, a woman bundled in black had paused while sweeping steps that didn't need to be swept. She was looking back down the street at him. Guilty . . . was she feeling guilty about something? Still she hesitated, her eyes watering as he sought her out. 'Frau Oberkircher?' he asked, causing her to dart indoors and bolt the door.

CLOSED, her little sign read. BY ORDER. She had eked out a living by making fruit-flavoured leathers and boiled sweets for schoolchildren, had returned from her brother-in-law's funeral to find her means of support had fallen prey to being classed as nonessential now that the Reich had finally gone to full mobilization.

The lace curtain was very French and he'd seen thousands like it, but what, really, had she been up to? Watching the street for himself or for Hermann, was that it, eh? A Gestapo informant? And why had God put her next door to the bookshop?

God often did things like that. He let chance play such a part these days, made surprises all too evident when least expected and only the more unsettling. Had she been questioned on her return? Had Hermann inadvertently let something slip while on that train?

Kohler waited behind the door to the laboratory and next to the foyer of the executive offices. He knew he hadn't much time. Sophie Schrijen hadn't hung around to be questioned while he had been closeted with her father. She hadn't even bothered to lock up, had left in such a rush her office door was wide open, but would Frau Macher leave that front desk . . .

It was empty. Muffled, the sound of Schrijen dictating a letter came faintly into the foyer where oil portraits of himself and Gauleiter Wagner flanked that of the Führer.

Closing the door a little, Kohler took in the office at a glance. Everything was in its place because she had so many things on the go. A table to the right held a beautifully made model of the *Karneval* as it had been. Brightly coloured, gay, exciting, tantalizing . . . the Ferris wheel, the Super Car Monte Carlo, Barrel of Love, House of Mirrors . . . were all to scale, but the time to have made it must have been considerable.

Behind it, on the wall, there was a diagram of the ruins with the locations and distances all keyed to the model and no problem at all in finding a potential victim, none either of fading away quickly or of watching someone put on her skis. Was that how it had been?

The left side of the desk was reserved for the volunteer work. Manila paper file folders overlapped in sequence: the

Women's Auxiliaries of the Nazi Party, among them the *Frauenschaft*, the mothers and housewives, the *Arbeitsmaiden* too, the Labour Service for girls from eighteen to twenty-one, also the BDMs—the League of German Girls—those from fifteen to twenty-one, and the *Jungmädel* from ten to fourteen, then, too, the Red Cross catering service at the hospital and the *Winterhilfswerk*. A busier lady by far than even that father of hers had claimed. Speeches to give, receptions at which to be the guest of honour, pins and other awards to hand out, the names of the recipients all underlined. The stress on her must be really something.

To the right was everything dealing with the Textifabrik-schrijen. Orders, letters to be signed, requisitions for supplies, production figures, fabric specifications . . . the Wehrmacht, Kriegsmarine and SS. Uniforms too, for the BDMs, and cloth for civilian needs. Dress fabric, blouse, shirt and suit fabric . . . man-hours expected, *Straflager* penalties handed out to slackers and troublemakers—as good an indication as any of how contented a camp was. Wages . . . seventy pfennigs per day per man, per twelve-hour shift but paid only to the French POWs, the Russians and the Poles receiving zero, but even at the base level of the official exchange rate and in *Reichskassenscheine*, the Occupation marks in France and other countries, that seventy pfennigs equalled *14 francs*, or *17 British pence*, or *32 American cents*.

Food was listed: potatoes, cabbage, sauerkraut, black bread in two-kilo loaves and lumpy, sour too, and soggy, horsemeat and bone, pork and bone, soup bones also, and calorie intakes required under the Oberkommando der Wehrmacht ordinance as per Karl Rudel.

Beside each of these intakes she had lightly pencilled in the normal minimum requirements for a healthy man at hard labour: 3,000 calouries per day instead of the 1,500 received; fats at least 100 grams instead of 30; protein the same; vitamin A 5,000 units, not the 2,000, et cetera.

Oh for sure, a voice should be raised, but from here and right next to the prime mover and shaker of the Works? It was suicidal.

Five hundred and ninety-three prisoners ate, slept, worked and did little else, and the quarry camp at Natzweiler-Struthof was always there if a vacation was needed.

She must have known Eugène Thomas quite well, must have had to consult with him often and but a step or two away, but had she known he had received that anonymous letter, had she known of the trinitrophenol and the cutthroat?

The bell above the bookshop's door rang well enough, but things were never simple, irony often deep, thought St-Cyr. Two buckets of sand, painted red and clearly marked by Civil Defence for use in case of fire during an air raid, were tucked out of the way inside the door. As would be expected, the regulations were clearly posted and signed by the *Luftschutzfeldwebel*, but here the name of one Werner Lutze was found, a fact that neither Frau Lutze nor Colonel Rasche had bothered to mention.

Leaded, diamond-pane, seventeenth-century casements gave crisscrossing shadows to the books. On the far wall, a large, framed photo of a book burning brought its stark reminder: 10 May 1933. Thousands and thousands of students had plundered public and private libraries, marching into the Unter den Linden and then following it to the University of Berlin, to set the mountains alight while *Zeig Heil*-ing at the top of their lungs.

All such fires, and there had been many of them, had awakened within him an ominous sense of foreboding that had been realized on 1 September 1939 with the invasion of Poland, but why had Victoria Bödicker chosen to hang that photo? As a protest or sign of loyalty, and if the latter, was that not wise, and if the former, not foolish?

Beneath the photo, three plump porcelain geese, like those found before the war in every second shop window in Strasbourg and Colmar to advertise *pâtés de foie gras*, were nestled in straw atop small stacks of newly received books, the geese sound asleep.

A protest, then, but hard for anyone in authority to prove.

'*Mein Herr*, can I help you?'

The voice was carefully modulated, yet warm and soft. A brunette with page-boy styled hair, she was perhaps thirty-two years of age. High, strong, almost Slavic cheekbones framed deep brown, mildly interested eyes, no lipstick, rouge or powder being worn, the skin clear and with the burnish of wind and sun.

She was also of the same height as Sophie Schrijen who stepped timidly from one of the aisles to stand apprehensively behind and partly to one side of her. Two of the original three, the one here to get the story of the other straight and make sure they both said the same thing, or here in fear of her life?

'*Meine Damen*, a few small questions, nothing difficult, but first, the automobile that is parked well down the street . . .'

And not outside the shop as a precaution—was this what he thought? wondered Sophie. 'It's my brother's. I left it there because, since a child, I've loved walking along that street to this shop. The *Schupos* will find me if it needs to be moved.'

The urge to say, *Ah, bon*, pulled at him, but it would be best simply to nod.

There were aisles and aisles of books: 20,000 new ones were published in the Reich each year. Sentimental novels of *Kameradschaft* in the front lines, dogma, too, and doctrine, the superiority of the *Volk*, the Germanic Nordic race and the unjust lack of living space. Stories of chivalry as well and of *Kinder, Küche und Kirche*—kids, kitchen, and church—for those were what girls were supposed to aspire to, though the church was definitely not in favour with the Nazis and hadn't been since 1933, especially the Protestants, and the slogan but one that had been borrowed from a deeper past and never quite expunged from the popular psyche and therefore used in various ways.

A sleeve of the closely fitted, trim brown velvet jacket of the Fräulein Bödicker's suit brushed against his overcoat as she put the lock on and turned the signboard to read CLOSED, her perfume causing him to start and she to smile softly.

'*Mirage*,' he said, as if baffled as to how she could have come by it, thought Victoria, but did he not know that Renée had bought her watch near that shop before the war and that Colonel Rasche had since been back and had, on one occasion, bought more of the perfume?

'It's lovely, isn't it?' she said. 'Very delicate, very feminine. Renée found it in a shop in Paris and gave me a little.'

The shop Enchantment on *place* Vendôme and the signature perfume of Gabrielle Arcuri, the chanteuse who had come into his life, but did God have to do this to him? wondered St-Cyr. 'Treasured,' he said, 'and now worn in memory of Renée Ekkehard.'

'Why, yes. I . . . I had to do something. She . . .'

Sophie Schrijen had reached out in comfort, or had it been to silence her?

Frau Macher was again at her desk and typing, the foyer a no-man's-land he'd have to cross, thought Kohler wryly. He also knew that at any moment Löwe Schrijen could ask for something in his daughter's office or ring Sophie up if he hadn't been told she had left. An intercom button connected this one to his and to Frau Macher, and opportunity enough to quietly listen in to the daughter, since there wasn't a light to give the game away.

In the rush to leave, Sophie Schrijen had forgotten her keys which lay in a bundle in the middle of the desk: keys to the administrative offices and this one in particular, those to the filing cabinets, the house in the country, the padlocks on the wagons at the *Karneval*, even a flat in town? he had to ask.

Keys were always going missing, girls always misplacing theirs, temptation the foremost of detective sins.

The sound of the typewriter continued. Things in here, though, were so tidy it had to raise alarm bells. Sophie Schrijen had even kept the desk drawers all but as her brother must have left them, and if that wasn't curious, what was? Only in the right front corner of the central drawer had space been set aside for herself. There was a newly purchased lipstick, of that horrible wartime *Quatsch* that burned the lips, but had it been used to write a suicide note? The urge to pocket it came, but if absent, she'd know that someone had been in and had lifted the keys.

An eraser-sized chunk of pink granite was curious. The quarry? he had to ask, but if so, why keep it so close it had to be a constant reminder?

A phosphorescent swastika button lay beside it—one of those that were meant to be worn during the blackout, but had obviously not been, and that, too, was curious. Had she been out and about in Kolmar?

A token, one of those little collectibles the *Winterhilfswerk* sold to parents and schoolchildren, was here too, the thing depicting a grim-faced Wehrmacht 1935-style helmeted soldier boy, strong and handsome, but this was not the only toy soldier. There was a broken lead one on a horse, one of those spike-helmeted unfortunates the Kaiser had let gallop into machine-gun and artillery fire until those had cut them down and killed good horses. Splendid mounts.

This one had lost a right foreleg but had also been scratched and picked at with a nail or pin, though elsewhere the paintwork was still like new. Had it been one of her brother's as a child and if so, why keep it here and not elsewhere? Had she stolen it in revenge perhaps over some childhood squabble, and if that, why, then, was she still feeling guilty about it?

Or had she found it at the *Karneval*?

The only sign of untidiness was a hastily removed sticking plaster, but why yank it off and not throw it into the wastepaper basket, why put it here in this little corner if not to hide it from Frau Macher or someone else, the basket bound to have been searched?

A forefinger . . . A single droplet of blood, now dried, had half-missed the gauze and hit the adhesive tape, indicating that the bandage had been hastily applied and then just as quickly removed. That ampoule? he had to ask and favour his own middle right finger. Had it been done by a broken neck of glass, the hand shaking so hard she had cut herself?

The sound of the typewriter had stopped. Rudel must have come into the foyer and said something, for Frau Macher's voice came clearly now. 'You're to go right in, Herr Oberstleutnant. Generaldirektor Schrijen is waiting.'

And in without even knocking.

Between where the keys had lain and the chair, there was a single file folder, a speech Sophie had been going over for a meeting of the *Frauenschaft* this coming Saturday, 13 February, at 8.00 p.m. Loneliness, Loyalty, and Constancy. Finding the Strength to Wait.

Pages of type held underlined words and passages. Beneath them were examples—advertisements torn from the Personals columns of the *Frankfurter Zeitung, Berliner Morgenpost* and *Deutsche Allgemeine Zeitung*, the *Kölnische Zeitung* and *Münchner Neueste Nachrichten*, the latest *Night Focus*.

To quote: 'Geli is eighteen, 160 cm in height (5′3″) and of good figure. Likes to dance and to party with friends. Loves long walks in the country or park and evenings at the cinema. Is happiest when with a loving, caring man who has a good sense of humour. Apply Box 183.'

Beside the advertisement, Sophie Schrijen had written, *'Geli misses her Ludwig terribly. When last heard from he was at Stalingrad.'*

Again to quote: 'Emmi is blonde, hazel-eyed and 42. Seeks male companion between 35 and 55 who can provide a caring home. Is experienced with children but past the age of child-bearing. Is willing and able to cook, clean and keep house for a widower and his little family in return for his respect, love and kind support.'

Here Sophie Schirjen had written, *'Emmi's husband, Heinz, is stationed somewhere along the Atlantic Wall in France and hasn't been home in two years. When asked, Emmi hotly claimed he was* "Ein böser Mench" *(a bad man) who beat her, but when pressed, admitted she was terribly lonely. "I haven't had a man in all that time," she wept.'*

'Anneliese is dark-haired and dark-eyed. A pleasantly plump girl, she is 22 years old, likes to grow vegetables, make preserves and mead the old-fashioned way, and to read while listening to recordings of Wagner by the Berlin Philharmonic, the *Götterdämmerung* especially. Seeks an older man who can give her guidance, friendship and much love. Apply Box 1521.'

The *Münchner Neueste Nachrichten*:

'Anneliese is married and has two children. Her husband, Gun-

ther, is stationed in Greece, she thinks. He does not write, she says, because he is too embarrassed to ask one of the others to do it for him. The loneliness is unbearable. The long nights and the children—I have only myself to rely on and must be both mother and father, she says. Her parents were killed in Köln during the firestorm.'

All over the Reich, and in France too, the lonely and the desperate were placing advertisements like these, the costs often negligible or given free of charge. Girls—women who needed companionship, security and sex, damn it, just like Gerda had. Women and girls who were seeing their youth and lives fly by. A tragedy.

Caught among the folds of the *Münchner Neueste Nachrichten* were two ten-by-eight-centimetre head-and-shoulders photos of company Sophie Schrijen or any other woman would definitely not want. One wore a white, thin-collared, too tightly buttoned shirt, black tie, heavy black woollen waistcoat and suit jacket. Round in the shoulders, his head was down on them, the perpetual evening shadow doing nothing to alleviate the expression in dark, half-hooded eyes that said, Ah, yes, you make the next move, *mein Herr*, and we'll see what happens.

The other one had a Hitler soup-strainer and eyebrows to match. Dissipated, a drinker too, and whoremaster who obviously sucked on more fags than he should, he was big in the shoulders, big everywhere and had the look of one who knew what he had to do and wouldn't give a damn about anything else.

'The colonel's detectives,' said Kohler softly. It hadn't taken a moment to decide, since photos like these were in every cop shop in the land and in France too, and each had its *Polizeikommandantur* number on the back along with the stamp and swastika. These were simply spares that had been, and were always kept in case false identity papers might be needed. Renée Ekkhard must have gotten them, and at some risk, too, but why tuck them in here unless watching for these two when in the street and before an audience?

Had Sophie Schirjen discovered she was being constantly followed and was that why she hadn't gone out to the *Karneval*?

'Herr Kohler, what is this, please?'

It was Frau Macher. '*Ach*, I was just trying to reach my partner but can't seem to figure out how to use the telephone.'

The tisane was not of camomile, that gentlest of nervines, felt St-Cyr, nor was it of peppermint or verbena. It was of motherwort whose pungent aroma and astringently bitter taste would have been lessened by lavender and honey. A tisane, then, to gladden and strengthen the heart in the face of adversity. *Leonurus cardiaca* in the Latin, the remedy centuries old and a favourite of medieval monks, but a bookseller who knew her herbal.

'Sip it slowly,' said this Victoria Bödicker to the Fräulein Schrijen, the bookseller now the one with a hand on the other's shoulder. 'Take deep breaths. Yes, yes, that's it. Inspector, you can see the way she is. Could the interview not be left until another time?'

The two of them were far from feeling easy. That neither wanted to be questioned was clear enough, but was it because each feared what the other might say?

'Another time . . . ? Of course it's possible, but my partner and I have only a limited amount of it and I've come on foot.'

The *Stube* they were in was directly behind the bookshop and gave onto a short, terra-cotta tiled corridor at the far end of which a heavily timbered and carved staircase rose steeply from a leaded window and rear door. On the limestone banquette of the tiled *Kachelhofen,* a grey tabby contentedly half-lifted sleepy eyelids to its mistress who was still tensely standing nearby with that hand firmly clamped on the shoulder of her friend—were things that desperate for them?

The Fräulein Schrijen sat with head bowed, clutching the cup and saucer in her lap, her blonde hair having fallen loosely forward over that shoulder and the other's hand. 'What did you find?' she managed, not looking up but shuddering at the thought. 'Please don't lie to me, Inspector. I can't take any more lies. I can't! I sent Renée out to the *Karneval* instead of going myself. It was all my fault. Mine! Had I not done, I could well have been the one in that . . . that horrible coffin the colonel had made for her. I *could,* don't you see? I *could*!'

The other was shattered by the outburst.

'Sophie, *please*. It wasn't murder. You mustn't think that.'

'Were you there, Victoria? Did you see her do it and not try to stop her?'

Tears . . . there were plenty of them, the hand of the bookseller tightening as if to stop the flood and give warning yet unable.

'You know I wasn't, Sophie. How can you even think such a thing?'

The bookseller's deep brown eyes registered both concern and despair. 'Inspector, Renée was very upset. She had seen a man hanged three times at Natzweiler-Struthof—that is how long it took for him to die, and when they had finally cut him down, one of them . . .'

'Victoria, please don't tell him. Please don't. I . . . I couldn't bear to have you do that.'

The tisane had spilled, the cup had rattled, a handkerchief was now being used, the skirt ineffectually dabbed at.

'Then stop this craziness. No one would have killed her. *Liebe Zeit*, why would they?'

'And Eugène, what of him?' challenged the other.

'Sophie, his death can't have had anything to do with what Renée saw. I made her swear she wouldn't tell another soul, not even yourself.'

Anxiously the hand that held her by the shoulder was grabbed and pressed against a cheek then kissed, the tisane again spilling. 'Why *didn't* she come back from the *Karneval*, Victoria? Why did she have to stay out there all night? That lorry was to have picked her up at about 5.00 in the afternoon. 5.00!'

'What lorry? *Meine Damen, bitte*, let us take this one step at a time. Did the Fräulein Ekkehard ask you to provide a lift in one of the firm's lorries?'

Why hadn't he been told? Why had no one let him know? 'Colonel Rasche telephoned the office to ask if I could arrange things. Renée had left the *Polizeikommandantur* by then to change and get her skis. He was going to give her a lift himself but had found he couldn't. Something urgent had come up.'

The tear-dampened grey-blue eyes were puzzled by his also not having known what had just been said of the facts.

'So a lorry was sent from the Works?' he asked.

She would let him see her tears. 'That is correct.'

'And was it sent to pick her up that same day?' he asked, she to touch the rim of her cup and no longer find the will to look at him.

Her voice was ashen. 'The driver waited a good half-hour. He . . . he honked the horn several times but when Renée didn't appear, he . . . he felt the colonel must have come by and taken her home. Colonel Rasche hasn't told you any of this, has he?'

Alarmed, she looked questioningly up at her friend, before

wincing and lowering her eyes to the tisane as if the truth were too hard to bear.

The shoulders were gripped, the hair brushed back into place, but it did no good. Instead, she said, 'Renée wouldn't have hanged herself, Victoria. Not even if Alain had shot that man, and I know he must have once they'd cut the poor soul down and turned him over so that the shot could be to the back of the neck as a further warning to the other prisoners.'

'Sophie, please don't cry. Renée didn't love your brother. She was trapped. Afraid not to say she'd marry him, and terrified if she did. You know what they're like up at that camp. You know the pressure that was put on her.'

'So she killed herself, is that it?' snapped the Fräulein Schrijen.

'I know it's hard for you to accept, but . . .'

'A good Catholic, damn you?'

'Sophie, I *held* her when she came back from that weekend at Natzweiler-Struthof. I tried to calm her just as I'm trying to calm you. Now drink that, please. Take all of what's left of it. You're overtired—exhausted. That father of yours has got you doing far too much. *Ach*, how can he expect so much of anyone, let alone yourself who has always to fill two pairs of shoes? Your mother's and your own. You know it as well as I do. Go and lie down on the daybed in the kitchen. Leave me to talk to this one. You *don't* always have to do everything.'

'Are you sure?'

Disconcerted by the swiftness of the response, the bookseller hesitated and then found her voice and said, 'Of course. Now leave us. Take an hour. Surely the Works can spare you for that long. Samson and I will wake you.'

Samson being the cat.

5

Ground wood was everywhere in the Pulping Shed, water everywhere, steam too, noted Kohler. Screens shook, pumps sucked, augers turned, pulley belts flapped and bounced as they spun and reached out warning everyone in sight to keep out of the way, but these sounds were as nothing to that of the debarkers. Each time a metre-and-a-half-long log of spruce was shoved into one of the tooth-wheeled strippers, the sound would begin with a crucifying chatter that instantly mushroomed into that of ten thousand demented woodpeckers, but there were six or seven of these Christly machines and hardly a moment's reprieve. Already he had a splitting headache. Already he was right on edge.

Russians in rags with mismatched boots—a laceless black dress shoe and no sock on one—yanked, pulled and threw the frozen logs down from atop mountain-high lorry loads whose heavy chains had been released, and *mein Gott* the danger to those boys, nimble as they were and all but bones.

Once the bark had been removed, the logs were then grabbed by other Russians and thrown or shoved—packed a dozen or so at a time—into the iron magazine boxes of the grinders where hydraulic rams held them lengthwise against grindstones that were half-sunk in the concrete floor and constantly spun in large vats of water. Jets of it too, the grindstones rotating at from eighteen to twenty-four metres a second.

In five minutes . . . ten . . . he didn't really know how long, ninety years of patient forest growth were reduced to a soggy mass of yellowish-brown wood pulp. Giant augers carried this draining mush upward to screens and towering tanks but then, farther down the cavernous length of the shed, in the cooking department, the redrained, resqueezed pulp was being conveyed to digesting tanks where it was boiled, stewed in a sulphate liquor of caustic soda and sodium sulphide, steeped, screened, washed, bleached and washed again and again to produce pure white cellulose fibre, the feedstock of the Textilfabrikschrijen.

A brief glance upward was all it took to add to the lack of safe working conditions. High in the corrugated iron roof above him, long daggers of ice had formed from the constant clouds of steam and hung there waiting to fall. The air, too, was either freezing or jungle-hot, the stench gut-wrenching, a pungent, eye-nose-and-throat irritation to which the cloying scent of spruce gum intruded. No man was idle. All sixty or eighty of them were busy, for Jakob Dorsche was right beside him and the Lagerfeldwebel far from happy.

Intuitively the men had sensed this.

'Herr Kohler, you will now do everything through me.'

'WHAT'S THAT? I CAN'T HEAR YOU!'

'Don't listen and find out the cost. You have fifteen minutes.'

Mein Gott, it would take that long just to walk to the far end of the shed and how the hell was he to find anyone in this?

'Look, I'm sorry Frau Macher misunderstood my being in that office. I only wanted to use the telephone. Rudel . . .'

'Sorry? How is it, please, that you even knew the Fräulein Bödicker's bookshop would have such an instrument?'

He had a point. In Paris, and especially in the rest of France, and here too, telephones were simply not that common. 'Okay, I didn't. Look, there are things—'

'You need to know. For a Detektiv that is, of course, understandable, but—'

'So where is the assistant machinist?'

One of the five who had worked at the *Karneval*. 'Find him, *mein Lieber,* since you are so good at finding things.'

Dorsche had been acidly chewed out by Karl Rudel who had been summoned to find a certain detective in an office where he had no right to be, but Rudel had not only done it in front of a woman and the chairman's secretary at that, he had done it in front of Löwe Schrijen. 'Couldn't you give me a hint?'

Had Herr Kohler finally seen the light and enough of the dangers of this place to unwanted visitors such as himself? A careless step, a missing leg or arm . . . 'Look beneath your feet. Look as if you had lost your last pfennig.'

Moody, a real son of a bitch when he wanted to be, Dorsche buggered off, leaving this Kripo to realize he had wounded the pride of the very man he should never have wounded.

Waist deep in a soup of fresh pulp, his hairy arms bathed by it, Martin Caroff, the assistant machinist, didn't acknowledge the summons. A wrist-thick, arm-long spanner had at last found its fist-sized nut just above mush level. A two-metre length of steel pipe, a lever, was fitted over the handle of the spanner. 'Now heave, you two!' he yelled in passable *Deutsch* to the Russians on the lever and, still not turning to look up, 'Loosen the old whore so that we can unscrew her.'

The heavy iron housing had been thrown back, the metre-and-a-half-long grindstone exposed. Kohler wet a forefinger in the pulp and tapped him on the forehead as the nut came loose. 'A moment, my fine one,' he said in French since that would be better.

The eyes were dark, the hair black, the stubbled, narrow face with its lines of worry and fatigue smeared with draining pulp. 'Who are you?'

'Kohler, Kripo, Paris-Central.'

'Paris . . .'

And forty or forty-two, thought Kohler. A Breton by the accent and a long way from home. Thin, bony, hairy-chested and angry . . . was he angry?

Grease- and nicotine-stained fingers fled over a break in the red sandstone of the grinding wheel. 'Thermal cracking,' spat Caroff to take the detective's mind off himself. 'The stone heats up with the friction. Normally these tiny, parallel grooves and ridges on the surface—the burrs, we call them—are sharpened every fifty to one hundred and fifty hours, but here they like to stretch things. Two hundred, two-fifty? *Merde alors*, I ask you, why shouldn't the stone burst? I've told that plant foreman of ours a thousand times, the Russians too. I also keep telling the foreman these old machines need to be replaced, but he keeps telling me the Führer knows everything and won't listen anyway. This is a new stone but there are also flaws in it. Thin partings of shale in the sandstone. Here . . .' A crack-nailed, tapping forefinger traced out a millimetre-thin layer. 'The bastards who quarry these stones patently ignore the flaws so that we'll get blamed, but you're lucky to have missed the bang. When a stone such as this bursts, the Russians usually shit themselves not because of cowardice, you understand. Because of the watery soup and black bread we have to eat. They'd play hell with anyone's guts. Mine especially, let me tell you. Dysentery . . . You should see the latrines, the—'

'Here, have one of these. Maybe it'll help.'

A small cigar, a fortune . . . 'For this, the hands must be dried. You two,' he called out to the Russians. 'Take five.'

'Make it ten and lead me to a place our Jakob will have trouble finding.'

The dark black eyebrows were questioningly raised, the look swift. 'The boilers, then. It's warmer there but watch the pipes. We had to undress them. It was best.'

Hawking up a lump of phlegm, he spat it out, causing immediate worries of tuberculosis.

'A cold,' he grunted. 'We have them constantly. Each is a little different from all the others so as to preserve some sense of individuality. Mine is deep down and I can give you the precise anatomy and symptoms if you wish.'

Leading the way, he found a narrow gap between two giant, wood-fired boilers whose shirtless stokers were bathed in sweat. The corridor narrowed. The pipes, totally bare of their asbestos wrappings, threatened. 'You can get the burn of your life if you're not careful,' he shouted. 'The Lagerfeldwebel once did and now is far too respectful to venture in here. We warned him and he obeys. After all, why should he risk it?'

Gauges and valves clung to the girders above Caroff. The hands were quickly dried on a filthy wiper rag, the cigar eagerly taken. 'Please, the light, Inspector.'

'Don't inhale.'

'*Ah, merde,* I would have. Still, to taste such a thing will be reward enough for a few answers—it is answers you wish, is it not?'

It was. 'Then you must take the cigar with you when you leave. I can't be singled out. The others would only accuse me of accepting something I shouldn't have and of yielding things they might not wish you to hear.'

A wise man, the assistant machinist drew on the cigar and sat on a wooden box, the remains of the French Army fatigues leaking all over the place as he leaned back against a girder whose rivets were rusty.

This one would want to hear it as it was, thought Caroff, and had already concluded that Chairman Schrijen was reinvesting zero in the Works while earning the maximum. 'Eugène's wife was spreading her legs behind his back, Inspector. When a wife bares that little orifice to others, she insults her man.'

'Or so the anonymous letter he was shown implied.'

'Letters like that are cruel, aren't they, but often contain elements of the truth. Did it tell you that Paulette Thomas had scraped up enough cash to buy a brand-new bicycle?'

It hadn't. 'Just how the hell did she get the cash then, Inspector, if not by offering herself to others? A nice one, too. A brunette. Thick, wide and curly, a real bush.'

Sex-starved were they all, or had it been said simply to reinforce Eugène Thomas's feelings of betrayal? In Paris, as this one must know, a new bike was all but impossible to obtain unless one had very highly placed friends and even then it would cost 8,000 francs, the prewar price of a brand-new two-door Renault or Peugeot sedan yet working-class wages had been frozen at those levels while everything else had had only one way to go.

The detective's mind was racing along the line of thought given, so that was good, felt Caroff, but a little reinforcement would be useful. 'Eugène's Paulette had about 7,000 francs a year on which to live, Inspector. Understandably he worried constantly about how she could possibly manage. When the parcels, a considerable expense, didn't come, he forgave her by saying she needed things for their little boy. When that letter arrived, he wept.'

Cigar smoke was savoured as it should be, a far-off look coming into those eyes.

'*Papa* used to buy these in England, Inspector, before returning home to Roscoff on the Breton Coast. *Maman* and us kids—there were eight of us then—grew the onions and shallots he carried round on strings draped over that old bicycle of his. Five months he'd be gone across the Channel. Swansea, Cardiff and Newport, Plymouth sometimes, though he preferred the Welsh simply because they could sing better and were closer to his ancestors. Women . . . I know he must have had several, but *maman*, she was very religious and never once mentioned it. But when I was old enough, she took me to the door and sent me to the naval yard at Brest, to her brother Martin, after whom she had named me. "Avoid loose women," she said. "Get a trade. Don't sell onions others are forced to grow. Become a machinist."'

In the Age of the Machine, and so much for nostalgia. POWs the world over would indulge in such reminiscences particularly if they thought they had a captive audience.

'We asked Eugène about his Paulette, Inspector. How was she in bed? Was she always wet or only at certain times? He didn't like to talk about her that way, was too protective of her, but the wire soon destroys all that. She had a way with her, he confided. A look, a gesture, sometimes even the simple touch of her hand and he'd know what she wanted and soon be hearing her cry out for more. *L'orgasme. Le grand frisson, n'est-ce pas?*'

The great shudder, but it was time to put an end to this. 'Look, my friend, I was once one of you and know all about what it's like, so let's cut the crap and you tell me what I need to know.'

Herr Kohler wouldn't be easy to convince but one had best try so as to reinforce what the others would confide. 'Eugène was really depressed. The poor bastard just didn't want to live anymore. Awake all night thinking terrible things were happening at home? Two men at a time, three . . . We tried to convince him his Paulette would never do such things, but . . .'

'Now listen, you. He had only one anonymous letter. There weren't any more of them.'

This could be checked if challenged but would the inspector then begin to wonder if someone here had gotten a friend or relative at home to write such a letter? Would it not be best to give him a little something else to think about? 'The guards in this place suggested all sorts of liaisons, knowing they would upset him further. The Jardin du Luxembourg when their little son was watching the puppet show or sailing one of the toy boats . . . *Sacré nom de nom,* but we had to keep an eye on him, though in a place like this, with all of us being worked to death, how could we possibly have stopped him?'

The fabric designer and test weaver having been deliberately forgotten since that one had a pass which allowed him to visit the laboratory at any time.

Fishing into a wet khaki pocket, Caroff pulled out a black armband of artificial silk. 'I only took it off because of that puddle I had to jump into. All of us are wearing them in honour of Eugène. We swore we would even though Herr Dorsche would bitch.'

'We?' asked Kohler.

'The other members of our combine to which Eugène was a member in good standing. Eat, sleep, fart and live together, all cooped up in one room in that place when not here at work? We shared everything we scrounged or got from our parcels, even though Paulette forgot to send him one last month and the month before that, the Christmas one.'

A member in good standing could only mean that some were not or had not been in the past, shunning being common in such cases, but it would be best to sadly say, 'A broken man, then.'

'Précisément!'

Pleased with this *détective's* conclusion, was he, this popgun fixer? 'Ping-Pong balls,' muttered Kohler. 'I seem to remember seeing your name plastered beside that on the roster.'

In the carnival's field office but what else had he found? 'I'm good at mending things. Those were for the shooting gallery. We've also made a bottle-fish for the ladies. At least, we will have if they are allowed to continue with their plans. Are they to be allowed, Inspector?'

And anxious, was he? 'It's too early to say. A bottle-fish?'

'Wine, *eau-de-vie,* cognac and champagne, if your comrades haven't drunk everything. It's easy. You tie slipknots that won't slip when the line is pulled after the little noose has dropped over the neck of a bottle. It's an old carnival trick I learned as a boy earning money for *maman's* apron pocket.'

This one would digress for as long as possible if allowed. 'Now tell me about the night he killed himself.'

Were knots no longer of interest, the suicide definite? 'Dorsche and his *Griefer* woke us up.'

His 'catchers', the 'grabbers', the plant's *Werkschutz,* its work police.

'They searched that hotel of ours from top to bottom for Eugène.'

'But he was found at just after midnight when the alarm first went out?'

Was Herr Kohler so green or had he forgotten that *Kriegsge-*

fangenen past of his? 'Dorsche had a good look anyway. After all, life is not exactly stimulating here, even for a Lagerfeldwebel who enjoys his job. We sleep like stones, Inspector. I was tumbled out of my bunk as were the others.'

Dorsche had wanted to see if they'd known of the suicide but they had obviously managed not to give him anything. 'Okay, okay, now tell me what Thomas was like?'

'Quiet. Studious. Very professional. He didn't cause trouble, if that's what you're after. He was one of us, a friend to all. He had no enemies, Inspector. This I must state emphatically.'

Just like the onions and the shallots, was that it? 'And with the members of the *Winterhilfswerk* Committee?'

'*Bien sûr,* they were skirts and they smelled like heaven, but Eugène knew his place.'

'Didn't the others? Yourself, for instance?'

'Inspector, we're not that stupid. Eugène always kept himself as clean as possible. That's what made the Fräulein Schrijen first notice him, and when she decided to fix up some of the carnival booths early last September, she went straight to him. Eugène then brought the rest of us in on it.'

Which was to say nothing about Thomas's having worked in the lab right next to her office, thought Kohler, but he'd leave it for now. 'Continue, I'm listening.'

'There are twelve of us in that cage we call home and our combine, Inspector—well, eleven now, until a replacement is found—but all of us had a hand in deciding . . .'

'Who best to help those naive young ladies, eh?' interjected Herr Kohler with all that this could imply about escape committees and other mischief for which a spell of *Straf* or a Natzweiler-Struthof hanging would be the reward. He had definitely found the cutthroat.

'There is no escape from this place, Inspector. We simply took a vote on who was to work with them.'

'No abstentions, no hard feelings?'

Like why should Eugène have been included when he already had such a cosy place in which to work and two—yes, two girls to talk to every day as well as the Fräulein Schrijen?

'None. We're one happy family because we have to be.'

And wasn't that twice at least that the assistant machinist had emphasized how well they'd got on? Best, then, not to mention the carpenters' nails and all the other things that had been accumulated to smuggle in here, best to say nothing yet of that cutthroat and the trinitrophenol, or of the colonel's also having been evasive. 'Enjoy the last of the cigar, then drop it in the soup. I'll be in touch.'

'You do that, Inspector. We wouldn't want to upset the Lagerfeldwebel any more than is necessary, but please remind him that I was ordered to come in here by a member of his Führer's Gestapo and dared not refuse.'

Were all Bretons so gabby? Louis's second wife had been a Breton, but Louis wasn't here to be reminded and definitely wasn't going to like what was bothering his partner. Löwe Schrijen had been right. Caroff and the others must have all agreed on what to say and that could only mean they really had been up to something more than handfuls of carpenter's nails and a few buttons but why, then, was Rasche being so evasive?

The aroma of the colonel's pipe tobacco seemed suddenly, thought Victoria, to fill the *Stube,* bringing warnings of its own the chief inspector could not realize. She had smelled it strongly on Renée many times. It had been soaked right through that lovely short-sleeved voile print Renée had worn out to the carnival on the twentieth of last August in the heat, the seams of its right sleeve and shoulder having been torn, the padding loose, and two of its rose-coloured buttons missing.

Dieu merci, there had been no customers in the shop. Colonel Rasche had simply dropped Renée off and she had run in here, run fast, the smell of that tobacco in her hair, her lovely hair. Spicy, plummy, sickeningly sweet and even more disconcerting than now because she herself hadn't known if Renée had said things she shouldn't have to the colonel.

Doucement, she said silently to herself. Go easy. Don't weaken. Sophie has left you to deal with this one.

Waving out the match he had used to light that pipe of his, the chief inspector studied her through the smoke. 'The Fräulein Ekkehard,' he began, 'I see that you've a telephone. Did she call to tell you she was on her way out to the carnival instead of your friend?'

'She said that she didn't mind going instead of Sophie. For her it was an unexpected opportunity not only to get out of the office but to be by herself. She loved to explore the carnival, was always delighted when she found something. A playbill that hadn't been picked to pieces by the local children, a ticket to the Ferris wheel or . . .'

'One of these?' he asked, dangling the droplet earring while watching her closely, too closely.

'Where . . . where did you find that, Inspector? In our biscuit tin?'

'A fake,' he said, capturing it in a pugilistic fist.

Some explanation had best be given. 'Renée had been searching for its mate. She was like that. Everyone will tell you this. Once she had found one of a pair, she had to find the other. I tried to tell her that we would never find it. *Mein Gott*, the size of that place alone defied us, not just the children who foraged constantly. We'd enough pieces and weren't going to use such costumes anyway, but still she kept it and others in mind. "Where there's hope, there's always a chance," she would say. If that is the mate, Renée would have cried for joy and clapped her hands like a ten-year-old then rushed to tell us all about it.'

He was not going to let her know where it had been found, nor was he going to ask how well or often she or Renée or Sophie had got on with the local children. Instead, he asked, 'When and where did the two of you first meet?' as if it had far more bearing on what had happened than that earring or the children, or the grief one had to conquer, the fear.

'On the ski slopes to the west of town in January of '41. I'd just come back from Munich and had gone there for a few days while the authorities searched through the deeds to this place, searched through everything, I guess, though the police don't tell people that, do they, and often it's done so well one doesn't even realize they've been in.'

If she had hoped to unsettled him, she had failed but had made certain he understood the shop and the house had been thoroughly searched more than once with nothing incriminating having been found.

'Renée came out to ski, late on a Saturday afternoon with Colonel Rasche, though he didn't and one had to wonder, I must admit, why he had chosen to come along. The ride, I suppose, as a little treat. We fell on one of the slopes and had a good laugh, and that is how we met. Sunday, 5 January 1941, at about 4.00 p.m. the old time and just as the light was fading.'

The old time and Colonel Rasche having stayed the night and all that might or might not mean. 'But you must have known who she was.'

'Of course I knew. Kolmar is not so big now, especially not

with a third of its citizens having left. Everyone knows what the Kommandant looks like because everyone has to. Renée often took my papers in to him to be signed and stamped, so of course it was only natural I knew who she was beforehand.'

The *Ausweise* and safe-conducts, the *Geleitbriefe* this one would have needed on the last Friday of every month.

'*Ach*, I admit I was lonely, Inspector. Terribly worried and desperately in need of a friend. Mother was in Besançon then, in the internment camp—all those women, the old, the young, the middle-aged, their teenaged daughters also, and younger children. No heat in that bitter winter, no running water or toilet facilities other than a latrine trench?—a terrible, terrible time for them and one from which she suffered greatly and still does. In March of '41 they were moved to Vittel, those with little children being finally allowed to go home. For the life of me, though, I still cannot understand what threat a sixty-five-year-old widow poses to the Reich, a nurse who came here before the Great War, got caught up in it, was married to an Alsatian, had me, lost her husband to an artillery barrage, ran a bookshop only to foolishly include among her keepsakes her British passport, not out of loyalty but sentiment, for she had no family left in Britain, none at all.'

She paused as if she had said too much, which she had, of course, had he not been a patriot himself, thought St-Cyr. She swallowed hard and then, still with an edge, said, 'And myself, you're wondering? I'd just lost my teaching certificate. I was a very good teacher who had been judged no longer fit to teach.'

The copy of the *Münchner Neueste Nachrichten* was dated Thursday, 19 December 1940. The photo showed a group of about fifty students, all of them Alsatian schoolteachers of varying ages from twenty to well past sixty.

'I was the only one who failed simply because of mother's being in the internment camp. Herr Ludin, the principal of that so-called school in Munich they sent us to for indoctrination, wouldn't listen, though I pleaded with him to let me continue teaching. I'd students who loved me, who then came to despise me for no other reason. I'd neighbours with whom I had always shared things but who would share no more. Understandably I am still bitter.'

'Yet you agreed to be a member of the *Winterhilfswerk* Committee.'

'It was my duty, wasn't it?'

'Good cover too, one might think.'

'Cover? Didn't I have to show people that I was a loyal citizen?'

'And your neighbour, Frau Oberkircher. Does she no longer—'

'Claudette? Claudette and my mother shared their widowhood, and now, poor soul, she has just lost her primary source of income.'

Dieu merci, that had made him pause. 'Sophie likes to ski, and when the three of us got together, we found we shared that love.'

'And the archery?' he asked, avoiding Claudette and whether she had been forced into watching the shop for the Gestapo.

'Sophie introduced us to it out at her father's country house. Renée was always keen to compete. We enjoyed ourselves. We skated too—there's a beautiful little lake in the forested hills behind the house and when the wind clears the snow, the ice is perfect and one can skate for hours in absolute peace. But . . . but how did you know of the archery?'

'Calluses on her fingers, feather cuts on the back of her right hand.'

Again he was watching her too closely but was he thinking of the knot that had been around Renée's throat, or that Renée hadn't committed suicide at all?

'She didn't love Alain Schrijen, Inspector. He hadn't given her time, had rushed her off her feet, but she'd been afraid to say no to him. Unlike Sophie, Alain has . . . well, he's been given far too much.'

'Why not say he's spoiled, Victoria? Why not say he's become a sadist who beats defenceless men who are already so broken, they can no longer work? That he enjoys what he does? That they're—'

'Sophie . . . Sophie, please go back and rest. You don't know what you're—'

'Saying? Don't you ever try to silence me, Victoria Bödicker. They even send young women to that place, Inspector. Experiments . . . they do experiments on them!'

The hush of the Steeping Shed had alarmed Herr Kohler, accustomed as he was to the noise of the Pulping Shed, felt Dorsche. Quickly this Kripo scanned the building, seeing the men in black rubberized boots, suits and long aprons, their gauntlets and goggles removed, their helmets those of a fire brigade. He would be wondering what was going on and where he was—in some sort of industrial spa perhaps, for long rectangular baths extended one after another and side-by-side from this end of the building to the other, the steeping tanks. He would see that rack upon rack of metre-square sheets of pure white cellulose from the Pulping Shed now waited to be bathed: two hundred of them to a rack, fifty racks side-by-side and to the far end of the building. He would note the fumes, the strongly alkaline odour of caustic soda, would know for certain that it was dangerously corrosive and that if splashed on bare skin or lips or in the eyes, one screamed in agony. He'd know that the concrete floor would most certainly become slippery once the roller presses, which were to the far side, began to squeeze the caustic from the sheets after their little bath of forty minutes.

'The carpenter,' managed Kohler, not liking things. 'You said he'd be here. Just why would a building like this need one?'

It being of corrugated iron in which there were no boards, only cellulose from wood fibre. 'Perhaps he's been transferred,' hazarded Dorsche, as a Lagerfeldwebel should.

'You're threatening me.'

'*Ach*, I am merely telling you that from now on all questions will be given and answered in my presence. Surely you must realize Lageroffizier Rudel will require thorough answers from me and that I must impart everything that has been said?'

'Where is he, then, this carpenter?'

'A moment, that is all. Herr Savard is learning the ropes, as they say.'

Dorsche had found and had the carpenter moved within the space of ten minutes, which could only mean he had a communications' network so good it could reach into every corner of the Textilfabrik in spite of superheated steam pipes. His *Werkschutz* must be everywhere, his *Spitzel*, too, his informants among the POWs, and he had just demonstrated this. An iron fist like the chairman's, only one with even far tighter control.

The chemist's suicide really couldn't have sat well with Dorsche—something like that happening right under his nose and he not knowing of it until after the fact.

When the last and most distant of the sheets had been hung in its rack, all fifty of the carriages trundled inevitably toward their respective steeping tanks where chain hoists lifted them.

The men—Poles this time, noted Kohler—covered their eyes with the goggles, pulled down their helmets, suited up with the gauntlets and lowered the racks into the baths, the sound of iron wheels changing to that of rattling chains, to that of gurgling, rising caustic.

One by one the men moved on to the roller presses to prepare things there. Water hoses were uncoiled, taps checked, buckets filled in case of needed emergency medical treatment, four-wheeled dollies placed nearby so that when squeezed of their juice, the sheets could be stacked and then transported elsewhere.

'You wished to see me, Lagerfeldwebel?'

In his late thirties and of less than medium height under a helmet that was too big, Henri Savard's watchful eyes remained obediently fixed on Dorsche. The dark brown moustache, not unlike Louis's, had yet to be shaved off, for in a place like this it could only soak up splashed caustic. The chin was blunt, the cauliflower ears big, the face drawn and pockmarked, the flattened nose encrusted with warts, the lips unsmiling, unanything, the vegetable silence that of peasant ancestors.

'Prisoner 220375, Herr Kohler wishes to know how you are finding your new employment.'

Eugène Thomas had been Number 220371.

'Very satisfactory, Lagerfeldwebel.'

And from Lille near the Belgian border.

'No complaints?' asked Dorsche.

'None, Lagerfeldwebel.'

'*Gut*. You may begin the interview, Herr Detektiv. Again, as before, time necessitates haste. Since others are filling in for this man, you may take'—Dorsche consulted his wristwatch—'twelve minutes, a little longer, of course, if you do not wish to also question Prisoner 220372.'

Savard didn't blink. He simply remained zeroed in on Dorsche.

'Number 220372?' asked Kohler.

Understandably he was puzzled since there were no windows in the shed. 'The glazier, Gérard Léger, is at the far end of the building, so I have allowed sufficient time for us to take such a walk. You don't want to be in here, though, when they squeeze the sheets. You are not suitably attired.'

Dorsche found and lit a cigarette. Exhaling, he said, 'It's perfectly safe to smoke in here. You may offer Prisoner 220375 one of Chairman Schrijen's small cigars if you wish.'

The pungency of motherwort returned as unexpectedly as Sophie Schrijen's sudden intrusion, and to this came the scent of *Mirage*, the bookseller having stiffened in alarm at what had just been revealed about Natzweiler-Struthof. Clearly the Fräulein Schrijen had come to a decision on how best to proceed and just as clearly, she had overheard everything that had been said in her absence.

'The Fräulein Ekkehard was afraid of men, Chief Inspector,' she said. 'Unfortunately I can find no other way of putting it unless I were to use the word *adrift*. Peripherally, of course. Certainly, in so far as I am aware, she didn't engage openly in such practices, given the threat of prison or worse, but when men got too close, the girl could become terribly distressed, though she hid it well during everyday circumstances, didn't she, Victoria? That little toss of her head that imparted so much, the dresses she chose, the lightness of her step. Everyone was taken in by her, myself especially.'

Still unsettled by the sudden intrusion, the bookseller could no longer find the will to look up. 'And had you known this about her?' asked St-Cyr.

'I would not have become associated with her at the outset, of course. There are rules—unspoken always—for people like myself, but as I came to know her better, I realized those rules were not always right, that some leeway would have to be given.'

A hard thing to admit to these days. 'And on the *Winterhilfswerk* Committee?'

'I had no qualms because by then I knew how carefully in control she could be. The girl also knew everyone and was, of course, the colonel's right hand and therefore extremely useful.'

Opportunistic though that must sound, but intentionally so? he wondered. Agitated, the bookseller began to knit her hands together only to realize this and press them flat against her thighs, indenting the dark brown velvet of her slacks, but was it because she understood only too well what must come next?

'Late last August, on a Thursday, the twentieth to be precise, Inspector, Colonel Rasche took the girl out to the *Karneval*—did he inform you of this? *Ach*, I thought not. You see, in her innocence, the Fräulein Ekkehard suspected nothing. They had been out there many times before, just the two of them, and had always enjoyed themselves exploring the ruins. Why should this one occasion have been any different? They entered the wagon we now use as a field office. There were some costume dresses scattered on the floor. Like most young girls who are dependent on their employers and on men they respect—after all he was her commanding officer—she became confused when touched, felt trapped, smothered . . .'

'Sophie, *please* don't.'

'She screamed, Inspector. She tried to get away from him and had to fight back. Like all such unfortunates must, she burst into tears when cornered, was driven to distraction by guilt—the shame of what was happening to her, her failure too, her inadequacy, was in a rage at herself and at a world she could not understand, and a colonel whom she had trusted. Victoria was the first to whom she ran, of course, I only hearing of it later. I very much doubt the girl would have confessed such a thing about herself to anyone else.'

Victoria, then, and 'confessed,' not confided, the 'Fräulein Ekkehard and the girl' being used and not Renée as before. Once again the bookseller found she could no longer look up at her but asked, 'And Alain, Sophie? What of him?'

Chairman Schrijen's daughter was now looking down at the bookseller but was it with deliberate contempt?

'That little indiscretion of Colonel Rasche's would have shaken any secretary's resolve, Inspector. My brother didn't know of it, of course. He had met the Fräulein Ekkehard several times at official receptions and gatherings out at Father's country house and the one here in town. Alain is impulsive and knows what he wants just like Father, and usually he gets it.'

Or takes it? The bookseller's fingers were again knitted in her lap.

'After the briefest of courtships, he proposed. One party is all it took. Early last December at which the girl became horribly drunk—she must have been, mustn't she, Victoria?'

There was no answer, not even a haltingly upward glance.

'A girl, Inspector, who seldom took more than one glass of wine and usually could make it last all evening? She didn't even like schnapps, did she, Victoria?'

'Sophie, please . . .'

'Dizzy, Victoria? Sleepy? So sleepy, she woke up naked in that room Alain had rented for her at Natzweiler's ski lodge, her shoulders and arms badly scratched, you said, her forehead and left knee bruised, the right cheek and eye also? A fall on the ski slopes you told me. A fall!'

There were tears, the bookseller unable to stop them. 'Sophie, *nobody* needed to know but us. Only us!'

'Understandably the girl wanted out of such a marriage, Inspector, but would never have killed herself.'

The bookseller's hands were twisted, defeat registering in the look she gave. 'Rape, Sophie. Why can't you call it that?'

Again there was that look, more fiercely given this time. 'Because I choose not to. She would have reconciled herself to being married to my brother, Inspector, would have tried her best to live that lie, and had even agreed to return this coming weekend for another party. After all, being married to him would have avoided so much, wouldn't it, Victoria? The fear, the shame, the certainty that others would discover she was adrift. Alain would be away on duty—only Kramer is allowed to have his wife and family at Natzweiler-Struthof. Renée would be here in Kolmar. Life would go on as before but it would be safer, for Colonel Rasche would never again attempt to lay a hand on her, not a girl who was married to an SS.'

'And what about the things she saw there, Sophie?' asked the bookseller in despair.

'Of course she detested what she had been forced to witness, and of course, she stupidly told my brother that they would all pay for it someday, but . . .'

There was only sincerity in the look she gave this Sûreté.

'Conditions are bad enough for the men at the Textilfabrik, Inspector, but at that granite quarry in such a winter? Any winter?'

'Why not make a *Karneval* hoarding of it, Sophie?' blurted the bookseller, this time looking defiantly up at her.

Was everything now lost—wasn't that what the bookseller's expression said? wondered St-Cyr.

'Renée Ekkehard must have let the truth about herself be known to that brother of mine, Inspector. Even though sleepy—drugged, was she, Victoria?—she fought back and others would have heard her terrified screams and then her sobbing after Alain had finished with her. That brother of mine would have become the laughingstock of the camp had he not done what he did. One of *those* as a bride, Victoria? Kramer would never have let a thing like that pass, not the Schutzhaftlagerführer Kramer!'

But had she said it to save herself? wondered St-Cyr. 'What, then, makes you so certain she was murdered, Fräulein?'

'I was being followed. The Fräulein Ekkehard and this one knew all about it. Everywhere I went, one or the other or both of those men would be there. At first I didn't know who they were and asked her to watch for them. She then . . .'

'A moment, Fräulein. How is it that you . . .'

'Didn't know them? Inspector, please don't forget that not only am I a very busy person with virtually no free time, but that Kolmar has seen its influx of new faces few of us, if any, know, not just myself.'

'Two men . . .'

'The Fräulein Ekkehard took it upon herself to find photographs of them, though I had not at any time asked her to do this.'

'The colonel's two detectives?'

'That is correct.'

Defeated, the bookseller found her voice. 'Renée and I soon began to watch for them. Either one or both of us would attend the meeting and while Sophie was giving her address or presenting awards, we would look over the gathering or watch the street outside. Renée knew at once who they were, for she saw them nearly every day and they would often speak to her, particularly if they needed to see Colonel Rasche on a police matter.

'There, Sophie. Now if you have the courage, tell him the terrible risk she took for you.'

'Unfortunately the girl had stolen the photographs from the police files, Inspector. These were kept in an entirely different department from her own and several offices away. Had I known that she would do such a stupid thing, I would have forbidden it.'

The bookseller started to object but then fell silent.

'Those two detectives, and I use the word loosely, Inspector, would most certainly have discovered what she had done and gone after her.'

'Sophie, I wanted to warn you that it might not be safe for Renée,' said the bookseller reaching out to her only to have the gesture ignored. 'When Renée told me she was going out to the *Karneval,* I tried to get Frau Oberkircher to mind the shop, only to remember that she was in France at her brother-in-law's funeral. I knew Renée might be in danger, Inspector, but also that she was terribly despondent and suicidal. I . . . I wanted to tell you, Sophie, but . . . but couldn't when you telephoned me from the Works to let me know Renée had gone out there instead of yourself. Alone, Sophie. You let her go out there alone!'

'The lines are constantly being tapped, Inspector,' said Sophie. 'What one says out of kindness or duty, another hears and seldom can a person put a face to that listener.'

A hard response. 'Then why were you being followed?'

'Do they need a reason, those people?'

'Please just answer.'

A shrug was given. 'I've no idea. I've tried to find out—have asked myself countless times did I unintentionally cross someone in an audience, not praise their efforts enough, insult some dignitary's wife by forgetting her contribution or making too little mention of it, but . . . but I still don't know.'

'And your father, Fräulein, what has he to say of it?'

'*Vati*? That I am to let them shadow me as much as they want, that they'll soon get tired of it.'

'Then tell me, please, Fräulein, why the colonel's secretary should have stayed out all night on her skis?'

And where she went, said Victoria silently. Could you not have seen this coming, Sophie?

The look the bookseller gave the chairman's daughter was ignored.

'She skied all night, simply to avoid them. They would have known from my call to the bookshop that the girl would be there. Since they must have discovered the photos of themselves were missing, they'—again there was a shrug—'they must have put two and two together and gone after her.'

'And tried to make it look like a suicide?'

'Why else would Colonel Rasche have brought you and Herr Kohler in, had he not trusted one word of what those two had claimed?'

Rubber boots weren't just for keeping water and caustic soda out, thought Kohler. The constant sound of splashing hoses and filling buckets made the carpenter want to piss, but of course, unlike a delinquent schoolboy, he couldn't ask Dorsche to be excused.

The reedy slash of a self-conscious grin was flashed as Savard let go. Dorsche knew it too. Nervous . . . was the carpenter nervous? wondered Kohler. Of course the poor bastard was, for he knew only too well what could quite possibly happen to him.

'Paulette a le diable au corps, Inspecteur. Eugène . . .'

The devil in her body . . .

'Deutsch!' shrieked Dorsche, the sound of him causing others to momentarily stop whatever they were doing.

'Elle prenait plaisir à . . .' She took pleasure in . . .

'Und bist du nicht willig, so brauch ich Gewalt!' shrieked Dorsche.

If you're not willing, then I will use force!

'She . . . she had . . .'

'Ja, ja, I've heard all about it,' sighed Kohler.

'Eugène couldn't take it any longer, Inspector. Lagerfeldwebel, forgive me, but some of your *Greifer* teased Eugène about his wife. They said that she couldn't get enough of your good German boys, that they were real men and had cocks like pick handles.'

The guards, the 'catchers', would have said it too, but Dorsche was far from happy at being told. The ruddy Burgermeister cheeks were sucked in, the wire-rimmed specs mirroring the feeble light as he gave the carpenter the slightest of nods.

That didn't stop Savard, though it should have.

'One of the *Postzensuren* had it in for Eugène, Inspektor. She's Alsatian and no doubt felt she was doing her bit to get back at us French, but no parcel at Christmas? None last month? It has to make you wonder if she didn't . . .'

Was Savard bent on suicide himself?

'All parcels are delivered,' muttered Dorsche. 'The *Lagerführung* cannot be held responsible for postal delays due to the hostilities. Copies of the Wehrmacht ordinance pertaining to all prisoners of war have been posted in the dining hall for all to read.'

'In each camp, cheap, mass-produced German dictionaries

have been issued, Inspektor, to assist in one language for all, but here there are only three copies!' swore Savard. ' "Our treatment must be firm but correct," eh? *Lieber Christus im Himmel*, Lagerfeldwebel, I'm sick of having to translate that passage for the Russians!'

Lead-blue behind those specs of his, Dorsche's gaze passed over the carpenter with a finality that made one shudder.

'The *Ostarbeiter* don't need to read that passage or any other, since they do not receive anything,' grunted the Lagerfeldwebel.

Were the Eastern workers, the Poles, the Russians and others denied Red Cross parcels? wondered Kohler, sickened by the thought.

'And mail from home, Inspektor, and are denied the freedom to write to their loved ones.'

Savard must have realized that the game was up, whatever that game was, but somehow it would be best to grin and try to make light of things. 'Now look, let's calm down, eh? Answers are needed, Lagerfeldwebel. Reports will have to be filed. Personally I'd like to . . .'

Cigarettes were found, one falling to be ruined, no small matter, but . . . 'I'd like to tell Berlin that everything I saw here was being done correctly and that everyone went out of their way to assist the investigation and that nothing was done to punish anyone for anything said while under questioning. *Ach*, who needs trouble?'

Or a transfer to the Russian front.

They lit up, Herr Kohler's offer of a light being held as still as death until that hand was gripped and withdrawn from Prisoner 220375, that one's cigarette being confiscated. 'Second-hand smoke is healthier for this one, Herr Detektiv Aufsichtsbeamter.'

How kind of him! 'Herr Savard, all of your combine are still in mourning, I gather?'

'Mourning?' blurted Savard, throwing Dorsche a terrified look. 'What is this, please? Lagerfeldwebel, the official three days are over, aren't they?'

'Definitely,' snapped Dorsche.

Only then did the carpenter realize that he had been so afraid, he had forgotten what the combine had agreed to say.

'Out of respect for those who died at Stalingrad, Herr Kohler,' said Dorsche, 'the prisoners decided to wear black armbands. I, of course, had the Russians make them.'

And never mind Martin Caroff's claiming he'd worn his out of respect for Eugène Thomas!

At the far end of the shed, one man in a rubber suit had removed his hat and was looking uncertainly their way. The glazier . . .

'The coffin,' managed Kohler. 'You would have had to measure that girl. Tell me everything you noticed about her. The knot, the position of her arms and hands, what she wore, her beret. All such things.'

'Knots all look much the same to me, Inspektor, but forgive me for contradicting you. There was no beret. Renée wore a woollen toque. It was very cold, the night she was out. A beret would hardly have been suitable or legal.'

'Mittens? Gloves?' demanded Herr Kohler, trying his best to recover from what had just been revealed, but would Prisoner 220375 forget what he and the others had agreed to say and yield a little more? wondered Dorsche.

'She wore mittens and gloves,' said Savard warily. 'Though I only saw the knitted cuff of one of her gloves, I knew them well enough. Renée often wore them when at the *Karneval*. She'd get so excited about something she had found, she would yank them off to touch it and then forget them, only to remember hours later where she had left them. She was like that. Days after she had found something, she could take you to the exact spot. It's a shame she felt she had to leave us. She was a lovely girl, very gentle, very kind. *Un ange, n'est-ce pas?*'

'*Ein Engel!*'—an angel—said Herr Kohler, the carpenter having momentarily switched into French.

'The Fräulein Ekkehard often broke the rules,' interjected Dorsche. 'When my back was turned, or that of one of my men, she would leave food or drop bits of string.'

'Or buttons, or a cigarette—even pieces of fruit leather. Black raspberry, red currant, apple or grape,' said Savard. 'She knew the *Karneval* so well, Inspektor. When Sophie . . . the Fräulein Schrijen wanted Raymond to draw her a map of the ruins and then make a scale model as it once was, Renée did a sketch map from memory. Raymond and Eugène then measured off the distances she had noted. I swear she knew that ruin like the palm of her hand. I'll never forget her enthusiasm for what we were doing. Our lives were brightened. *Ach, mein Gott,* in this hellhole of ours, she was a saint, even if she did break the *gottverdammt* rules!'

'Raymond Maillotte is the Textilfabrik's test weaver and fabric designer,' grunted Dorsche, pinching out his cigarette to save it for later. 'Now please, Inspektor, your time is up with this one.'

Savard couldn't leave it at that. 'Eugène and Raymond were working on a new process, Inspektor. Viscose rayon has long filaments and when these are still in their plastic state, they can be chemically treated to produce a much tougher, more resilient fibre that withstands frictional heat, deformation and impact bruising far better than ordinary rayon.'

Dorsche looked about to bash the carpenter. 'For rubber tyres?' asked Kohler, stepping between them.

'The synthetic ones, since no others can be made. Eugène called it high-tenacity rayon.'

'And now he's dead. . . .'

Dieu merci, sighed Savard inwardly, the detective had swallowed the bait and would understand, for sure, that the process was top secret and perhaps believe that Eugène, as a loyal Frenchman should have done, had dealt with the matter in the only way possible and had taken his own life.

'*Bitte,* Herr Kohler, I really must insist,' grumbled Dorsche. 'Your visit here is already overextended.'

'Then make sure I can interview this one again, eh? Otherwise Berlin . . . Well, you know how they are. Didn't the OKW assign you to this posting?'

'Of course they did, but they, too, know that accidents happen, especially when that same High Command has ordered myself and my men to get the maximum work out of our guests.'

And also what truths we can pry from them, said Dorsche silently. 'Prisoner 220375, be sure to wear your goggles and gloves. Remember, too, that the floor can be very slippery when the caustic is squeezed from the cellulose sheets and that men have, unfortunately, accidentally slipped and fallen into the baths. A tragedy, of course.'

From one end of the shed to the other, the glazier, still with hat in hand, never ceased to look their way. Uncertain of what was to come—apprehensive, no doubt—he waited for them, but was he also watching what went on behind them? wondered Kohler. Was Prisoner 220372 seeing other workers leave their stations to skirt the roller presses and converge on the carpenter? Could the 'accident' not be stopped?

'Herr Kohler, we haven't time to look back,' said Dorsche, hurrying on ahead.

Everyone behind them seemed busy, no notice being taken of them, yet notice taken all the same. *Verdammt*, the tension in the shed was everywhere. Had Dorsche organized one of his *Spitzel* to take care of the carpenter? If so, the camp's mouth radio would have spread the alarm even as the Lagerfeldwebel had hauled these two in here to give them rubber suits. Dorsche wouldn't be the only one with informants. The POWs would have their own among the guards, as well as a network of watchers among themselves. It was always like that. Always.

Savard had filled his buckets with water in case of a caustic spill and was now about to put his goggles on. Others had already done so. Hidden like that, who was to know who had pushed him? Wasn't that really why the glazier watched?

When the scream came, the shrieks would follow until there were no more.

Prisoner 220372 was older than the others—maybe fifty-two and a veteran of both wars. A man who knew himself and could look life in the face, grim though that might be.

The hair—what there was of it—was reddish grey and crinkly, the balding head freckled and sun-blotched by childhood years, the stubbled, square-jawed chin and cheeks sagging prematurely, the nose that of a Walloon for sure, so from Lille or Roubaix just as Rasche had said.

There were cuts and scars on the big hands, the result of poor quality glass cutters. The lips were compressed, the moustache red-grey, the attention still very much focused on what was happening at the other end of the shed.

When a hand was politely extended to him, the one with the gauntlet refused to budge and to hell with Dorsche or any other Boche, even a Gestapo. Beneath the widely spaced, reddish brows of this defiant patriot, the eyes were decidedly greenish-brown and devoid of feeling.

'Look, I'm here to help,' said Kohler with a grin.

'Help? There's plenty needed.'

Offer nothing, eh, while still concentrating on the other end of the shed? One had best give him what he wants. 'I gather Eugène Thomas was very depressed and suicidal.'

'One could say that, yes.'

'Listen, *mein Lieber,* I know that even the most hardened criminals can look down the tunnel of their sentences to see the end, whereas a POW can never know. He longs for word from home, takes out his snapshots several times a day if possible, and kisses those of his loved ones at lights out. I know what it's like, *mon ami. Bien sûr,* we'll speak *Deutsch* as is required, but believe me, I have been behind the wire.'

'But not, I think, required to work, or am I not speaking to a former officer?'

Touché. 'I did ask to be sent out to the nearby farms but they wouldn't allow it, though the widows there sure could have used the help. Kids as young as three were grubbing for potatoes at harvest. The cows were not being milked. That's not good for cows. I used to worry about them.'

Herr Kohler had even learned to speak French but if he thought that this would make him more acceptable than others of his kind, he was sadly mistaken. 'Eugène refused to be an NCO.'

Which, along with its consequent loss in pay, had made him a hero to his mates, for soldiers were always complaining about their officers and the combine must still have been blaming theirs for the Defeat, but was there no way to break the ice? 'Did one of the *Postzensuren* tease him? Hitch up a garter belt to let him have a little look? Leave a photo mag' of female flesh in that toilet for him to peruse while he was having a smoke?'

'Keep his parcels from him when rations are so short those

little boxes can mean the difference between starvation and life—is this what you are implying, Inspektor?'

'Did she?'

Good for Henri and Martin. 'We think so, but can, of course, have no proof, can we, Lagerfeldwebel?'

Dorsche didn't answer. Was he waiting for that shriek, wondered Kohler, or did he just know that this one was the combine's leader and would therefore have to watch him closely?

'She teased Eugène mercilessly about his being too familiar with his lab assistants, Inspektor,' said Léger. 'Paulette was always his only love and the girl knew this. "A married man without a wedding ring?" she would taunt. Eugène's was taken from him when he was captured, so he had Martin make him one to shut her up.'

Martin Caroff, the assistant machinist. 'And when Thomas had been away working at the *Karneval* and came by for his mail?'

'She would always snicker and ask him what had gone on out there, implying mischief even with Sophie Schrijen, of all people, or with Renée or Victoria. The *Idioten* didn't know.'

'What?

'The boss's daughter? The Kommandant's secretary? Our guards . . . we were always under guard. We're not fools, are we?'

'And if there was mail?'

'It would be so blacked out, Eugène would be driven to despair. He was far too sensitive. Behind the wire one can't be, can one?'

'So when the anonymous letter came, he went over the edge?'

'That is how we see it, yes.'

The tourer had leather seats and a heater that not only cleared the windscreen of its icy fog but kept the hands and feet warm.

Sophie Schrijen drove carefully through Kolmar's streets, avoiding cyclists and pedestrians, an excellent driver, thought St-Cyr, but was she also taking her time so as to impart yet a further *confidence*?

It wasn't long in coming.

'Eugène would never have killed himself, Inspector. Paulette and he had grown up in Chartres on the same street. Having to move to Issy-les-Moulineaux welded them together. Both had come from family bankruptcies. First her mother died, then his parents. They had no one else, were totally dependent on each other and happy, I'm certain. Very happy. A love like that is hard to find.'

She did not give it pause, but slowed the car further.

'One of the *Postzensuren* was particularly vicious. She had been very fond of one of the junior sales' staff, who had been killed in action, and was taking it out on Eugène—we all knew this, but nothing was done about it. Like other such girls, she has now probably taken to placing advertisements in the newspapers. Young man wanted . . . Old man, what does it matter so long as it's a man and she can find a lover? Lonely like most of them, she is also bitter.'

'And with his mail?'

'It was the most heavily censored of all but you see, we had a slight advantage. After everyone had left the office, Eugène could sometimes find his postcards and take down what Paulette had written before that girl got at it. That way he only had to contend with what Vichy's censors had blacked out. His despair was a total fabrication. The girl never knew—I'm sure she didn't—and I don't think any of the men of his combine did either. For him to have said anything to them about my unlocking that office door would have been far too risky for me. He was totally selfless, Inspector. A very dedicated worker and the truest of friends, and he taught me a great deal about things at the Works. The chemistry and mechanics of the process, you understand. Without him as my teacher, I don't know what I would have done.'

The chemical equations and formula on that scrap of notepaper . . .

'I'd never even been in the Works for more than an hour at a time before this war made it necessary for me to take over as its assistant manager. *Vati*—my father—hasn't the patience or time to teach me, a girl, a woman with no technical training or mind for chemistry. I had to have help.'

And had become dependent on Thomas. 'And when this anonymous letter arrived?'

Karl must have given it to Kohler. 'Eugène would have been badly shaken, of course. It . . . it would have been totally unexpected. The girl would have gloated over it and made some comment when he came out of Oberstleutnant Rudel's office after having read it, but Eugène must have known it was nothing but lies. He must have!'

Or had he? wondered Sophie. Had that *Postzensure* discovered he had been reading his mail and taken care of the matter in her own way? 'A friend or relative in Paris could easily have written that letter for her, Inspector. She has a sister in Paris, a translator at the Kommandantur on *place* de l'Opéra. Their father is an ardent member of the Party.'

6

Between the root cellar and the barn-board latrine, across a distance of perhaps fifteen metres, St-Cyr found that the snow had not only been trampled flat. It had been stained and splashed by human waste which had been emptied, bucket by bucket, from the pit into rusting sheet-iron barrels on wooden sledges that had been pushed and drawn by ropes.

Behind, and parallel to the low-roofed latrine, the washhouse was in the adjacent ground-floor corner of the barracks block, its windows small and grimy and stuffed with rags and straw where broken and not. One man, a Russian, stared out from the floor above the washhouse. It was impossible not to notice him, but was he pleading for some awareness of their plight, wanting to know the truth about the chemist and Renée Ekkehard, or simply hoping for a delivery of potatoes?

Sophie Schrijen had driven into the *Arbeitslager* without so much as a word of challenge or nod. The gates had simply been flung wide at the tourer's approach, but if she could enter that way, could she not just as easily leave like that taking others with her unnoticed?

'We had a slight advantage,' she had said of Thomas's reading his mail, but by not informing the members of his combine, by in effect deceiving them, had he not betrayed their confidence and would that not have had repercussions for him had they found out?

'This case, this investigation,' he said, turning away from the Russian without so much as an indication of having acknowledged his existence since to do so would not be wise and he was probably being watched himself, and yet . . . and yet one must turn back.

The Russian now pressed a hand flat against the glass, his fingers splayed. One must touch the brim of one's fedora in salute. One must.

Again it was damp in the root cellar. It was fiercely cold, still stank to high heaven, and when the lights came on, the first sight of the potatoes was not of their number but of a pinkish-grey to yellowish-purple-brown frozen, glistening mush where the rotten had been trampled or split in half to be left geode-open on the tiers.

'Leave me. I'll come to the gate when I'm finished, but if you see Herr Kohler tell him to wait, then come and get me at once. Don't let him down here.'

'*Jawohl*, Herr Oberdetektiv.'

The guard closed the doors, and since Hermann wasn't available to talk things over, why . . . 'One murder, one suicide, or two of the former,' he said to the second victim, his breath billowing. 'You see, since Sophie Schrijen made it possible for you to steal a look at your mail, did your friendship not also extend to hiding what my partner and I greatly fear that committee of hers was up to? *Bien sûr*, she would have begged you not to tell anyone and she now wishes to distance herself from Renée Ekkehard and in no uncertain terms to warn the bookseller in front of this police officer that it is only herself who will speak for the two of them. She also hints that perhaps the Fräulein Bödicker knows more of Renée Ekkehard's death than that one is letting on. And early in December, you ask? That party at Natzweiler-Struthof? Is it that Renée Ekkehard betrayed not only herself but the others of that committee? Isn't that why Sophie Schrijen knows perfectly well the girl's death was murder? Isn't that why those two detectives the colonel doesn't want us talking to have been following her, and isn't that why she and Victoria Bödicker now fear they are to be next?

'She gambled, didn't she, when she interrupted my questioning the bookseller to reveal so much? It was almost irrational of her and certainly desperate. She accused that brother of hers of being not only brutally cruel but impulsive, claimed that either he or her father would have taken care of the matter—a "suicide," but made sure that my partner and I would have to visit the quarry to question him. So I must ask, in our absence, has she laid the groundwork for yet another suicide, that of the bookseller, and would that then distance herself sufficiently?'

The dust was everywhere in the shed and like pastry flour, felt Kohler. The tattered blue coveralls of Raymond Maillotte, the test weaver and fabric designer, were caked with it, his face, ears and neck stark white under a dust-covered cap, the goggles clouded, the filthy rag over the mouth and nose useless.

As thick stacks of the metre-square sheets of pure white cellulose were fed by him into the machine, they were grabbed by the rotating blades, sucked in and ripped from his hands. No gloves, for they'd already been lost. Not much purchase for the sabots either, for he was standing perched up there on a narrow, steel-meshed gantry at about four metres from the concrete floor. Bins and chutes caught the mountains of dust. A conveyor hurried metre-high stacks of the sheets up to him, giving no time to do anything but hustle them bunch by bunch into the blades. No time to pause like the dust which had to age before it was treated with carbon disulphide to turn, as if by magic, to a brilliant orange in the 'crumb' factory at the far end of the shed.

Pungent with the stench of rotten eggs, the eyes weeping, the throat tight, the Xanthate Shed converted the purified soda cellulose to sodium cellulose xanthate which was, in yet another shed, dissolved in dilute caustic soda.

Sprayed through spinnerets that were drowned in sulphuric acid, the xanthate became 'viscose' rayon—artificial silk.

The weaver was but one of many. Stopping his conveyor belt, Dorsche motioned for him to come down. Blinking, choking—trying to brush himself off and still terrified of being sucked into the shredder, Raymond Maillotte looked like death in white on a ramrod.

He coughed. He tried to clear his eyes, sneezed maybe thirty times and broke a blood vessel. '*Excusez,*' he blurted and, finding another rag, clamped it over his nose and threw his head back.

'Sit, *mon ami,*' said Kohler. 'Tilt your head forward a little and breathe through your mouth while you pinch your nose tightly. Take five. Don't blow.'

Holding him by the back of the neck, he looked questioningly at Dorsche, for the bastard had deliberately chosen this man for this job. The weakest link in the combine, eh?

Maillotte's neck was scrawny, the crinkly black hair matted with sweat, though this end of the shed was freezing.

He began to shake. Like Savard, he had to piss but had, unfortunately, no rubber boots. Tufts of straw stuck out of the sabots—straw to prevent his feet from slipping and to keep them warm, but sabots the Russians would have carved.

Gently Kohler patted Prisoner 220374 on the shoulder. 'Rest for as long as you need,' he said sadly. 'No one's going to hurt you while I'm here. I promise.'

'Eugène . . . Eugène had been sentenced in absentia, Inspector.'

Finding two of Chairman Schrijen's cigarettes, Herr Kohler lit them, placing one between Prisoner 220374's quivering lips. It fell, of course, noted Dorsche, and the Detektiv tried to rescue it from the piss-soaked dust only to fling it away and donate the one he'd lit for himself. 'Sentenced?' he asked in *Deutsch*.

The head was nodded. Tears and blood streaked the pancake makeup of dust. The harried dark brown eyes were gaunt. A bronchial cough was given.

'To death?' hazarded this Detektiv, still not wanting to believe that prisoners could well attempt to hide such things from their Lagerfeldwebel.

'*Ja*, but . . . but we could not agree on how to carry out the sentence,' managed Maillotte, 'nor could we decide who should do it.'

And so much, then, for Victim Number Two not having had any enemies.

Almost imperceptibly Eugène Thomas trembled, and when one laid a hand on him, the vibrations were transmitted.

'It's the Works,' said St-Cyr. 'It's all that heavy machinery.' Pipe smoke drifted from him and he waved it away. 'I need to put myself in your shoes. Sophie Schrijen would have seen you nearly every day. Among her many duties she would have liaised with you on fabric quality, production problems, dye batches, the length of each run, the types of cloth planned, all such things. Is it not safe to say, then, that over the past two and a half years you became the dear friend she has claimed?'

There are friends and there are friends, Inspector.

'And certainly you, or any other POW, would have encouraged such a friendship, but did it grow to much more than that, and if so, then when she learned that Renée Ekkehard had been found hanged, did she not come to you at some point? Understand, please, that she desperately needs help and will sacrifice the bookseller if necessary. Of this I'm certain.'

A bookseller, a secretary and a chairman's daughter, Inspector—three, who though they took terrible risks to help us in such tiny ways, were definitely not equals.

'Two soft, rose-coloured buttons from a summer's frock, monsieur? I've been a fool, haven't I? These were lost last summer on the twentieth, of August but why, then, did I find them in your pockets?'

Renée had a blanket pass to the Works and could come and go after hours without the colonel.

'And Renée and Sophie had much to discuss. Löwe Schrijen would often work late . . .'

But could have been asked for much needed materials.

A carnival . . .

'Colonel Rasche would have gone through your pockets but given that failed seduction of his, would not have left those buttons for us to find which means, of course, that they must have been left *after* you had been laid out here.'

And since Victoria Bödicker doesn't have a pass, that leaves . . .

'Either one of your combine or Sophie Schrijen.'

Who must have become very close to Renée.

'Victoria was the odd one out.'

A girl whose notebook was then taken by Yvonne Lutz.

'At the request of Colonel Rasche.'

A torn page being found crumpled in my pocket.

'With the precisely written chemical equations, much simplified, for making viscose rayon, something Sophie desperately needed to understand.'

And I was well able to teach.

'But didn't write down the formula for trinitrophenol. Instead, it suggests that it was quickly done by someone who was leaning over your shoulder and since Raymond Maillotte, the fabric designer and test weaver, is the only other one from your combine who has a pass allowing him to come to that laboratory of yours . . .'

Experiments, Inspector. Didn't Sophie tell you of them? Since May of 1941 that camp at Natzweiler-Struthof has been in those granite hills to the southwest of Strasbourg. We learned early on of what was happening to some of those who had been sent there. A failed hanging, isn't that what her friend had to witness?

'The Fräulein Schrijen is ashamed of her brother but why would he have forced that fiancée of his to have witnessed an execution unless he had already overheard the girl crying out things his sister would not have wanted anyone to hear?'

Renée really didn't want to marry him.

'Victoria Bödicker not only knew that girl was in danger but also despondent and suicidal.'

POWs always have three things in mind, Inspector. First there is the hope of mail from home, then that of a parcel once a month, and then . . .

'Escape.'

That cutthroat your partner found yet left behind the photograph of a striptease artist.

'Trinitrophenol, monsieur, especially if in its dry, crystalline form, which it would have been in a place like this and used well up into the late twenties or early thirties as a yellow dye. Unfortunately even unscrewing the lid of a jar of it can set it off. It's highly unstable and definitely highly explosive. You see, though we in the trenches of that other war all knew about it under its other name, picric acid, others around the world soon learned. Halifax, Nova Scotia, 6 December 1917 the news flashed: WORLD'S BIGGEST MAN-MADE EXPLOSION. It still is, though we're in another war. Sixteen hundred dead in that city; 9,000 injured, the sight taken from 200 by the flying glass from their very homes, 250 hectares of factories, et cetera absolutely flattened by the blast whose plume reached nearly two kilometres into the sky, or by the tidal wave* that quickly followed, or by the fires that were caused as walls collapsed onto household stoves. Two vessels, the Belgian *Imo*, and the French *Mont Blanc*, collided in the harbour at 8.45 a.m., and at 9.06, you ask?

'Two thousand, seven hundred and sixty-six tonnes of picric acid, gun cotton and TNT destined for the European conflict to be made into munitions, detonated in the *Mont Blanc*'s hold. Granted flaming benzol draining into the hold was a major factor, and granted that the shock of the collision by itself did not set off the cargo, but picric acid is still nothing to fool with.'

* Recent studies at the Bedford Institute of Oceanography have called into question the presence and extent of the tidal wave because of the configuration of the harbour and the nature of its bedrock. Though damage from the blast was essentially as given here, the size of the wave was greatly exaggerated and probably not much more than a metre high.

A dyestuff.

'Which both you and the firm's test weaver could well have discovered overlooked in some storeroom.'

Kohler was only too aware that the forced march from the Xanthate Shed had been just that but voices hadn't been raised, not yet. Cap tucked under the left arm of a still snow-dusted greatcoat, Dorsche stood rigidly to attention inside the open door of the chairman's office, while Karl Rudel confided to Löwe Schrijen what Prisoner 220374 had revealed.

'A sentence in absentia, Kohler,' sighed Schrijen as if savouring the matter, his dark blue eyes flicking briefly over this Kripo to settle beyond him. 'Lagerfeldwebel Dorsche, the highest commendation will be in my monthly report to Colonel Rasche. A citation at least. If our Kommandant didn't have such a one to look after his *Arbeitslager*, Kohler, where would a man in my position be? Always in the past I've trusted implicitly the judgement of our Lagerfeldwebel, as has Colonel Rasche and with good reason. A *Grossfahdung* was thought necessary when you arrived this morning. You asked me to stop it and out of misguided courtesy I reluctantly agreed. Now surely you must see its need.

'Lagerfeldwebel, I'm certain Lageroffizier Rudel will concur with what I have to say. Please proceed with your search.'

'Now just a minute,' objected Kohler. 'The death of Eugène Thomas could well have been murder. Until our investigation is—'

'Murder, Kohler? A man's comrades sentence him to death and he learns of it? His wife in Paris is letting our boys have her repeatedly? There's a brand-new bicycle few can afford?'

'He killed himself, Kohler,' said Rudel stiffly. 'Don't push it any further.'

'A fait accompli, is that it, *meine Lieben*? Gestapo . . . I'm one of them, remember? If we're stopped, Gestapo Müller hears of it, not just Gestapo Boemelburg.'

'Kohler, Kohler, what is this you're saying?' exclaimed Schrijen. 'That what the Gruppenführer Müller most wishes to hear from you has finally come to pass? That once again you consider yourself one of us?'

'And loyal,' said Rudel. 'Please don't forget that even in Berlin they've heard of you.'

Raymond Maillotte would be sent to Natzweiler-Struthof to be interrogated, no questions asked here, no interview taken down by either Louis or himself. 'What can a few minutes matter? Allow my partner and I to have a go at their quarters before Maillotte gets his things. If we find anything, we'll be sure to let you know.'

Kohler wasn't going to learn how to behave but why, suddenly, was he so agitated? wondered Schrijen. Concern for the prisoner or had something else been uncovered that he was holding back, something even Dorsche, as yet, knew nothing of? 'Pick through the rubbish afterward. Let Lagerfeldwebel Dorsche know if you find anything he and his *Greifer* have missed. Make a little contest of it. Your eyes against theirs.'

Only the Russian watched from his window. Even the guards up in the nearest tower hadn't yet taken notice, felt St-Cyr. If he could scoot round the corner of the kitchen, could he make it down that side of the administrative block unaccompanied? It was worth a try but first the root cellar doors would have to be closed. The guards on the gate would have to continue thinking he was still with the victim.

Certainly he couldn't search through the laboratory under

guard. There would still be Thomas's assistants to deal with. He would have to go carefully, couldn't have anyone finding out what he was after.

At a signal from the Russian, he realized that the man could see the gate quite clearly and that the guards there were momentarily preoccupied. Running, he darted round the corner of the kitchen, kept on going through the ankle-deep snow, cursed his broken shoes, found stacks of old machinery, broken grindstones, boxes of rusty bolts . . . Was nothing ever thrown out?

Found that even so, a cleared space of ten metres lay between him and the perimeter wire, its single warning strand no more than two-thirds of a metre above ground, with short lengths of dirty white rayon cord tied every ten metres to mark it, beyond this, the no-man's-land, beyond that, the first of the three-metre-high fences with their inwardly leaning overhangs, the barbed wire complete with continuous nests of concertina wire atop the overhangs and between the inner and outer fences.

The boot prints of the *Hundeführerin* and the dogs on their nightly patrols were clear enough. When a voice, given over a megaphone, called out, *'Halt! Was wollen Sie?'*—Who goes there?—he was right back in that other war and cried out, *'Nicht Schiessen!'* Don't shoot! *'Ich bin der Oberdetektiv Jean-Louis St-Cyr der Sûreté Nationale, meine Herren.* I am merely trying to find the entrance to the laboratory and administrative offices.'

'Ach, the other side. *Kommen Sie her. Beeilen Sie sich!'* Come here. Hurry!

They would have him in their sights. Others in further towers would be notified if they hadn't already seen him. With a wave, he shouted, *'Danke!* I'll go this way as ordered,' and kept on, the wire always there, the guns too. No prisoners ventured here unless they had to. All were either at work or in their compound.

A black Mercedes four-door sedan was in the garage he entered just beyond the far end of the administrative block, having felt it best to duck out of sight where possible.

Beside the sedan, its bonnet up, was the tourer. Two lorries were also being worked on but there were no guards and it looked as if no one here had yet seen him.

Hobnailed boots rained on rough-timbered stairs that were shoulder-narrow and too *gottverdammt* steep, thought Kohler. Doors burst open ahead of him, wire-meshed dividers were thrown aside as, caught up in the rush of Dorsche and his *Greifer,* he was carried along.

Floor by floor the bastards went, the sleeping tumbling from their bunks to blink myopically in the pitiful light, a bucket of piss pouring over a bare, plank floor as the men, their stubbled faces lined, confused, terrified or empty, fought to stand upright beside bunks that were tiered four to the ceiling timbers.

The Russians, but this was only the third storey of the brick monolith that had, in 1870 or '80, been the original works. On and on Dorsche went. Everywhere the muscle was applied. He seemed to thrive on it, for he'd a lead-weighted, black leather truncheon in hand.

The French POWs were on the fifth floor and directly under an attic that must be huge. Here there was a little more headroom allowed and bunks that were only layered three high. Stiff, closely woven, timber-held wire mesh ran from floor to ceiling, dividing up the space and separating them from the four-tiered bunks of the Poles as though the two peoples must treat each other as untouchables. But even here, those who had been asleep after a twelve-hour shift, poured from their bunks to stand rigidly to attention, though the *Grossfahdung* was to be conducted in one 'room' only.

Shaking, Kohler tried to light a cigarette. The 'room' in which Thomas's combine lived when not at work was large by what had been seen so far, yet still it couldn't be any more than eight metres deep by five in width. There were two small, wire-meshed windows at one end, and within this space for the past two and a half years were bunks for twelve. Armoires—cupboards, closets, whatever they'd called them—were being emptied. Everything was being yanked out, glanced at and thrown to the floor, the lumpy mattresses and pillows spilling their cellulose when ripped apart.

Photos of loved ones were torn from where they had been pinned, letters strewn, books fanned and flung aside, mess bowls dented, banged, crunched, the remains of last month's Red Cross parcels no longer budgeted but trod on, the tins of meat, fish, butter and condensed milk being bayoneted first. Even the bunks were pulled down, their slats and timbers scrutinized for hidy-holes.

A refuse dump remained and it hadn't taken any more than ten minutes. Dorsche had already had a look early this morning. 'Satisfied?' demanded Kohler. The bastards were sweating, he himself still shaking, still remembering those first days behind the wire.

'*Ach*, now it's your turn.'

Clutching the wire, the Poles silently watched from its other side. The French POWs who had been asleep, simply waited.

'Leave me, will you?' he said to Dorsche. 'I need a little time.'

'Take as long as you wish. One man will remain while the

rest of us visit each of the prisoners who occupied this room but are currently on shift.'

'They're not to be harmed nor sent anywhere, not until we've had a chance to interview them.'

'Prisoner 220374 will be the first of them. He can then join you to collect his things.'

'I'm warning you, Lagerfeldwebel.'

'That, too, is understood.'

The snowflakes were large, and when they struck the window of the entrance door to the garage, they hesitated as if unsure of themselves, and only then began to melt.

Standing just inside the door, still catching his breath, St-Cyr knew with absolute certainty that not only had he a perfect view of the eastern end of the administrative block, chance had come into play and he was onto something. He could feel it, almost taste it, but could he find it and would it then lead him to the trinitrophenol?

Diagonally across a cleared lane of no more than ten metres lay the private entrance to the executive offices. Above this entrance, Löwe Schrijen's windows looked out from the first storey, those of his daughter also. And when the big garage doors are opened? he had to ask. Both could easily see if a lorry or van was available and that their respective vehicles had been serviced. So, too, would Eugène Thomas have seen this if in Sophie Schrijen's office, and also Renée Ekkehard.

But had it really been luck, his crying out in *Deutsch*, 'Don't shoot'? Hadn't he done the same thing in that other war; wouldn't audacity be what the POWs would believe was the only way to defeat their masters? A gamble, swift and unexpected?

'*Mein Herr*, is there something I can do for you?'

It was the mechanic who had been half-hidden under the tourer's bonnet. '*Ach*, my shoes. I was giving them a little rest.'

'They don't look good, do they?'

'And haven't for some time.'

It could do no harm to help; indeed it might well do some good. 'Lucien Weber at your service, Herr Oberdetektiv. You're a long way from home and I greatly fear those shoes will not last without a few stitches. Fortunately this was once the stables. Though the firm's horses are still used in the logging operations, none are kept here now but we do have the tack room where harnesses were mended and I still do a little of that work. If you would be so kind as to follow, I think we can settle this, at least until you get back to Paris. Things are satisfactory there, are they?'

Dry shoes to a detective were as necessary as pipe tobacco, but it would not be wise to tell the truth. 'Things are fine. There's a shortage of small coins, but it is only to be expected.'

'The *métro* still busy?'

'As ever. My partner and I are hardly there, so we really haven't noticed any changes.'

'It's not good, is it?' confided Weber when they were alone.

'But far better than Stalingrad, Berlin or London.'

'Inspector, please don't worry. We can at least talk to each other like civilized men. Now give me those shoes. Sit in the other room if you wish. This won't take long. What one learns as a boy, one never forgets. My father was *Stalldirektor* here.'

'Which other room?'

'That one. The barbershop. The gift of a wealthy French businessman who wished to ease the plight of those who had been taken prisoners of war. It has never been used. Most of those men were only here for such a short time, they missed its arrival, but Chairman Schrijen felt we should at least install it, so a room was found.'

Un salon de coiffure pour hommes, ein Friseurladen. 'I could use a shave.'

Had nostalgia swept in on the chief inspector? 'Then please help yourself. There's plenty of hot water, towels too, and a lovely aftershave.'

Alone but for the guard, Kohler surveyed the refuse heap as a POW would have done. Frustrated, angry at the injustice of it and yet exhilarated, for now he had to find what had been missed, and hadn't it all been a game: them against the guards, those against them, the hidden and the most hidden?

Where utensils had been needed—the knives, forks and spoons of common decency—Martin Caroff, the assistant machinist, had fashioned these out of pieces of tin cans salvaged from their parcels. Nothing was ever wasted. The rivets, forged with the aid of one of the tin-can blowers and shaped on a small anvil, were perfect. Not only had the Breton an eye for utility, he'd one for artistry. Brightening their lives, each utensil, the plates and tin cups too, had incised designs that curved continuously, circling round and round. Celtic those designs and thousands of years old.

The blowers themselves had been fashioned out of soup, butter and sardine cans. Each tiny, clay-lined firebox would be fed with wood chips, cellulose, bits of paper and the odd pea-sized piece of stolen coal. A fan, rapidly cranked by hand, kept a stream of air directed into the firebox, above whose chimney, either a mess bowl or home-made saucepan would be heated at the end of each day.

Unlike the others, the French POWs were allowed to dine in comparative luxury. Not for them the day's final meal in the crowded mess hall that was next to the *Lagerküche*. They drew the slop the kitchen dished up and brought it here to eat with their other rations, twelve men sharing everything because only then could they survive.

Two-kilogram loaves of black bread—one per man per week—added a further sourness to the air which was heavy with the stench of old sweat, body heat, bad sauerkraut, unwashed rags, urine, rotten eggs—that chemical smell—and stale tobacco smoke. A puddle from a bayonetted can of condensed milk had engulfed photos from home. Meat paste of questionable age and origin had the greasy slickness of pâté to which Norwegian fish-oil margarine had been substituted in quantity.

Letters had been stained. Postcards had their uncensored remaining words blurred. A bead of solder rolled from under a partly unravelled woollen sock whose holes outnumbered the rest. Elation filled him. Solder—lead and tin from the seams of the cans—was being gathered and that could only mean they'd a definite use for it.

Tunic buttons, cap badges and Iron Crosses, et cetera, the beads melted in one of their blowers and cast into those blanks to be later meticulously painted but where? Not here, he knew, letting his gaze sift slowly over the rubbish, asking too, Had Dorsche removed the evidence of those blanks early this morning?

He couldn't have. He would have had the combine put on *Straf* and would have cleaned this place out.

A much needed pair of work gloves awaited further stitching, having been fashioned out of scraps of cloth. A bit of grey-green fabric—nothing more than a tunic's lapel in size—matched the shade of the uniforms of those the French had come to call *les haricots verts*, the green beans, the Wehrmacht's finest.

Newspapers had been sewn into a hood to give warmth—he

and others had done the same in that other war. The smell of a smashed bottle of cheap scent rushed at him as he lifted a soggy wad of newspaper from the remains of that hood, dehydrated peas and carrot cubes now underfoot.

Caught among the rubbish, the fist-sized carving of a long-haired, voluptuous naked woman gazed fiercely up at him from her chariot. Armbands of beaten gold, a torque of the same and a quiver of javelins completed the attire, the one in her hand broken off during the search.

Rescuing the carving that the assistant machinist must have done, he cleaned it off with pages from the *Kölnische Zeitung* of Monday, 4 January 1943, only to hesitate, to pocket the carving and to quickly scan the columns. Kathe . . . Maria . . . Angela . . . 'Karen is at the age where a girl desires children. She is 175 cm tall (5'9"), weighs 54.4 kgs (120 lbs.), has a good figure if just a little big in the bust, likes to dance and to party, to go to the cinema and take long walks . . .' *Ach*, hadn't he read this before? 'Reads romance novels but finds them insufficient for her needs. Wishes to meet a man who is gentle and kind and older than herself so that a mature hand can give guidance to a sometimes frivolous nature. Preferably he will appreciate Herr Wagner's music as much as she does. *Der fliegende Holländer* perhaps.' The Flying Dutchman. 'Apply Box 1043.'

Pages from the *Berliner Morgenpost* were here too, from the stuffing of that hood. Those of the *Deutsche Allgemeine Zeitung* and *Tageblatt* but earlier issues, and then . . . Wednesday, 20 January 1943, the *Münchner Neueste Nachrichten*. 'Beate is blonde, blue-eyed and lonely. At the age of 27, she finds herself still a virgin. Friends say she is too rambunctious, that she needs guidance and should seek someone much older. One who likes swimming, sunbathing and the superb *Deutsche Grammophon* recordings of *Das Rheingold* and *Die Walküre*. If you are that man, apply Box 1379 and include a snapshot, please.'

Dorsche hadn't seen this either.

From one of the wire-meshed windows there was a view of the root cellar's entrance, still closed—Louis could take forever talking to a corpse. There was also a view of the administrative block and all the way down it to a garage.

To his right, to the south and just beyond the outer perimeter, a goods train was backing along a siding, the slogan *RÄDER MUSSEN ROLLEN FÜR DEN SIEG!* splashed in sooty white paint on its engine and coal tender. Wheels must roll for victory.

These boys would have worked out the schedules. Once loaded, that train would go to the station where Louis and he had waved *auf Weidersehen* to Frau Oberkircher only to find that it hadn't been good-bye after all.

Astounded by what he had inadvertently come upon, St-Cyr took a moment to survey the barbershop. There were four reclining chairs with cushioned leather upholstery, hand-lever controls and nickel-plated footrests that gleamed. Bevelled wall mirrors, all but to the ceiling, were behind a countertop of variegated grey marble with inset basins, taps and retractable shower-hoses.

'*Merde*, why send it here and not use it?' he sighed. Individual cabinet sterilizers were also on that counter, atomizers too, each with its little plunger-pump. Bay Rum, cologne and hair oil, the standard three bench bottles every *coiffeur* had for men's hair, were here, but these bottles, and many more of them, were of cobalt-blue glass webbed with silver to give a decidedly spice-trade look. Everyone who sat in any of these chairs would automatically see those elixirs and think of Arabia and of desert caravans, of dusky-eyed maidens bathing *toutes nues* in palm-treed oases or plump, honey-skinned Turkish belly dancers in an Istanbul café whose aroma would most certainly be of pungently black tobacco and strong, dark coffee.

There were bars of scented Castile soap that had been made in Aix from 'pure olive oil' before the Defeat. These days to get anything like this in Paris, or that oil, was to get the impossible. 'Would the monsieur like the lemon-, the rose-, or the lavender-scented?' he taunted. 'A coconut shampoo, *peut-être*? A little of the Old Master Brilliantine for glossing the moustache? The *Vieux Seigneur*?'

Tweezers, nail clippers, hairdresser's smocks of white drill were here and had never been used. A honed, brand-new cutthroat razor gleamed, its balance perfect, the blade of Damascus steel.

Cutthroat in hand, he couldn't help but see himself in the mirrors: jaundiced, hollow-eyed, no light in his eyes anymore, just the fear of defeat, of worry too, eh? Worry over Hermann and his Giselle and Oona in Paris, worry over Gabrielle and her son too, and what was to become of them all and, yes, worry over trinitrophenol and just how was he to find it, yet not let anyone know he was searching for something like that?

Among the cutthroat razors there was a choice like no other and one would not be missed. Had Eugène Thomas managed to pocket it and then taken it to the carnival against all risk of discovery?

'Like the colonel, we're digging a hole for ourselves and it just gets deeper and deeper.'

Choosing the Crème de Vichy, silk-velvetine shaving soap and using a brand-new badger-haired brush from . . . 'Harrods of London,' he said, and fleetingly had to smile at the magic of a war that could be so utterly tragic. Lathering up, he was careful with the razor.

When Lucien Weber rejoined him, the chief inspector favoured cheeks that hadn't been shaved as closely in years.

'My partner must see this,' he said, patting them a last time and feeling like a new man. 'He's always going on about setting up some little business. A bar, a café . . .' And never mind that it was to be on the Costa del Sol and well out of France before it was too late. 'A small hotel perhaps, of which business he knows nothing though thinks he has all the answers. Something like this would suit him far better. If he was with us, I'd get him to give me a proper trim just to prove he really can do such a thing when he puts his mind to it. By the way, that lavender aftershave you mentioned is perfect, but I prefer the jasmine. Ah, my shoes. *Danke*.'

'I've found you some overboots as well, from the *Volksopfer*. Alain . . . the Fräulein Schrijen's brother brought them for the collection the last time he was here. Sophie . . .'

'Is chairperson of that committee also. The people's offering of winter clothes for the boys along the Russian front.'

'You may choose others if you wish, Inspector. I don't think the Fraulein Schrijen will mind. The pair I've selected should suit but . . .'

They did. They weren't new, of course, had been purchased in '39 probably, and from the Bon Marché in Paris, so not expensive yet still with years of life. A full thirty centimetres high and of natural rubber, with a fleece lining, they even had snow excluders, and when the trousers were tucked in, why no less than five buckles had to be done up.

The storeroom, just beyond the barbershop and complete with sorting tables, shelves and boxes, held not only overboots and shoes, but overcoats, scarves, hats, heavy pullovers, shirts, blouses, trousers and skirts even underclothes both male and female, though there were far fewer of the latter and certainly BDMs and nurses would also be stationed near the front.

'The young master is always bringing her things.'

'Nothing is ever wasted these days, is it? Everything has a use.' Even a dead man's overboots.

One table, small and rough-hewn, had been set up just outside the cage, one straight-backed chair on which to sit as he interviewed each of the combine, but that wasn't going to be of any use. Kohler knew Dorsche would wring each of them dry before they ever got here. Dorsche would start with Raymond Maillotte, would ask the test weaver only one question: Why had Prisoner 220371 been sentenced to death?

Maillotte might hold out, having already betrayed himself and his friends. He might take the blows and the shrieks, but even if he did, the others wouldn't know what he'd said. There was only one way to help them. Nothing else really mattered now. He had to get the colonel to intervene, had to convince him that his visiting detectives desperately needed time.

Stuffing the coat-hood with its wadding of newspapers into a torn pillowcase, grey from use, he headed for the exit, pushed past the guard who'd been delegated to watch him, heard that one's startled objections, the sighs of observant POWs as he started down the stairs, cramming the pillowcase into a pocket, going faster, faster until the cold light of day and the gently falling snow hit him.

Far along the soot- and snow-covered lane that ran between the steam plants and sheds to one side and the administrative block to the other, Dorsche and two of his *Greifer* were escorting Prisoner 220374 toward him. The Lagerfeldwebel was in the lead and clearly in a rage; the other two each had Maillotte by an arm, their Mausers slung. POWs dropped their shovels and stood to attention, snatching off their caps and baring their heads. Outside the kitchen, one of the Russians deliberately threw a bucket of potatoes across the trampled snow in front of them but was ignored.

Between the latrine and the root cellar, the ground was filthy, Dorsche livid. 'WHERE IS THAT PARTNER OF YOURS, HERR KOHLER? WHY HAS HE NOT OBEYED THE ORDER FROM THE TOWER TO TURN BACK?'

A cigarette would do no good, a grin certainly wouldn't help. 'Louis will turn up, Lagerfeldwebel. He can't have gone far.'

'ALLE WERDEN BESTRAFT, KOHLER. ALLE!'

All are going on punishment.

'STRAFLAGER IST KEIN ZUCKERLECKEN!'

Punishment camp is no picnic.

'Bitte, find your friend and quickly,' said Dorsche, suddenly out of breath and realizing that the POWs in the barracks block would be at their windows watching the scene he'd created. 'Tell him he must not do this, that you both, at all times, must be with one of the guards for your own safety, of course.'

Cigarettes had best be hauled out now, for Dorsche badly needed to save face.

'Danke, Herr Detektiv Aufsichtsbeamter. Prisoner 220374 can give us both the answer to the question I asked him.'

Maillotte was brought forward, the men in the background not moving from where they stood to attention, simply watching as POWs had done in every camp that had ever been. Maillotte hesitated. He flicked his dark brown eyes uncertainly over Dorsche and this Kripo, was still caked with that white dust, had slipped a hand into the right pocket of the blue coveralls whose faded fabric showed through only at its creases.

'You are to answer,' said Dorsche, still catching his breath.

The test weaver lifted his gaze to the barracks block beyond them. Perhaps he tried to find the two windows his combine had shared, perhaps he simply begged the Russians and the others to forgive him, but one thing was certain. The two guards had stepped back and to his left; Dorsche and himself were now facing him, and between them there was perhaps no more than two metres.

'Don't,' Kohler heard himself saying, but by then it was too late, though he ran. He slipped and nearly fell as he chased after Maillotte but the Frenchman had kicked off his sabots and had somehow found the wind of the gods. Maillotte leapt easily over the warning wire, didn't stop, didn't wait for the shots, grabbed the barbed wire and started to climb, the white dust of him being sprayed with blood and brains, the teeth erupting from his mouth as he coughed once, Kohler grabbing him and what he had tried to swallow . . .

A bloodied lump of partly masticated papier-mâché and a phosphorescent swastika button.

Dorsche hadn't seen him take them, not really. Inherently suspicious because he had to be, the Lagerfeldwebel grunted and said, '*Für ihn ist der Krieg zu Enden,* Kohler.' For him the war has ended.

'No one is to be sent anywhere without the Kommandant's order, Lagerfeldwebel.'

Was the Detektiv about to throw up? '*Straf* cells are in the attic and that is where they must now be taken. You could have been shot. *Ach,* had you been patient, I might still have helped you, but now can do nothing.'

'Then put this one in with the other one.'

'Certainly, but your hand. You've cut it.'

'The barbed wire.'

'Are stitches needed?'

'I don't think so.'

'You must go immediately to the *Lagerführung* in any case. They have a first-aid kit and euflavine, an antiseptic, also some of the sulphanilamide powder. Sepsis you do not want. There is no doctor here, but as soon as possible, have one look at the wound or . . . *Ach,* there's a woman pharmacist in town who is excellent. The Unterlindenstrasse, near the bus terminal. I go there many times.'

And hadn't that same pharmacist already been mentioned? 'I'll just rinse this off in the washhouse before I go to the *Lagerführung.*' Louis . . . Louis had to be in the one place Dorsche and his *Greifer* hadn't thought to look.

St-Cyr knew that no shots had been heard in the garage. There had been far too much background noise from the servicing of the lorries, and from the Works out there. A goods train was also being loaded, but still the news had travelled quickly.

'To each saint his candle, Inspector,' said Lucien Weber, using a decidedly French expression but prudently giving it in *Deutsch* while sadly shaking his head.

Honour to whom honour is due, but was Hermann all right? Had he thrown up? Did he have the shakes that damned Benzedrine sometimes caused? They'd not eaten. His blood sugar would be low. It was nearly 3.30 in the afternoon.

'The Fräulein Schrijen will be terribly upset, Inspector. Sophie had her heart set on those men bringing some of the *Karneval* things to life for the *Winterhilfswerk* fundraiser. Three deaths. First Renée Ekkehard . . . Such a lovely girl and her dearest friend. Those two . . . To see them together was wonderful. But then Herr Thomas on whom Sophie depended for virtually everything she had to do here. No task was too difficult, no schedule too complicated. He would work it all out with her and was extremely patient, a real teacher.

'Inspector, you must know she is convinced Renée's death was not a suicide. Now she'll be worrying all the more that it could well have been herself had her brother, Alain, not come home unexpectedly. The car is his. Sophie never forgets.'

'And on Saturday, 30 January?'

Not two weeks ago. Eleven days to be precise. 'She went to the train station that afternoon to give him the car as she always does. Alain then drove here without her, spoke briefly with his father and then went on to the house at Kaysersberg. It's always been his first love, that house and its vineyards.'

'Could he have gone out to the *Karneval*?'

'I don't think so.'

'Didn't he want to see his fiancée?'

This one was going to press for answers that had best not be given. 'He told me he was going to the house in the country.'

'And his sister?'

Must the Inspector make things difficult? 'Sophie would have stayed in town and taken the bus home, to the house Chairman Schrijen has in Kolmar.'

'It's a beautiful car, isn't it? A dark forest green, with a bonnet that seems to go on forever, and two spare tyres up front under white duck covers.' Unheard of these days.

'The 540K of 1938, Inspector. A birthday gift from the chairman. The four-speed, supercharged *Überwagen* whose overdrive is so smooth one hardly notices its kicking in. A hundred and seventy kilometres an hour, from zero to one hundred in 15.6 seconds. I've clocked it many times for Herr Schrijen and his son.'

And that with a weight of nearly two and a half tons, to say nothing of the five passengers, should each seat be occupied. 'The Fräulein Schrijen must really enjoy having the use of it.'

'She worries all the time and lives in fear of getting even the slightest scratch or dent, though there are so few cars on the roads, who hears of an accident? We take good care of it too, so she really has no need to concern herself.'

'And when with the Fräulein Ekkehard?'

'Only then would we see her get behind that wheel and smile.'

'Yet still she must have fretted?'

'Certainly.'

'And on Sunday, 31 January? Come, come, Herr Weber?'

The day of Renée's suicide. 'Alain took the late afternoon train back to Strassburg. I believe he was to stay over with the Fräulein Ekkehard's parents to discuss the wedding. Renée didn't want her parents spending much; Alain and Chairman Schrijen wished a somewhat larger celebration since the Gauleiter Wagner was to be among the guests of honour.'

'I'll just sit in the car for a moment.'

This one was trouble. Anxiously Weber looked across the garage to see if the others were busy and finally taking no notice of them. 'Inspector, there's no need. Sophie has the Mauser pistol my captain once carried in the Great War. She asked me to quietly find something for her and I . . . *Ach,* I gave it to her. It's fully loaded and in the glove compartment. It's crazy of her to think she's in any danger but what could I have done except to have humoured her? Please don't inform Chairman Schrijen of this. I . . . I would not just lose his trust and respect.'

The Wehrmacht's version of that pistol would most probably be the 7.63mm, with a ten- or twenty-round box magazine. The overall length was nearly thirty centimetres; the barrel a good fourteen, the weight almost one and a half kilograms, the muzzle velocity 480 metres per second. Somewhat clumsy and not as well balanced as the Luger, it was still every bit as effective. Indeed it had a third more muzzle velocity and was simply not a lady's gun.

Concrete laundry tubs, each with a lone and dribbling tap, flanked the washhouse walls on three sides, while at the far end, four goose-necked shower heads serviced nearly six hundred men.

Kohler hesitated; those who were doing their laundry paused. For perhaps thirty seconds, the two long lines of waiting, naked men, each with a bundle of clothes and a postage stamp of grey face cloth for drying off, waited.

They were all staring at him, even the guards who hustled the men into and out of the shower bath at intervals so short no one could possibly clean oneself properly.

Without a word, one of the Russians stepped away from a laundry tub, indicating that he should use it.

'*Danke*,' he managed, but the shakes came so suddenly it was all he could do to get his left fist under the tap. Ice-cold water helped but again and again the shakes came, again and again he kept seeing the dead in the trenches of that other war, the heaps of rotting corpses, those of this one too, Louis among them. Louis. Gabrielle and Oona and Giselle—*Gerda?* he demanded. Their boys, Jurgen and Hans—how had they died at Stalingrad?

Searching for answers to it all did no good. Throwing up didn't either. The mush of papier-mâché in his hand held a tight wad of off-white threads. *Rayon?* he demanded. Like an eggshell, the papier-mâché covering had been.

'None of you saw this,' he heard himself saying first in French and then in *Deutsch*, for he knew no Russian or Polish.

The phosphorescent button with its enamelled red swastika stared up at him from amongst those threads and why the hell would Maillotte have tried to swallow a ball they had made for the *Jeu de massacre*?

There could be only one reason. The dry heaves hit and he shook so hard, he almost wet himself.

'Your tears, tovarisch. It's not good that you should be seen with them.'

Washed without hot water when the steam plants could have supplied endless streams of it at no cost, the rag, a woollen sock, was far from clean but he used it anyway.

'Is it true what we hear of Stalingrad?' asked the prisoner.

A nod would suffice. Suddenly he was too exhausted to do otherwise.

'Are your people building an Atlantic Wall in France?'

A continuous line of fortifications. True again.

The Russian considered this gravely. Frowning, he deferentially hazarded, 'It's impossible your Führer could have made the same mistake as the Maréchal Pétain and Monsieur Maginot when they helped to convince the French Government to build a similar line from Southern Alsace to the Belgian border but still, isn't wisdom as foreign to great leaders as poverty is to wealthy men?'

During the Blitzkrieg of 1940, the Maginot Line had been gone round and taken within the blink of an eye but there were more important things to discuss. 'Did any of you do laundry for Eugène Thomas?'

Had this detective once been a POW? 'We do it for the French when they feel it necessary.'

'Cigarettes?'

'One for the socks, the underwear and undershirt; two for the trousers, shirt and pullover. Though we would like to haggle, the price is nonnegotiable and has been set firmly by the French. Without Lagergeld, Red Cross parcels or those from home, it is the—'

'The only way you can get a smoke, but did the others of his combine make certain his clothes were always the cleanest you boys could get them?'

This one was thinking clearly. 'That is as it was, Inspector.'

'Good. Here, take these. Share them up for me.'

Fumbling, the Gestapo's detective pressed cigarettes and small cigars into waiting hands, matches too. 'I'm not one of them,' he said of the enemy. 'If Dorsche or any of his *Greifer* ask, forget I was here.'

Four dried, boiled sweet chestnuts mysteriously appeared from the depths of a pocket. 'Shave them,' said Herr Kohler. 'Don't break a tooth.'

'We will soak them in water for as long as it takes and make a paste. Perhaps a little of the boiled potato or black bread could be added if it is first soaked. Salt is out of the question, of course, but . . .'

'Enjoy. I only wish there was more. Maybe someday there will be.'

'Then let us look forward to it, Inspector. Now go, please. It's not good for me to be seen talking to you.'

Again the men were staring at him, again he had to pause just inside the door. Standing out in the wind and the snow, a handkerchief tied round his hand, Kohler knew they would have endless days and nights in which to think over and discuss what had happened in those few moments. Something strange, something decidedly different. A miracle.

When Louis, hurrying between the nearest of the steam plants and the kitchen, caught up with him, Kohler quietly confided, 'Ask that God of yours to be with us, *mon vieux*. I think I've found the trigger element.'

7

Long shadows fingered the carnival where a coal-black Renault, the two-door Primastella—the 1934, St-Cyr thought—sat at the end of the snow-covered lane on a gentle rise up near the Noah's Ark and the dangling, shattered biplanes of the Pilot in the Sky. Two men in grey fedoras and broad-shouldered overcoats, their cigarettes alight, stood waiting all but in darkness with hands in their pockets, one on either side of that car.

'The colonel's detectives,' sighed Hermann.

Perhaps one hundred metres lay between the two vehicles. From the Textilfabrikschrijen it hadn't taken twenty minutes with Hermann at the wheel. There had been no time, really, to talk things over, and yet word had gone ahead and these two had come out here.

'Löwe Schrijen must have called them, Louis, as soon as we left the gates.'

'The trigger element, Hermann.'

'Guncotton wrapped in papier-mâché. I'm certain of it. If we didn't have company, I'd touch a match to it.'

'Burns with a very hot flame; explodes if a detonator is

used. Is made from pure cellulose, of which Eugène Thomas had plenty. Cold nitric acid too, and sulphuric acid.'

'But they wouldn't have needed a detonator, not with the trinitrophenol.'

'The flame of the one would have been perfectly adequate for the other, but why had he been sentenced in absentia? Surely he would have wanted to escape as much as the rest of that combine?'

'But they'd asked him to do something and he had refused. He must have, Louis. One for all and all for one because that's the way it has to be.'

'That cutthroat you found in their office wagon . . . Had they been planning to use it on someone?'

'They must have. They've been gathering solder and making uniform buttons, badges and collar pips which Dorsche doesn't yet know of.'

'And that tourer of Sophie Schrijen's brother enters and leaves the Works without challenge.'

The two up ahead were still patiently watching them. 'Löwe Schrijen says his son was at Natzweiler-Struthof the weekend Renée was hanged,' said Kohler.

'Yet the boy couldn't have been. Weber, the garage mechanic, has stated that Alain unexpectedly arrived at the railway station on that Saturday afternoon and that Sophie had to drive the car there for him to use. That's why the Mademoiselle Ekkehard went out to the carnival alone instead of her.'

'But if we are to believe Schrijen, the girl then left a note in lipstick that said, "I can't go on. Please forgive me," and what do I find in Alain Schrijen's desk, in the corner that sister of his reserves for herself, but a lipstick and a little piece of granite from the quarry camp.'

This hole they were digging for themselves seemed bottomless. 'Did the son kill that girl, Hermann? Did he discover what that *Winterhilfswerk* Committee was really up to and attempt to put an end to it?'

'She skis and or walks all night, and could well have caught one of the local trains or thumbed a ride. Neuf-Brisach and Alt-Breisach aren't that far. Maybe seven and a dozen kilometres from here.'

'And, if she could get across the Rhine between them, where to, then? A girl who wears a beret that is forbidden.'

'She wasn't,' said Kohler. 'She was wearing a woollen toque, according to Henri Savard, the carpenter who made that coffin. Rasche must have removed the one and replaced it with the other, but why would he do a thing like that if they were up to something and where did he get it? From her rucksack?'

'Or a room at the Lutze residence.'

Still the colonel's two detectives hadn't moved. 'This isn't looking good for us, Hermann. Schrijen sends van-loads of his wine to the Gauleiter Wagner.'

'At no charge and guess who has been invited to the wedding now a funeral and also to the fundraiser a certain combine must still want to know is continuing, especially in view of what's happened to another of their members and with a visit to Natzweiler-Struthof a distinct probability.'

Merde but they needed a cigarette to share.

'Saturday, 6 March, is the target date,' said Kohler. 'Nearly everything is ready, including buckets of papier-mâché balls that just need a bit of paint and a match. What the hell were those boys really up to, eh? Guncotton flaming to trinitrophenol?'

'And three young women, each of whom was a rebel in her own right. A bookshop that reminds its customers of book burnings, its proprietor a fired teacher who admits to being bitter about a mother who is being held in the internment camp at Vittel which she visits on the last Friday of every month, and if that isn't opportunity enough to make contact with the Francs-Tireurs *et Partisans*, what is?'

'A chairman's daughter who, beside what they are actually receiving, impulsively jots down the calorie intakes necessary for men at hard labour, and a secretary who steals police snapshots of those two so that her friend—'

'Her lover, Hermann. I'm almost certain of it.'

'And yet another reason for her to insist that death was murder. Snapshots so that she can see who's been following her and not following that same secretary.'

'Whom Frau Lutze tells us brought to the house or bookshop the travel papers Victoria Bödicker needed for Vittel, rather than have the bookseller visit the *Polizeikommandantur* too often. Good of the colonel, wasn't it? No wonder he's worried.'

'Frau Lutze, Louis, formerly Fräulein Yvonne Eva Ellmann. Schrijen made a point of telling me "she was one of those on her father's side."'

Which discretely meant half-Jewish. 'A woman who has a daughter, Hermann, at the University of Strasbourg in Clermont-Ferrand.'

'That marriage is a puzzle, isn't it, since Rasche was once hot and heavy with Yvonne and Löwe Schrijen knows all about it even to asking me what the colonel hoped to gain by claiming murder instead of suicide?'

'Which we now know it definitely was, at least in the case of his secretary.'

'An ampoule and a droplet earring that girl was searching for . . .'

'A girl, Hermann, who didn't even like the taste of schnapps or an *eau-de-vie* and who could make a glass of wine last all evening. Drugged was what Sophie Schrijen asked the bookseller, that one in turn demanding to know why she hadn't accused her brother of raping the Fräulein Ekkehard at that skiing party. An event which causes the sister to wonder if the girl hadn't cried out the truth about her feelings for men and for herself.'

'And all the rest of it, like moving deserters through to the Vosges.'

'Talk to those two. Use your charm. See if they'll tell you why they were following Sophie Schrijen. That Primastella is no match for a Citroën *traction-avant*. I'll go round them and leave the car up by the Devil's Saucer. I'll get to that office wagon before the three of you.'

'You'd best have these, then.'

Her keys. 'I knew I could count on you. Now reach under the seat and hand me my Lebel.'

'It's back at the house. I didn't think we'd need the firepower.'

'Then think again!'

'Have you any more matches?'

The last of the light was fast fading. 'Haven't you?'

'I gave them all to the Russians.'

'*Merde*, what is it with you? Now I'll have to head over to the farmhouse for lanterns *and* matches!'

'Ask for bread, marg' and a bucket of their potato soup. It's the least the Army can do, seeing as we're working for one of them.'

Alone, St-Cyr stood where the Primastella had been. 'Hermann,' he heard himself saying. They'd taken him. 'To Löwe Schrijen?' he demanded and knew it must be so.

'They can pick me up at any time,' he rebelled, for here in Elsass he was an alien on a temporary pass.

Hermann's footprints were next to where the taller one had stood—the other one hadn't come round his side of the car. He would have held a gun on Hermann, forcing him to get into the car.

Turning toward where the Citroën idled, its headlamps blinkered, he said, 'Things have finally caught up with us, haven't they? The honesty, the dogged pursuit of common crime no one seems to want to bother about but ourselves.'

The snow in the Primastella's ruts was packed down hard. He'd walk along one of them even though the new overboots were perfect, would turn to look back at where those footprints had met.

'A pillowcase,' he muttered. While squeezing himself into the backseat of that little car, Hermann had managed to drag it from a pocket and flick it behind himself. Unseen by either of those two, it lay forlornly between the ruts, caught in the light of a borrowed Wehrmacht torch.

'Newspapers,' he hazarded, much puzzled, 'and a little carving, though not a child's toy. Boudicca, Hermann. Queen of the Iceni in what is now Norfolk.'

And freedom.

To the west, the iron and slatted skeleton of the Ferris wheel raised dark and silent circles to the night sky. Closer in and even darker, were the remains of the *Salon Carousel* and Ideal Caterpillar, and when he brought the Citroën to a halt deep in this lost city of theirs, the House of Mirrors waited.

'Renée Ekkehard,' said Kohler with a sigh, his knees jammed uncomfortably against the back of the front seat. 'She got away from the two of you on that Saturday, didn't she?'

There was no answer. There hadn't been a word from either of them. The taller one was behind the wheel and solidly filling that seat, the one with the bullfrog neck, the shoulders and the gun feeding lighted cigarettes to himself and his partner.

They weren't taking him back to the Textilfabrikschrijen. They were heading off into the hills to the northwest of town and with the headlamps unblinkered, were taking him to the vineyards near Kaysersberg, but first they'd ask him a few questions. 'She knew that *Karneval* like the palm of her hand, didn't she?' he taunted. '*Ach*, just when you thought you had her cornered, the little *Schlampe* would slip away. The Devil's Saucer, Maze of Darkness, Super Car Monte Carlo . . . She wasn't about to let you kill her, was she, so she grabbed her skis and buggered off as soon as darkness fell but you knew she loved to find things and that she'd have to come back, and you knew that either of her friends on that committee could easily have sat down beside her, pretending to have found a little something she wanted, but that was on Sunday, wasn't it?'

Kohler was just pissing about, said Hervé Paulus to himself. He'd light another Gauloise bleu for Serge and see if this Kripo had figured out how they'd come upon such a supply. Burnt, ground parsnips for coffee? A lovely oil from beechnuts? 'Floaters'—hadn't Kohler told the woman he and St-Cyr worked in the 'never-never land of shadows'? 'Missing persons,' Frau Oberkircher had blubbered. 'Fraud and bank robberies,' she had coughed and crapped herself.

He and St-Cyr had even hired a horse-drawn sleigh to take the old bag home from the railway station. Home to fruit leathers and boiled sweets she could no longer make to sell to schoolchildren!

'That girl fingered you, didn't she?' said Kohler. 'She stole mug shots of you so that Schrijen's daughter could get a better bead on the two of you, but what I can't understand, *meine Schatzen,* is why he had you follow his daughter and not Renée Ekkehard. Chairperson of this and that, wasn't she, this Sophie of his? Paragon of Nazi virtue and favourite of Gauleiter Wagner?'

'Silence!' shrilled Paulus. 'You're some treasure yourself! Refusing to tell Herr Schrijen what he wishes to know? Looking for trouble when he told you there couldn't possibly be any? Are you too stupid to listen to someone like that?'

'Hervé, leave it,' muttered the other one. 'We'll find a place up ahead and soon.'

'*Dummköpfe,*' swore Kohler. 'Renée definitely wasn't what Schrijen wanted for that son of his, so he told you to make it look like a suicide, even to your scribbling a note in lipstick. Where'd you get the war paint, eh? From one of your *Huren*? Hey, you two left things lying around you shouldn't have and guess who found them?'

There wasn't a murmur from either of them, which wasn't good. At least now he knew Schrijen had been telling them what to do, but that could only mean there were others who would be after Louis. 'She was up to mischief, wasn't she, that daughter of his? She didn't like what was going on at the Works. Starving the men while working them to death? Freezing the poor bastards? Unsafe working conditions and no doctor? *Lieber Christus im Himmel,* is it any wonder she rebelled?'

Still they didn't respond but now the car was climbing more steeply into the hills. The rear wheels skidded, clouds hid the moon, but with the snow cover there was still sufficient light. Vineyards were on either side. They couldn't be far from the house now, but they'd have to stop first, have to soften up this Kripo.

'This will do, Hervé,' said the one behind the wheel. Banks of plowed-up snow lay on either side and, of course, there was no one else about.

'I don't need to take a piss.'

'When we're done with you, *mein Lieber,* you will,' said Serge Deiss. He would leave the engine running, would let Hervé get out first and then pull the back of the seat forward for this *Schweinebulle* from Paris.

One lead-weighted leather truncheon, taken from the floor, came softly to rest on top of the car and was slid over to the driver's side, the other kept to hand. 'Look, I'll stay here. I've no need to get out.'

'Don't be difficult,' said Deiss. 'We have our orders.'

Both now had their guns out. '*Ach,* my shoelace has come undone. Hang on a minute.'

The wind was down, the silence of the carnival absolute. On the ring of keys Hermann had taken from Sophie Schrijen's desk there were those to the executive offices and others in the administration block, but also those to various sheds and storerooms, even one to the garage, no doubt, and those to the houses in town and in the country. And if left once in haste on that desk of her brother's, could they not have been left another time and copied by that combine's assistant machinist so that doors that needed to be opened for trinitrophenol could be, or was her association with Eugène Thomas so trusting she simply let him borrow her keys when needed? Certainly she would miss them, but would she ask Frau Macher if they'd been seen, would she dare to ask that father of hers, since by now she must have realized who had taken them?

Six others, all nearly identical, were to the padlocks on the wagons here, only two of which they had yet been in and yes, Renée Ekkehard must have had a set of her own, though no mention had been made of them by Colonel Rasche. Had he taken them; had her killer?

The bread was hard, coarse, sour, and being dry, rather difficult to swallow. Gripping the chunk between his teeth, he found the appropriate key and, ignoring the Wehrmacht no-entry notice, removed the padlock only to pause, to listen again and to look over a shoulder. The bare branches of the Kastenwald being nearby, one could not help but think of that girl going in there on skis, but had she done so in the afternoon of that Saturday or only after dark, and why, please, had she been out all night, if not to escape her killer or killers?

With the wagon's door tightly closed behind him and one of the full-length, heavily framed mirrors leaning against it for good measure, the coffin screws came undone and its lid was gently drawn halfway back.

'So that I can use it as a table,' he said. 'We haven't much time, mademoiselle. I greatly fear we are about to have company.'

Her face was now more livid and swollen, the lips of a darker plum-purple. Decay would be rapid if she was allowed to warm. The blotches would meld and take on iridescent hues, the sprays of petechiae also; the once sea-green eyes that must have been lovely and full of life would soon collapse and drain.

More flecks of gilding and sawdust had fallen into them, and for this he apologized. 'An autopsy,' he muttered. 'We absolutely must have one but are being denied it.'

Setting the bread aside, he opened Hermann's little sack and arranged everything on the lid. 'Boudicca,' he said of the carving. '*Bien sûr,* nothing seems new in this world of ours, does it? Stripped of her family's holdings by the Romans, she objected loudly to the loss and was publically flogged naked and forced to watch as her daughters were raped. In rebellion, she rose up to lead most of the Celtic tribes of the British Isles against them. Camulodunum, the Roman capital, fell and was sacked and burned, other hillforts and settlements too, their collaborationist Celts put to the sword, and then Londinium, but in A.D. 62 she was betrayed, it is said, by one of her own. Rather than suffer capture, she and her daughters took poison. Three females, mademoiselle. The number three just keeps turning up, doesn't it? Three ravens, the three of you on that *Winterhilfswerk* Committee?'

He would give her a moment, would run his eyes down these stained scraps of newspaper Hermann had gathered from the living quarters of those men, would smooth each of them out.

'As a boy of five I was rather sickly,' he said, for sometimes it helped to recount such things to a victim. 'Cod-liver oil was of no use, iron tonics neither, and not just the stone-filings from a carpenter's nail. Fifteen francs a bottle my dear papa paid for that stuff. Weeks in bed were prescribed. "He needs rest," the doctor said, giving my poor mother little to hope for but a lifetime of nursing, and *grand-maman* little patience. "Courage," she said to *maman*. "Don't flood the house with your tears. The boy can't swim though I've warned him he'd best learn."

'She read to me.' He indicated the carving. 'Of course at such a tender age the word *defilement* meant little, but to be stripped and flogged by an enemy was sufficient for what my grandmother most wanted to implant. That wherever oppression exists, there will be those who rise up against it. *Boudicca* is from the Celtic word *bouda*, meaning *victory*, mademoiselle. In English, the equivalent name is, of course, Victoria. Many of those from Lille, and from Brittany too, have Celtic/Gallic ancestors. Was it the assistant machinist who carved this as he did the buttons for the waistcoat the colonel was having made? A boar, a stag, a salmon . . . these too.'

He set Thomas's wedding ring and one of the spoons down on the lid. 'Let's admit that this artist and artisan remembered the centuries of his ancestors, but what is more important, did so deliberately and not just to improve the lives of his comrades. And as to his having instructed you in such things, though you loved the woods, you constantly felt a forbidding presence, and in this the colonel was, I believe, telling us the truth.'

Three ravens, three crows . . . The Phantom Queen.

'The supreme goddess of all that is perverse and horrible amongst the powers of the supernatural. My second wife was a Breton and at times very superstitious, as are many Bretons.'

Morr'igan . . .

'And Badhbh, the Crow-Raven, and Nemhain, that of Frenzy and Panic. There are always the three, though really they are but one and the same.'

Morr'igan. But showing herself as three solitary ravens or crows.

'Was it that assistant machinist who pumped you full of Celtic mythology? More importantly, please, why did he do so? Admit it, you were desperately afraid, mademoiselle. You knew that what you and the other two were involved in could only end in disaster, but did he and the others then find out and plan to use it for themselves?'

Sophie was being followed. . . .

'That father of hers learned what the three of you were up to, didn't he? That is why those two detectives of the colonel's came and took my partner.'

But did Colonel Rasche also find out? Did Werner and Yvonne? A *Winterhilfswerk* fête, a little *Karneval* of our own?

Games of chance, target shooting and a *Jeu de massacre?* A Bottle Fish . . .

The carving of the chariot and its rider had a short round peg under it and could not be set quite upright. 'My partner and I haven't had a chance to discuss things thoroughly, mademoiselle. There are still things he knows that I don't; those that I do, and he doesn't.'

Opening the cutthroat which must have come from that barbershop for it was every bit the same, he flashed its blade and asked, 'Did you know of this? Come, come, you weren't exactly the blithe spirit you wanted others to perceive.'

Staring at the ceiling, surrounded by hideously garish masks, murals and distorting mirrors, she lay silent.

He'd sigh, then, thought St-Cyr, and say, 'You didn't know about this razor, did you? You're as shocked as I am that those five men for whom you and Victoria and Sophie would risk so much, should in turn contemplate betraying you with something like this. Admit it, mademoiselle, of all of those five men, Eugène Thomas had the best chance of taking it, since he had the confidence of Sophie Schrijen.'

The Primastella's engine didn't idle well. Each time the engine faltered, the beams from its headlamps would dim and a breath would be held, but then the damned things would brighten.

'You should have that looked at,' said Kohler. Caught in the light, he waited, facing them, and as they advanced, their shadows were thrown ahead of them: pulled-down fedoras first and then the rest; Gauloises bleues being sucked on, tobacco smoke drifting into the cold night air, the one much taller, bigger in every way than the other who was to the right. '*Ach*, can't we talk this over?'

They hesitated. A split second passed, but on they came and well apart. The tall one would start it, the shorter one would wait but momentarily. Breath billowed—his own. Light from the car was blinding him. Silent still, they drew closer. Both cudgels would now be raised. The tall one would hit first and high—the left shoulder or forearm. The other one would try for the back of the right calf or knee. They would want him to fall over.

The headlamps dimmed, the engine coughed. Kohler lunged at the tall one, grabbed the cudgel in mid-stroke, felt the jar of it, the pain, found himself slipping, losing balance as he cried out. Over and over they rolled, fists flailing, hands grabbing, forehead trying to smash him and smash him. The bastard was too strong, too heavy. An ear was bitten, eyes were gouged, blood tasted, a hand thrust under a bristled chin to force the head to stop butting him, the other one's truncheon glancing off a shoulder. Now his back was being clobbered and instinctively each time it was hit, it arched, causing him to lose his grip.

From one side of the road to the other, they rolled, grabbing, choking, punching, struggling, the tall one trying desperately to tear the shoelace from around his throat but the cord cut too deeply.

Knees jammed hard against the son of a bitch's back, Kohler spat hard and tried to avoid the other one's truncheon, had best kill this one. Couldn't avoid it. *Verdammt!*

'Don't!' yelled Hervé Paulus, backing away a little. 'Serge, I'll try to get him to stop.'

Arms flailed, eyes bulged, the tall one's struggling began to slacken . . . 'Toss that thing of yours away. Don't and I really will kill him.'

'Serge . . .' hazarded the shorter one, pitching the truncheon to the road but not far enough.

'Your gun,' managed Kohler, catching ragged breaths as the weapon bounced and skidded to the edge of the road but didn't bury itself in the snow like it should have. 'Now go and put your hands flat on the bonnet of the car. Stand with your back to us.'

They weren't done with Kohler, swore Hervé Paulus. Serge would get his breath back and come at him when he least expected it. And then Kohler would get a fistful of handcuffs in the mouth. They would both fall on him and beat him senseless.

Coughing, his chest heaving, Serge Deiss toppled over and lay there repeatedly flexing himself into the fetal position as he clawed at his throat. Blood from his right ear stained the snow and oh for sure, it wasn't good, that ear, thought Kohler. They would really hate him now, these two, the Kolmar SS as well and even Kramer at Natzweiler-Struthof.

The flame of the lantern stirred but otherwise there wasn't a sound. Though he listened hard, St-Cyr swore he could hear nothing. The wagon was indeed like an ancient, albeit garishly decorated and cluttered tomb—a long barrow of its own, he thought, remembering the Gallic and pre-Gallic tumuli and standing stones of the Quiberon Peninsula and the Morbihan in Brittany.

'*Ah, bon,* mademoiselle, a crudely fashioned coat-hood with its insulation of daily newspapers. Inoffensive and logical enough under cursory examination, nor does it matter particularly if the hood was that of Eugène Thomas instead of one of the others, but did he often go into Sophie Schrijen's office? Isn't that where he first discovered these newspapers? "Karen is at the age where she desires children."

Loves Wagner, mademoiselle? "Beate is blonde." Likes *Das Rheingold* and *Die Walküre*, from Wagner's magnificent tetralogy, *Der Ring des Nibelungen*? Wants a man, a lover who will appreciate the same? "Guidance" is needed. In each of these personal messages it's more or less the same, yet they are separated by many others and by time and location from city to city forcing me to ask, Is this how you three were contacted?'

She gave no answer. Quickly he glanced over the lid of the coffin. The carving was to the left, then the personals columns and that partly masticated papier-mâché ball. The phosphorescent swastika button was next, after it the desperate bead of solder Hermann had found and the weeks and months of secrecy and planning it must imply.

Spread open at its torn page, the school notebook of Victoria Bödicker made him murmur. '*Bouda*, Munich, the *Münchner Neueste Nachrichten* and freedom.'

Again St-Cyr read the chemical equations for viscose rayon and the single formula for picric acid. 'It was Raymond Maillotte who wrote this last, wasn't it? He came into the lab to lean over Eugène Thomas and remind him of it. Only he and Thomas had passes to be there.'

Again she offered nothing. 'There are also these,' he said. 'The tip of the glass ampoule that cut my partner's finger and the earring that was taken from that biscuit tin, most probably to distract you. And then, there are these.'

He held up the three delicately stemmed liqueur glasses, but did not ask who had sat down beside her in that other wagon. Instead he said, 'Those men were planning a breakout, mademoiselle, but for some reason Eugène Thomas refused to do what they had asked of him which is unfortunate, for they could not have known of the pistol Sophie Schirijen keeps in the glove compartment of her brother's car when that one is not around, and yes, she would not have told anyone of it, not when desperately afraid for her life. Which leaves us with the cutthroat, doesn't it? And an explosion. A big one.'

Frau Oberkircher's suitcase had never been much, yet as he took it from the Primastella, Kohler remembered he had gotten such a kick out of talking to her on the train. It had really felt like coming home, like it used to be.

And now? he wondered as he set the case on the bonnet. 'Now what have you two done to her, a war widow well into her sixties?'

'Contraband,' spat Hervé Paulus. 'She was planning to sell them on the black market.'

The son of a bitch had tried to smash this Kripo with *Polizeikommandantur* bracelets and had found he couldn't. Legs spread widely for balance, hands now cuffed behind them, the colonel's two detectives sat in the faltering light from the headlamps. Fedoras were lying about, coat buttons were missing, blood was splashed everywhere, that ear of Serge Deiss's now so cold the bleeding had all but stopped, though it still must hurt like hell.

He would open the suitcase and see what they'd done, would say, 'If you've harmed her, I really will have to leave you to freeze to death. Then I'll come back to remove the bracelets and let the car go off the road so as to make it look like an accident.'

They'd been helping themselves to her cigarettes. Sick with apprehension, he turned to look at them.

Alarmed, Deiss shouted, 'Kohler, be reasonable.'

'Why should I? What did you have her doing? Watching the street for you?'

'And the comings and goings at that bookshop.'

He would pick up a truncheon with each hand, would simply ask, 'For how long?'

'Kohler, listen. Back off, will you?' said Paulus shrilly and spitting blood.

'Look, I want an answer. Don't force me to use these.'

It was Deiss who yelled, 'Only since you and St-Cyr got off the train with her but why did Rasche ask for the two of you? He had to have a reason, didn't he?'

'A man who walks over corpses,* Kohler,' said Paulus, his left eye now closed. 'One who doesn't want autopsies done?'

They'd get Kohler going now, thought Deiss. 'He finds that secretary of his missing on a Saturday afternoon but doesn't bother to look for her until the following Tuesday?'

'Returns to the *Karneval* to open that box he had made for her and sits with her for hours, when another suicide turns up? Finally calls Paris?' said Paulus.

'Doesn't want those French POWs to be taken to the quarry camp. Is afraid of what they'll reveal under reinforced interrogation,' shouted Deiss.

'There has to be a reason,' managed Paulus, having to spit out a tooth.

'Ask yourself why that colonel of yours didn't leave it at a suicide, Kohler?' said Deiss. 'Ask why he had to claim it was murder. What could he possibly have hoped to gain?'

'Rasche has a daughter at the University of Strassburg in Clermont-Ferrand,' said Paulus.

'The daughter he had by Yvonne Eva Ellemann, now Lutze,' said Deiss.

---

* ruthless, shows no mercy

'Maybe the Detektiv should ask himself what Frau Elleman-Lutze hopes most to hide, Serge?' asked Paulus.

'No request for the *Sippenforscher* at the Office of Racial Affairs? No check back through the ancestors as is required by law?'

'Three generations at least, isn't it, Serge, before the *Sippenbuch* can be given if clean?'

The record book laying out a family's lineage to prove it Aryan. They had worked it all out.

'That of the daughter too, Kohler,' said Hervé Paulus. 'Those students and their professors at the University of Strassburg in Clermont-Ferrand are a hotbed of trouble the Gestapo there are most anxious to stamp out.'

This was true enough and they'd known it too.

'Is Geneviève Rasche-Lutze one of the *Mischlinge*?' taunted Deiss.

The mixed offspring of a Jew and a non-Jew.

'Bad for the colonel if true, Serge,' said Paulus. 'Guilty of racial disgrace which can only lead to a court-martial.'

But that fire at Colmar's town hall during the Blitzkrieg had put all of the records up in smoke. These two couldn't prove a thing and neither could Löwe Schrijen, but these days did that really matter, and why should Schrijen feel he had to prove anything unless, of course, he had damned well found out what that daughter of his and her friends had really been up to?

'Don't leave us, Kohler. *Bitte*, there are wolves,' managed Deiss, the one with the bullfrog neck.

'*Ach*, don't worry. The Generaldirektor will take care of you both, not only for failing to soften me up as ordered, but for drawing attention to him he can't afford. Not with friends like the Gauleiter Wagner, and with a son in the SS at Natzweiler-Struthof and a daughter who is chairperson of this and that and one hell of a lot else. Just jump up and down. Then I can tell him you won't freeze to death.'

It wasn't far. From the smokehouse, they would soon enough find, came an aroma that was hard to resist, from the stoves in the house, the perfume of seasoned beech. Schrijenhaus, Löweshaus or whatever Schrijen called it, was at the end of the road among spruce and pine and not like many in Alsace, not one of a cluster, but isolated. Half-timbered, one storey and an attic, it had a railed, narrow porch under the overhang of a steeply pitched and stepped roof across which moonlight, having broken fee of layered cloud, shone.

The house was at least a hundred years old. Nothing ostentatious, thought Kohler. Just solid comfort and tradition.

Down over the vineyards which crowded close, lay the Plain of the Rhine Valley, and well to the southeast, the carnival, the Kastenwald and Louis. To the west and here, too, at their edge, were the Vosges and a route through to France if one had the stamina and guts, and wasn't the isolation perfect? No dogs had challenged him and that was a puzzle. No lights shone but that was normal these days. Schrijen's black Mercedes had been parked in the drive shed next to the stables, but there'd been no sign of the tourer. Had the daughter gone out to the *Karneval*?

Most of the help would live a short distance away at the farmstead, but there'd been no dogs there either and no one had come out, though they must have heard the car. Had Schrijen given them a night off, they taking one of the horse-drawn sleighs into Kaysersberg or Kientzheim? Only the geese had given warning of this Kripo. Was Schrijen deliberately keeping the dogs close until needed?

That, too, was a worry. Behind the floor-to-ceiling black-out drape that hung just inside the front door, the entrance foyer was crowded with boots, coats, skis, trout rods, creels and hip-waders. Had Rasche been a frequent visitor, his secretary with him?

Anoraks, mittens, scarves, gloves and *bleus de travail* were here with rucksacks too. Father, son and daughter—it was almost too easy to tell them apart. Of all, the daughter's was the most worn and it seemed clear enough that she must spend time alone hiking in the forest, but then he found, under an anorak, another worn rucksack, and yet another and had to ask, *Renée Ekkehard and Victoria Bödicker*?

No one had thought to remove them. Pruning clippers lay on a side table. Bundles of vine cuttings were in the wood box near the tiled stove, a freshened stack of sawmill slab-waste too. A man, then, who liked his comforts yet liked to get back to the land.

The corridor wasn't long but in semidarkness with here and there a rack of staghorn beneath which were framed photos of past hunts, past harvests, too, *les vendanges*, and through the far door, light enough to see a cabinet with shotguns and sporting rifles under the shaggy head of a magnificent wild boar whose curved tusks gave warnings of their own.

Leather club chairs sat about the ample room with scattered throw rugs. Oil paintings of standing and reclining nudes hung between superb racks of antlers. Voluptuous girls; turn of the century—from a brothel? he wondered.

A plain, dark green, long-necked bottle of the Riesling had been uncorked. Two glasses lay on the pewter tray next to it, the one on its side and broken at the stem, with droplets of blood nearby on the cloth, and a spill of wine.

Another bottle, one of those pale, washed-out blue unlabelled things the French kept and had used for centuries was not on the tray. An *eau-de-vie* or marc and reminder of that wagon at the *Karneval*.

Schrijen, who had been watching him all this time, was sitting behind a plain wooden table, cigar smoke in the air and one old dog, an arthritic Doberman pinscher, on the floor at his feet, its sad eyes taking in this Kripo, only to then glance questioningly up at its master.

'Well, Kohler, you continue to surprise me. Those two idiots won't freeze to death, will they?

'Generaldirektor . . .'

'Löwe. Please grant me that. I'm at home here.'

'Your daughter's in trouble. Those two were told by you to follow her.'

'To keep her out of it.'

'Safe from herself?'

'If necessary.'

Lead soldiers filled a nearby vitrine: shelf after shelf of the Kaiser's uhlans—his cavalry armed with lances and a reputation that had, by 1914, made them legendary. Dragoons too, and horse-drawn artillery. 'The Crown Prince Wilhelm's hussars also,' said Kohler. 'The Death's Head, though the name's since been borrowed, hasn't it?' And hadn't Sophie Schrijen had one of them in that desk drawer of her brother's?

Its place in the vitrine had yet to be refilled and was glaringly empty, though it could have been filled so easily before this war. A symbol, then. A constant reminder?

'Those were mine and then my son's,' said Schrijen, still watching him closely. 'Alain was always allowed the only key, but one day lost it.'

'Your daughter . . .'

Kohler had been through that desk. 'Told the boy it must be

in the secret hiding place he kept from all eyes but his own and that he had simply forgotten where that was.'

'And the Death's Head colonel that's missing? She took it, didn't she?'

Kohler could think what he liked, but would never learn that the boy had come upon his sister and one of the girls that had then been employed as housemaids, that Alain had seen the two timidly kissing in one of the barns, and had informed on them as was only right and proper. Nor would he learn that the girl had been taught a lesson she would never forget and had been sent to live with distant relatives. 'That lead soldier was never found. Miata,' he said softly to the Doberman. 'It's all right, dearest. Herr Kohler will put away the pistol he took from one of those men. You've no need to fret.'

'Miata?'

'It's a Japanese family name. A visiting delegation of textile manufacturers from Kyoto came through early in '29 when my friend here was newborn. One of them was quite taken with her and kept calling her Miata-san, Fräulein Miata. The name stuck, which showed how intelligent was my choice. Try as I did, though, I couldn't get her to come unless I said *Miata*. She can hardly walk now. I should have her put down but can't bring myself to arrange it. Alain needed our Alsatians at the quarry. Magnificent animals Miata tolerated but barely, but what can one do these days? I couldn't refuse the boy.'

And no dogs to cause a fuss if deserters were being moved through to the west but he'd better be sure of it. 'You've no hounds?'

Kohler indicated the boar's head but did he think him a fool to have missed the trend of thought? 'Not at present. We still hunt, of course. Now why don't you take off that greatcoat and sit down? You're making Miata nervous. That's bad for her heart.'

There was an enlarged photograph of the daughter at the age of ten. A funeral, the kid grief-stricken, skinny and trying hard not to cry. The blonde hair had been braided into a diadem, the photo a constant reminder of her new and vastly increased responsibilities to the family. Nearby there was another of her in a shift, mortified and trying hard to smile while standing with her back up against the wall, her height being measured by some doctor who had his hands on her. The brother, in his underpants, was laughing at her.

There was a map of the vineyards, the house, farmstead and forest, including streams and a lake. Hunting trails were clearly marked, as were the locations of three *Jagdstande,* three hides.

'Archery,' said Kohler.

He and St-Cyr must have discovered that too. 'My Sophie took it up for relaxation.'

'As did Renée Ekkehard and Victoria Bödicker?'

'Kohler, what have those men who were helping them been up to?'

'When we know, we'll tell you.'

'*Ach,* don't try my patience. Prisoner 220374 was sentenced to death by his comrades. Haven't I a right to know the reason and you a duty to tell me?'

'There are two glasses on that tray, Generaldirektor, and we both need answers. Where is she?'

'My Sophie? Available as always. Now look . . .'

'No, you look. My partner and I believe Renée Ekkehard was drugged and then hanged, and maybe we've a good idea who did it and why, and maybe we don't, but before I say anything further, who have you sent to that *Karneval* to take care of Louis?'

Such concern was touching, and hadn't Paris's Gestapo warned of it? 'No one, *mein Lieber*. Why should I trouble myself when there are others who desperately want silence?'

'Colonel Rasche?'

Deiss and Paulus had at least accomplished something. 'I think you and that partner of yours will discover that suddenly our Otto regrets entirely having asked for you, and that he has much to hide and knows others are now fully aware of this and will use it if necessary.'

They really were at each other's throats. 'Is Werner Lutze with him?'

'His Oberfeldwebel, his constant companion, the one who takes care of so much? Now sit, please. Have a shot of our schnapps. Sophie . . . Sophie, *mein kleiner Liebling*,' he called out. 'There is no need for you to find refreshed bandages and iodine. Herr Kohler can't possibly have cut himself on that barbed wire as Lagerfeldwebel Dorsche has insisted, but bring a little snack for our guest. The *Hiriwursch*—pork and beef sausage I smoke myself, Kohler. The *Schiffala* also, the pork shoulder with the hash potatoes. My cook, one of the farm's women, is always most generous. Some sauerkraut too, Sophie, and the *Zewelewai*, an onion flan. Coffee afterward and strong. He looks hungry and probably is.'

They were at the door of the wagon and St-Cyr knew there was no stopping them. Torch in hand, Rasche entered in what would have been a shower of glass had the mirror not been caught. 'KOHLER . . . WHERE IS KOHLER?' he demanded. Oberfeldwebel Lutze was right behind him, a Schmeisser crooked in his good arm.

'Taken.'

'SCHRIJEN?'

'Apparently.'

'Werner, those two must have come for him.'

'Your detectives,' said St-Cyr. 'I had no chance to stop them. Neither of us were armed.'

'Why was Eugène Thomas sentenced to death by the others? Come, come, don't waste my time!'

'We're not certain. Hermann and I really haven't had much of a chance to . . .'

'Do you think I'm a fool? What did Kohler find in that cage of theirs? Did Dorsche miss something?'

'This, I think, and these.'

A carving and a wad of wet newspaper. 'Anything else?'

'Are they not enough, Colonel?'

'That bead of solder?'

'When and if Hermann and I are able to . . .'

'Kaysersberg,' muttered Rasche, but would Kohler have been forced to tell Diess and Paulus everything? 'What's all the rest of this rubbish?'

The bits and pieces were indicated. 'Evidence, Colonel. My pockets always seem to carry a bankroll of it just as did those of your second victim.'

'Werner, close the door. Let's hear what this one has to say.'

Rasche nudged the glossy peak of his cap up and let his dark blue eyes flick over everything, missing nothing now. 'Renée Ekkehard, Colonel. You lied to us. You knew she was coming out here on that Saturday because you had telephoned the Fräulein Schrijen to arrange a ride for the girl.'

Mirrors tossed her reflection back and forth, distorting her even more hideously, thought Rasche. They made the eagle and swastika on his cap expand only to quickly contract and fold in on itself as he set the torch down on the coffin lid and took out his pipe and tobacco pouch, then found his matches.

'That telephone call, Colonel . . .'

'I was detained. Something had come up.'

'What, exactly?'

'We had learned that Alain Schrijen was to arrive unexpectedly on the early afternoon train. As Kommandant, I'm not without my sources. Stationmaster Krencker and I often go fishing.'

'And?'

'As I had some business to discuss with the boy but had said I would drive his fiancée out to the *Karneval*, I then had to find her a lift. The Fräulein Schrijen said it would be no problem, that the firm had a lorry in the garage. She then apologized for any inconvenience she might have caused by her not being able to go there herself as planned.'

And what would Renée have whispered had she been alive? wondered St-Cyr: You see not only how he gets around things, Inspector, but how he has emphasized who really was responsible. Aren't *boy*, *fiancée*, *lorry* and *planned* all well chosen? 'And this business you had with the Untersturmführer-SS Schrijen, Colonel?'

'The Gauleiter Wagner, myself and the Generaldirektor Schrijen are to officiate at the opening ceremonies of the *Winterhilfswerk* fund-raiser on Saturday, 6 March, at 1000 hours. Kommandant Zill and Schutzhaftlagerführer Kramer were also to have been included but through some oversight on the Fräulein Ekkehard's part, the pressures of work perhaps, an invitation had not been sent. Wanting to correct the matter, I was going to ask the Untersturmführer-SS Schrijen to personally carry my formal invitation and apology to the quarry camp on his return the following day, Sunday, that is, 31 January.'

Clearly the colonel is no ordinary adversary, is he, Inspector? she would have whispered. 'Wanting to correct the matter,' and avoid any unpleasantness? *'Boy,'* now becomes Untersturmführer-SS but the colonel doesn't blink an eye at your having corrected him? He even reminds you of the date of leaving so that you will think what you must. Werner is watching everything too, isn't he? Ready at a moment's notice and ever loyal but would he do things to protect his colonel that even that one hadn't sanctioned? Isn't *this* what you are now wondering?

St-Cyr was still waiting for more, thought Rasche, and had let a hand come to rest on the edge of the *verdammt* box, forcing him to look at her again; therefore it would have to be said plainly. 'Unfortunately I was detained and when I got to the station, the Untersturmführer-SS had already left in his car. The Fräulein Schrijen was, however, still waiting for a bus and only too glad to take the invitation to her brother. I was able to offer her a lift back to the Works but she declined. A matter of some errands in town, I think. I then returned to my office at the *Polizeikommandantur*.'

Step by step, Inspector, the Mademoiselle Ekkehard would have said, thought St-Cyr, but notice, please, how he has deliberately left out any mention of Sophie's being greatly distressed and nearly in tears. Alain suddenly arrives and there has to be a change of plan? She has to give up the use of his car, must drive it to the station when it's badly needed, has to then send me to the carnival instead and has to wait for a *bus* not knowing what must happen?

And now a hand-delivered message to Natzweiler-Struthof when of course the *Polizeikommandantur*'s telex or telephone would have done just as well. 'Colonel, by your own admission, you didn't bother to search for the Fräulein Ekkehard until the following Tuesday. Forgive the persistence, but I find that hard to believe.'

There must be no hesitation. 'I sent Werner out to look for her.'

'When?'

'At about 1600 hours on that Saturday, the thirtieth of last month.'

And again he's taking care to give you the times, Inspector, and emphasize the date, but didn't Sophie tell you that the lorry from the Works returned here at about 5.00 and waited a good half-hour, its driver repeatedly honking the horn? *Bien sûr,* Herr Lutze could have left by then, but please don't forget that a man like the colonel is inevitably one step ahead. 'And yet you told us that Herr Lutze and his wife were quietly asking around town if anyone had seen her?'

Momentary shadows from the lantern kept flickering over Renée's reflection, St-Cyr knowing only too well that this could not be missed. 'I had my reasons. I knew Werner hadn't been able to find her. Instead . . . *Ach,* Oberfeldwebel Lutze, be so good as to enlighten him.'

You see how he'll play it every way he can, Inspector, the girl would have whispered. He'll bounce it off his sergeant, off the mirrors, too, that you've forced him to watch. Now a hard, if distorted glance at them, now a deep frown as some further thought comes, but notice, please, that he has completely forgotten to pack and light that pipe of his. And Werner? you ask. Werner feels his colonel is taking care of things but wonders why you made a point of saying neither yourself nor Herr Kohler had been armed. Were your weapons still at the house, in that grip of yours? he wonders. One that Frau Lutze must surely have gone through.

'*Ach,* come, come, Werner, tell him.'

'*Jawhol,* Oberst. The Untersturmführer's tourer had been parked well up among the ruins here and next to this wagon's House of Mirrors. I felt that he might have trouble getting the car out, as the snow then was quite deep, and that he must have been in a hurry, since he is usually very careful with such things.'

Careful with that car, Inspector, she seemed to ask, or with murder?

'He had gone into the woods after her,' said Lutze, watching him closely. 'On foot, Inspector, the girl on skis.'

It has to be asked, she seemed to whisper. Please don't avoid it, Inspector. 'And how, precisely, did you get here yourself?'

'Our police van was the only spare vehicle,' sighed Rasche. 'From the woods Renée would have heard and most probably seen it, Alain Schrijen also.'

'And what was she to have thought, Colonel. *Die Grüne Minna** and immediate arrest?'

'*Ach*, I admit, in retrospect, that I should have been more circumspect and given Werner the use of my own vehicle, one that girl would easily have recognized and come to without being alarmed.'

'Of arrest, Colonel, but for what, please?'

'For what I have since been forced to believe they might well have been up to.'

'They?'

'Those three girls to whom I had granted so much.'

'And is that why you removed her toque and replaced it with her beret?'

'Which the little fool had in her pocket.'

Sophie Schrijen, those grey-blue eyes of hers wary, had braided her hair as in the photo of herself at the age of ten. There had been recent tears—Kohler was certain of this—and just as cer-

* the Green Maria, the equivalent of the Black Maria

tainly she was still extremely upset and terrified, probably, of what was to come and of what this father of hers could well do. After all, it wasn't every day that two detectives were hired to beat another into submission, not every day a man you had worked with and trusted to fix up *Karneval* things deliberately climbed the wire to end his life.

Resilient she might normally have to be, but now she was like the proverbial eggs in a *résistante's* carrier-basket as her bicycle was stopped at a control and her papers demanded.

The dress and full white linen apron were much like those of Yvonne Lutze, the neck-chain with its cross the same as when he had first encountered her. Even Miata sensed that she was far from self-assured and sorrowfully watched her as slices of oven-warm *Kugelhupf* gave off their aroma.

Stopping her from leaving, Kohler noticed the bandaged cut the broken wine glass had caused, then the shock the nearness of him brought, and as it passed through her, the instant of panic and revulsion.

'What is it?' she demanded.

'*Ach*, forgive me, but I want to get something clear. What was so important at the Works that you had to send Renée Ekkehard out to the *Karneval* instead of yourself?'

'Eugène was experiencing difficulties with one of the dye batches. One can't shut down a Works like ours. It stops for nothing.'

'And the problem?'

'The strike-offs—swatches of coloured cloth Eugène had done. He couldn't get any of them to match the shade Raymond had recommended. Dress fabrics are sometimes not easy.'

'Printed patterns, Kohler, for summer wear.'

'For next year's season in Berlin, *Vati*. Why not tell him that?'

'*Liebling . . .*'

'The depth of colour wasn't clean, Inspector, nor bright enough. Sharp outlines are necessary, otherwise the pattern becomes blurred. You can't have a dye that bleeds. Consistency across larger areas—the blotches we call them—is also critical.'

Realizing that her cheeks had reddened under his scrutiny, she caught a breath. 'We use synthetic dyes. Ciba-Geigy, Durand and Huguenin. They're in Basel—others, too, when we can get them. I did go to the railway station to pick up some we were having sent from a supplier, but that didn't take more than an hour. Eugène and I then worked on things until well after 5.00 that afternoon. 6.00 probably.'

'While Renée . . .'

She winced, could not have avoided it. 'Look, I don't know who killed her or why. How could I?'

But still feel you could have been the victim yourself. Herr Kohler didn't say this. Instead, he asked, 'Would Victoria Bödicker?'

'Have killed her? *Ach*, I meant to say, *have known* who did? I can't see how. I telephoned the shop to ask if she would go out there but Victoria said that she couldn't. Frau Oberkircher, her neighbour, was away and couldn't fill in for her. A customer was coming to collect a book. An SS major.'

It had sounded so futile, felt Sophie. Herr Kohler would demand the name of the major and the title of the book.

'Her brother-in-law's funeral,' she heard him saying of Frau Oberkircher.

'I . . . I had to ask Renée to go. There wasn't anyone else I could turn to.'

'Couldn't it have waited until the following day?'

That Sunday. She must force herself not to glance at *Vati*, must try to be calm and self-assured. 'We had a deadline to meet with the *Karneval,* and still have, Inspector. As it is, not everything we need will be ready.'

'The *Jeu de massacre?*'

Why had he chosen it? 'That and the shooting galleries, the Hall of Mirrors also, and Wheel of Fortune.'

'The Bottle Fish?'

The look she gave was swift. 'That too, and . . . and the Ring Toss.'

'*Liebling,* I know this is all very unsettling for you,' interjected Schrijen, 'but could Colonel Rasche's secretary have been involved in something?'

'Something illegal, Father? What, please?'

He'd say it gently, thought Schrijen, would go on as if Sophie hadn't known a thing and would use gestures to soften the impact. 'She took things into the *Arbeitslager,* Sophie. Only little things, of course. Bits of string, carpenter's nails, buttons, bread from time to time and cigarettes. It was foolish of her, but . . .'

'Of this I know nothing, *Vati.* Is Lagerfeldwebel Dorsche trying to blame me for something I could not possibly have had any connection with?'

'Not at all, dearest.'

'Then did Victoria give her things to take in there for her, since she didn't have a pass to the Works? Well, did she?'

'Your friends, Sophie . . .'

'They were *not* my friends! They were associates. People with whom I had to work.'

'Yes, yes, of course. Perhaps it is, though, that Herr Kohler can enlighten us further. One murder, if indeed it really was, and we'll never know, will we, unless Kommandant Rasche agrees to an autopsy, which I very much doubt.'

And one suicide, *Vati?* wondered Sophie, but he went on

with, 'Now another death for the colonel to explain in his weekly reports to Berlin and to Kommandant Zill at Natzweiler-Struthof, Kohler. So again I must ask, what were the men of that combine up to? Blood on your hand and yet no cut across its back or palm? Blood from Prisoner 220374's mouth, I think.'

What had he coughed up, eh? snorted Kohler silently, and just what had Schrijen said to this daughter of his to make her so wary? 'Blood and brains, Generaldirektor. I needed a moment to myself. That's why I left Dorsche and went into the barracks block washhouse to clean myself up.'

'Where there was a crowd of men.'

And so much for his having a moment to himself, thought Sophie. 'Eugène and the others weren't up to anything, *Vati*. If they had been, he would have told me.'

'But took his own life instead, *meine Liebe*?'

'He had no reason to.'

Mein Gott, but she could be tough when needed, felt Kohler, only to hear Schrijen ask, 'Another of your associates, Sophie? Isn't it true that you spent a lot of time in his company?'

'I had to! Alain would have done the same had he not been away.'

'*Ach*, that is so, of course. Before he volunteered to join the services, Kohler, my son kept in close consultation with the lab, myself also, as I still do. Always it is the lab that has to get things right before production commences.'

'Raymond Maillotte was our fabric designer and test weaver, *Vati*. Where are we to find another? We've orders to fill well into next year. Where will we find another Eugène?'

Gut, the child had come through. 'I'll see to it. I'll put in a call to Gauleiter Wagner who will understand and get on to Berlin for us. A sweep of the Gauleiter Saukel's foreign workers. Somewhere we'll find replacements. For now we have a little time, ten days until the current run is finished. By then they'll be here.

'Now, Kohler, since the colonel's two detectives have yet to arrive on my doorstep, why not bring them in from the cold.'

'They're warm enough in your smokehouse, probably, but I'll go and have a look if you like.'

'You do that and I'll build up the fire.'

8

Grey and congealed, its aroma repulsive to a palate far too sensitive even after two and a half years of Defeat, the glutinous mass of the Wehrmacht's soup glistened in the lantern light but was waxy otherwise and hot like boiled synthetic rubber. The bread was just plain terrible. These two staples—could he call them that? wondered St-Cyr—had fed, and often did, the world's largest and strongest army, but was it still that, the Americans having at last entered the war and the Russians having done the impossible at Stalingrad?

He didn't know—how could he? Boiled onions were here in the stiffened pudding of the soup, salt in plenty, and far too much of it. 'Colonel,' he said dispassionately as he set the galvanized bucket aside, 'why was that beret in her pocket and why, please, did you then put it on her thereby condemning her to an illegal act a coroner or undertaker would most certainly have noted and had to report?'

'First, I didn't know why she would have had it at all, a secretary of mine. Secondly, I removed it when we laid her out here. I wouldn't have said a thing of it but . . .'

'Only to put it on her *after* Eugène Thomas was killed?'

'*Verdammt*, that one was murder too! *Ach*, I'll admit that what I did was impulsive. I was angry. I was certain Alain Schrijen must have had something to do with her death but I couldn't understand the chemist's hanging. *Mein Gott*, why kill such a much-needed man? Löwe Schrijen was aware of how dependent on Thomas that daughter of his had become. I sat with Renée's body in that other wagon for hours trying to sort it all out. It didn't make sense.'

'Admit it, please. You were afraid Löwe Schrijen and his son were about to point the finger at you for having let that *Winterhilfswerk* Committee have the freedom they had, but let's also not forget Frau Lutze and your daughter were at terrible risk.'

Löwe must have told Kohler of them. 'He's a bastard, that man. Families like his always breed them. You've only to meet the son.'

'*Ah, bon*, Colonel. Now, please, by putting the beret on her what did you hope to accomplish?'

Paris had said it would be step by step with St-Cyr. 'I knew Löwe Schrijen would find a way in here to have a look at her, even though I had posted a guard.'

'So you left a warning for him that you knew things weren't right.'

'Then called Paris. I had to have someone I could trust.'

'But, Colonel, you had given Herr Schrijen ample time to have had a look at her *before* putting that beret on her?'

Paris had said this too, that St-Cyr and Kohler would lead one on. '*Ach*, the warning was for yourselves, and for this I apologize.'

'Don't try to avoid it, *mein lieber Oberst*. You knew we had a reputation and that this, if nothing else, would divert Herr Schrijen from yourself and your loved ones, especially if we could prove it really was murder and would then be stupid enough to point the finger at the guilty.'

'Löwe Schrijen and that son of his.'

Now ask him again about the beret, Inspector, whispered Renée, though her coffin had been sealed in that other wagon. 'Was she to have used that beret as a sign to others she hoped to meet, Colonel? Those personal columns that are spread before you. The *Münchner Neueste Nachrichten*?'

'Yes, yes, Wednesday, 20 January. *Das Rheingold und Die Walküre*. Were they moving two of those bastards?'

Deserters. 'What do you think?'

Did he have to hear it? 'Guidance, *verdammt!*'

Now force him into a corner, Inspector, Renée seemed to whisper. 'And on the following Wednesday, the twenty-seventh, Colonel, you and the Fräulein . . .'

The big hands came together, the fingers tightly locking as Rasche took him in.

'We were here. That girl . . . The Fräulein Ekkehard wanted me to stop in.'

'"Stop," Colonel? You were passing by, were you, from . . .'

Gott im Himmel, must St-Cyr persist? 'All right, all right! She begged me to bring her out here. "For an hour," she said. "There's a little something I want you to see." She was like a child, a girl I once knew.'

Yvonne Lutze, or her daughter Geneviève, Inspector? Ask him! demanded Renée only to be told, It's not the moment. 'The *Jeu de massacre*, Colonel?'

'Those,' grunted Rasche, indicating the buckets of papier-mâché balls that had been recently made and others that had been found.

Oberfeldewebel Lutze, his Schmeisser slung, continued to

tend the fire in the stove using scraps from the coffin. Rasche got up to reach across the table and take one of the balls that had yet to be painted. 'How could she have hidden such a thing from me, Inspector? A girl I'd as much as adopted.'

In disgust, he crushed the ball in a fist and tossed it to Herr Lutze who dropped it into the stove. *Dieu merci*, there was no whoosh of flame but this did not mean there wouldn't be with others that were, no doubt, hidden. 'Colonel, tell me what happened on that afternoon.'

Paris had also said this one and that partner of his would keep a suspect talking by asking seemingly incidental questions. 'I busied myself in here while Renée went out to open up the wagon in which those helpers of theirs had stored the game. When she called, asking me to bring a bucket of those things, she was happy—excited and jumping up and down. The butcher, the baker, schoolmaster, old maid, village policeman and priest had all been finished and those she had set out on their turnstile pedestals, their colours bright against the sunlit snow. "Now you first," she said, and fool that I was, I enjoyed myself.'

A confession of sorts, whispered Renée. Normally the men in our *Arbeitslager* aren't allowed to see complete newspapers only selected articles which have been posted for all to read. Tell him this!

There is no need, mademoiselle. Your colonel understands.

'*Ach*, newspapers were needed in order to make the papier-mâché. I allowed Renée to bring whichever she wished from the office, since we get far too many, though there's virtually nothing of value in any of them.'

'The *Kölnische Zeitung*, *Berliner Tageblatt* and others, Colonel, the personals columns which those men must have avidly read and gradually found in them a further meaning.'

'*Mein Gott,* how could I possibly have known? Never in my life have I bothered to read such trash!'

As Beate desires someone older, Inspector? Renée seemed to ask. Wouldn't a vanity that is huge have caused him to peruse them in private?

Don't deride him, mademoiselle. It will only hinder the investigation.

Then please ask him if he ever dipped those hands of his into the papier-mâché. Ask if he ever helped me to make some of those missiles. Ask if the men, our now knowing that they had been making *guncotton,* would have laughed at the two of us behind our backs. Ask . . .

'Colonel, when did you first begin to think that something must be wrong?'

Was this safer ground? 'When Löwe Schrijen began to have that daughter of his followed.'

'And when did you notice that this was happening?'

'In mid-December. I saw them in the street outside one of the meetings the Fräulein Schrijen was addressing but they left in their car as soon as they noticed me. I'd gone there to ask Renée where she had put a file I needed. The girl came out of a nearby café and was flustered to find me there, but I thought no more of it. She'd been unsettled and definitely not herself since that skiing weekend at Natzweiler-Struthof. Victoria Bödicker had an arm locked in hers and was obviously keeping a very close eye on her. I . . . well, I didn't pursue the matter.'

'Had anything else happened to her while at the quarry, Colonel?'

Anything, thought Rasch, beyond witnessing the same hanging three times until successful. Sophie Schrijen must have told St-Cyr this, and if not her, then Victoria Bödicker.

'Only a skiing accident. At least that is what she claimed. Personally I doubted it but felt it a private matter. The girl was an excellent skier.'

But does he now suspect what really happened to me, Inspector?

'She had become engaged then, had she, Colonel?'

'That didn't happen formally until Christmas Eve.'

And three weeks of absolute terror over what Alain Schrijen must do, Inspector? Didn't Sophie tell you and Victoria that I must have betrayed my true self and them too?

'And after Christmas, Colonel?'

'Look, I'm certain that boy must have found out what those three were up to. Perhaps the girl inadvertently said something while at Natzweiler-Struthof. Löwe Schrijen then started having his daughter followed. Renée was then murdered. How could I not have felt her death far from being a suicide? A devout Catholic? A girl who was gentle, kind and full of life? *Mein Gott*, everyone had a warm spot for her, myself especially.'

Ah, bon, mademoiselle, and yet another small confession on his part and reassurance that he could not possibly have had anything to do with your actual killing, though that still leaves us to deal with Herr Lutze, and certainly if you were to have lived, you would have been a distinct threat to them, since Herr Lutze and his colonel are virtually inseparable. 'Thomas was then hanged . . .'

'But you've not yet settled that, have you, even though he was condemned by his own men, only one of whom, other than Thomas, had a pass to the administration block. Raymond Maillotte, Inspector. The weakest link in that combine and one whose weakness, I must emphasize, Lagerfeldebel Dorsche knew of only too well and used.'

'Hermann may have something.'

'Then let's hope that nothing has happened to him.'

'Your detectives, Colonel . . .'

'Believe me, neither of those two would have bothered to sit down with Renée to discuss a bauble. They'd have strung her up and gladly and could easily have got at Thomas if ordered to by Löwe Schrijen or that son of his.'

'Yet you've not let us see their report.'

'Because there is nothing in it but lies. It's all a cover-up, and the smoother the better as far as Löwe Schrijen is concerned.'

'Herr Oberdetektiv,' interjected Lutze, 'the Untersturmführer Schrijen was well aware of how much Renée wanted to find the mate to that earring. Renée was always looking for such things. He would have known how pleased she would have been.'

'And distracted,' muttered Rasche, motioning Lutze to join them at the table. 'Tell the Oberdetektiv about that boy's last visit to the house.'

A cigarettte was offered and accepted, the colonel sliding his tobacco pouch and matches over to this Sûreté.

It was time to let St-Cyr know where things really stood, thought Lutze. 'The Untersturmführer came to take Renée to his father's house in town on Christmas Eve, Inspector. He spoke of the biscuit tin they kept in one of those trunks here—she had shown it to him early in November when they'd all come out here for a picnic. He asked if she and Victoria or Sophie had found anything new to add to it. "A veritable treasure-trove, that tin," he had said with a laugh. "If only those things were real, my sister could auction them off and would have no need of fixing anything for that fête she plans to hold."'

It would have to be asked, 'Had Alain Schrijen access to a means of drugging her, Colonel?'

If only the answer could be served on a platter. 'They've plenty of ampoules at the quarry camp.'

'Ampoules . . . Then we will have to have the autopsies done.'

'And the others of that combine, Inspector?' asked Rasche. 'Will you then stand idly by when they are sent to that camp for reinforced interrogation?'

And what will they cry out? demanded Renée. That he had given them so much freedom they'd taken advantage of it?

'There are ten of them being held in *Straf,* Inspector,' said Werner Lutze. 'The three who are left of the five who were released under guard to work here, and the rest of their combine.'

Those men would face certain death and St-Cyr knew it well enough, thought Rasche. 'Find Kohler, *mein Lieber*. Look at things thoroughly but in the light of present realities.'

'Suicides . . . Is it that you now wish us to say it definitely wasn't murder?'

'I want answers. Nothing else but the truth.'

'And Löwe Schrijen, what will he do if it was his son, as you and Herr Lutze have tried to suggest, as has Sophie Schrijen?'

'Believe me, Chief Inspector, Löwe will do whatever suits him best.'

The smokehouse was far from lonely but had been locked, its latch now solidly in place. Coughing came from inside, first from Hervé Paulus, Kohler felt, and then from Serge Deiss.

'Please don't open it, Inspector,' said Sophie Schrijen, stepping from the shadows to stand in moonlight. 'I've only just closed it. I once locked my brother in there for a few minutes. He'd been spying on me, and for days afterward stank of wood smoke and complained of tears, but otherwise was fine. *Vati* will deal with them.'

She'd a bow in hand, an arrow pointed at him, and a quiver on her back.

'You took my keys,' she said. 'I'd like them back.'

'Louis has them.'

'What were Eugène and the others up to?'

'There was a little carving . . .'

'Of a chariot and Boudicca, its rider. It's for the Wheel of Fortune which is to be mounted horizontally so that when spun, the chariot will go round and round until it stops and Boudicca points her spear at the winner. Martin Caroff, our assistant machinist, carved it. Martin liked Eugène. They all did. They couldn't have been planning to kill him.'

She wasn't going to appreciate it, but had best be told. 'Maillotte said nothing further, Fräulein. He made sure of that.'

'Raymond,' she said with longing, the bow faltering as she bit back the tears. 'He and Eugène were the very best of friends. They always got on and worked well together. He wouldn't have killed Eugène. How could he have?'

She was desperate. 'He did say the combine couldn't decide who and how best to carry out the sentence.'

'But . . . but you've just said . . .'

Again the bow and arrow faltered but only for a moment. 'That was earlier, when he confessed.'

'To Dorsche? Does the Lagerfeldwebel now know what they were planning?'

'Ask him. Maybe he'll tell you.'

'I can't. I mustn't.'

He took a step, she cried out, 'DON'T! Just . . . just stay where you are.'

'Then give me a cigarette.'

'I haven't any. I don't often use them and left mine at the house. Renée . . . Renée used to get them for me.'

'From Werner Lutze?'

'In fun she used to call him our acquirer which always pleased him, for he's really quite shy. Junos, Lord Chesterfields . . . whatever was going, Herr Lutze would have some. He knew she was getting them for me or for Victoria, that she didn't use them herself. Charcoal for the braziers we'll use at the fête to warm the hands was no problem for him. Tallow and beeswax, also, for the ceremonial torches all such events must have at their openings. Prizes too. Teddy bears, china figurines, vases, artificial flowers, wine, of course, and schnapps. Lots of things. Donations, all of them.'

And the *Karneval* was still very much on, but whoever had sat in that field office of theirs beside that girl on that Sunday had dribbled cigarette ash and had tried to remove it. 'Why not lower the bow? Arrows are no fun. My partner and I once had to deal with a crossbow and quickly found out what it was like.'

'What were those men up to?'

'Had they realized what you and the others were doing—isn't that really what you desperately need to know?'

'If Renée and Victoria were up to anything, I knew nothing of it.'

'Taking things behind the wire? Buttons, bits of string, bread and cigarettes, carpenter's nails . . .'

'The packets out at the wagon.'

'There are thirty or more of them, all in tidy little bundles.'

'For prizes, Inspector. Prizes!'

And wouldn't you know it! 'Who suggested this?'

'Gérard Léger. We were always finding lots of nails. There are far more bundles than you saw. They're in with the rest of the papier-mâché balls. Most of the nails were bent, but when cleaned and straightened, they were fine and perfectly acceptable.'

And weren't nails as scarce as hen's teeth in France too, and wasn't that glazier a veteran of two wars and most probably the leader of that combine?

Shrapnel, sighed Kohler inwardly. Torches, charcoal fires, bundles of nails and utter chaos. 'How close will the nails be to the *Jeu de massacre?*'

Why did he need to know such a thing? 'There's to be a table with prizes between it and the Wheel of Fortune's booth.'

'And the braziers and torches?'

'Why should it matter?'

'Please just answer.'

'There's to be a brazier at each table, with torches at either side of each booth. If you'd not been so intent on stealing my keys, you would have seen the plans on my desk for the fête. There'll be music too. Tambourines, drums and recorders, the musicians all in period costume. The Renaissance. Renée . . . Renée had a fabulous imagination and had planned it all. A jester, a troubadour, a magician and fortune-teller, a puppet show for the children.'

'You three were moving deserters through to the Vosges.'

'If Renée and Victoria were mixed up in anything so illegal as an act of terrorism, Inspector, and I very much doubt they would have been, I knew absolutely nothing of it. How could I have? Aren't I busy enough? Didn't I have to delegate virtually everything to them?'

'Drugged . . . was that girl drugged before you hanged her?'

'I didn't! I could never have done something like that. Not to Renée, not to anyone. I wasn't even there. I was busy at the Works!'

'And on that Sunday?'

'I was here with Father.'

'And your brother, Fräulein?'

'Alain? He was on duty at Natzweiler-Struthof. Didn't *Vati* tell you that?'

'It's what he didn't tell me that's interesting.'

'Did he send those two men after Victoria?'

'I think so.'

'Then may God be with her.'

Alone again, St-Cyr stood under clear moonlight. The Devil's Saucer hung at a crazy tilt. The *Tonneau de l'amour* that Yvonne Lutze and her husband had explored was long, low and silent. Behind it, and not seen from here, would be Dr. Bonnet's Travelling Museum of Anatomy. Broken glass, she had said. Shattered jars, Werner Lutze having forced a way into it, she thinking only of formalin and a daughter who had begun a 'preserving stage' at the age of ten.

'*Merde*, it gets to one, doesn't it, this place,' he muttered to himself.

Rasche and Lutze had gone back to town, to the house. Obviously the colonel had felt threatened when he had asked Paris for them. His office was being bugged; things could not have been right between him and Löwe Schrijen and those two detectives. Hermann was, of course, quite able to take care of himself but had always counted on backup from this partner of his. 'And now?' he had to ask. 'Now Hermann could be gone from me, the frontier closed.'

An Antarctica of leather covered the Citroën's front seat, the ignition was irresponsible, the engine recalcitrant. Again and again it refused to start. Had Lutze and the colonel made certain he would never leave the carnival, had someone else?

It started. It idled. It grew more confident and settled into a rhythm that was music to the ears, but the sigh he gave was caught in his throat.

There was someone behind him. As yet there was no sight

of them in the rearview, only this feeling, this sixth sense that he wasn't alone.

Deftly, silently, he found the cutthroat and held it at the ready. Still there was no sight or sound from this unwanted passenger. Perhaps they would think to wait until his hands were on the steering wheel and gear shift; perhaps if he turned off the engine . . .

Switching on the heater, its sound seemed more desperate than usual. '*Mirage*,' he said. 'Fräulein Bödicker, that scent Renée Ekkehard gave you haunts me.'

'Have they really left?' she asked of the colonel and Werner Lutze, the muffled quaver betraying her fear.

'Gone,' he said. 'Why not come and sit up front?'

'It's best I don't. Then, if necessary, I can hide on the floor.'

'You came on skis from the bookshop?'

'A cigarette . . . Have you got one?'

Putting the cutthroat away, he opened his coat. Suit and waistcoat pockets were dug into. 'Emergency rations,' he muttered. 'Hermann and I always try to have a little something. *Ah, bon*, mademoiselle. The match, it is necessary.'

It flared, lighting up the interior, but she'd hidden herself well.

'I didn't even see those two detectives of the colonel's,' she said as the match went out. 'Claudette was watching the street this afternoon because they had told her to, and when she saw their car racing up it, she knew they must have been coming for me. There's a passage behind the courtyards. She and *maman* were always using it when they wanted things to be private. She . . . she said she would . . .'

'Hold them.'

'She risked her life for me, Inspector. I hid. Coward that I am, I didn't even go back to see if she was all right.'

'Just returned later for your skis.'

He would have to be told. 'They wrecked the bookshop and house, searching for something but must have gotten tired of waiting for me and . . . and took Claudette back to her place. Now I don't even know what's happened to her.'

'Then we'd best find out, hadn't we?'

'Sophie lied to you, Inspector. She and Renée were deeply in love. It was a very tender and secretive thing, and it developed over time. Oh for sure, I was the only other one to know of it until Alain found out, and he must have. Renée would have panicked when he took her back to that room he had rented for her at the Natzweiler ski lodge. She would have tried to get away from him.'

'But had she also been drugged, mademoiselle?'

'I . . . I don't know. How could I? It . . . it was wrong of Sophie to have implied that I must have known and that I might have had something to do with Renée's death. It was a suicide, Inspector. Renée was dangerously depressed and Sophie certainly knew of this, as I did. That brother of hers is a sadist. Renée . . . Renée didn't just see a man hanged three times. Alain proudly told her of the scientific experiments they'd been conducting.'

Experiments, Inspector, whispered Renée Ekkehard as if also present. And now what do you think are your chances of returning to Paris? What are those of your partner?

Out of the darkness of this crooked, narrow street that had seen the centuries, one light glowed a paltry phosphorescent blue.

'Our air-raid shelter,' whispered Victoria. 'The shop isn't far now.'

'It's at the bend,' said St-Cyr, having switched off the headlamps some time ago. 'Let's leave the car here, mademoiselle, and continue on foot.'

'Must I come with you? Is it really necessary?'

'Those two detectives of the colonel's will have heard the engine.'

He pointed to something up the street, the houses crowding closely on either side. Where things were not totally in shadow, there was light from the snow cover, but always there had been lamps in this street she had loved, the rue Madeleine of her childhood, the Madeleinestrasse. 'Another car.'

'Their Primastella.'

'Claudette's flat is on the second floor.'

He paused to peer into the car, muttered, 'A suitcase.' Listening first to the street, he shone a blue-blinkered torch briefly over the Chantilly lace *maman* had given Claudette years ago.

'Closed, by order,' whispered this Sûreté, 'but not closed at all.'

The door hadn't been smashed in. Claudette must simply have left it off the latch when she had run to the bookshop. Her broom had fallen, and there it was still lying on the pavement. No one had dared to touch it.

Gently he nudged the door and it swung in a little. Immediately Victoria felt the tiles underfoot and knew the staircase would abruptly rise. Step by step, and feeling his way, the Inspector paused at each to listen closely. No torchlight now. None. Always as a child she had been in such a hurry to climb these stairs.

'Breathe silently,' he whispered.

It took forever to reach the flat but here, too, the door was open.

'Otto, what is happening to us?' asked Yvonne Lutze. 'You've both been keeping things from me.'

'They're not good. I'd be less the man I am were I to tell you differently.'

The *Kachelofen*'s firebox had been banked long ago, but all about her in the kitchen behind the *Stube*, the aroma of red cabbage and sausages mocked her. She would have to use the terrine to keep the meal warm for the detectives, would put the lid on, then the lock, wouldn't look at Otto or at Werner, would simply take the key from her pocket and press it to her lips. 'Did either of you kill that girl?'

'Of course not.'

'You both knew she was going out there. You both knew those three must have been up to something. Werner . . . Werner knew exactly where that notebook of Victoria's was kept. How is it, please, that my husband knew you had best get it before someone else did?'

Still she wouldn't look at him or at Werner. '*Liebling*, I gave it to St-Cyr and Kohler.'

'Don't you dare *darling* me. Geneviève is in danger of arrest and not because of any student demonstration.'

'Arrest? Not yet. Not if cool heads prevail.'

The urge to shout was with her, but she wasn't a shouter and he knew it. 'Let's see it through—is that it, Otto? Please don't forget that child of ours doesn't even *know* what's been going on here or that it must threaten her life. You ask for detectives from Paris? You claim Renée's death a murder, yet *still* you tell me nothing? Nor will you, Werner. Aren't I your wife?' she asked as he stepped from behind his colonel to look at her in that way he sometimes did, as though the two of them were one against all others.

She would never understand how he felt, thought Lutze, would always see him as his colonel's Oberfeldwebel. 'We think they were moving deserters through to the Vosges.'

What could have been plainer? 'I knew it. I felt it. And now

I'm broken. What you smashed when you deserted me, Otto, you've smashed again!'

The white milk jug, the crinoline from the Soufflenheim pottery was near, but she wouldn't dash it on the floor, not Yvonne, thought Rasche. Not the girl he'd known. 'You were aware that I had a wife I couldn't divorce.'

A barren woman five years his senior, he had claimed. One he could barely tolerate. The daughter of a wealthy landowner, with lands she had inherited. 'I came to know you for what you are, Otto. Now get out. Get out of my family's kitchen, the two of you. Leave me to my memories of the daughter I held and taught to use this terrine.'

'Did you leave everything you found in Renée's room as I asked?' demanded Rasche.

'Renée's room, Otto? Was it not Geneviève's?'

'*Ach*, just answer. Did you take anything from it?'

'And if I did, what of it?'

'No one must suspect that you did.'

Alone at last, she took down one of the biscuit cutters that hung in a row before her: the mayor, the priest, the schoolmaster, others too. With each of them the child had first admonished the biscuit for crimes committed and then had explained the sentence before apologizing and eating it.

'They are so perfect, aren't they, *maman*,' Geneviève had often said as she had cut them out or sprinkled sugar decorations on them, sometimes chips of candied fruit. 'How could such good citizens possibly do the bad things they do?'

A *Jeu de massacre* of her own.

'Geneviève,' she said and wept, only to feel Werner pull her round to let her bury her face against him.

'*Doucement, mon amour. Doucement*,' he said in the French he had sometimes used for Geneviève's benefit. 'Go easy. Don't panic. Kohler and St-Cyr were not asked to come here without good reason.'

Little by little the eyes became accustomed to the lack of light in Frau Oberkircher's flat. An armchair had been tipped over, a gramophone also. Bakelite recordings had been smashed.

'Her *Deutsche Grammonphon Platten,*' said Victoria, drawing in a breath as he pressed a finger to her lips. 'Claudette . . .' she managed, her voice seeming to shock the silence.

A cheek was touched, and only then did she realize St-Cyr had a cutthroat and not a gun.

He left her. At first she thought he must be close but soon realized that he must have moved well away from her, but he didn't show himself against the leaded windows that overlooked the street below. He made no sound at all. Claudette, she silently cried. Claudette, forgive me.

How many times had she climbed those stairs as a child? How many times had that good woman shown surprise and delight as she had welcomed her in and they had sat at the table here and had a tisane of camomile or linden or rosehips sweetened with honey? Biscuits too, they playing a game of cards, herself as a young child and then as a teenager? The three of them close. The three!

Maman often in the bookshop or out on an errand.

Der Ring des Nibelungen, Inspector, said Victoria silently. Claudette listening to those treasured recordings, not just those of Herr Wagner's music, but also of Chopin, Camille Saint-Saëns, Bela Bartok and many others. Recordings that brought back memories of a husband who had been killed in that other war but had loved opera with a passion and all that was beautiful in music, and had played third violin in the symphony orchestra and the lead in a trio of his own, with cello and piano at weddings, anniversaries and whatever for a little extra cash. 'To be a musician is to always embrace poverty, *mes petits,*' Claudette had often said, 'but to possess far greater riches.'

Fruit leathers and boiled sweets, said Victoria silently. I betrayed you and for this I beg forgiveness.

St-Cyr would have to hand her over to the Gestapo. He would have no other choice; Sophie wouldn't, couldn't, mustn't intercede.

They'll kill me—she knew it absolutely. They would beat her senseless, bring her round and start in again, trying to force her to tell them what she knew must never be yielded.

'I should have killed myself,' she whispered.

By the smell alone, St-Cyr knew Frau Oberkircher was in the pitch-dark bedroom. As elsewhere in the flat, the room was a shambles but here there was someone else—he knew it, felt it, could not avoid it.

'Hermann, *c'est moi, mon vieux.*'

'Louis, I can't take any more of this. I can't!'

Firmly but gently the chief inspector spoke to him as one soldier would to another over fallen comrades. Perhaps ten minutes passed, Victoria felt. Perhaps a little more. One thing was certain: St-Cyr had been the one to examine Claudette's body.

With a finality that hurt, he closed the bedroom door behind him, nudging his partner ahead, that one much taller and bigger and, now with a bit of light, appearing ashen and badly shaken by what had happened.

The chief inspector set the table upright and placed the *chaise de mariage* at it, the chair Claudette had been given as a young girl for her dowry. 'Sit,' he said.

Half a glass of milk was set before her. Miraculously the

blue stoneware jug with its raised design of daisies hadn't been smashed. The triangular earthenware dish Claudette had bought years ago held a clutch of the small round biscuits she had always kept on hand. Not dusted with sugar, though, for that could no longer be easily obtained and what Claudette had managed had had to be saved for 'the shop.'

'Eat something,' muttered Herr Kohler, the blackout drapes now drawn.

'I can't. I couldn't.'

'Just take a bite and have a sip. They'll help to settle your nerves.'

My terror, Inspector? she silently demanded, quickly doing as told and setting the biscuit down to scatter crumbs, Claudette always saying, 'Crumbs, *ma petite*? Won't they taste as good if not better than before, when you gather them?' Or, 'Those biscuits of mine, have I not followed the recipe correctly? Come, let's go over it again.'

'I loved her. She was like a second mother to me.'

When they didn't respond, she asked, 'Why won't you let me see her?' but found she couldn't face them anymore, for they were standing at the other side of the table, looking down at her and St-Cyr had placed pieces of broken recordings in front of her: *Das Gotterdammerung, Das Rheingold* and *Die Walküre*.

Again she heard herself asking why they wouldn't let her see Claudette. Moisture in her deep brown eyes made her appear *très tragique et vulnérable*, thought St-Cyr. *Bien sûr*, the tears emphasized despair and of course Hermann, still in his present state, would perhaps weaken even more. That page-boy fringe of auburn hair . . .

Defiantly her gaze grew unwavering but was there now also an emptiness? 'We need answers, mademoiselle, and haven't much time. Start talking.'

Or else—was that it, eh? '*Sprechen Sie Deutsch, Herr Oberdetektiv*. Otherwise I won't be able to understand you.'

'Louis, if she tries that with the resident Gestapo, we'll never be able to save her.'

'Perhaps she's beyond saving, Hermann.'

'You were moving deserters through Alsace, Fräulein,' said Herr Kohler.

'Is that what Sophie told you?' she asked.

'This one skied out to the *Karneval*, didn't she, Louis?'

'What if I did? It's not against the law, is it?'

'But avoiding arrest is,' countered St-Cyr.

'You ran,' added Herr Kohler, now looking her over carefully.

'I ran because of what you must have found in there.'

From a coat pocket, the chief inspector took her school notebook, and opening it at a page whose corner had been torn away, fitted a scrap back into place.

'That notebook has always been kept in my mother's desk for when I might again be allowed to teach.'

'When Elsass is returned to France?' he asked.

'I didn't say that. You know I didn't!'

'Louis, her lips are sealed. We'd best leave while we can.'

'And leave the Primastella for others to find.'

'Cuff her then and let them have her, eh?'

'Why not? She might hold out. It's possible.'

'But not probable.'

'Some clothes,' she said. 'These . . . these things are fine for skiing but not for . . .'

'One of the camps?' asked Kohler. 'Don't worry about it. Believe me, Fräulein, you won't get a chance to leave Kolmar.'

They'd let her take a moment to think about it. She could see this in the way they glanced at each other, but then St-Cyr dragged out the framed photograph Claudette had kept beside her bed.

The glass had been broken. Droplets of blood had been sprayed across the photo and these had congealed and frozen, but still the faces in the photo grinned up at her, still there was that moment's sharp happiness to mock her.

'That is Blaise Oberkircher and myself, 15 June 1938. We had just become . . .'

'Engaged, Fräulein?' asked St-Cyr.

'I'd known him all my life. He became a fellow teacher until called up but was killed during the Blitzkrieg. Along the Meuse, I think. At Monthermé most probably, and on 12 or 13 May 1940. I don't know for sure. No one really does.'

Whether the Lutze house slept or not was of little concern to the chief inspector, thought Victoria. Alone with him in the bedroom Renée had used, she waited for his questions to begin again.

Still wrapped in tissue and never worn, the brassiere Alain Schrijen had given Renée on Christmas Eve was of the sheerest white Calais lace, the step-ins of silk but trimmed with that same lace. Beneath them, in the bureau, she knew there was other lingerie. A fortune these days, things so hard to come by, few even bothered to think of them.

'My partner is a connoisseur of such,' muttered this Sûreté who had insisted, step by agonizing step, that she examine with him everything in the room, even if it took the rest of the night. 'The Textilfabrikschrijen's ex-assistant manager has taste or access to someone who does.'

She had to stop him from prying further. 'Why not ask Frau Bisch of the *Naturfreundeklub* (the Nature-lovers Club). *Die Erektion* is how it's known to those who regularly visit it, as Alain

Schrijen does, or you might try Frau Voigt, of the *Goldene Adler* (the Golden Eagle). The woman took the name from the inn where Goethe is rumoured to have written some of his best works. The *Götz von Berlichingen* or *Faust*, who knows? Certainly I couldn't find out when I was there in . . .' *Ah, merde, merde,* why had she said it?

'Fräulein, when were you last in Innsbruck? Come, come, we haven't time to waste.'

He would think the worst of her now. 'In the summer of 1938. Hiking. A fortnight. Blaise . . . Blaise Oberkircher took the train first and then I followed. Claudette . . . I think she always knew but never once said a thing, was simply content that we were happy as was my mother.'

But to have entered Austria in that summer was to have entered a nation that had only just been absorbed by the Third Reich during the Anschluss of 12 March. Czechoslovakia and the Sudetenland crisis had remained very much in the news until 29 September when, after the Munich Conference, the British Prime Minister, Neville Chamberlain, had returned to London promising 'peace for our time' and waving a guarantee the Führer had signed on the thirtieth.

Two teachers, two hikers. 'You took a chance in going there, Fräulein.'

'Blaise belonged to an international hiking club. I . . . Well, I simply tagged along.'

He dragged out her school notebook, quickly thumbed through pages until he had what he wanted.

'"Is self-reliant and exceedingly capable," mademoiselle. "As a student spent her summer holidays camping and orienteering."

'And then there is this,' he went on. ' "Refuses to adhere rigidly to the dictums of the Ministry of Education. Looks for ways to enhance and enliven the learning experience? Children are happiest then," she says. "Shouldn't learning be among the happiest of experiences?"

' "Is far too rebellious," one inspector has noted. "I'm not a monkey with a tin cup. If you want a robot, get someone else."'

But those inspectors had all been French.

There were other things in the notebook, Victoria knew: "Smokes cigarettes; wears roll collars and Norwegian trousers, yet uses expensive perfume; is happy; is in love and lets it show," and then . . . "Is engaged to be married. Is inclined to let misdemeanours pass. Stresses comprehension not the rote memorization, as demanded by the curricula. A love of each subject is, to quote her, the truest route to learning."

'Is rebellious, mademoiselle,' said St-Cyr, putting it away for now, not mentioning anything else. 'You were telling me about Alain Schrijen's leisure activities in Kolmar.'

'Der Goldene Adler is known for its *Sonnenanbeterinen.*'

Its habitual sunbathers of the female kind. '*Gruppensex?*' he asked as Hermann would have done, and saw her suck in a breath and nod a little too quickly.

'The men who frequent it watch them first and then . . . then choose the one or more they want to share.'

Hermann would also have asked, as would this partner of his, 'Is it a rough house?'

She seemed relieved that he had asked it.

'Personally I wouldn't know, Inspector, but it's rumoured that sometimes things have to be hushed up.'

'Then is it true to say you've made a point of finding out all you could about Alain Schrijen?'

'Only what his sister has told me.'

'And no impressions of your own from the picnic the four of you had out at the *Karneval* in early November?'

'None. He . . . he spent most of his time with Renée.'

The chief inspector did not say, You're lying, mademoiselle. He simply dug deeper into that bureau drawer, lifting the neatly stacked lingerie out until she heard him suck in a breath and say, 'Fräulein, what is this, please?'

The blouse Renée had worn to that party at Natzweiler-Struthof was torn and missing several of its sky-blue buttons. Though laundered, no attempt had been made to mend it.

'Bloodstains are often among the hardest to remove,' he said, gingerly unfolding it and then . . . '*Evipan*, Fräulein? Two ampoules lying side by side and cushioned, but leaving vacant what would not be noticed by most, the impression of a third?'

Each was of clear glass and contained an all but clear liquid, their slender necks thin and with a frosted necklace so that when snapped off, the spine would not splinter, but sometimes did, the name clearly given.

'A hexobarbitone, Fräulein. Usually of the sodium salt. Slightly bitter but very soluble in alcohol or water. Given intravenously as an anaesthetic whose reaction is swift. Taken orally also, in capsule form or in a glass of schnapps or *eau-de-vie*. Within as little as fifteen minutes it causes a deep and comatose sleep of from two to four hours, depending on the dosage of course.'

There was panic in her.

'I . . . I didn't know she had those, Inspector. I swear I didn't.'

'Mademoiselle, let's dispense with subterfuge. You have often been in this room. As we went from item to item, including the flacon of *Mirage* on that dressing table, or stood momentarily looking around us, you betrayed a familiarity your reflection in its mirror could not deny. Renée Ekkehard wasn't just your friend who brought home the travel papers you would need to visit Vittel on the last Friday of every month. She was a fellow *résistante.*'

'We weren't moving deserters. We wouldn't have done such a stupid, stupid thing. *Ah, mon Dieu,* Inspector, I've my mother to think of and . . . and I'd Claudette as well. Renée was simply very depressed and suicidal. She had seen things no decent human being could ever tolerate and had felt how hopeless her life was. I tried to tell her that she didn't have to marry Alain but she kept on insisting that if she didn't, she had only one other choice. She took it to save Sophie.'

'Her lover.'

'Alain found out about them—he must have. That . . . that is how I see it.'

'Then think on it, mademoiselle. Think hard.'

He left her, left the bureau drawer open, the lingerie not replaced, the ampoules still lying there. Made her ask herself would two be enough?

Alone, the chief inspector sat at the table in the *Stube,* having still not gone to bed. Pipe smoke billowed from him so lost was he in thought, felt Yvonne, having come down the stairs as quietly as possible. Everything—all the bits and pieces of this investigation of theirs, this tragedy—was laid out before him. The two rose-coloured buttons that had come from that dress Renée had worn out to the *Karneval* last August. Snapshots, some torn, others not, of the wife and little son of Eugène Thomas were there. A wedding ring made of beautifully worked tin, the missing corner of that page from Victoria's notebook. Chemical formulae and wouldn't he have noticed that among Geneviève's schoolbooks there were those that dealt with chemistry?

'An anonymous letter,' said St-Cyr, not looking up. 'An earring, Frau Lutze. While the house sleeps or doesn't, let us contemplate each of these items.'

He indicated the spread before him, asked, 'Are Hermann and I to take them with us tomorrow when we go, as we must, to Natzweiler-Struthof to question Alain Schrijen and try to put an end to this matter?'

'Please, I . . . I know so little . . .'

'A second-class ticket for Strassburg for this coming weekend?'

The thirteenth and fourteenth of February to be precise and the second party Renée was to have attended at Natzweiler-Struthof.

'Had she been told, do you think, that she had best come or else?'

An ultimatum. 'I . . . I think so, yes. Yes, now that you mention it, I do recall her saying she had to go, that . . . that if she didn't, Herr Schrijen's son would be very angry.'

The pipe was companionably removed. '*Ah, bon,* you should have told us that before, shouldn't you?' he said *en français.* A roll of bills, bound with a rubber band, was touched. 'The Lagergeld Eugène Thomas was probably going to pay the assistant machinist for making this.'

The wedding ring.

The chief inspector then touched the pocket watch Renée had had to borrow but said no more of it. Pages from Kolmar's *Morgenzeitung* were fingered, a reminder of the lunch that girl had taken and something she, herself, would definitely have known of but had said nothing of. Did he think her guilty?

A bead of solder, a swatch of grey-green cloth the size of a tunic's lapel were there, the dying of this last really quite good.

'Boudicca,' he said, fingering the small carving. 'Unfortunately her javelin broke off when the cage those POWs call home was turned upside down.'

Other newspapers, scraps torn from the personals columns, were underneath a bloodied papier-mâché ball that looked as if partly chewed.

The ampoules were not here, of course, nor was the lingerie.

'Please sit across the table from me,' he said. There were three pieces from broken gramophone recordings in front of her and she had to ask herself, Had he anticipated her coming downstairs?

'*Das Rheingold und Die Walküre,* Frau Lutze. Was that girl to have found two deserters waiting for her at the *Karneval* on Saturday, 30 January, or was she to have gone farther east to collect and guide them back, and then hide them among those ruins?'

'How could I possibly know?'

'Please don't lie to me, not when my partner and I must leave early to interview Alain Schrijen whose fiancée carried a man's pocket watch while hers . . . Where did you tell me it was? At a repair shop, 3 Schöngstrasse, wasn't it? A Maurice Springer. Am I to assume that Victoria Bödicker and Sophie Schrijen also knew of him, or am I to ask Alain Schrijen? Repeated repairs to an expensive wristwatch that Colonel Rasche could easily have returned to Brequet's on *place* Vendôme when next in Paris? Has this Springer a relative living on the other side of the Rhine, especially if one goes through Neuf-Brisach and Alt-Breisach?'

'Herr Springer's brother lives in Vogtsburg and has a string of hides in the forest leading up to the Totenkopf. He's the Kaiserstuhl's *Wildhüter.*'

Its gamekeeper and probably at least twenty-five kilometres from the carnival.

'Is he involved?' demanded Yvonne, now desperate. 'Is Maurice, whom I've known all my life, as has Victoria and Sophie? If so, I must blame myself. You see, Inspector, Maurice Springer would stop me in the street to tell me when Renée's watch would be ready for pickup and to ask if I would please let her know. Three days, a week, sometimes ten days, seldom more. I didn't ask why he would bother with such advance notices. I simply felt the girl was anxious to have her watch back and that he had understood this. After all, she was the Kommandant's secretary and must have needed it.'

There were tears and that was understandable. 'But those who should have been waiting at the *Karneval* weren't there, so the girl went east to find out why and then came back exhausted.'

'I didn't kill her, nor would my husband.'

'Yet he went out there in the *Polizeikommandantur*'s *Grüne Minna* on that Saturday afternoon at about 4.00 p.m., your having told me that the two of you always did the shopping and afterward visited the *Winstube* of a friend, returning home at around 3.00.'

'My husband and Otto tell me very little, often nothing.'

'Of course, but you knew that girl was going out there instead of Sophie Schrijen, and you knew that upstairs in your daughter's bedroom there were three ampoules of Evipan that girl must have brought back from Natzweiler-Struthof. Everything that is in that room is known to you.'

'Geneviève is my daughter. It . . . it helps to keep me close to her.'

'And to Renée Ekkehard?'

'After she came back from that party, I . . .'

'Frau Lutze, I haven't time. You've been keeping an eye on that girl ever since she first arrived on your doorstep. You even went through that grip of my partner's and mine and had a look at our guns.'

'She was so pretty, I . . . I couldn't help myself. Otto—'

'Has let her and the other two drag us all down, hasn't he?'

Through the gilded letters of an altered name, history fled in faded outlines: APOTHEKE FERBER . . . PHARMACIE FERBER . . . and there, again, APOTHEKE. Impatiently scraping at the frost on the inside of the Citroën's windscreen, St-Cyr peered at the shop. This war, he lamented silently, the Occupation of France, the Annexation here, the interwar years and those from 1870 until 11 November 1918. Weren't they all coming home to roost to make the statement that humanity would never learn because it couldn't?

Hermann stood before the arched, dark-mullioned windows of the shop, framed by trusses too many and a reminder of the impediments guaranteed by war, but other items too: a pyramid of tooth powder to his right, but even there one had to ask, Chalk dust, soot and peppermint, as in Paris and the rest of France?

It was 9.57 a.m. Berlin time, Wednesday, 10 February and they had a long way to go and an interview neither of them looked forward to.

Pedestrians brushed past Hermann who seemed stuck in memory and still looking into the shop. Twin demijohns of pickled snakes, a favourite of all such shops during the *fin de siècle*, simply presented their owner—this girl who, at the age of nineteen, had rescued him in 1915 and had then spoken in his defence to Colonel Rasche—with a problem of disposal.

Posters flashed the benefits of Sirop Ferber, a spring tonic whose *belle fille* had once adorned a similar poster: *Régénérez-vous par le Sirop Vincent.* It had been in every pharmacy and she had simply cut the figure out and slapped it on to a poster of her own making: *Deutsch* as ordered.

A girl then, a middle-aged woman now, he reminded himself, one who must have little patience and absolutely no free time. As in France, and here still, unless one was on their very deathbed, one always consulted the pharmacist, never, God forbid, a doctor. The former had to undergo a rigorous training—three years or more—but acquired none of the arrogance and pathetic ignorance typical of the latter.

Harried, Hermann finally tore his gaze from the window to take in the crowded bus terminal which was diagonally across the Unterlindenstrasse and next to the *ancienne cloître* where Augustinian nuns had established their convent in the thirteenth century. He gave the whole thing the quick once-over, realizing as did his partner, that there would be twice-daily *autobus au gazogène* runs to Neuf-Brisach that anyone could have taken if needed on that Sunday, a distance of probably not more than fifteen or so kilometres, the *Karneval* and the Kastenwald being about halfway between it and Kolmar.

Strains of 'Deutschland Über Alles' came from the Platz where fresh-faced recruits in their early twenties and late teens stood rigidly to attention, their single suitcases behind them, each casting its shadow on the snow.

Hermann had ducked into the pharmacy.

The line-up was the length of the display cases whose glass tops were curved and still the same as they'd been in 1914 and '15, thought Kohler. To one side, a woman in her sixties handled the nonprescriptive trade, giving him the look-see as he rushed past. Coughs echoed, for the ceiling was high and of embossed tin plate, just as he had remembered it. 'My chest,' he heard someone saying. 'The usual,' grunted another.

The dispensary was still at the very back of the shop and behind the lift-up of an oaken countertop that had been scored by the years of use. The register which contained the dates, names and prescriptions filled, still weighed probably thirty kilos and was bound by brass rods and to his left. Behind the counter, he setting it back in place, an open doorway led discreetly into that alchemy of alchemies where jars and glass-stoppered bottles filled narrow shelves and a roll-away ladder sometimes had to be used.

The auburn hair that had been soft and long and had touches of dark red was now worn much shorter, prematurely greying and had hastily been pinned into a bun. The eyes . . . they'd once been of the warmest shade of greenish-brown and lively too, were now faded, puffy-lidded and behind black-rimmed specs that made her look like a forty-seven-year-old tyrant.

The rosy cheeks were no longer firm and smooth but flaccid and pale. In waves, her voice broke over him.

'Hermann . . . Hermann, is it really you?' *Ach*, he had aged. Too many late nights, too much tobacco and alcohol, but was he also on an amphetamine—Benzedrine perhaps?

She was not tall, this woman who had been lithe, willow-shoot thin, quick-witted and quick on her feet. She was rounded in the shoulders, chunky in the hips about which an off-white smock-coat's ties were bound, and though she hesitated, she couldn't stop herself from saying, 'I always knew you'd come back.'

'Lucie, I need your help.'

'When have you not?' Was it really Hermann? That scar down the left side of his face from eye to chin—how had he come by such a thing? That graze across a brow to which she had clamped cold compresses to bring down a raging fever? A bullet, she tersely nodded to herself, but there was no longer that mischief she had seen in those blue eyes of his that were now faded, no laughter anymore. He was harried, desperate and obviously on the run again.

Kohler set the mortar and pestle she had been using aside, took them right from her as she heard herself telling the morning's patients to please wait but a few moments. 'An old friend.'

Deliberately he blocked their view by filling the doorway, knowing though that, like all who ventured here, they would strain to listen.

'I haven't much time, Lucie. I meant to come back after that other war. I really did.'

'But didn't.'

A floor-to-ceiling curtain shielded the dispensary from the audience and this he quickly drew, knowing also, of course, that now those waiting would begin to imagine what must be going on behind it. There would be talk, and talk was not good these days.

'*Evipan*,' he said, his voice kept deliberately low.

'You're one of the detectives Colonel Rasche requested. When I heard that you were actually in Kolmar, I . . .'

He touched her lips. Fondly he let that hand stray to her left cheek, and she heard him saying, 'I've wanted to see you ever since that bastard Lutze came and took me away.'

Under arrest and dragged from bed, but a lie, of course, for in all those years since there had never once been a letter, not even a postcard. He had been a skirt-chaser—she had seen that right away. A breaker of hearts. Even then, she had had the sense not to try to fool herself when he'd come to her 21 February 1915, a Sunday, at 10.02 in the morning. *Papa* had been at church, she at her studies, the shop closed as Hermann had banged on the door and then had collapsed into her arms. Had God sent him to her? she had foolishly wondered. *Liebe Zeit*, he had been handsome, still was, but now . . .

'What can I do for you this time?'

He took a handkerchief from his jacket pocket, laid it on the counter and unfolded it to reveal a 10cc ampoule, some two and a half centimetres long from base to tip.

'Just tell me if taken orally in alcohol or straight up, would one or two be enough.'

'To cause death—with no other drug in the system? But . . . but I thought Renée . . . the Fräulein Ekkehard had hanged herself.'

'You knew her?'

'Of course. Most come to the shop.' Had it been murder after all as some were whispering? Why else would he have come?

Holding the ampoule under a light, she ran a thumb over its label and fine print. 'One gram of Evipan dissolved in ten cubic centimetres of distilled water is a lot to down, even if needed, Hermann. Usually for intravenous injections before surgery, much less is used. From one-quarter to three-quarters of a cc of such a solution—maybe even as much as one and a half ccs, sometimes, but this . . .' She closed her fingers about it. 'If taken orally, it would, I think, not cause death but certainly sleep would come and it would be profoundly comatose. As to someone's orally taking two of these, I don't know what would happen. A lot depends on the age of the person, their state of health. Many factors.'

'And intravenously?'

'Surely no one with any sort of training would think to do such a thing unless the patient was . . .'

'Death?'

'Even then with the one gram, I doubt it, but . . . but with Evipan the rapidity of injection is, perhaps, the determinant.'

'The more rapid the injection, the harder and faster the hit.'

How could the young man she had known, if but briefly, speak of such things in such a way? Had all innocence been lost?

As they went toward the front of the shop, they passed the litre bottles of Vittel and Hermann, he could not help but notice them and had to ask and harshly too, 'How did you come by those?'

A mineral water from the springs at Vittel that was taken orally for the relief of gout, hepatic colic and other ailments of the liver, arthritis too. A still water with tiny amounts of bicarbonates and sulphates. 'Victoria Bödicker always brings me some when she visits her mother at the end of each month. The bottles are only for show, of course, since everyone brings their own containers. I have four of the milk cans from a farm. She fills them for me.'

'Get rid of it. Deny ever having it.'

'And my customers? What of those who know I stock it for them? Victoria can't have done anything. How could she?'

'Don't ask. You're not involved. You know nothing of what she was up to. Deny it.'

There was frost on the windows and as they hurried by outside, people seldom bothered to glance in. It was always best these days to appear busy and bent on one's destination.

At the kerb, though, a Wehrmacht Citroën sat idling. 'Who is that?' she asked.

Kohler felt her take him by the hand, felt the nervousness in her. 'My partner.'

'I meant the woman in the back.'

'Lucie, forget I was even here. Remember always that for those of us in my line of work, friends are the hardest thing to come by. You're one of them and I won't rest until I've done all I can.'

Then Hermann was gone from her again, just like that, she standing out on the pavement. Gone this time, right out of her life? wondered Lucie, but knew she would simply have to wait and see.

One thing was certain. Renée Ekkehard had come back from a skiing party early in December wanting to ask what few unmarried girls like to ask but need to know. And as for Hermann, were he and his 'partner' on their way to Natzweiler-Struthof, and if so, why please, were they taking Victoria Bödicker with them?

Not until Goxwiller, just to the south of Obernai and in the shadow of Mont Sainte-Odile, did Herr Kohler, having floored the car nearly all the way, pull off the road. They were perhaps some forty kilometres to the north of Kolmar, felt Victoria, and there was now no longer any doubt in her mind as to where they were taking her.

St-Cyr had dozed off; Herr Kohler had said so little, it had been and still was all too evident that he dreaded their destination, but in spite of this he had been kind. He *had* asked if she was warm enough and, though tobacco was obviously in extremely short supply, had found, lit and passed back to her his only cigarette.

Now he broke out the lunch Yvonne Lutze had hastily thrown together for them. A vacuum flask of lentil soup; sandwiches for more than two, and of dried, smoked sausage, mustard and Munster wrapped, of course, in newspaper. Had Yvonne done it to remind her of what Renée had taken from the Lutze kitchen? If so, she silently asked, how is it that I could possibly have known of its contents?

St-Cyr had found her in Renée's room, the ampoules in hand. He had suspected she might well try to take her own life and had deliberately left them with her, only to then suddenly intervene. 'You will give up all your secrets,' he had gently said as he had taken those from her. 'Willingly you will betray your friends—please don't think it cowardly of yourself, or hateful of me to state it. One holds out for as long as possible to give others a chance to learn of the arrest and to then escape—that's an unwritten rule of the Résistance, but the Gestapo's interrogators have their ways and like as not, they'll be Alsatian, as in France they are invariably *gestapistes français*. It helps to know with whom one is dealing, *n'est-ce pas*, and what better way than to question a suspect by using a countryman or woman?'

And now? she asked. Now both he and Herr Kohler had turned to look at her as she cradled the vacuum flask's cap of soup for warmth and let its aroma rise.

'Louis, she isn't going to cooperate.'

'Mademoiselle, we're not torturers, nor would we turn you over to such people, but by taking you into protective custody—and, please, it was necessary, as I'm sure you understand—we endanger not only ourselves. There are others at home, in Paris.'

'I can't help you. I know nothing.'

'No one else need hear,' offered Herr Kohler. The engine had been switched off, the silence was intrusive. Freezing, the wind found every little crack, but from the snow-covered vineyards, the perfume of burning vine cuttings came. Iron barrows, with little fires in them, were being pushed between the rows by men whose *bleus de travail* stood out sharply. Beyond them, and perhaps no more than three kilometres away, the forested hills of the Vosges quickly climbed. Mont Sainte-Odile was some six kilometres almost due west; the convent clearly seen atop its rampart cliff. Beyond it, and a little to the south, was Neuntelstein, some eleven kilometres from them and at an elevation of 971 metres. Superb views of the Champ du Feu, Mont Sainte-Odile and the Haut-Koenigsbourg could be had from there, also on a clear day from the Champ du Feu, at 110 metres, the Black Forest. Blaise Oberkircher and she had stood there many times. Blaise . . .

Beyond Neuntelstein, a further six or so kilometres—a total of seventeen as the crow flies from here—were the quarries, at an elevation of about 800 to 1,000 metres. Bare and windswept, utterly cold and absolutely cruel.

'She isn't going to answer, Louis.'

The sound of church bells came. A wedding? she asked herself. A christening? It wasn't Sunday. Not yet. It was Wednesday, 10 February 1943, and she would never have children.

'Renée was despondent, Inspectors. Eugène . . . I still can't believe he took his own life.'

'Your notebook,' muttered St-Cyr, and turning from her, set his sandwich amid the dust and clutter next to the front windscreen that was rapidly fogging. 'It's a puzzle,' he said, dragging the notebook out. 'Frau Lutze . . .'

'I realized Yvonne had taken it.'

'Yet you didn't demand its return?'

'Werner Lutze must have known exactly where it was being kept. As our air-raid warden, he had had opportunity enough to have found it, and that could only mean he had felt his colonel had best see it and that Colonel Rasche had probably wanted a look at my background. The comments of the school inspectors and each of my directors.'

'So you let Frau Lutze steal it?'

'Yes.'

'It was that or let the local Gestapo get their hands on it,' said Herr Kohler.

The best of a bad bargain, was this what he thought? wondered Victoria.

'Frau Oberkircher's death has fingered you, mademoiselle,' said St-Cyr. 'Those two—Deiss and Paulus—won't let it lie. They can't. You ran from them and you now know exactly what they did. They'll have to put it out that you were involved in something.'

'Book selling, that is all.'

They'd get nowhere with her, Kohler told himself. Too proud, too loyal, too . . .

'Patriotic,' said Louis, having realized his partner's trend of thought.

'Stubborn,' said Kohler. 'Brave, of course, Louis, and oh for sure, there's always a time for that but this isn't one of them.'

'Mademoiselle, we have reason to believe that Renée Ekkehard discovered that the two who needed guidance and were to have been brought to the carnival by their courier hadn't arrived.'

'Others then came looking,' said Herr Kohler. 'First there was Alain Schrijen and then Werner Lutze.'

'To avoid one or the other or both she skied into the woods and stayed out all night.'

'Headed east, Louis, to Neuf-Brisach, either skiing, walking or catching one of the local trains, buses or a lift, and then went on to Alt-Breisach which is just across the Rhine.'

'And from there, Hermann, went to the northeast and into the Kaiserstuhl, that little range of volcanic hills whose lower slopes are covered with vineyards, the woods above.'

'And?'

'To the Totenkopf, and a gamekeeper's hut, after which she then returned, but having found out what?

'Answers . . . we are always needing answers, mademoiselle,' continued St-Cyr. 'It was perfect, wasn't it? Messages hidden in the personals columns of the daily newspapers, a resident repairer of watches as a go-between along with his gamekeeper brother, the carnival as a way-stop on the route through to France and one that Colonel Rasche had repeatedly and unwittingly sanctioned.'

'Even to allowing you to make trips to Vittel to visit your mother,' said Kohler, 'thereby allowing contact with the Francs-Tireurs *et Partisans* on that side of the frontier and in the Vosges but what none of you realized was that while the three of you were busy, so were the men you had convinced the colonel to let help you.'

'They had a plan of their own, mademoiselle.'

The chief inspector reached out to take the vacuum flask's cap from her. 'But Eugène Thomas wouldn't go along with what they wanted him to do—and I think this must have been how it was, Hermann, for of all of them he was the closest to Sophie Schrijen.'

'So they sentenced him to death, mademoiselle, and *voilà*, die he did.'

'Murdered? Eugène? But . . . but why? He . . .'

They left her then to think it over. They knew they had already told her far more than they should. Taking the rest of the soup and sandwiches, they slammed the doors on her, slammed her in.

'She didn't know those boys were planning to escape, Louis.'

'Nor did Sophie Schrijen.'

Lunch in hand, the wind tugging at its newspaper wrapping, they moved away from the car so as not to let her overhear, thought Victoria. Backs to the wind, and to her, they began to talk, St-Cyr gesturing with a sandwich at which he frowned perhaps, for one did not spoil Munster with mustard, and both Renée and Yvonne had done that.

'All things are of interest, Hermann. Frau Lutze is far too good a cook to have done such a thing unless intentionally.'

'And that can only mean one thing, can't it?'

'She feels that the one behind us here could well offer answers but will refuse.'

'Rasche wants us to go for the son. He and Löwe Schrijen have been at each other's throats over this little venture of Sophie's, and all along we've been dumb enough to have stepped between them.'

'But neither will now want the men of that combine to be sent to Natzweiler-Struthof for reinforced interrogation.'

'Because each is afraid of what will come out of that should Kramer and the rest of the SS hear of it,' sighed Kohler. 'Lagerfeldwebel Dorsche will do his damnedest to prise what he can from them—he'll have to. Karl Rudel will insist on it, but Schrijen won't let Dorsche use the machinery of the Works to terrify those poor bastards, not while they're being held in *Straf*, and the colonel knows it. Both he and Schrijen will want us to question those boys alone, if anyone does.'

'So he cries murder, not suicide, Hermann, and asks himself where he can find two honest, hardworking, dumb *Schweinebullen* who will look for the truth he'll present to them.'

'And sends us to Natzweiler-Struthof. We can't take her into that camp.'

'Schrijen and Rasche both know this but have given us no other choice.'

'Yet Renée Ekkehard was forced to watch an execution. Only Kramer could have given that boy the permission to bring her into the camp.'

'Which can only mean he knew all about what that girl had cried out.'

'Or had been told enough by Alain Schrijen to sanction it. We've no authority there, Louis. Even I haven't. Camps like those have laws of their own.'

'We'll leave her at the ski lodge. If we can, we'll bring Alain Schrijen to her. Maybe that will force the truth from him.'

'He'll never tell us, and you know it.'

'Of course he won't. They'll all lie, but between the lies will be the mustard and the Munster.'

9

The modest guesthouse, the Gasthaus Struthof, a ski lodge, was much as Victoria remembered from the winter of 1936: grey, weather-beaten boards and timbers whose carvings were beautiful and in the traditional style, with a long, railed, first-storey porch that overlooked the slopes. Racks of staghorn were on either side of the entrance. There had been lots of skiers back then, were quite a few still, though apparently oblivious to, or welcoming the swastika that hung from the crown of the roof high above her. Snow-deep, the single roadway out in front was no more than ten metres wide. Beyond its ends, downhill pistes cut through the fir trees to the west and east, clouds of powder snow trailing each skier. There were uniforms but not that many: the black of the Schutzstaffel, its newer grey-green, and that of the Wehrmacht, and here a Mauser rifle over a shoulder, there a Bergmann submachine gun or an officer with a holstered pistol.

'Go in and have a cup of coffee,' said Herr Kohler. 'Try to just relax. Don't do anything stupid.'

'I have no reason to.'

Across from them, across the road, was the building that had been used for overflow guests, kitchen storage, extra showers and a washroom.* It all seemed so innocent: at least twenty degrees of frost, with drifting smoke from isolated farm chimneys being caught by the gusting wind, and in the distance, the sight of snow-covered hills and forest that she had always found so exhilarating.

Dismayed, she watched St-Cyr and Kohler drive away. Two decent men. Patriots? she asked. The Frenchman certainly; the Bavarian . . . Where, please, did he really sit in this tragedy?

The road to the *Konzentrationslager* was only three kilometres long. All of it was steeply uphill, and there were several tight bends the prisoners had cut and built with their bare hands. Laughing, two skiers pushed past her to stand their skis and poles in the nearby snowbank, both already pulling off their caps and unbuttoning their jackets to hang them up with all the others. No one seemed to pay the slightest attention to a woman with an overcoat, scarf and hat she quickly removed but took with her. The patterned pullover would blend in as would the slacks, but could she find the strength to behave exactly as if on holiday?

'*Einen Kaffee mit Milch, bitte.* A table by the window, if possible.'

The lace-trimmed blouse the waitress wore was white, the straps of the dress, the deepest of reds, the braided hair under the primly tied kerchief, flaxen and long, but not perfect, for in the haste to wait on so many, several strands had come loose.

---

* In the summer of 1943 the shower-baths became part of an experimental gas chamber that would have held about twenty at a time.

The girl had rosy cheeks, an enviable complexion, exquisite brows and beautifully formed lips, the eyes of the darkest blue. 'Are you from Schirmeck?' asked Victoria.

Flicking her gaze hesitantly to a table far to the left of them, the girl said, 'Now that I am needed here, Fräulein, I live in and share a room with two others. It . . . it is best that way.'

'Have you been here long?'

Again there was that apprehensive glance toward the table where a lone man sat smoking a cigarette. 'Not long. Since late last autumn when the skiing began.'

The dining room was large; there was a dance floor and a stage, everything that a party would need and, from the window, the view across the Bruche Valley stretched to the hazy outline of the Donon at 1,009 metres. Seemingly endless fir forest covered this part of the Vosges, with beech trees in the lower reaches, the snow deepest among them and thinnest over the crests of the hills, some of which had been cleared for pasture well before the Middle Ages. There would be utter silence out there, utter peace, the frost so hard, the branches would creak. The ski runs were perfect here, and wasn't it this that made it so hard? Renée had loved to ski; Sophie had too, and herself, and it hadn't been wrong of her to have brought those two together. They had been happier than ever before, content in themselves, so many things.

Of course it had been wrong, she said silently, for look where things are now, look at what has happened to Renée.

Her coffee came, and with it, a glass of schnapps. 'Who . . .' she blurted as the girl tossed her head in the direction of the *Kachelofen* and that other table. 'I can't accept it. I'm sorry.'

'*Bitte*, Fräulein, if I were you, I would thank Herr Meyer and call out *Ein Prosit*. It costs nothing and will keep him happy. It's always best with those people.'

'Who is he?'

'The Obersturmführer? He is Head of the Political Department at the Natzweiler Lager.'

Somehow she did as advised, even to smiling at this Nazi in mufti. She would concentrate on the ski slopes, would let the good-natured camaraderie of this place wrap itself around her. St-Cyr and Kohler would want to sit Alain down in front of her at this table and confront him with what they knew must have happened, but did they now suspect that Renée, on seeing that car of his arriving at the carnival, had thought Sophie must have come out after all, only to then realize that it was Alain and to scramble to put on her skis and head into the Kastenwald to avoid him?

Did they now know that the *Polizeikommandantur*'s *Grüne Minna* had then arrived and that Renée, on looking back, had seen it and had immediately thought all had been lost? They could only assume that she had been out all night. They could not possibly know that she had forced herself to do the impossible and had gone east to the Totenkopf, to the hut to find out what had gone wrong and to warn the others along the line, only to then find that none of them were there either.

Two boys, two deserters and their courier were supposed to have been coming through from Munich. Instead, she had found cold ashes in the firebox of the hut's little stove and an emptiness that would not go away.

Exhausted, Renée had had no other choice but to return to the carnival. Despondent, yes, poor thing, and terrified of arrest.

'Might I join you, Fräulein?'

'*Ach!* Why, yes, of course.'

'A cigarette?'

'That would be lovely. The two who dropped me off used up all I had.'

'Then we had best see that you keep better company.'

The camp was quiet, the wire fences barbed and electrified, the ground-storey, barrack blocks low-roofed in tiers, paired two by two and stepped up the hillside, perhaps thirty of them in all and without a whisper of wood smoke or sign of a chimney except from the kitchen hut. Guard towers were at each corner of the wire and midway between, but even here, little sign of life was evident beyond that of the wood smoke from their portable stoves. Even the dogs, in the fenced runs, had sought the shelter of the kennels, these being well insulated with straw.

Had Hermann and he happened upon an execution? wondered St-Cyr. Though they'd been seen, and their approach closely followed, no challenge had been given. 'The administrative block is uphill, Hermann, and just outside the gate.' They had parked some distance down from it.

'Be quiet. *Mein Gott*, can't you listen? What's that sound?'

Hermann was really edgy. 'Skiers.'

'Not those. That other sound.'

Now it came and now it didn't, for the wind from the west was intermittent. Again and again they heard it, both looking uphill questioningly. From the camp to the nearby bald crown of the hill it couldn't be any more than two hundred metres. Tangled, windswept brush was up there. Stunted beeches, bilberry and gentian, the snow cover thin and trailing to leave uncovered a litter of round boulders.

'A dinging,' swore Hermann, not liking it.

'Iron on iron.'

'Countless blows.'

A steep, wide path, its snow beaten down by many, disappeared over the crest of the hill. Slippery, the path was a son of a bitch to climb, but looking back over a shoulder and beyond the wire enclosure of the camp, the view was straight out of a storybook.

'Louis, maybe we'd best leave this. Let's just go down to the Kommandant's office, that one right down there, the one with the window and the binoculars that are staring at us.'

Hermann was afraid and with good reason. 'We'll go through the motions, *mon vieux*. We'll do exactly as they want, and then, suitably chastised and conditioned, we'll confront them.'

There were two quarries beyond the crest of the hill, sharply stepped, amphitheatre openings in the rock, other, lesser ones distant among the beech and fir. Against the green and grey of the trees, the snow and the blue of the sky, the pink of the granite was startlingly bright, the sound of the hammering constant. 'When cold, there is no other sound quite like that of iron on iron,' muttered St-Cyr. 'It's distinctly resonant and acutely so.'

Perhaps four thousand men in mud-brown tattered coats, trousers and the oddest assortment of footgear were at work. No one took any apparent notice of two detectives standing out against the skyline on the crest of this hill. To have looked up would have been suicidal. Each man either knelt on the broad ledges among innumerable rectangular, snow-covered blocks yet to be removed, or swung a ten-kilo sledge to hit a drill rod that was being held, and certainly one waited apprehensively for the scream as a hand or wrist was smashed or an eye blinded by a splinter of iron or rock. Hoists and pulleys, logs, skids, ramps and finally wagons, on to which blocks of stone were being loaded for transport downhill to the railway siding at Shirmeck, also offered places where a man could easily be crushed.

Iron, two-wheeled barrows held the waste rubble and were being pushed, pulled, heaved at and dragged to a tip where they were dumped on to a roadway that was being built. Beyond these were lorries that could just as well have been used. Three of them were parked with two grey tourers next to the neat row of SS barracks from whose parade ground flew a large swastika.

Guards were nearly everywhere and warmly clothed, their steel helmets, rifles and Schmeissers sharply outlined against the frost, the sky, and a sun whose glare was blinding.

When a drill rod accidentally fell, it added its more rapid dinging until hastily stilled. On one ledge, the rock suddenly cracked and the long, long splitting of it was clearly heard above the undertone.

'Their hands, Louis. They don't have gloves, only rags.'

'Their faces, Hermann. Many of them are sunburnt.'

The coffee was real, but she must not in any way indicate that this was anything but normal, felt Victoria; the schnapps, an *eau-de-vie de framboise*, a raspberry liqueur for which Alsace was justly famous; the cigarette a Juno.

Skiers came and went, paying no attention to them and yet . . . and yet, she wanted to cry out that things were far from normal, that at the camp, men were being systematically worked to death.

Instead, she must smile softly at this Obersturmführer, this gaunt, rake-jawed SS with the jutting chin and intense grey eyes whose rank was equivalent to that of a Kriminalinspektor in the German Police. She must make idle conversation, must lie if necessary and consistently, must then remember every little thing she had said because he would remember it.

'A bookseller!' marvelled Bruno Meyer. 'But that is extraordinary, Fräulein. Really, you must meet our Schutzhaftlagerführer Kramer. He collects books for the Standartenführer Sievers, the Executive Secretary of the Ahnenerbe, the Institute for Research into Heredity, and Director of the Institute of Military Scientific Research. Standartenführer Sievers was a bookseller before the war and here, at the camp, Schutzshaftlagerführer Kramer has been patiently gathering quite a collection for him. Velum-bound manuscripts written entirely by hand and in Latin or in Old German. Examples of the earliest of printings too, and of the French. I'm certain you would find much in common.'

Again the Fräulein Bödicker found herself saying, 'That would be lovely. If there is time, I would like that very much.'

'Time . . . Why should there not?'

'The two who brought me here. I . . . I simply don't know how long they'll be.' His eyes darkened.

'It's about the suicide of Untersturmführer Schrijen's fiancée, isn't it?'

Cher Jésus, save her now. 'Alain's fiancée, yes. Renée . . . Renée Ekkehard.'

'You knew her well?'

He must know all about it. 'A little. We worked together on the *Winterhilfswerk* Committee of Alain's sister.'

'A fête . . . I seem to remember seeing something about one your committee was to hold in mid-March.'

It was impossible to read his thoughts. 'The sixth, yes. That's when it's to open.'

'*Ach*, now I have it. Gauleiter Wagner is to officiate. Did you know he was a former primary schoolteacher, as was yourself?'

'Did I say I'd been a teacher?'

'A difficult one, if I understand the reports of your directors and visiting school inspectors. Not a strict disciplinarian, as was Herr Wagner. Little got past him, let me tell you. Minor offences must always be severely punished if discipline and absolute obedience are to be firmly instilled.'

Just what was he after? 'I . . . I felt it best to overlook certain misdemeanours. If a child is placed in a position of trust and responsibility, he or she invariably feels useful and there is both a learning process of immense value and a sense of self-worth that engenders harmony.'

'Then you don't agree with the Gauleiter Wagner's methods?'

Ah, merde, she had fallen right into it. 'I didn't say that.'

'Then what *did* you imply?' Her cheeks were colouring.

'Breaking a child's spirit isn't necessarily the best form of discipline, Herr Obersturmführer. Humiliating them in front of their peers by using a birch rod or leather strap simply reinforces the underlying problem which may have nothing whatsoever to do with the school and everything to do with what's been happening at home. Children love to be busy learning new things and to feel useful. Always if there is that sense of their making progress, even if only at their own speed, you will seldom have discipline problems.'

'Then it is that you really do disagree with the Gauleiter?'

'I didn't say that, Herr Obersturmführer. I merely said that I . . .'

'You disagreed.' Her eyes had moistened.

'Is Herr Wagner some sort of expert in the education of children?'

'Would it interest you to know that we have a copy of your school notebook?'

On microfilm? 'I . . . I assumed my mother's house and bookshop had been searched while I was in Munich for retraining with other teachers in the late autumn of 1940. I . . . I didn't know anything had been photographed.'

Like all the other students, she had been required to take that notebook with her to Munich but had felt he would be unaware of this, thereby avoiding any mention of later searches! 'And now you do, Fräulein. Page by page.'

Steel wedges, one face flat, the other curved to fit against the wall of the drill hole, and perhaps fifteen centimetres long, were being slipped into each hole. An iron wedge was then jammed between them and each wedge hammered into the rock in succession until, with a muted cracking, a *pop*, or *bang*, the rock split.

'It's much the same process,' said Louis, 'as the Egyptians would have used to quarry stone for their magnificent obelisks and the rose-coloured lid of Tutankhamen's quartzite sarcophagus at Karnak.'

The boy-king's tomb had been all the rage of Paris in the last half of the '20s and early '30s. Louis, like most Parisians, had been fascinated, but unlike most he still remained wrapped up in it.

The quarries here had been opened in the summer of 1941 and inspected by Himmler, head of the SS, the securing of 'a much-needed' source of pink granite hailed as a 'triumph.'

Men from all of the occupied territories were at work. Several languages were being spoken, their hurried, harried shouts a biblical Tower of Babel of its own while shoulder patches gave red for the politicals and a deep, inverted equilateral triangle with the black letter *F* for French, a lighter red and a *B* for Belgian, and in between these, shades and letters denoting Czechs and Italians, while yellow was for the Hungarians, green for the Germans, and an *S* on the latter's patch denoting that the man was a 'security risk.' And in addition to the inverted triangles, there were the large red crosses on the backs of the *N und Ns.*

As each short drill rod was hit and hit hard, it was then given a quarter turn by the man who held it. No goggles were worn, no protection whatsoever and, with each blow, there was that terrible shock to rag-wrapped hands, for the drill rod would vibrate. 'And at subzero temperatures like this,' muttered Louis, 'the iron is work-hardened by the constant hammering.'

'Becoming more brittle, *mein Lieber*, it burrs and tears more easily at the top, the rod being turned to rotate the fucking tungsten-carbide bit!'

Still no one had come to question their presence. Was it that the rule of silence had been invoked, a shunning as was done in some religious sects, the smell that of what? wondered St-Cyr. Of long-unwashed clothing and bodies, of sweat, pus and old blood, but . . . but to these was added a sulphurous taint.

'The mineral pyrite, Hermann. A disulphide of iron. There must be grains of it in some of Herr Himmler's rock. A variety of fool's gold, it will weather, rust and stain the monuments that are to record for all time the glories of the Third Reich unless those sections containing it are removed.'

Splinters—the 'shrapnel' Hermann had experienced at Vieil-Armand—were a constant hazard attested to by rag patches over an eye here and there, the expressions of the men universally gaunt and empty, even more so than at the Textilfabrikschrijen. One man paused to snatch and hastily down a handful of snow, and for a brief second there was the thought that he would be severely beaten, and then the thought that such a punishment was merely being delayed due to the presence of visitors.

Perhaps one hundred guards were on duty, perhaps a few less but under these were the *Kapos*, the block leaders, prisoners themselves and armed with pick handles. But at any moment, all of the prisoners could have rebelled were it not for the machine guns that were trained on them from the heights, and of course there were also the everlasting hunger, the extreme weather and lack of any form of suitable clothing or transport to consider.

'The remoteness, Louis. God Himself couldn't escape from here. Kramer must be in the next quarry.'

Fortunately they hadn't attempted to bring Victoria Bödicker with them.

It was freezing in the communal shower bath across the road from the guesthouse. Caught, seized, dragged up and propelled from the restaurant without coat, scarf or handbag, Victoria held herself by the elbows and tried not to shake. 'I know nothing, Herr Obersturmführer. *Nothing*!'

'THE FRÄULEIN EKKEHARD TOLD YOU OF THE EXPERIMENTS THAT ARE BEING CONDUCTED HERE FOR THE LUFTWAFFE AND OTHERS.'

'SHE DIDN'T!'

'And yet she leaves a note: "I can't go on. Please forgive me"? Come, come, Fräulein, you can do better than that.'

He wasn't going to listen. 'Why not ask Alain? Surely if everything was so secret, he'd not have boasted of it to Renée?'

She hit the wall, hit it hard, was momentarily blinded and felt herself sliding to the floor. Blood wet her hand when she wiped her broken lips. 'Am I also to have a skiing accident?'

He smiled. He said nothing. Through the buzzing in her ears she heard him laugh. Perhaps two metres now separated them, perhaps a little more. The room was simply large and bare, but with gooseneck nozzles and taps, and a drain in the concrete floor. He had closed and locked the door. They were all alone and no one would hear her cries, not St-Cyr and not Herr Kohler.

' "Boasted," Fräulein? Would it interest you to know that the Untersturmführer Schrijen brought his fiancée here during that party?'

'But why? Whatever for?'

Punched hard, blood burst from her nose and lips. Her head hit the wall again, his fist, her left eye. There was now no hope. None at all. The pain was excruciating.

'Experiments, Fräulein. You will tell me what that lesbian whore told you of them.'

Seized by the hair—dragged up and propelled into an adjacent room—she was thrown to her knees. *'OPEN IT!'* he shrieked.

The small, circular well, one of three that had recently been sunk into the floor, was lined with the green and white tiles of a *Kachelofen*, the smell revolting. 'Please. I know nothing of this, Herr Obersturmführer.'

When he shrieked again, Victoria cringed and did as asked. The well was brimful and stank of formaldehyde, and on its surface, a mat of blonde hair had floated up and out.

Crouching, Meyer wrapped the fingers of his left hand through the hair and pulled the corpse up until the head and torso were free and staring at her, the formalin draining from the breasts, the blue eyes wide open.

Slowly it sank back down and she watched it disappear. 'This one will soon be on her back in the cutting room at the

University of Strassburg, Fräulein. Be thankful it's not yourself. Now come. We will go up to the hospital at the camp. Perhaps we can do something for you there. That eye . . . I don't like the look of it.'

Although the main quarries were now behind, there still hadn't been a sign of Kramer and Alain Schrijen, nor challenge from any of the guards. 'Do they intend to kill us, Louis?' managed Kohler.

There could be no way of their knowing ahead of time. They passed among firs, the haulage road well trodden and cutting through deep snow, the sound from the quarries carrying. At a pause, Louis tried to roll a cigarette from the contents of his little tin but had to give it up. 'The wind,' he said. 'My fingers are too numb.'

But did he have to look at his partner in such a soulful way? 'It's not my fault,' said Kohler. 'You know how much I hate these bastards and damn them all to hell.'

The urge to say, *This is hell*, was there, but . . . 'Paris, *mon vieux*. Paris.'

'Giselle and Oona, Louis.'

'Gabrielle too, and the boys and their families on my street.'

The rue Laurence-Savart and his precious Belleville, the little friends who endlessly discussed the ins and outs and private life of this Sûreté with whom they kicked a soccer ball as often as possible.

In time they came to a quarry where no men worked but where five stood out on a ledge against the rock and the snow. Dressed in rags, their camp coats, with painted crosses faceup, were neatly folded on the ground in front of them, their hands tied tightly behind their backs, their heads shaven.

On their haunches, two splendid Alsatians waited obediently, one on either side of what must be Alain Schrijen.

Josef Kramer was with him.

The surgery was overly warm and reeked of disinfectant. Left to herself while Meyer went to find a doctor—what sort of doctor?—Victoria forced herself to look into the mirror of one of the medicine cabinets. Blood had spattered the front of her pullover. Shaking, she shut her good eye and tried not to cry. They were going to kill her. She'd be submerged in formaldehyde and cut open . . . They would kill St-Cyr and Kohler. They couldn't let any of them live.

Everything was exactly as on that Sunday morning, 6 December last, when Alain had brought Renée here. Syringes still lay on their glass shelf behind the window doors of their cabinet. Ten cubic centimetre ampoules of Evipan were in flat, thin grey cardboard cartons. All it had taken Renée had been two steps, and three of those had gone into a pocket. Alain hadn't seen her. She'd been positive of that.

The dark brown, glass-stoppered, 250 cc bottle of phenol was here too. 'Phenol,' wept Victoria softly. 'Twenty cc's. The girl in that well?' she had to ask.

When dead, that girl had been stripped, her clothing taken away and donated by Alain to Sophie's *Volksopfer*.

There were bandages and rolls of gauze, tins of antiseptic powder, splints—everything needed should any of the SS guards require them, for this was not the camp hospital behind the wire. This was for its personnel and Kramer's family.

Steps sounded in the corridor. The ampoules of Evipan were not cold but warm, their glass paper-thin and smooth, and yes, it would shatter easily when in her pocket but would the cuts be deep enough, would sufficient of the drug get into her bloodstream? Would its reaction be fast enough?

The steps had ceased just outside the door, the one whispering urgently to the other, 'But no *Vollzugszettel* has been received from the RSHA in Berlin, Obersturmführer?'

No execution order from the Reichssicherheitshauptamt, the Reich Security Office.

Alain had enjoyed telling Renée about the experiments. Sometimes men were inflicted with typhus, their arms cut open to be swabbed with the disease, they to die in agony as its progress was studied, but not here, of course, in that other 'surgery' behind the wire. In other experiments some had been forced to inhale or swallow Lost gas—mustard gas—to then die of bleeding lungs and other organs that had often burst. The Herr Doktor Professors Hirt, Bickenbach and Haagan regularly came from the University of Strassburg to conduct their research. In turn, cadavers were sent to them for autopsy. Sometimes only the heads were hermetically sealed in tin boxes of formalin for delivery. Girls too. Girls like that one she'd been shown. All selected as test specimens by that former bookseller, the Standartenführer Sievers, who would follow the professors' requests and make certain they were filled.

Renée had been drugged on the night of that party. Dizzy, in panic and confusion, she had tried to fight Alain off, but had he known beforehand that she and Sophie were lovers? Had Löwe Schrijen told him to take care of the matter but keep it within the family? Hence the invitation to that first party. The skiing, the dancing and the good times, then the threat of the experiments, the rape and Renée crying out what she should never have cried out.

From the window, the camouflaged, grey-green Citroën Herr Kohler had parked some distance from the gate still appeared unoccupied. Across from the hospital, there was the building that housed the officer's barracks and the mess hall, beyond this, the Alsatian-style villa the Schutzhaftlagerführer Kramer had had built for his family in the autumn of 1941. Kramer had been here right from the start, had served as one of the interim Kommandants. From the chimneys of the villa's gabled roof, smoke was plucked away by the wind to drift quickly over the camp, while below the railed, first-storey balcony that was still decorated with fir bows and gilded ornaments, children played.

Beyond the house, beyond the kennels, lay the camp and, right next to the outermost wire, the large square of ground over which the grey dust Renée had spoken of was again being spread. Under guard, two of the *N und Ns* used coal shovels to empty a wheelbarrow, the wind playing havoc with the distribution.

In season, that plot was the Kramer family's vegetable garden.

'Fräulein, this is the Herr Doktor Professor Haagan.'

'I'm really quite all right, Obersturmführer. I'll just wait here if I might for the Hauptmann Detektiv Aufsichtsbeamter Kohler and the Oberdetektiv Französisch der Sûreté Nationale Jean-Louis St-Cyr that Gestapo Boemelburg sent from Paris on orders from the Gestapo Chief, Herr Müller, in Berlin. They should be along soon. I've had a bad fall. A patch of ice that was hidden under the snow. Nothing more. Colonel Rasche, the Kommandant of the Ober-Rhein, will be certain to ask when we get back to Kolmar, and that is what I will tell him, since he and those two Detektivs are responsible for me and must report everything to the Reichsführer Himmler.'

'Fräulein, sit, please. It's best that way.'

'And if I refuse?'

'Suit yourself.'

Already the shadows were spreading. Already one-half of the quarry had acquired the bluish tinge snow gradually gets as daylight recedes.

'Schutzhaftlagerführer Kramer at your service, *mein Herren*. Apologies for not having welcomed you at the gate. Always these days there are things that must be done, always orders from Berlin. Those five are to go up the chimney this evening.' Kramer indicated the condemned. 'Untersturmführer Schrijen,' he called out sharply, for that one had moved away from them.

'*Jawohl,* Schutzhaftlagerführer?' came the immediate response amid the clash of heels.

'Take the Oberdetektiv St-Cyr along on your final review. Be so good as to accompany him, *mein Herr*. Make sure each man accurately gives you his full name and former place of residence. The Untersturmführer, who does not speak their language, will then check these off against the clipboard's list.'

'And the dogs?' asked Louis.

'Those will accompany the Untersturmführer as always,' said Kramer. 'It's best that way. Perhaps you will soon see why.'

This former guard at Dachau, Buchenwald or Sachenhausen, thought St-Cyr, this 'family man' in shiny black jackboots, grey whipcord breeches and a black, three-quarter-length leather coat, would have been an all but nondescript, quite ordinary-looking individual had he been dressed differently. Blocky in the face, below the peaked, black military cap with its white death's-head, the brow was wide, the dark reddish-brown eyebrows hooded, the look in the greenish-brown eyes at once belligerent and cold.

He was not tall, but of medium height and with the build and stance of a barrel-maker or stonemason, the nose prominent, a vertical crease directly above it giving a perpetual frown. But what would Hermann say to him in the absence of his partner? Would Hermann turn his back on all that had happened to them since their first meeting in Paris on that Thursday, 13 September 1940? Would he weaken?

Feeling the end was close, would Louis be defiant? wondered Kohler as Kramer, cupping his hands about the lighted match, lit a cigarette for him. *'Danke,'* he managed. A last smoke, was that it? The firing squad of ten hadn't moved a muscle, and there was Louis striding toward the condemned. There would be two shots into each of those boys up there and no white cardboard patches to mark where they'd best go, just stern faces on the squad. Like steel-helmeted robots and yes, the memories of that other war were coming quickly, especially those of that other firing squad and Colonel Bloody Damn Otto Rasche with one Werner Lutze at his side.

'Well, Kohler, we could use a man like yourself,' said Kramer. 'One thoroughly familiar with explosives, though we don't use anything but black powder and only to bump up the key stone in each quarry's floor. A former officer of a trip-to-heaven detail, former artillery officer . . .'

'Let's cut the *Quatsch,* Schutzhaftlagerführer. It's too damned cold for one thing.'

'And for another?'

'That boy has a lot of answering to do.'

'But answers need not be given?'

'Not unless they're necessary.'

'Gut.'

Louis had paused to confront Alain Schrijen. Neither of the dogs was on a lead; both watched that Sûreté with consummate interest; both waited for the single command they felt certain was to come.

I love dogs, said Kohler silently and then, 'Those are beautiful animals, aren't they?'

Kramer drew on his cigarette, the black kid gloves almost brand-new. 'Let's hope that partner of yours doesn't ask too many questions. Always after a detail like this, we give the boys a stiff drink. You'll join us, of course.'

He wasn't going to let them leave the quarry. It was really that simple. An order was an order, and there was Louis going on and on as if they had all day.

'You killed that girl, didn't you?' said St-Cyr when Alain Schrijen and he had reached the lowermost ledge of granite. 'You were not here on January thirtieth and thirty-first, as that father of yours has claimed, but had taken the noon train to Kolmar on the Saturday for just that purpose and would have arrived at perhaps 2.00 or 2.30 that afternoon.'

'I was here. The day log is proof enough.'

'Your sister drove to the station to leave you your car. You then drove to the *Karneval*, parking up by the ruins of the House of Mirrors. Renée Ekkehard saw you get out and, putting on her skis, headed into the Kastenwald, causing you to shout and run after her.'

'What if I did?'

'She was afraid of you, *mein Lieber*. Why, please, was she afraid? A girl whom you were to have married?'

Four years younger than his sister—twenty-eight at most—Alain Schrijen was not as tall or fair or lightly boned, nor was he anything at all like Hermann had said of the father, but something in between. 'Why did you treat that girl so abominably?'

This *Schweinebulle* from Paris would soon learn the truth, not that it would much matter. 'Renée didn't understand. Girls who are virgins sometimes don't.'

'*Salaud*, don't piss me off! And don't try to deny that you understand our language. You and Sophie grew up under French jurisdiction.'

'I didn't kill Renée. I broke her in and that is all. She enjoyed it.'

Ah, mon Dieu, what was Hermann doing? Saying to that other one that they wouldn't interfere? 'You will accompany us to Colmar, there to answer truthfully all questions that are put to you.'

'And if I don't?'

'You will be handcuffed and forcibly taken.'

'Arrested?'

The smirk was there and one had best say, '*Sans aucun doute.*' Without a doubt.

'Then why not wait and see, Inspector?'

'It's Chief Inspector.'

'Wait, then. Duty calls and even you, a former frontline soldier for the French must at least recognize that in a time of war, duty takes precedence.'

Louis went up the ledges ahead of the Untersturmführer who let him hurry on. Soon he came to the first man and for a moment, they looked at each other, but did Louis say, Listen, *mon ami*, I'm not one of them? Did he say, *Vive la France libre*?

Kramer watched the proceedings while budgeting his cigarette. Spat at by the first of the condemned, Louis stood his ground, not even wiping his face. One by one, the Untersturmführer and the dogs following, they went along the line and at each man, spittle erupted to hit that Sûreté but still he wouldn't pause to remove it.

Only as the last of the condemned was passed by did St-Cyr take his place, noted Kramer. Dumbfounded, sickened, Herr Kohler was at a loss for words and aghast. This disgrace to the Service, this 'conscientious doubter' who had caused so much trouble in Paris and elsewhere in France by pointing the finger of truth with that French partner of his, started forward only to hesitate, to look over his shoulder in panic.

Kramer flung his cigarette away.

Ah, Jésus, merde alors, Louis, what the hell am I to do? silently demanded Kohler. Cry out to you, Get away from there; stand well to the side? Let's claim both deaths were suicides. Let's be realistic?

There was only one way to settle this and Kramer had known it all along. Louis would hate him. Everything that had ever been between them would be destroyed and yet they would never be allowed to leave unless it was done. Berlin must have ordered it.

Shoot the five or else. Snatch away the nearest rifle and be that firing squad.

The dogs were going back and forth in front of the line, now to nip at a tattered shoe or rag-covered ankle, now to bite a Sûreté's 'new' overboots.

Suddenly one of the prisoners panicked. Turning, the man tried to climb the ledges to get away, to cry out God knows what, for the dogs were instantly upon him. Dragged down, torn at the crotch, the throat, he threw himself about, blood everywhere in the snow, his shrieks echoing until wave after wave of shots finally broke over Kohler, one of the dogs leaping up as it was hit and then madly thrashing its legs until still, the other simply flipping over to lie half on a ledge and half over its edge.

Shaking, he thrust the rifle back at its owner. Curtly Kramer gave the detail a nod and the crash of rifle-fire began again to rebound from the walls of the quarry until stilled as three ravens, black against the fading light, flew up and away.

Only Louis stood out on that ledge, but why hadn't those birds flown away earlier? Why had they to wait until now?

Seen through the windscreen's ever-moving wiper blades, the snowflakes were like an endless cloud of tiny parachutes caught in the searchlight's feeble beam from the headlamps, felt Victoria. Alain Schrijen had not come with them but was to follow.

Still to the west of Molsheim, and deep in the Bruche Valley, St-Cyr, who had constantly glanced into the rearview, became increasingly apprehensive. Though speed was necessary, and they desperately had to put distance behind them, he anticipated difficulties ahead, but now he suddenly speeded up, now he began to take chances. He could not know that there were ampoules of Evipan in her trouser pocket, could not know that she would break them when necessary and that there really were things she must never reveal to anyone.

Herr Kohler still stared emptily out his side windscreen, and one sensed absolutely that whatever had happened to them at the quarry, it had had a profound effect. Both, beyond a few terse words of commiseration to herself, had remained withdrawn, each waiting for the other to say something. Kohler, she knew from what had happened at Claudette's, must be feeling that death really did follow him everywhere and that, in spite of what he stood for, he must share the blame and that nothing he could do or say would ever renew the friendship he had once had with his partner. St-Cyr, one sensed, was well aware of this, the revulsion, the horror of what they'd seen, and perhaps it was that he felt Herr Kohler needed to sort things out for himself, perhaps it was that he was simply too angry and appalled to reach out to his friend.

Both had been shocked by her appearance as she had run from the hospital, no coat, no hat, no handbag, just a terrified, badly beaten woman. They had been solicitous, had wanted to take the Obersturmführer to task, only to realize that they had best leave while they could.

And now? asked Victoria. Now she sat between them, neither knowing when the SS would overtake them, each wanting to reach out to the other, herself the gulf, the quarry between.

Perhaps some sixth sense alerted St-Cyr, perhaps he had seen the glint of unshielded headlamps well behind them. Snowbanks crowded closely. There were no lanes that she could see, no side roads onto which they might turn. Again and again St-Cyr glanced into the rearview. 'Two lorries, Hermann.'

They didn't have a chance. 'Kramer must have gotten through to Berlin and they've now told him what to do,' said Kohler. 'Pull over. Switch off and douse the headlamps.'

The lorries didn't stop. They roared past in clouds of billowing snow. 'They're going for those boys in *Straf*, Louis. There's nothing we can do but follow and they know it.'

'That doctor, mademoiselle,' said St-Cyr, darkness now enveloping them.

'The Professor Haagan. The Obersturmführer Meyer wanted him to include me in his experiments, but Haagan had to have his little piece of paper. Fortunately I overheard them and was firm enough to tell him that if he so much as touched me, word of it would get back to Berlin. Had I not done, I would, I think, no longer be alive but immersed in formalin.'

Neither of them said a thing. They just looked at each other for what seemed the longest time. 'Phenol,' Victoria heard herself saying at last. 'Twenty cc's. That is how much he uses in one of his "experiments."'

'Not Evipan?' asked St-Cyr, sickened by what she had just said.

Involuntarily she shivered, Herr Kohler managing to drag off his greatcoat and wrap it about her. Again St-Cyr asked, and she knew that this much she had best tell them. 'The phenol is given intravenously in the guise of a tetanus or typhoid-fever shot. Perhaps it is that Berlin wants the professors to find a quick and easy way of killing that does not entail anything so overt as hanging, decapitating with an axe or shooting. Perhaps it is that . . .'

'Phenol's strongly caustic, Louis. The pain would be—'

'Excruciating, *mon vieux*. Unconsciousness and death would certainly follow.'

'Agony, Louis,' muttered Herr Kohler emptily.

'Inspectors, Alain told Renée of the torture in the faces of four girls who had been selected and sent to the camp. All of them were *N und N*s. He spoke of how, as they fell unconscious, their expressions softened. He thought it curious. Among his duties, he has to watch and record everything that happens so that the professors and their students will then have an independent observer's comments.'

Tonelessly she told them of the other experiments and the autopsies that were being done both at the quarry camp and at the University of Strassburg.

'Rasche would have had to visit that camp often enough, Louis, and must have known.'

'And yet, Hermann, he made no mention of it beyond saying that they were doing autopsies all the time.'

'He knew Renée Ekkehard would be at the carnival,' said Herr Kohler.

'He sent Werner Lutze there in the *Polizeikommandantur*'s *Grüne Minna*, Hermann.'

'Knowing damned well she would see it and panic, Louis. He knew Alain Schrijen would be there and that the boy would chase after her.'

'Had the best of reasons for wanting that girl dead,' said the chief inspector sadly. 'A daughter in Clermont-Ferrand. One of the *Mischlinge*.'

'Then why call us in?'

'If not knowing we'd be certain to point the finger at Alain Schrijen.'

'Since that one had every reason as well,' sighed Herr Kohler, 'but wouldn't have dared to do it at the camp or ski lodge, not the Kommandant's personal secretary.'

'And knowing, too, Hermann, that Alain's father had every reason to want her silenced, but quietly.'

And Sophie? wondered Victoria. Did these two not consider that Sophie might have done it? Sophie who had come to realize that her father must have learned of what his daughter and her committee had really been up to?

'Mademoiselle, when I went through Eugène Thomas's pockets, I found a bankroll of four hundred and seventy-one Lagermark.'

'They'd not have been of any use outside the *Arbeitslager*,' muttered Herr Kohler.

'But they were, Inspectors. You see, there are among Colmar's tradespeople, some who will accept Lagergeld. *Bien sûr*, it's risky and they try to do it as unobtrusively as possible, but still . . .'

'Then the money wasn't to pay Martin Caroff for crafting the wedding ring Thomas wore?' asked the chief inspector.

She could not smile though she wanted to. 'It was for toothbrushes, tooth powder, hair combs, medicines and other personal items at the pharmacy.'

'Lucie Ferber, Louis. I might have known.'

Hermann's pharmacist, but now was not the time to console him. 'And the two rose-coloured buttons that were torn from Mademoiselle Ekkehard's dress last August?'

'Eugène found them in our field office and put them in the fruit jar with the others. I . . . I then gave them to Sophie who always kept them close as a reminder of what had happened. She would have been beside herself with grief at Eugène's death. He was like a brother should have been to her. Always kind, always helpful . . .'

'Would she have had to see his body, mademoiselle?' asked Herr Kohler.

'But why?'

'Tell her, Louis.'

'*Ah, bon*. Because I then found those buttons in his pockets.'

'But after Rasche had had him laid out and had gone through the damned things himself,' said Herr Kohler.

'He having called Paris, she then wanted us to look a little closer at things, mademoiselle.'

'But was Thomas murdered, Louis?'

It would not hurt to tell them, thought Victoria. 'As a fire warden, a *Luftschutzfeldwebel*, Inspectors, Werner Lutze can come and go at the Textilfabrikschrijen any time he likes and has a blanket pass for just such visits.'

'Whereas you have none,' said the chief inspector.

'That is correct.'

'Then what about that scrap of notebook paper, Louis?'

'*Ah, bon*. Your notebook, mademoiselle. Trace for us, please, how it came to have chemical equations for the viscose process written across the corner of an otherwise empty page and then—'

'The formula for picric acid?' she asked.

'A yellow dye,' said Herr Kohler blandly.

This could not be avoided. 'When Sophie decided that Renée and myself should serve on her *Winterhilfswerk* Committee, she asked Renée to find out what she could of my background and I, learning of this, told Renée to take the notebook to her. But . . . but that was in the late spring of 1941. That is how long I've been on her committee.'

'But did her father see it then?' asked St-Cyr.

'He must have, Louis. That's why his daughter asked for it. Löwe Schrijen told me he hadn't approved of his daughter's choice.'

'Inspectors, I've known Sophie for years, through the bookshop. She had no need to find out anything about me, and didn't let her father stop her from asking me to join her committee.'

'And when was it written in by others?' asked St-Cyr.

'Eugène apologized for having done that. Sophie can sometimes be very impulsive. You've seen how she is. He had been teaching her everything he could about the viscose process—she was new to it all in that spring of '41. They needed a bit of paper and Sophie had my notebook in hand and thrust it at him, he then jotting down the sequence of equations for her as they went over them.'

And weren't the simplest of explanations often the most elusive? 'And the formula for trinitrophenol?' asked St-Cyr.

'That was jotted down much later. About a week after Renée had come back from the party, I noticed that the notebook was again missing. I really didn't know what to think. It wasn't like Renée to have taken anything of mine. She was distraught and badly frightened. Herr Lutze . . . I did wonder if he might have taken it, for he'd come that week to check the house and shop for the fire-prevention measures in case of an air raid, but I had stayed with him every step of the way because he had asked it of me.'

'And Sophie?' asked Herr Kohler.

'Was keeping her distance.'

'And then?' asked Louis gently.

'There it was. I went through it page by page. Someone had written the formula for trinitrophenol under the equations. Raymond . . . I was certain it must have been Raymond Maillotte.'

'And a warning to our second victim to cooperate with his combine or else, Louis, but did Löwe Schrijen then get another look at it?'

'He . . . he might have,' said Victoria. 'I . . . I really don't know, nor why Sophie couldn't have simply asked me for it herself that second time.'

She hadn't because her father *had* asked her for it again, said Kohler silently, and Renée Ekkehard must have inadvertently let Rasche know of the interest. 'Mademoiselle, I think you know very well why Sophie didn't.'

Raymond and a highly unstable and very violent explosive—she would have to tell them, thought Victoria, since St-Cyr had gone through Renée's bedroom with her. 'In her haste to join the other students in Clermont-Ferrand before the Blitzkrieg of 1940, Geneviève Lutze left some of her chemistry textbooks behind. One of them gave me the formulas. Renée . . .'

'Was the Mademoiselle Ekkehard with you at the time?' asked St-Cyr.

'It would not have mattered, not in the state she was. Outside of her room, Renée could barely control her despair, alone with Sophie or myself, or both of us, she invariably broke down.'

And Yvonne Lutze must have known of it, and of the formulas, thought St-Cyr.

'Wasn't Sophie keeping her distance by then?' asked Hermann.

'She *was*. She would, in any case, have thought of it only as a dye stuff, but what, please, were Martin and Gérard and the others planning? To escape? If so, then why would they have condemned Eugène to death?'

'That's something we've yet to answer,' muttered Herr Kohler, 'but if what you say is true, Colonel Rasche must have learned of Löwe Schrijen's interest and decided that he had better have another look at that notebook himself, and when Yvonne Lutze got it for him, he tore the corner off that page and left it for us. I might have known, Louis!'

'Our second victim, Hermann. Hanged with full pockets and a fisherman's knot!'

South of Sélestat, and now within twenty kilometres of Kolmar, the snowfall suddenly ceased. One minute it was there and comforting, felt Victoria, the next it had vanished and with it all thought of the freedom that must someday come. On the road ahead the snow was rutted, hard-packed and had been glazed over by earlier traffic. Herr Kohler was driving, his greatcoat still wrapped about her, and it was warm and kind of him, but St-Cyr was constantly nervous. Every time the car skidded, he flinched, she did too, there really being very little room to spare and she keeping herself as far from Herr Kohler as possible for fear of breaking one of the ampoules. Every time the car speeded up, the chief inspector would suck in an impatient breath at such a terrible driver, yet still his inquisition of her hadn't let up.

'This fête, mademoiselle,' he asked. 'Were any of those men who helped the three of you to have run the booths?'

Model prisoners were always considered useful by the Nazis as examples to others, especially visiting delegates from the Red Cross and other organizations. Seldom, if ever, though, were *Arbeitslagern* visited by them, in part because the numbers of men were much greater in the other camps. 'Sophie did ask Colonel Rasche if he would allow such a thing, but he flatly refused. "The security alone would be far too tight," he said, "with the Gauleiter Wagner officiating at the opening."'

'And with Löwe Schrijen there too, Louis, and himself.'

'And Kommandant Zill, Hermann, and the Schutzhaftlagerführer Kramer.'

'One happy little gathering,' said Herr Kohler, speeding up again as they entered the Forêt de Colmar, the Kolmarwald.

She had best tell them something, felt Victoria, so as to give the lie of cooperating while holding back what couldn't be revealed. 'The fête is to be held in what we used to call *place* de la Cathédrale. Since the *Polizeikommandantur* is right there, and it would be good for relations with the public, the colonel was going to let some of the staff help out.'

'Diess and Paulus?' asked Herr Kohler sharply.

'Why, yes, their . . . their names were on the list he had drawn up. The Gauleiter Wagner and Herr Schrijen are to light the ceremonial torches and then he and Herr Schrijen and the colonel are to have a game of *Jeu de massacre*, after which they will spin the Wheel of Fortune.'

'As will Zill and Kramer, Louis. Those torches, mademoiselle. Have they already been made?'

'Gérard . . .'

Softly he swore, but did not slow the car, simply said, '*Verglas*, Louis.'

Black ice lay beneath the snow, the tree trunks dark and crowding closely. If they went off the road, could she try to get away long enough to . . . 'Gérard and . . . and Raymond looked after those,' she said. 'Beeswax and tallow Herr Lutze found for us; dried rushes and sticks they had gathered in the Kastenwald and had tied into bundles with vine-cuttings Sophie had brought from the Schrijen vineyards. The torches are almost the length of the wagon they are stored in.'

'And behind them, Louis, pyramids of papier-mâché balls.'

'Why, yes, and . . . and charcoal braziers at which to warm the hands before throwing them.'

'They thought of everything, didn't they, Louis? Packets of nails as prizes. Lots of them. Teddy bears too, and bottles of wine.'

'And each packet tied with a bowstring knot, Hermann, some of them done by the colonel himself. It was perfect, wasn't it? *Mon Dieu*, who would have suspected there would be any problem?'

'Musicians, Louis. Tambourines.'

'Recorders and drums,' Victoria heard herself saying hollowly.

'Everything that would be needed to distract them,' said Herr Kohler, the car now skidding round and round, they holding on tightly and gasping as lights ahead were flung over the road, the branches of the trees now in shadow, now not.

A horse-drawn wagon had been hit by the first of the lorries; the second completing the destruction. Dead, one of the horses lay entangled in its harness, the other neighing in terror, poor thing, and trying to get up. Firewood logs, destined for Sélestat, were scattered everywhere, the wagon now matchwood. Two of its wheels protruded from the edge of the forest, a third was propped against one of the lorries whose left front tyre was flat, and whose headlamps, bonnet and windscreen had been smashed. There were bandaged SS heads, a broken arm . . .

'No one's happy, Louis,' said Herr Kohler, his gaze, like hers and the chief inspector's, fixed on the wreckage. Perhaps two hundred metres separated them from the SS, perhaps a little more, the Citroën having miraculously turned to face them.

Caught in one of the floodlights, the driver of the wagon did not look well. Slumped against the back right tyre of the other lorry, he must have broken something too. A leg? she wondered. One of the SS trained a Schmeisser on him. Others had begun to clear the road but had stopped to take note of their arrival and to await further orders. Still others had gone into the forest to search for someone.

'I'll deal with it, Louis. Stay here and that's an order.'

'I'll just get behind the wheel again.'

'Don't. The least little thing could set them off.'

He got out of the car, no coat, only a rumpled grey suit and that fedora of his to ward off the cold. He walked toward the horse that kept trying to get up and, though Schmeissers and Bergmanns and pistols were anxiously touched as he took out his own pistol, put an end to the misery, the shot crashing and rolling over them, St-Cyr sucking in a breath and still concentrating on his partner, willing him to remain safe? wondered Victoria.

Alain Schrijen was standing next to the Obersturmführer Meyer. At a sharp command from the latter, her handbag, coat, scarf and hat were brought from the first lorry and given to Herr Meyer, her scarf accidentally falling at his feet to be left lying in the road.

'Mademoiselle . . .' began St-Cyr, only to feel her hand grip his own.

10

From the depths of the woods came the cry of, '*Halt!*' and then a burst of firing, from the road, a stillness as every man paused in what he was doing and the driver of the wagon looked up with hesitation at the man who was guarding him. Was there nothing he could do to stop the madness? wondered Kohler.

Dragged to his feet, forced to run on that bad leg, the wagon driver stumbled and lay prostrate. 'My son . . .' he babbled. 'My Étienne . . .'

Struck in the back by the Schmeisser's fire, he arched his spine, stiffly flung out his arms, coughed blood, clutched snow and lay still.

Meyer flung his cigarette away in disgust. 'These black marketeers, Kohler. They will never learn.'

The urge to throw up was there but wouldn't be wise. Maybe Meyer was forty years old, maybe ten years younger than the grey and stubbled driver of the wagon, but one thing was certain. As Head of the Political Department at Natzweiler-Struthof, he was independent of the camp administration and considered a law unto himself. Interrogations were always overseen and often personally conducted by Meyer. Hence he'd been on the road to the Textilfabrikschrijen not just to catch up with them but to interrogate Martin Caroff and the others and to take them back with him. Hence the hurry too. Had Deiss and Paulus sent him a little something?

They must have, hence Alain Schrijen's helpless look, the lamb too, and ready for the slaughter if necessary, and Meyer taking in the two of them at a glance before saying, 'That woman in your car, Kohler, is wanted for further questioning.'

'She doesn't know anything. She's just a bookseller who once a month is allowed to visit a sick mother.'

'Then why did you bring her to Natzweiler-Struthof?'

'To hear what this one has to say about his fiancée.'

Meyer didn't start shrieking, he simply smirked. 'Really, I must insist, Herr Hauptmann der Kriminalpolizei. You see, we feel she has been a party to top secret information and therefore cannot be allowed to leave the camp.'

'She's with us. You don't need to worry.'

'If she knows nothing, her conscience is clear.'

Victoria Bödicker's coat, hat and handbag were thrust at Alain Schrijen, the boy, the young man startled and now uncomfortably looking off toward the Citroën, for of course she knew far more than she was letting on and Alain Schrijen knew it too, but also what he had kept from this one when questioned himself at the camp, otherwise the whole can of worms would have had to be opened.

'Untersturmführer, I believe I gave you an order,' said Meyer. 'Please see that it is carried out.'

'My scarf . . .' blurted Victoria helplessly.

She had every reason to be sickened, felt St-Cyr. The scarf

still lay at the Obersturmführer's feet but now not only was Alain Schrijen coming toward them, others of the SS were dragging the body of a teenaged boy out to the road.

'Mademoiselle, was there anything in that handbag of yours that you wouldn't have wanted Herr Meyer to find?'

'I . . . I'm trying to think.'

'Your papers . . . There wasn't anything wrong with them, was there?'

'Why should there have been?'

'Please just answer.'

'None, then. My compact, it . . . it has a small mirror.'

'Which could have been used to see if anyone was following you—that is what he can and will claim.'

'My cigarette case. It's of silver and could have been used for the same purpose, I suppose.'

'Given to you by whom? Come, come, mademoiselle, before Alain Schrijen reaches us, it's best you confide everything.'

'Blaise Oberkircher gave it to me on my birthday. Its . . . its inscription reads, "Victoria, our traverse has only begun." And . . . and then there is "with much love" and his full name and the date, "27 May 1939."'

The inscription wasn't good and she knew it and need not be reminded. 'A lipstick?' he asked. Schrijen, though heading straight for them, seemed uncertain, his stride not the usual for an SS with more than enough support behind him.

Tersely the chief inspector repeated the question, but why had he to persist? 'A lipstick, no. At least, I don't think there was one.'

'You seldom use it,' he muttered, reminding her that he never forgot a thing and that Renée's farewell note had been written in lipstick. 'Anything else?'

'An Opinel. Ah, no, I'd lost that. I'd set it down when we

were last making up the packets of nails and . . . and forgot I'd put it on the table.'

'In the wagon that was used as a field office?'

'*Oui*. It . . . it was Mother's and had been in our kitchen for years.'

Hermann had found just such a knife in the trunk from which the rope had come that had been used to hang Renée Ekkehard. 'The colonel, mademoiselle, could he have taken it?'

'Renée and Colonel Rasche had been tying the packets. Sophie and I had been counting them.'

'And Eugène Thomas?'

'Was standing at the drawing table with Raymond Maillotte. They'd been going over the schedules. Eugène had turned to ask Sophie something, but . . . but then didn't. He . . . he just gave me the oddest of looks and turned quickly back to the table.'

Having seen Sophie Schrijen or the colonel pocket the knife, or had either of them? 'And when was this? Come, come, mademoiselle. We haven't much time.'

'Before Christmas. A week, I think, or ten days. I . . . I can't remember.'

Because you don't care to? he wanted to demand, but asked, 'Well after the party?'

'Yes.'

'Anything else? Women's handbags invariably contain countless items yet you've had trouble mentioning three.'

'Some sticking plasters. I always try to carry a few, though one can't buy them easily now. Before the war, I used to help Mother parcel books in the evening to take to the post the next day. That brown paper we used was always sharp. I . . . I often cut myself.'

A creature of habit who has an answer for everything if

pressed—was that how she was? Hermann had, of course, found a used sticking plaster in the drawer of Alain Schrijen's desk, in the only corner his sister had set aside for herself, and Hermann had cut himself on the spine of an ampoule while searching through the jewellery.

'Matches?' asked St-Cyr as Alain reached the car.

'Yes! But . . . but I'd no cigarettes and don't use them often. Only when I . . .' *Ah, Sainte Mère,* why had she let him make her say it? 'Only when I feel the need.'

Cigarette ashes had been found on a corner of the tin trunk that the killer and Renée Ekkehard had sat on. 'It's stuck, Untersturmführer,' said St-Cyr of his side windscreen. *'Ein Moment, bitte.*

'Photographs?' he asked her.

'I . . . I can't remember.'

'Not even one of Claudette Oberkircher's son?'

Would that, too, be used to condemn her? 'Of Blaise, yes. In uniform, but . . . but also the telegram Claudette received. It was she who came to tell me of our loss.'

Meyer was far from happy and could hardly wait until Alain Schrijen was out of earshot.

'Kohler,' he shouted, jerking up on the toes of his jackboots for emphasis, 'what has been going on at the Textilfabrikschrijen of that one's father? Kommandant Rasche asks Section IV in Paris for you and that French *Schweinebulle* to investigate what are clearly suicides? Prisoners are being given unheard of freedoms without proper security clearances and now . . . now those same men are being held in *Straf*? *Straf,* Kohler! And I receive no official notification of this and no request for any such clearance but must learn of it from Kriminalinspektor Serge Deiss and Kriminaloberassistent Hervé Paulus? Seasoned detectives who investigated the deaths and concluded they were suicides? Detectives, Kohler, who had advised Colonel Rasche of this very fact and who, I must add, you saw fit to nearly beat to death!'

'It was all a misunderstanding, Obersturmführer. Deiss and Paulus mistook me for someone else. I simply defended myself—you'd have done the same. Finally I was able to convince them to listen. *Ach*, they even apologized for the mistake, as I did too, of course.'

And trust Kohler to try to lie his way out of it! 'Deiss believes that bookseller of yours was also involved in highly illegal activities. That is the reason—the very reason, let me tell you—why the Untersturmfuhrer Schrijen's father had them follow her.'

And not his daughter Sophie, eh, which could only mean Deiss and Paulus had been bought off by Löwe Schrijen but then . . . why then they had let Meyer know of the men in *Straf* just to cover their own asses in case needed! 'Look, at present my partner and I have to take things a step at a time. Berlin . . .'

He'd teach Kohler not to shoot good guard dogs but to execute *N und Ns*. 'Berlin, Kohler? Berlin has insisted that the matter be settled. The men in *Straf* are to be given reinforced interrogations after which the Untersturmführer Schrijen is to be allowed to take the body of his fiancée home. A corpse, I might add, Kohler, that Kommandant Rasche clings to for highly dubious reasons, even to sitting with her out at that carnival, thinking he was alone and not being watched by others.'

By Deiss and Paulus, but had Rasche been blind to their presence, or had he damned well known of it?

He'd known. He must have. Hence his call to Paris-Central.

'A hearse has been arranged to take the body to the station, Kohler, at 1000 hours. We are to be the guard of honour at the funeral.'

'You think of everything, Obersturmführer. I'm sure the boy and his father and sister will be grateful.'

'As will the Gauleiter Wagner, *mein lieber Detektiv*. The very one who personally requested that I form the guard, and who is to attend the funeral himself along with Colonel Rasche, of course. Kommandant Zill, Schutzhaftlagerführer Kramer and Frau Kramer will also attend.'

Every seat taken and still no mention of Renée Ekkehard's family. 'When?'

'The day after tomorrow.'

Friday, 12 February. Even a blizzard wouldn't stop them.

'In Strassburg Cathedral, Kohler. After which the body is to be cremated.'

With a tired but dismissive wave, Kohler left the bastard. It would be the longest walk ever to get to that car and Louis. Meyer was going to have them killed. Berlin must have ordered it. Eliminate Kohler and St-Cyr, get rid of the Bödicker woman. Silence them, but first find out what's been going on. Once they got to the Schrijen Works, Meyer would soon pry answers from those boys in *Straf*. If not one, two would confess, or three. Not only had they planned to escape, they'd factored in the perfect assassination of the Gauleiter Wagner and all those who were to be with him. Nearby citizens too. Men, women and children.

Rasche would have to admit to having inadvertently assisted the *Winterhilfswerk* Committee; Löwe Schrijen to having harboured a daughter who was one of the *Banditen*, a *résistante*.

They'd all be taken to the quarry. Meyer hadn't just brought the honour guard along for Renée Ekkehard's funeral, he had brought enough men to take care of everything.

When Kohler reached the car and opened the door, he found his greatcoat neatly folded on the driver's seat. No one said a thing. Alain Schrijen, sitting behind her, had a pistol jammed against the back of Victoria Bödicker's head. 'Louis, Meyer doesn't know damn all yet but thinks that boy in the back needs a little help and is willing to go that far, even to giving him the task of making sure we follow them. Trouble is, what's going to happen when he does find out?'

'Hermann, just hand Herr Schrijen your gun and get in.'

'Or he'll blow her brains out and shatter the windscreen? *Jésus, merde alors, mon vieux,* hasn't he realized we're all he's got? Can't he see that if he kills Victoria, he has to kill us and then he and that father of his will have no one? The sister too? Not Deiss and Paulus, and certainly not Meyer or Kramer or the Kommandant Zill.'

'Monsieur,' said Louis, 'those men in *Straf* were planning to escape on 6 March.'

'The fête . . . ' gasped Victoria, wincing as the muzzle of Alain's pistol was pressed harder against the back of her head.

'They'd stolen a cutthroat,' said Kohler.

'And had planned, I think, to cut his sister's throat, *mon vieux*. You see, monsieur . . .'

'It's Untersturmführer, damn you!'

'*Ach*, one forgets the little things, doesn't one, Hermann?'

'Just tell him, Louis.'

One by one, on the road ahead, the floodlights were being extinguished as the SS prepared to leave. 'You see, Untersturmführer, Eugène Thomas was close to your sister. He had, I'm certain, become her trusted friend. She, in turn, genuinely wished to make his life easier and had gone so far as to let him read his mail before the censors in the office got at it. This had to have happened after hours, but Thomas often worked late, as did your sister. She by choice perhaps, he out of necessity, but also to avoid the cramped living quarters and close company of his fellow prisoners. At times he would go into your former office to discuss plans for the carnival with your sister, or some problem with the Works. More often, the two must have met in the laboratory where it was safest for them to have been seen together.'

'Sophie couldn't stand to have Eugène being hurt by the constant teasing,' said Victoria, 'and by a censor who wanted only to get back at us French, but if he read his mail—and please, I was not aware of this—didn't the men of his combine know of it? Surely he must have told them?'

'He couldn't,' said St-Cyr. 'To protect her, he had to remain silent.'

Meyer would find that out too, thought Alain. 'And with the cutthroat?'

'Both your father and sister would be at the Works early on the morning of the sixth. For your father to do anything else would be out of character and out of the question.'

'And from there, they would leave for the fête at about 0830 hours, Louis.'

'Eugène Thomas must have known of this, Hermann, and had confided it to the others.'

'The cutthroat was then stolen.'

'By Thomas, Hermann. He was, I think, the only one who could have crossed to the firm's garage to take it, having gauged when best to do so.'

'But it had to be kept somewhere safe, otherwise Lagerfeldwebel Dorsche would have found it.'

'And was hidden at the carnival until needed, Thomas no doubt hoping that it would stay there and not be used.'

'But when he refused to go along with their killing Sophie,' said Victoria, 'they—'

'Sentenced him to death,' said Kohler.

'Not realizing then that one of the *Postzensuren* might well have had him sent an anonymous letter, Hermann.'

'But that's only a part of what Meyer's going to find out, isn't it?' He would turn to face Schrijen now, thought Kohler. He would try to get that gun from him. 'Once Meyer gets at those boys in *Straf,* he's going to discover that they knew what your sister and Renée Ekkehard and this one were really up to and that those boys also had plans of their own.'

'The trinitrophenol, Hermann.'

'The guncotton, Louis.'

They were following the lorries now. Soon they would be in the outskirts of Kolmar, soon at the Works, Victoria knew. The Obersturmführer would beat the truth out of Martin and Gérard and the others, and then would start in on her. Everything would come out. She'd not be able to stop herself. 'Chief Inspector,' she heard herself saying quite calmly, turning so as to face him, 'how is it that you realized I must have something fragile in my pocket?'

'You constantly favoured your left side. Whenever I was behind the wheel, you crowded Hermann; myself as at present.'

'You killed Renée, Victoria,' said Alain, having realized the significance of the explosives. 'You went out to the carnival on that Sunday morning. Haven't you two thought to ask her where she was?'

On the last Sunday of January. 'I was at church.'

'You weren't. I checked.'

'I was seeing to Claudette's cat.'

'Her door was locked and when I rang the bell, you didn't answer.'

'Untersturmführer, a moment, please,' said St-Cyr. 'How is it that you knew to try at Frau Oberkircher's residence?'

Hermann sighed as only he could. 'Sophie was with him, Louis.'

'Had you taken the bus out to the carnival, mademoiselle?' asked St-Cyr. 'It would have dropped you off at the side of the road.'

'We found her footprints in the snow, Inspector,' said Alain.

'At what time, please?'

St-Cyr had again taken hold of her right arm and would move quickly to stop her from crushing the ampoules. Herr Kohler would also try to stop her.

'At close to 1200 hours,' said Alain. 'My train didn't leave until 1730. My sister said she had to see if Renée had come back.'

' "Come back," Untersturmführer?' asked Louis.

'I'd been there on the Saturday, hadn't I?' said Alain sarcastically.

'I only wanted to hear it from yourself, monsieur.'

These two couldn't be allowed to live, not now, thought Schrijen. 'We saw her footprints next to Renée's ski tracks up by that wagon they used as a field office, but when we went inside it, neither of them were there. That's when we went to the House of Mirrors and found her body.'

'But didn't search elsewhere, did you, Alain, because Sophie knew where to look,' said Victoria. 'She led you to her. She showed you what you'd driven Renée to do that morning, at 10.00 perhaps, or closer to 11.00. That is as close to the time as I can get, Inspectors. Renée knew he couldn't let her live, that that father of his had told him what to do.'

'Invite her to a party. Tell her of the experiments. Drug her to confuse her. Beat the truth out of her and all the rest of it, and when she comes to the next morning, force her to witness an execution,' sighed Kohler. 'What did she cry out before you raped her?'

'That the sluts were moving deserters through from the Reich.'

'And that she was deeply in love with your sister, Alain. Wasn't that as much the reason you did what you did to her? You couldn't stand to have one of those in your family. A lesbian? Sophie has always had to fill two pairs of shoes, Inspectors. Those of her mother and of herself. Always she has had to be proper, to never do anything that wasn't totally acceptable to that father of hers, to always be on hand for receptions and dinner guests, always to smile and look her best, but never to be herself. She's terrified of you, Alain. She knew you would tell your father about her and Renée.'

There wasn't time for him to respond. They had entered the gates, the wire closing behind them. Now steam billowed from the boilers and the smell of rotten eggs intruded.

Unbidden, Victoria crossed herself and saw that the chief inspector also did, Herr Kohler simply staring at the tarpaulin-covered back of the closest lorry. All too soon, though, Meyer and several of the armed SS were rushing them up a steep and narrow staircase where, through the dimly lit haze of each freezing floor, hundreds of men, some of them clad only in grey underclothes, silently watched her. Old men, young men, gaunt, haggard, hollow-eyed and with longing in their gazes, lust too, and fear. 'A girl . . .' 'A woman . . .' 'Beaten . . . she's already been beaten,' they murmured, the hush of their whispers travelling, she not knowing their languages, yet knowing what they said and thought as their fingers, with dirty, blackened, broken nails, clung to the closely meshed wire that kept them in and kept them so crowded they could longer remember how it had been to live decently.

Under the cobwebbed, soot-blackened roof timbers of another century, the *Straf* cells waited. One, a box so tightly constructed its occupant could only stand, not turn, was flung open and she was taken, pulled, dragged away from St-Cyr and Kohler toward it until Herr Kohler yelled, '*Halt!*' and then said more calmly, 'That's enough, Obersturmführer. She's a suspect in a murder case and until that's been settled, she's with us.'

'Questions . . . there are questions,' stammered Meyer, obviously stricken by the continued insubordination.

'You'll have to be patient.'

'*Patient!*' he shrieked.

'Why not start with the men you came to interrogate?'

There was no one being held in *Straf* and Hermann had sensed this but there was now, St-Cyr realized, no sign of Alain Schrijen either.

'He's gone to talk to his father, Louis,' said Kohler, having taken Victoria Bödicker's hand in his.

No cell had room in which to move more than two paces, no furniture beyond three planks.

'The head office, I think,' said Kohler. Only then, as Meyer and the others momentarily stopped, did they realize that beyond the constant sound of thousands and thousands of shuttles, there was the silence of the barracks block, for none below them moved. They only listened hard, all eyes lifted to them.

'Inspectors,' wept Victoria, the three of them standing a little apart from the others. 'Inspectors, please forgive me.'

'For being brave?' asked Louis. 'Mademoiselle, you humble me.'

'But still will seek the truth?'

'We have no other choice,' confided Kohler. 'We hadn't when we began this thing, and haven't now.'

'His colonel made certain of it,' said St-Cyr.

'Alain Schrijen murdered Renée Ekkehard, Louis. It's what Rasche has always wanted.'

'Because he, too, has had no other choice, Hermann. None at all.'

With the blackout, the darkness of the Works was often all but complete at ground level.

'Louis,' said Herr Kohler softly. 'Louis, take a look above us. You too, mademoiselle.'

Beyond the billowing, grey-white pillar of ever-expanding smoke that poured from the tall brick chimney of the first of the steam plants, the stars were incredibly beautiful. Pistons throbbed, gearwheels meshed, shuttles endlessly went back and forth, but above them, all seemed as if totally at peace.

St-Cyr and Kohler couldn't know what Löwe Schrijen had forced Martin and the others to reveal, nor what he had done with them or even if they had also planned to set off explosions here during their escape, but they would have to have answers before being confronted when they reached the office.

St-Cyr was looking at her, not at the stars. 'Mademoiselle,' he said, and she felt a shudder go through her.

'When Alain was with us in the car, Chief Inspector, and accused us of it, I didn't deny that we had been moving people through Alsace. There would have been no point in my doing so, but we weren't just moving deserters. Escaped prisoners of war came to us, also politicals and others on the run. We did what we could because we felt we had to.'

This one was tougher than even she, herself, believed. 'Then all along you've known Renée Ekkehard must have told him?'

'She must have, mustn't she? I didn't know for sure, since Renée always maintained she had been so drugged and terrified, she couldn't remember.'

'But the thought was clear enough?'

'Afterward, yes. In the weeks following that . . . that "party."'

'And the Fräulein Schrijen, did she also know of it?'

'That brother of hers and her father would have made her abundantly aware of it as they found out everything they possibly could. Why else would Sophie now deny we were close friends, Renée especially?'

'And yet you still maintain that Renée Ekkehard's death was a suicide?'

How could it possibly matter to him now in these last few moments? 'That is for you and Herr Kohler to decide.'

Still he didn't look up at the stars. 'That wasn't what I asked,' he said, and she knew he was impatient with her.

'Then *oui, oui, Monsieur l'Inspecteur premier. Un suicide, n'est-ce pas? Très tragique et très regrettable.*'

'Louis, don't be so hard on her. Think about those men. Planning to escape from a place like this under cover of darkness is one thing, in broad daylight another. Oh for sure they would have taken one of the cars—the tourer—but . . .'

'Not the other car,' sighed the chief inspector, now turning away at last to look up at the stars.

'They couldn't have,' said his partner. 'If Schrijen didn't show up at the fête, the whole thing would have been off. They had to let him leave in that sedan of his and believe emphatically that his daughter was following right behind him.'

'Two cars, Hermann, when petrol is rationed and in such short supply?'

'Inspectors, Sophie wouldn't have gone with her father. She had to avoid his questions and would have found any excuse to follow him. The need to stay all day at the fête, the need to drop by the Lutze house first to collect Renée . . .'

'Then those boys must have been planning to take one of the lorries, Louis.'

'There were two of them in the garage for servicing when I was there, Hermann.'

'And they'd have had the schedule at that garage pinned down, but though they'd been harvesting solder and dyeing scraps of cloth, they couldn't have made uniforms for all twelve of that combine. At most, only two of them would have been in uniform and even with those, the greatcoats they'd fashioned or stolen, the caps, the trousers and boots, would have been enough.'

'Eugène and Raymond,' said Victoria sadly. 'Eugène as an officer.'

'Maillotte would have driven the lorry, Louis. Thomas would have gotten into the tourer with Sophie.'

'Who wouldn't have helped them, Inspectors. Once Sophie had realized what was going on, she would have thought only of Renée and of what must happen to her if they succeeded.'

'Thomas would have had the cutthroat, Louis. Timing would have been everything. Schrijen would have to catch a glimpse of that daughter of his in his rearview as the gates were being opened.'

'He'd see the "officer" beside her,' said St-Cyr.

'And think it Karl Rudel perhaps, though Sophie would have been in a fluster and trying to figure out what to do,' said Kohler.

'Löwe Schrijen would also see the lorry, Hermann.'

'It would probably have had to slow momentarily outside the *Lagerküche* so that the others could scramble into the back and pull the tarp back down. Maybe there would have been two brief pauses before the gates. One thing's for sure, those boys would have had it all figured out.'

'And?' asked St-Cyr.

'They'd not have detonated anything here.'

'Because they couldn't have, Hermann, not without jeopardizing the rest.'

'The assassinations, mademoiselle,' sighed Herr Kohler. 'Those they planned to hit at that fête you three had dreamed up.'

'Löwe Schrijen having invited the Gauleiter and others; Colonel Rasche also,' said St-Cyr.

Then everything needed—at least some of it, felt Victoria—must now be at the carnival. If only she would be taken there, if only she could reach that one wagon before anyone else did: the *Jeu de massacre*. 'Eugène and the others must have discovered we were bringing people through, Inspectors, and that Sophie would then take them to the farm in her brother's tourer. On the day of the fête's opening she would have had to turn to the northwest, off the main road into town in order to get to Kaysersberg. Her father would no longer have been able to catch glimpses of the tourer behind him.'

'But would have had to hurry on,' said Herr Kohler.

'Thomas was to have cut her throat soon after they reached that turning point, Hermann.'

'Those boys who were helping you, mademoiselle, wouldn't have taken it kindly your using them as cover while getting others to freedom. Even Thomas would have felt it.'

'But once at the farm, they would have put as much distance as possible behind them, Hermann. They'd have split up, some going west, others north or south, but all into the depths of the Vosges, even though it's winter.'

'Having stolen the father's collection of sporting rifles and shotguns, mademoiselle,' said Kohler, 'and so much for your having tried to make their miserable lives a little less miserable.'

What they had said was true. 'Sophie wouldn't have gone with any of them as a guide, not even Eugène, Inspectors, and they must have known this. She would never have left Renée to face things but would have tried to stop them, they knowing they would have had to kill her or be taken.'

Assuming, of course, that Renée Ekkehard would not have been hanged, and that Eugène Thomas would not have refused to cut Sophie's throat and was still alive. A foolish, foolish gamble all the same, felt St-Cyr. Desperate as all such attempts must be, and invariably doomed to fail.

As they passed the Xanthate Shed, identifiable simply by the rankness of its stench of rotten eggs, Kohler couldn't help but recall how Raymond Maillotte, the test weaver and fabric designer, had been chalk-white and terrified of being sucked into the rotating blades that had reduced the sheets of pure soda cellulose to the dust that had coated him.

Outside the Steeping Shed there was the smell of caustic soda, overlain like everything else by that of carbon disulphide. Here he couldn't help but think of how Gérard Léger, the glazier and no doubt leader of that combine, had stood at the far end of the shed and watched as Henri Savard, the carpenter and coffin maker, had panicked at the thought of being deliberately pushed or accidentally slipping into the steeping tank to which he'd been assigned by Lagerfeldwebel Jakob Dorsche.

At the Pulping Shed, the noise of the debarkers was sufficient, and here he remembered Martin Caroff, the Breton, neck deep in a soggy mush of ice-cold wood pulp, the assistant machinist bellyaching about a cracked grindstone.

Caroff had been the source of Renée Ekkehard's Celtic/Gallic mythology and carver of Boudicca for a Wheel of Fortune, but just what the hell had Löwe Schrijen done with those boys?

At the far end of the administrative block, the colonel's two-door Juraquatre was parked in darkness next to the entrance to the head office.

'Mademoiselle, a moment,' said St-Cyr. 'The ampoules you're carrying. Please hand them over.'

'Must I, Inspector?' she asked, wincing at the loss.

'Louis . . .'

'*Merde alors*, Hermann, we can't have her falling asleep. Even that much Evipan wouldn't kill you, mademoiselle, but drugged you will be of no use, only a pronouncement of guilt.'

'But I'd have been in dreamland, wouldn't I, Inspector, and soon in the Land of Everlasting Life those ancient peoples believe in?' she said, pressing them one by one into his hand.

Armed SS crowded the dimly lit staircase and the foyer above, their weapons cradled as they parted to let them pass. Most were young and in belted greatcoats under steel helmets, some of them not much older than the boy they had shot, but men who looked at her with an emptiness that filled her with dread.

A Scharführer crashed his heels, curtly ducking his head in a pre-emptive salute as he opened the door to the office. Löwe Schrijen, in a flannel shirt, its sleeves rolled up, and a dark green waistcoat with brass boar's-head buttons sat behind his desk, a cigar in hand trailing smoke. Colonel Rasche, in uniform with cap still tucked under the left arm, sat stiffly in front of that desk, having turned sideways a little to see her standing here as if alone.

Obersturmführer Meyer, his greatcoat flung carelessly open and peaked cap perched jauntily atop that angular, rake-jawed countenance, was here too, and staring emptily at her.

Alain . . . Alain, looking foolish and decidedly uncomfortable, stood to one side, the white death's-head on his cap far from terrifying now, a wineglass in his left hand and bottle of ice-clear schnapps in the other, the glass having been hastily filled at least twice already.

There was no sign of Serge Deiss or of Hervé Paulus; there was no sign of anyone else. The colonel could not even take out his pipe and tobacco pouch.

'Kohler,' he croaked. 'Kohler, what is this I hear?' He had even worn his Iron Cross First- and Second-Class, the Pour le Mérite also, and other medals.

'Yes, tell us, Kohler,' said Löwe Schrijen. 'Don't keep us waiting any longer.'

Two big, strong, powerful men at loggerheads.

In panic Herr Kohler tossed his partner a desperate glance. 'We still have work to do, Colonel. Louis and I have to revisit the crime sites. I'm sorry, but that's the way of it.'

'*Gut*,' grunted Rasche. 'A suicide, Kohler. When I contacted Gestapo Boemelburg in Paris, I expressly informed him that I wanted the matter cleared beyond question.'

A suicide . . . Was this what he was now wanting? wondered St-Cyr.

'There's little doubt, Colonel, that it was a sad affair and unfortunate,' went on Hermann, quickening all too readily to it.

'Then Untersturmführer Schrijen did not kill her and try to make it look like a suicide, Kohler?' asked Rasche.

'That . . . that's what we're working on, Colonel.'

'But you're almost certain it was a suicide?'

'Almost.'

Ah, Hermann, Hermann, how could you do this? asked St-Cyr silently. The years they had been together, the struggles always in the search for truth.

'And the Fräulein Bödicker, Kohler. Was she involved in anything illegal?' demanded Rasche.

The crunch at last, thought St-Cyr, though Hermann didn't have the guts now to glance at his partner and former friend for advice, sanction or even support.

'Involved in nothing, Colonel. That was all a misunderstanding.'

'Then there you are, Obersturmführer. Deiss and Paulus were incorrect in their assessment of her.'

'Very, Colonel,' said Hermann, having failed entirely to anticipate where things were leading.

'She must still be interrogated,' snapped Meyer. 'I insist.'

'As is your right and duty, of course, Obersturmführer,' said Rasche levelly. 'Kohler, is it that you are now free to release the Fräulein Bödicker into such worthy hands, or do you and the Oberdetektiv St-Cyr require further from her?'

'Further, Colonel. With your permission, we would like her to accompany us to the site of the first suicide.'

The carnival.

'*Ach*, it's late and you've had no sleep,' said Rasche. 'Perhaps at first light, and before the Obersturmführer and his men arrive with the hearse to remove the body.'

At 1000 hours, *mon vieux*—could you not have seen this coming? asked St-Cyr silently.

'We'd best go out there now, then,' said Hermann, the quaver in his voice revealing how betrayed he now felt, fool that he'd been to have tried to appease them.

'As you wish. There is one thing, though,' said Rasche. 'The detail I had out there have all had to be recalled and sent east to the front.'

To Russia.

Kohler gripped the steering wheel as he floored the Citroën. Ahead of them, through the darkness and the snow, lay the Kastenwald; behind them Kolmar and the wire. Victoria was sitting tensely beside him, Louis on the other side of her, both not having said a thing because they knew they'd never get out of this alive. For himself, he'd never see Gerda again, would never be able to warn her to leave the Reich while she still could, never be able to tell her that their splitting up had been his fault, that the work, the months and years away from her and the farm had done it. No chance to comfort her now over the loss of Jurgen and Hans, no chance to even say he was sorry and that he had missed them and herself.

Again he anxiously glanced in the rearview. Again he was forced to admit that no one was following. Rasche had simply left them on their own until 1000 hours. Rasche had cut himself off from them and had made a deal with Schrijen. He must have. 'Louis, if Löwe Schrijen has had those boys in *Straf* killed, I don't know what I'll do.'

'Agree with your colonel, Hermann. Without our weapons, there is little else, is there?'

'And I've let him walk us right into the shit, haven't I?'

'You said it, I didn't.'

'*Ach*, don't get huffy. *Merde alors*, what else was I to have said? That I was certain Alain Schrijen had hanged Renée Ekkehard?'

'Admit it, you couldn't bring yourself to arrest the boy.'

'Be reasonable. I had to go along with Rasche. He was in such a tight spot, he made me squeak.'

'Because he knew you would, Hermann. He knew you inside out. When the chips are down, mademoiselle, patriots like you and me have nothing to lose but our lives and self-respect!'

'Louis . . .'

'Hermann, you caved in. You let him lead us to this. Even in my darkest moments, and I have had many of them, mademoiselle, I have felt . . . *Ah, mon Dieu,* what have I felt? That my faith in this partner of mine would be restored. All a detective ever has is his sense of right and wrong, his judgment, *n'est-ce pas,* but that colonel of his has left us to face the libretto he has composed with the compliance of this . . . this player of triangles, gongs, bicycle horns and squeak boxes!'

The Citroën skidded, turning itself round and round until facing east again and at idle. '*Sacré nom de nom,* Louis, was I to have slapped the bracelets on Alain Schrijen in front of that *salaud* Meyer?'

These two, were they now to start yelling at each other, wondered Victoria, only to hear the chief inspector snap, 'An arrest. We've done it before. Why not now?'

'Because there were far more of them and we don't even have our weapons.'

'You didn't then, and neither did I.'

'A château near Vouvray,' managed Herr Kohler.

'Are you absolutely certain Alain Schrijen murdered Renée Ekkehard?' demanded the chief inspector. 'Come, come, Herr Detektiv Aufsichtsbeamter of the invincible Gestapo's Kripo, swear to it!'

'Louis, what the hell's this you're now implying?'

'*Ah, bon, mon vieux,* that as the boy has claimed, he may not have killed her.'

'But then that leaves . . .'

'Your colonel, Hermann. Why else would he have planted a

beret on that girl's head, one that we would notice right away and wonder why she would have worn such a thing?'

'When a woollen toque would have been far more appropriate,' muttered Kohler bleakly.

'Why else would he have all but accepted our concluding that if she'd been out skiing all night, she must have been up to something illegal?'

Like moving deserters.

'Why else would he have torn off that scrap of notebook paper and stuffed it into Eugène Thomas's pockets unless he knew we would find it and think the worst?'

The trinitrophenol.

'Not only is that colonel of yours ruthless, Hermann, he's shrewd enough to have swindled us to save himself, his daughter and her mother.'

'Yet he didn't know what those boys had planned, Louis. Tell me he didn't.'

'Of course not, but would have figured it out even as we were struggling to do so ourselves.'

A man who could walk over corpses. 'Then it must have been Rasche, with or without Werner Lutze, or Werner himself, or . . .'

'*Ah, mais alors, alors,* Hermann!'

'Louis, it was Rasche.'

'Finally, even when in the face of great difficulty, he's beginning to think again as a detective should, mademoiselle, though still not quite clearly.'

'Sophie, Chief Inspector . . . Is it that you now believe she killed Renée to save herself?'

Pilot in the Sky, Maze of Darkness, Danceorama—one by one Victoria located them as she waited beside the Citroën. Always at night, the last hours were the darkest; in winter, the cruelest. Beyond the Devil's Saucer, the tall silhouette of the Ferris wheel's iron girders could not be seen but even so, she could hear the frost working at them. 'It's as though it has to move,' Renée had sighed on a night like this. They had come out to meet and hide a German corporal the courier had brought through from the Totenkopf. The sounds had frightened Renée who had immediately thought of Martin Caroff's tales of the Phantom Queen, only to softly laugh at herself when told their origin and say, 'It wants to turn for joy, Victoria, for all the pleasure it brings, the magic.' The freedom from life's cares, from life itself. Renée had often revealed her innermost thoughts, the childlike wonder too, the intense delight and surprise she had immediately felt when presented with some long-sought little treasure.

That earring, Sophie, said Victoria silently. Those lovely greenish-brown eyes of hers, would have widened, wouldn't they, become incredibly clear, if only to quickly return to the fear and despair that had so often of late shadowed her. The terror, Sophie, of your being followed. Her absolute conviction of what must happen not only to herself but to us—wasn't that how she felt?

The Noah's Ark was nearest and just beyond the tourer, behind which Herr Kohler, its ignition and lights switched off, had let the Citroën come to a stop. St-Cyr had opened the door on the passenger's side and was rummaging about for something. Herr Kohler, having moved a little from her, was now closer to him. They wouldn't know where she was; would never be able to find her until it was too late. Only Eugène and Raymond would have known there was picric acid, long forgotten at the Works and where and how best to get it. Only they would have had access to Sophie's keys. They could have brought it out here, little by little.

They must have been terrified it would explode in transit, would have hidden it in the wagon with the torches and all the other pieces of the *Jeu de massacre* Renée had loved. Renée who had been so special to them.

'Hermann, there's no sign of the Mauser. Mademoiselle, you had best . . .'

'Louis, she's gone. I didn't even get a chance to tell her we'd do everything we could to see that she escaped and wasn't harmed.'

The two sets of tracks were divergent, the one heading from the tourer toward the House of Mirrors and its wagons. The other was elusive: now to the ruin of a round stall between the Noah's Ark and the *Salon Carousel,* a ruin whose once candy-striped canvas tilt had shed rain and sun from the suckers who had attempted its hoopla of square pedestals which would have been but a whisper shy of being too big for the hoops to drop over. These little posts littered the snow-covered rubbish among scrolled and gilded panel boards that had peeled and faded.

From here, this second set of tracks, having picked its defiant way through that rubbish, headed for another stall, somewhat closer to the *Salon Carousel.* Hermann played his torch fitfully over the ruin until it settled on the tracks, as once garishly painted, plaster clown heads stared emptily up at them with gaping mouths.

'Ping-Pong balls,' he muttered. 'The clowns would all have been ranked in line, eyes to the right or left, or facing straight ahead. You feed a ball into the mouths of the ones you think will win and the ball drops down a gullet slot and either rings a bell or doesn't.'

'Carpet-sweepers, duvets, tureens and chamber pots as prizes, but few if any winners. Don't linger.'

'My Gerda used to love going to carnivals, fêtes and fairs. We would have such a time of it, the two of us.'

The tracks, when again found, led into the depths of the *Salon Carousel*, their torch beams flickering as they passed over the once gaily coloured menagerie. A band organ had been pulverized by the budding musicians among the local tribe of farm children. A stallion now wore charcoal horn-rimmed spectacles, the swan-chairs, the crayoned grimaces of white-winged witches.

'Louis, if we ever get out of this, we're going to have to get out of France. Neither of us will be allowed to stay, not now, and you know it.'

'The Résistance . . .'

'Will be after both of us, and if not them, the SS and Gestapo, and if not them, the collabos, and if not them, the *Bonzen*, and if not those . . .'

'The French Gestapo of the rue Lauriston and others.'

Gangsters the SS and Gestapo had let out of the Santé, Fresnes and other such prisons and had put to work. Gangsters, several of whom Louis had consigned to those very prisons.

'Come on, *mon vieux*,' said St-Cyr, 'we can discuss it later.'

'There won't be time and you know it.'

They shook hands, and through the darkness, looked steadily at each other. Hermann had taken far more Benzedrine than he should. The hand was warm but quivering until gripped more firmly. '*Merci bien, mon ami*, let us count on each other.'

'As always.'

'Yes, of course.'

'You didn't answer Victoria when she asked if you felt Sophie had killed Renée.'

'There was no need and she knew it.'

'And now . . .'

'Un moment!'

'The *Tonneau de l'amour*, Louis.'

Victoria Bödicker had fallen and the startled cry she had given was repeated, the echoes torn from it. 'She's been leading us away from what she has in mind, Hermann.'

'The *Jeu de massacre*, but she'd not have cried out like that had she not been terrified.'

'And followed by Sophie?'

Who must have heard the Citroën's approach and then watched as they had got out of the car. 'That Mauser pistol, Louis . . .'

Light spilled from a canted doorway behind the long, dark silhouette of the Barrel of Love. It gave small shadows to footprints that shouldn't have been here had he been doing his job, felt Kohler. Hesitantly he touched Louis on the shoulder, heard him suck in an impatient breath and knew that this partner of his was trying his damnedest to figure out what best to do.

'Hermann, find another way in. Let me confront the Mademoiselle Schrijen.'

Above the spindled, horn-winged arch over the broken entrance, drunken letters gave the name in French of Dr. Bonnet's Travelling Museum of Anatomy.

Light seeped from among splintered panel boards whose faded, peeling posters gave the lie of pseudoscientific credentials, once luridly dyed wall hangings portraying obscure surgical operations: Transfusion of Goat's Blood; et cetera, et cetera.

'Hermann, leave me. Either Sophie Schrijen has set the lantern down to distract us or to shine it at her friend.'

'Take care. I mean it, Louis.'

'You also.'

'Batteries okay?'

'Hermann, there isn't time!'

They parted. A last glance over the shoulder gave the blocky, dark silhouette of Louis as he quickly ducked into the entrance, totally committed and utterly reliable . . .

St-Cyr drew in another breath. Everywhere he looked there was broken glass. Cork-stoppered bottles had once held deformed and perfectly formed fetuses that had been drenched in formalin. Jars of the same had held pickled organs: the heart, the lungs, liver and kidneys, the brain of 'a real live man,' the reproductive organs also.

Against a broken, blue-, white- and gold-tiled mural of a gowned and bearded ancient Hippocrates holding a sick child, the hourglass of time had shed its last grains of sand.

Cobwebs caught the gently falling snow as they stretched from spine to spine of shattered glass. Autumn's dead leaves, blown in from the nearby Kastenwald, were everywhere. Stains were everywhere: grey, dark red, brown, the shards of glass most often fogged and smeared, the light catching everything that had fallen from the displays.

The battery-powered lantern, its stiff wire handle upright, was on the ground at Sophie Schrijen's feet. Caught in its spotlight, Victoria Bödicker stood well out in the middle of this exhibit whose roof had fallen in. The canted cross-poles, with their rotten, now frozen canvas, were all around her, her shadow large and looming over a still standing wall whose hangings cried out: *Embryologie et Maternité* and the Damnation of Illicit Sex.

Kohler couldn't stop shaking. Caught in the beam of his torch, the skulls that littered the floor of this little room he was in, this cul-de-sac, spoke for all those he had had to see in the trenches of that other war. Shells screamed overhead as if he was right back at Vieil-Armand. Thrown up, the stench of rotting flesh, of blood, guts, brains and shattered granite mingled with those of mildewed earth and spruce gum. Panicking, he was suddenly terrified he would die without ever seeing Gerda again, wept as the skulls accused him, cursed him, mocked him; those also from all the murders he'd had to investigate.

'YOU KILLED HER, VICTORIA!' shrieked Sophie Schrijen, the sound of her voice breaking over him.

'MADEMOISELLE, SHE DID NOT MURDER RENÉE EKKEHARD!'

Louis . . . was that Louis shouting?

'SHE DID! MY BROTHER DIDN'T!'

'But could and would have.'

Louis had said that.

'MY FATHER DIDN'T GET ANYONE TO KILL HER EITHER!'

'But would have seen to it. Now, please, mademoiselle, put the gun down.'

'INSPECTOR, STAY WHERE YOU ARE!'

Ah, merde, she was going to shoot Louis.

'Sophie, please listen to me.'

That had been Victoria.

'Sophie, you know how despondent she was.'

'A SUICIDE, YOU SAID!'

'MADEMOISELLE, THE GUN, *S'IL VOUS PLAÎT*!'

Louis must have moved closer. He'd have his hand stretched out to take that gun . . .

'Give it to him, Sophie. He and Herr Kohler will try to help us.'

Postcards littered the skull-strewn floor at Kohler's feet: stained, frozen, faded photos of cadavers swathed in blood-soaked, white muslin or not; wounds . . . horribly gaping wounds. One who'd just had his head blown off—how many times had he seen just such a thing? Another without his limbs. No morphia, the poor bastard just staring emptily up at him like others he'd seen. Deformities too: twins linked at the hip, the shoulder or trunk but also pornographic shots the doctor must have sold on the sly. Shots of beautiful young girls, those of boys too. Several displays of *sadomasochisme . . .*

A shaving brush.

Kohler shook his head to clear it. The brush stood upright on a little shelf before the splinters of a mirror. A drinking glass held a toothbrush. An all but empty bottle of grass-green shaving lotion held clots of last autumn's flies. A tin of boot grease had been left in haste. Regulation issue and if found by others, an automatic sentence of death for Renée Ekkehard, Victoria Bödicker and Sophie Schrijen unless *Vati* could intervene.

Shards of glass were almost everywhere, but near the shaving brush there were none of them. The chipped enamel of the tin basin was whisper clean. 'Louis . . .' he muttered. 'They hid those boys in here until Sophie could drive them to the farm and send them on their way.'

There was a chair, a stool, the dust of cigarette ashes. A key hung on a nail—*Ach,* how naive of them. It was to the wagon they had used as a field office. At night, the one or two they were moving would have crawled out of here and had something to eat in that office. They would never have stayed long at the carnival, but as sure as he was standing here, Martin Caroff, Eugène Thomas and the others had begun to notice that something was going on.

'Sophie,' pleaded Victoria, 'Renée didn't want to live.'

'YOU DRUGGED HER!'

'Mademoiselle, your lover took ampoules of Evipan from the SS hospital at Natzweiler-Struthof,' said Louis.

'YOU CUT YOUR FINGER WHEN YOU BROKE THE TOP OFF ONE OF THOSE THINGS, VICTORIA!'

'Mademoiselle Schrijen, you found the sticking plaster she had used. You found the lipstick also, with which she had written the suicide note your lover begged her to write. Now, please, the gun.'

'INSPECTOR, IF YOU COME ANY CLOSER, I WILL HAVE TO KILL YOU!'

Louis was going to try to stop her. Kohler knew it, felt it, would have to get to them, have to distract her . . .

'Mademoiselle, your brother came out here on Saturday, 30 January, to kill her but she got away from him. The deserters or escaped prisoners of war the three of you had expected were not here either. Renée then went well to the east, to the Totenkopf.'

'She found the hut empty, Sophie,' said Victoria. 'They weren't there, and neither was Herr Springer's brother. She had skied and walked and had even hitched a lift in a Wehrmacht lorry all for nothing, and had then made her way back here because she had nowhere else to go. Nowhere, Sophie.'

'Alain . . . Alain had told Father where to find them, Victoria. Renée must have said something at Natzweiler. *Vati* . . . *Vati*, saw to it that they were stopped.'

'WHY DIDN'T YOU TELL ME, SOPHIE?'

'I couldn't. By then it was too late. None of them were interrogated. They were all simply taken out and shot. Herr Deiss and Herr Paulus did it for Father, for money.'

Sophie Schrijen stood with the lantern at her feet; Louis within two metres of her now and simply not close enough.

'She was exhausted, Sophie, and convinced that the only way she could save you was to take her own life.'

'You're lying. You thought only of yourself.'

'She begged me to help her.'

'You sat with her,' said Louis. 'You had a cigarette, a little schnapps, something she didn't really care for. You talked. You rummaged about in that tin box where the three of you kept the bits of costume jewellery that you'd found and took out the earring.'

'Renée had wanted so badly to find its mate, Inspector, we pretended that we had. She cupped it in her hands, held it to the light and pressed it against her cheek, and as she became sleepier and sleepier, she said, "Tell Sophie to try to forgive me."'

'By committing suicide, Mademoiselle Schrijen, your lover felt that your father would do everything he could to protect you.'

'But not myself, Sophie. Not me. Renée and I both knew that it was only a matter of time until he sent someone for me.'

'LOUIS, DON'T!'

The Mauser leapt, the sound of the shot reverberating as Victoria was knocked off her feet and thrown back. She cried out for her mother, cried repeatedly for the woman to come quickly. Cried for all the things she hadn't done, for the children she would never have, for Blaise Oberkircher and for forgiveness, but cried it ever more faintly in darkness.

Gently St-Cyr lowered her to the ground, having held her at the last. 'Hermann . . . ?' he managed.

Hermann had gone after Sophie Schrijen but that could only mean . . . 'HERMANN, LET HER GO! HERMANN, PLEASE!'

Two shots were fired and then another, the blast smashing things all around him as he cringed and held on to Victoria Bödicker. In wave after wave, the sound of the explosion came until a last shower of broken glass and other debris had finally settled.

In the ever-deepening hush that followed, he bowed his head and let the tears fall. 'Hermann . . .' he said. 'Hermann, I needed you. Together we might have made it through this lousy war; alone, I have no chance.'

Little by little the snow in the pot began to melt. St-Cyr held his hands to the stove. Alone in this world, in this carnival, this field office wagon, he waited. He would have a tisane of hot water. Miraculously the three ampoules of Evipan that Victoria Bödicker had handed over had been spared. He would set them on the drawing table in a row beneath that of the liqueur glasses Hermann had found.

The carving he would put at the top—*ah, oui, oui,* that would be best. 'Boudicca who rode again and with such bravery.'

A bead of solder, a swatch of grey-green cloth, the cutthroat and partly masticated, bloodstained ball of papier-mâché followed. The phosphorescent swastika button a uniform would need was next, and the pieces from broken phonograph recordings of *Das Rheingold und Die Walküre.* The personals columns from the newspapers Hermann had recovered were laid to one side, especially that of 20 January 1943's *Münchner Neueste Nachrichten.*

The pocket watch was placed there too, and the earring. The copy of *Schöne Mädchen in der Natur* was followed by the rusty nail and pebble against which it had been ground. Torn photos from home were added, those of Paulette Thomas who would soon receive notice of her loss. To these he added the Lagermark, the two rose-coloured buttons, the wedding ring with its Gallic scrollwork, the notebook and lastly its torn corner-scrap with the chemical formulae and equations.

So many items, the bits and pieces of lives lost, their last register. Should he burn them all? Could he leave the investigation unfinished or go it alone?

'Eugène Thomas,' he said, sipping from the pot and blowing on the water. 'Renée Ekkehard commits "suicide" and this has a profound effect on Sophie Schrijen, as it must have had on Victoria. But Sophie's the one closest to Eugène and they talk—they must have. He's been sentenced to death by his comrades and, though he would not have been told this by them, would have sensed it. She tells him Renée was murdered. He already knows why that has happened and sees no hope even in the plan of he and his fellow prisoners, all of whom would most surely be arrested, interrogated and then executed. He knows only that the killing has just begun.

'I don't think anyone murdered him, Hermann,' he said. Though Hermann was gone from him, it did help to talk to him just as it had with Renée Ekkehard and Eugène Thomas. 'Our chemist would have been in daily contact with Löwe Schrijen. He would have known that for him, it was only a matter of days. We'll have to leave it at a suicide, a touch of doubt I don't like, of course—*merde alors,* it's not in my nature but with no chance of my interviewing either of those two *Postzensuren,* his laboratory assistants either, or any of his combine, what else can I do, and what, please, has happened to those men?

'At some point after Eugène Thomas's death, Sophie Schrijen put these two buttons into his pockets. She must have wanted us to look closely at your colonel, Hermann, and to not accept everything he would tell us, must also have wanted to distract us from that father of hers. Brokenhearted, she had rebelled at everything she and her comrades had stood for, was in fear for her own life, and had been told, I'm certain, that she had no other choice.'

They would never know for sure, of course. Like so many aspects of this war, too much was bound to remain unanswered.

The carved staghorn buttons the colonel had left lying on his desk were here too, with the three beechwood bobbins still wound with their thread, and the swatch of wood-fibre silk.

'Raymond Maillotte didn't kill Eugène Thomas. He told you, Hermann, that they hadn't decided on who was to carry out the sentence or how.'

Warmed a little now, St-Cyr took to searching through the diagrams those men had drawn and when he had one of the fête, longed for tobacco and his pipe, and for time to pursue the investigation.

'There was to have been a brazier at each table, Hermann.' He pointed them out. 'The torches at either side of the booths. Torches dipped in tallow and beeswax, and containing guncotton no doubt.'

The torches were to have been held in place by ropes that ran from side to side above the Wheel of Fortune's booth and that of the *Jeu de massacre*, but those ropes were then to be linked to another that made its way to the back above the table that separated the two booths. 'When lit by the Gauleiter Wagner and Löwe Schrijen, Hermann, they would have torched the sky before toppling inward to shower flaming debris onto the pyramids of papier-mâché balls to trigger the trinitrophenol.

'Boudicca,' he said, and picking up the little carving, held it a moment as if undecided, for always he liked to have a memento of each investigation, yet now of course, there would be no sense in that. '*Adieu*, my queen. I regret that I met you only in my imagination.' Dropping it into the stove, he quickly pocketed the watch and tossed everything else in except for the ampoules and the cutthroat. These he would keep.

'For later, *mon vieux*. For later.'

At first light, the memories came hard and fast, but it was bitterly cold. Hermann would have said, Why wait out here when you can stay by the stove?

Hermann . . .

So hard was the frost, a three-metre thick blanket of icy fog shrouded the carnival and adjacent fields, the Kastenwald also. When sunlight finally touched the topmost girders of the Ferris wheel, St-Cyr started out. He would have to find Hermann's body, would have to see that it was laid out properly and covered with something. He couldn't leave him and simply walk away to be arrested.

Silent as always at such times, three ravens took flight. Startled, he watched them, the heart racing. Would they lead him to Hermann, had they pecked out his eyes?

All too soon he lost sight of the Phantom Queen. 'It's that kind of place, Hermann,' he said.

One brightly painted iron standard lay on the ground, and then another, and through the fog, he could see that they were bent and twisted and blood-spattered. The village cop, the priest, the bailiff and schoolteacher. 'Hermann,' he cried out. 'Hermann, where are you?'

As if he could have answered.

A crater was all that was left of the wagon that had held the *Jeu de massacre*. Debris was scattered. Sophie Schrijen lacked both face and hands and most of her clothing. Had Hermann found her, he would have gone right out of his mind. Frost-numbed Sûreté fingers dragged a bit of frozen canvas over her, St-Cyr making the sign of the Cross, though would it do any good? 'God has forgotten us, mademoiselle. The SS won't. At 1000 hours they'll be here in force.'

Sounds were muffled, blood was everywhere in the snow, this life of theirs, no life at all. 'Hermann,' he said.

The sound grew but faintly, and when he stumbled toward it, he passed by the House of Mirrors, much of which had been flattened, found the Ideal Caterpillar ghostlike in the fog, the Noah's Ark no better.

'Colonel,' he heard himself saying as Rasche got out of that little car of his.

There wasn't any sense in asking St-Cyr where Kohler was. It was written in the way he stood, the tears that were frozen to his cheeks. 'Get in and I'll take you to the station at Rouffach. It's to the south of Kolmar where, hopefully, you won't be stopped from boarding.'

'Not until we find my partner. You sent Herr Lutze out here on that Saturday afternoon but didn't bother to discover Renée Ekkehard's body until the following Tuesday?'

'I needed time.'

'You knew Victoria Bödicker would come out here on that Sunday, that Alain Schrijen would also have been here with his sister.'

'He killed Renée, didn't he? He and that father of his.'

'They had to stop them, Colonel, and those three women knew it and lived in terror until the one begged her friend to help her, that friend now having paid for it.'

'And the other?'

'Why not come and see for yourself?'

The ravens had returned. Two of them flew silently from the body while a third watched from a nearby branch at the very edge of the Kastenwald where a field-grey giant madly shooed them away, waving arms and gloved hands but making no sound whatsoever.

Still dazed, Hermann broke through the edge of the woods. Wandering uncertainly toward them, he looked frightened, lost, puzzled—ah, so many things—had bound his head with his scarf, had pulled the collar of his greatcoat up and had buttoned it tightly. Bloodstains were everywhere on him; the cuts and nicks having congealed. 'Hermann,' said St-Cyr. 'Hermann . . .'

'He's in shock,' grunted Rasche. 'He can't hear you.'

'He's frozen. He's hungry and exhausted, has had nothing to eat but Benzedrine and snow.'

'Get him into the car. Get him out of here now. You mustn't miss that train. This is perfect. Löwe Schrijen will cry foul about the *résistants* and terrorism and claim his daughter had to put a stop to it but died in the process.'

'Colonel, you came out here to find out what had happened to us and to them.'

'Listen, you, get in. With luck we'll make it and you'll be well on your way to the frontier before Meyer and the others find out. I'll stall them all I can.'

'Papers . . . The *Ausweise* and safe-conducts we'll need?'

'In your grip, your weapons also. Alain Schrijen found he had no choice but to give them to me.'

'*Danke*, Colonel. It . . . it was the least you could do.'

'There are some sandwiches and a vacuum flask of soup Yvonne insisted she pack in case you had . . .'

'Solved the matter and survived? Settled it as best we could, given the circumstances? But, please, what has happened to those men who were being held in *Straf?*'

'When I sent the ones I had here to the front, I sent them along to stalags. I couldn't let Löwe Schrijen pry answers from them.'

'Be honest, Colonel. You needed the insurance their continued presence on this earth would provide to keep him from pointing the finger at yourself for allowing it all to happen.'

'He'll have dealt with Deiss and Paulus.'

'No, Colonel, you will already have had that taken care of. Seeing as Herr Lutze did not accompany you this morning, I assume he has . . .'

'Silenced them. As it turns out, another "terrorist" attack.'

'And the watchmaker?'

'Yvonne insisted I send him to relatives in Provence.'

At Belfort there was an hour-long stopover. Leading Hermann by the hand, St-Cyr took him into the station and sat him down next to the stationmaster's stove. Everyone went out of their way to be kind. 'Shell-shocked,' they whispered. 'An RAF bomb. A stray one, hung up in the bomb bay and finally jettisoned.'

Cigarettes, one after another, were found and lit and placed between his lips, those faded blue eyes still vacant, the continued silence a tragedy to compound tragedies.

In silence, they ate. What Hermann needed most was sleep.

'Don't even think of it, Louis. If you feed me Evipan, I'll never thaw out.'

'Hermann . . .'

'*Shh!* You're across the frontier, aren't you? You're on your way back to Paris. *Paris*, Louis.'

Ah, merde, he had been faking!

At Dijon a telex from Gestapo Boemelburg, Hermann's boss at 11 rue des Saussaies, caught up with them. *Return HQ immediately. Streets being terrorized by blackout crime. Heil Hitler.*

A tapestry . . . that's what this life of theirs was like. A wall-hanging to keep out the cold until the fortress on high was finally taken and its occupants thrown from the walls.

Historical Note

Hermann was incorrect when he stated that God Himself could not have escaped from Natzweiler-Struthof. On 4 August 1942, five prisoners—a Czech, an Austrian, a Pole, a German and a Frenchman of Alsatian birth—after considerable planning, stole SS uniforms and a car and drove out of the camp. The first two made it to England where, in January 1943 the Czech government-in-exile was given a full report of what was happening at the camp, news of which was then broadcast over the BBC. The Pole was imprisoned in Spain but later managed to join the Free Polish Army, the Alsatian Frenchman joining the Free French in Tunisia. Only the German, a 'political', was captured and returned to the quarry where, in November 1942 under Josef Kramer's orders, it took three attempts to hang him. Details of the 'experiments' and the involvement of the doctors, all of whom were professors, have been documented and need no further comment here.

Four young women, all of them *N und Ns*, one French, two British, and one whose name was never recorded, were executed on the night of 6 July 1944 and cremated in the camp's furnace. Although the subsequent War Crimes Trial went to great lengths to establish whether Evipan or phenol had been injected, no firm conclusion could be reached due in large part to all the lies. Phenol was, however, used at Auschwitz and at Bergen-Belsen, where Kramer became Kommandant in April 1944.

At the time of *Carnival*, the overflow building across from the ski lodge would not have been surrounded by the barbed wire that later became necessary when an experimental gas chamber was installed there in the summer of 1943 and the ski lodge reserved for visiting personnel. Natzweiler-Struthof, though small in comparison to other such camps, had up to forty-seven work camps and probably at any one time, about 200,000 prisoners under its umbrella but also tested methods of killing that were subsequently used in the much larger camps. In total, perhaps as many as 45,000 men passed through the quarry camp itself, perhaps as many as one-half never leaving it. Many *N und Ns* from all over occupied Europe were sent there, among them nearly 5,000 from France, as well as groups of up to a hundred men and women from other camps who were then used in the 'experiments' but had been arrested solely because of their race.

One last point needs to be stated. During the background research, brief reference was found of a young Alsatian girl who spoke fluent *Deutsch* as well as French, knew the terrain extremely well, and had guided escaped French POWs from the Reich through to the Vosges. Eventually she was arrested and sent from prison to prison in Germany until finally ending up in France, in the women's section of Fresnes Prison. Was she released or executed? The author of this report, a prisoner herself, could give no definite answer, only the slim hope that perhaps the girl had been released. The date was between April and June of 1943 and one of the girl's brothers had already been executed at Fresnes, hence her having been sent there. As one who was related to an *N und N* and guilty, too, of an act of 'terrorism', it is doubtful she would have survived and I have to wonder if she wasn't that unknown young woman who died at Natzweiler-Struthof on 6 July 1944. The names of the others were Miss Vera Leigh, Miss Diana Rowden, and Miss Denise Borrell, all of whom were imprisoned at Fresnes before being sent to the quarry camp.

Well after I had written the above, I finally came across the identity of this fourth victim: Sonia Olschanesky, a Frenchwoman who had become a courier for the British F (French) Section. Because she had not been commissioned into the British armed forces, as she would have been if she had fled to Britain and then come back, her name had been left off the monument to the others, all of whom, I am certain, would have wanted it to be there.

THE ST-CYR AND KOHLER MYSTERIES

FROM MYSTERIOUSPRESS.COM
AND OPEN ROAD MEDIA

Available wherever ebooks are sold

MYSTERIOUSPRESS.COM

Otto Penzler, owner of the Mysterious Bookshop in Manhattan, founded the Mysterious Press in 1975. Penzler quickly became known for his outstanding selection of mystery, crime, and suspense books, both from his imprint and in his store. The imprint was devoted to printing the best books in these genres, using fine paper and top dust-jacket artists, as well as offering many limited, signed editions.

Now the Mysterious Press has gone digital, publishing ebooks through **MysteriousPress.com**.

MysteriousPress.com offers readers essential noir and suspense fiction, hard-boiled crime novels, and the latest thrillers from both debut authors and mystery masters. Discover classics and new voices, all from one legendary source.